THE DEADER
THE BETTER

Leo Waterman Mysteries
by G.M. Ford

WHO IN HELL IS WANDA FUCA?
CAST IN STONE
THE BUM'S RUSH
SLOW BURN
LAST DITCH

THE DEADER
THE BETTER

A LEO WATERMAN MYSTERY

G. M. FORD

AVON BOOKS, INC.
An Imprint of HarperCollins*Publishers*
10 East 53rd Street
New York, New York 10022-5299

Copyright © 2000 by G. M. Ford
Interior design by Kellan Peck
ISBN: 0-380-97723-0

Library of Congress Cataloging in Publication Data:

Ford, G. M. (Gerald M.)
    The deader the better : a Leo Waterman mystery / G. M. Ford—1st ed.
    p.   cm.
    1. Waterman, Leo (Fictitious character)—Fiction. 2. Private investigators—Washington (State)—Seattle—Fiction. 3. Seattle (Wash.)—Fiction. I. Title.

PS3556.O6978 D42 2000
813'.54—dc21   99-052652

First Avon Twilight Printing: February 2000

AVON TWILIGHT TRADEMARK REG. U.S. PAT. OFF. AND IN OTHER COUNTRIES,
MARCA REGISTRADA, HECHO EN U.S.A.

Printed in the U.S.A.

FIRST EDITION

QPM   10 9 8 7 6 5 4 3 2 1

www.harpercollins.com

To Merla . . .
when it was good, it was good.

LAN 22.00 INGRAM 7DAY

THE DEADER
THE BETTER

1 NOWADAYS, HE WAS JUST A PIMP WITH A LIMP. A WIRY SPEC-
imen with a head too big for his body and a string of
two dozen call girls he ran out of a limousine service in south
Seattle. The girls called him Baby G, but I remembered a time
when he was plain old Tyrone Gill, a playground legend who
could take you off the dribble and stick it in the hole with
the best of them. The Rocket Man, we'd called him . . . after
that old Elton John song. That was back before he made what
he now liked to call "a series of unfortunate self-medication
choices." Back before a rival procurer tried to amputate his
foot in a Belltown alley. Back before a lot of things. For both
of us.

"Gonna call it Ho-Fest Two Thousand."

He nudged me hard in the ribs. "Can you see it, man?
The tents. The banners. The food stands."

"Food stands?"

I caught his feigned astonishment from the corner of my
eye. "Man do not live by pussy alone," he said gravely.

When I reckoned how he might be right, he went on.

"Culturally coordinated, too, my man."

"How's that?"

"You know, man, like we got one tent set up for the regular trade. Missionary position types. Right next store we got
some comfort food. Strictly meat and potatoes. Grits and
gravy. That kinda shit."

"Oh?"

He cut a swath with his hand. " 'Cross the way we got the Greek tent. You know . . . for the backwards types."

I pulled one hand from the wheel and held it up. "No. No. Let me guess. Dolmas, kabobs, and rice pilaf."

He grinned and nudged me again. His big head bobbed up and down like one of those spring-loaded dolls. "I knew you was a man of vision, Leo."

Vision was precisely what I didn't have. The Explorer needed new wipers. Despite slapping back and forth at breakneck speed, the worn blades merely flattened the intermittent rain across the glass, smearing the muck into pulsating blobs of form and color that reminded me of long-ago light shows and psychedelic drugs. The unwanted memory tightened my lower jaw and sent a shiver sliding down my spine. I clapped my free hand back onto the wheel and scrunched down in the seat, peering out at the thick traffic through a small, unsullied crescent of glass at the bottom of the windshield.

Baby G snapped me back.

"That's why you got to help me out wid this," he said. "Ain't nobody else could do it but you, man."

I shook my head. "You got to get real here, G. No way anybody is going to give you a city permit to stage . . ." I looked over at him. "What did you say you wanted to call it?"

He wore a blue silk suit. Three-piece. Tailored to him like it was made of iron. And a bright yellow tie.

"Ho-Fest Two Thousand," he said.

"Not gonna happen in any city park, man. No point even talking about it."

As G opened his mouth to protest, I leveled him with the coupe de grace. "Even my old man couldn't have pulled that shit off," I said.

He recognized this as a serious rejoinder, indeed. His face clouded. He closed his mouth so hard he looked like a large-mouth bass and then began staring sullenly out through the windshield.

My old man had parlayed an early career as a union thug into eleven terms on the Seattle City Council. In the course of his storied thirty-year career of public service, Wild Bill Waterman had tilled previously unimagined ground in the fertile fields of influence peddling, insider trading and familial hiring preferences. When I turned forty-five, I was in line to inherit a bundle of ill-gotten downtown real estate, and to this day, twenty-five years after my father's death, nearly every city department is still being run by somebody related to me either by blood or by marriage.

That's how come G had spent the ride from downtown filling my ear with his nonsense about wanting me to use my connections to help him get a permit to use Discovery Park for some kind of a superbowl of suction. Mostly, though, he was just talking to hear himself talk. He was nervous about our errand tonight. He wasn't letting on, but I could tell. Those huge hands were twitchy.

"There's Darlene," she said.

First time she'd spoken. G had introduced her as Narva. The professional makeup job made it hard to tell, but I made her to be about thirty. Better than six feet, light green contact lenses, short blond hair, smooth and curled under. Impeccable in a blue microfiber raincoat, she sat in the center of the backseat, her perfect face as smooth and unmoving as a figurine's. If I hadn't known better, I'd have made her for a corporate type. Big-time Ivy League. Stocks and bonds. Maybe a junior partner attorney. Never for a hooker. No way.

Up ahead on the right, wedged between Watson's Plumbing Supply and a boarded-up beauty college, the Pine Tree Diner lurked in its own shadows, like one of those Edward Hopper paintings. At once welcoming and onerous, a classic silver diner, back before they added on and became "family restaurants." From a distance, the rounded silver edges and the solid band of light along the front facade made it look like a jukebox buried to its neck in asphalt. I moved the Explorer into the right lane.

Just as you'd never make Narva for a whore, you'd never make Darlene for anything else. The girl had the look down. Texas teased hair, a white fur bolero jacket over what appeared to be a red rubber dress. Knee-high white boots that laced up the side.

I pulled off the highway and into the parking lot. Sliding along the front of the building to the far end, I turned the car back toward the highway, killed the lights and shut off the engine. The silence was broken only by the soft ticking of the motor as it began to cool.

G pulled a fresh photograph of Misty McMahon from an envelope and passed it over the seat to Narva.

"Show her this," he said. "And make goddamn sure that crack-smokin' bitch knows what the hell she's talkin' about, too."

Narva made no move to take the picture. Her gaze was level. "You want to make an anti-drug speech to her, G, you go on out there and you talk to her."

He scowled and began waving the picture about. "You know goddamn well she ain't gonna talk to me."

Only her eyebrows moved. "Perhaps, if you'd didn't beat people up, you'd create more long-term goodwill," she said affably.

"You tellin' me how to run my business?"

"I'm merely suggesting that when one uses beatings as exit interviews, one severely compromises one's future credibility."

"Hey." He waved the picture again. "You hold that college girl crap of yours, you hear me? I don't want to hear it."

"Just trying to help," she said.

The way Darlene was wobbling across the lot toward us, you'd have sworn the heels weren't attached to the boots.

G turned in his seat and met Narva's gaze. "She was holding out on me," he said. "And you know, baby . . . that just can't be. You let one ho hold out on you and the next thing you know, they lose all respect. Two weeks"—he snapped his long fingers—"you got no girls. You sellin' yo own ass out on Jackson Street."

Narva favored him with a small smile. "What do you charge for that bony little butt of yours, G . . . three, four bucks a pop?"

A vein bulged in his temple like a thick brown worm. I unhooked my seatbelt and got my hip out from under the steering wheel . . . G didn't take much shit from his girls. Way I figured it, he was going to go over the seat after her and I was going to have to stop him, and no matter what happened after that, finding Misty McMahon and returning her to her grandmother was going to get a whole lot harder.

To my amazement, however, he merely smiled back, matching her tooth for tooth. His voice was calm. "Please," he said. "Just show her the damn picture."

She shot me a quick victory glance and then plucked the photograph from his stiff fingers. We sat in silence as she got out of the car and ambled away with one of those languid one-foot-in-front-of-the-other walks designed to pop coffin lids open. She met Darlene out in the center of the lot. As the women embraced, Darlene kept her wide eyes locked on the car. Sensing the woman's discomfort, Narva threw us a quick look, took Darlene firmly by the elbow and moved her away from the car, back toward the rusted chain-link fence running along the north side, talking as she walked, moving the woman back behind the Explorer, into the deepest recesses of the gloom.

G read my mind. "She ain't like the others. I got a different arrangement wid her than wid the regular girls."

"So I see," I offered.

He couldn't let it go. "Her and I work a straight percentage. She do her business, slide me ten percent for keepin' the riffraff off her ass. That's all. Nice and clean."

"Nice and clean," I repeated.

He folded his arms across his chest, lifted his chin and made his surprised face. "I showed her that other picture you give me, and lo and behold if she don't jump all over it. I mean, this honey ain't exactly the whore wid the heart of gold, if you catch my drift, Leo, so when she says she'll get some copies out to the street girls, I figure, you know . . . she wants to go to a bunch of trouble . . . you know . . . what the hell, let her. 'Sides"—he looked around furtively—"that way nobody know it comin' from me. Figured we might get better results that way."

"On account of that credibility problem of yours that Narva was talking about?" I inquired.

He sneered at me but didn't answer. I sat staring out the side window into the gloom, squinting my eyes at the abstract pattern of leaves plastered to the fence and ruminating about how the problem with missing kids is that you've got to find them in a hurry. The street eats them up. You leave them out there too long and there's nothing to bring home. At least nothing Grandma was gonna want around the house.

I had met Constance Hart in the coffee shop of the Westin Hotel. Her message on my voice mail said she was going to be in town for the day and wanted to meet me for lunch to discuss me finding her granddaughter for her. Finding runaway kids is among the most frustrating and heartbreaking assignments a private investigator can take on. Most of the time I make up reasons why I'm too busy, but since she hadn't left a number where I could call her back, I felt like I had an obligation to show up and give her the bad news in person.

I put on a nice pair of gray gabardine trousers, a blue silk shirt and my best black blazer. Poised and professional, five minutes early. Figured to get myself settled with a cup of coffee on the upper level, looking down onto Fifth Avenue. Firmly in charge of the high ground, moral and otherwise.

She was already there when I arrived. Drinking tea at the exact table where I'd envisioned myself turning her down. She rose as I ascended the final pair of steps. I checked her shoes. Flats. One tall woman, six-two if she was an inch, with thick salt and pepper hair, wound into an elegant braid that circled her head and then ran down her back. A black wool dress, understated but classy. Diamond as big as the Ritz worn on the right hand. Staying at the hotel. No coat . . . no purse. She extended the hand with the rock and I took it. Her palm was callused and her grip strong.

"Thank you for coming," she said.

I told her not to mention it, settled into the chair across from her and ordered coffee. We traded pleasantries until the waiter delivered my order, inquired as to the state of my immediate needs and then left.

The secret of turning down a case is not to give the prospective client a chance to tell their story, so I brought my big guns out right away. "You said on the phone that it was your granddaughter you wanted me to find. Is that right?"

"Yes."

"You said she was thirteen years old."

"That's right."

"Are you the girl's legal guardian?"

I figured this would be the end of it. She'd tell me that she wasn't, and then I'd tell her that working for anybody other than the legal guardian was considered extremely poor form by the local constabulary and generally resulted in things like kidnapping charges. Wham bam, no thank you, mama.

"Yes, I am," she said.

Before I could close my mouth, she reached into the pocket of her dress and produced a folded piece of paper. I took it. A copy of a court document. Indeed she was the kid's legal guardian. Peninsula County, September fifth this year. Constance Pierce Hart was awarded full-time permanent custody of Misty Ann McMahon, her granddaughter.

Now I really didn't want to hear the story. The state of Washington exercises the greatest reluctance—some say entirely too much—in separating children from their parents, and on those rare occasions when they deem the child's welfare to be better off elsewhere, they are far more likely to remand the child to the foster care system than they are to award custody to a relative. I groped for an excuse as I slid the paper across the table to her.

It's like any lawyer will tell you. Don't ask questions that you don't already know the answer to. Curiosity got the best of me.

"What's with the parents?" I asked.

I slouched in my seat, waiting for the painful dance that inevitably precedes a person admitting that the seed of his or her loins is the scum of the earth. Tales of how he'd always been a difficult child. Of how he'd always been far too sensitive for the other children to understand. How maybe that unfortunate incident with Mrs. Zahniser's cat and the electric charcoal lighter should have alerted them all. I'd heard it all before. In my business, denial isn't exactly a river in Egypt.

Constance Hart, however, was made of far sterner stuff. Instead of making excuses, she pulled herself erect, looked me hard in the eye and said, "My son Mark is a pederast, Mr. Waterman. He molested his own daughter, Misty"—she averted her eyes—"probably since birth."

The air between us felt magnetized, as if the leaden weight of her sudden admission was now partially mine. It's a feeling I get when people are forced to let me further into their lives than either of us would prefer. I changed the subject.

"And the mother?"

Her black eyes rolled back my way.

"Mona's weak. She's whoever and whatever Mark tells her she is, and nothing more."

She could tell I understood. Back before no-fault divorce, I used to meet a lot of people like that. People who had somehow gotten the threads of their identities tied up with those of their mates. People who'd spent twenty years driving minivans and beginning sentences with "we," as if they had tapeworms, only to awaken one middle-aged morning to find the fabric of their lives unraveling before their puffy eyes. Divorce work had been steady, but somehow I didn't miss it a bit.

"Did she know?"

"Of course," she snapped. "She was right there in the house. How can she say she didn't know?"

When I didn't respond, she went on.

"Which is why Misty has to be told that she's not going to have to go back home. Ever," she added. "That she will stay with me for as long as she chooses. If she thinks you're taking her back home, she won't come with you. You'd have to—"

I held up a palm. "Whoa, now . . . I haven't said anything about taking on the case."

She didn't argue or plead. She simply said, "You must."

I knew what I was letting myself in for, but I asked her anyway.

"Why's that?"

She told me her story. Mark McMahon was her son by her first marriage. Raised by his father after the divorce. Over in eastern Washington. He and Mona had been married for nearly fifteen years. Three years ago, Mark had been transferred to the Seattle area, affording Constance Hart an opportunity to get to know the granddaughter she'd hardly met. From the beginning, she'd sensed something was terribly wrong.

Misty had always been a timid, withdrawn child, seemingly more content to play alone indoors than to be outside with the other kids. A poor student. Unable to concentrate on anything for very long, she was adjudged to have a learning disability and was assigned to classes for the differently abled. And it might have ended that way, too. She might have just been another misdiagnosed kid who slipped through the cracks in the system and was never seen again.

Three months into the fifth grade, all students at Westwood Middle School are shown a videotape designed to inform them as to what is and is not appropriate touching on the part of grown-ups. The tape is no big deal. Mostly drawings and arrows. Most of the kids have seen it twice a year since second grade. Many nap.

This time, however, when the lights were turned back on, something was amiss. Misty's seat was empty. The halls and restrooms were checked. Then the school grounds. The police were called. Nearly an hour after her teacher reported her missing, Misty was found huddled and nearly comatose in a supply closet at the back of the maintenance room.

Subsequent sessions with the district psychologist revealed a pattern of sexual abuse dating back to Misty's earliest memories. Unfortunately, while the girl was able to speak quite cogently of her father's abuse within the confines of therapy, Misty proved unable to handle cross-examination in open court and eventually, despite three criminal trials, the protests of the school district and the best efforts of Constance Hart's attorneys, the girl was remanded back into the custody of her parents, from whom she then proceeded to run away at every opportunity.

Misty's father Mark made his fatal mistake about three months ago. He'd kicked in his mother's front door, thrown her to the floor and then dragged his runaway daughter, kicking and screaming, back out through the shattered portal. Big mistake.

What Mark McMahon overlooked was that Constance Hart's front door was in Peninsula County, not King County, and in Peninsula County, Ms. Constance Hart was both extremely prominent and astonishingly well connected. Seems her late husband Frank had not only left his widow extremely well fixed, but had shown the remarkable foresight to have gone to college with both of the county's district judges, one of whom, after a suitable period of mourning, now considered himself to be a serious suitor for Constance Hart's affections. She only had to ask once.

Within forty-eight hours, Mark McMahon had been arrested on a Peninsula County warrant charging him with kidnapping, felonious assault, child molestation and breaking and entering. As Misty was witness to the alleged crimes, the county insisted that she be present at her father's arraignment. Once they had her back in their jurisdiction, they ruled that Mark and Mona McMahon were unfit parents and awarded permanent custody to Constance Hart. Halfhearted protests from King County fell on deaf ears. That was the good news. The bad news was that Misty's previous experience with the social welfare system had, quite understandably, failed to foster a great deal of faith in the judicial process. While Constance Hart was in the Peninsula County Courthouse, on the very day when she was awarded custody, Misty ran away. That was three months ago yesterday.

Constance Hart gave me a rundown of her efforts to find her granddaughter. First the cops. Overworked and understaffed. Runaways not a high priority. The shelters. Doing the best they can. The CPS folks. Barely holding their own. The missions. Same deal but with religion. Somebody said maybe she ought to try a private firm. Hired Consolidated, the biggest firm in town. For the past six weeks, they'd had an army of suits papering the city with posters of the kid. No go.

"What makes you think she's in Seattle?"

"She called. About a month after she ran away." Her spine stiffened. She took a deep breath. "She . . . she sounded like she was on drugs. She kept saying she was fine. Just kept repeating that she was fine. I tried to explain the court order . . . but she hung up." She took a sip of her tea.

"I'm afraid you're my last resort, Mr. Waterman."

Par for the course. Nobody comes to me first. At least not with anything legal. In my business, you get over any romantic idea that you were their first choice to help them with their problem and come to realize that by the time they worked their way down to your yellow pages ad, they'd already consulted everything from the cops to the I ching.

"Why me?"

She eyed me carefully. "I heard—in several places—that you were quite skilled at finding people and things that didn't want to be found. They said you were tenacious and knew people on the street."

Tenacious was a pretty big word for most of the people I knew on the street, so I asked, "Who said?"

"They asked me not to use their names."

Couldn't say I blamed them.

"What else did Misty say?"

"She said she was okay. She said she'd seen her picture on a poster and wanted me to know that she was okay."

"That all?"

"I tried to tell her about the court order, but she kept repeating that she was okay and that I should stop looking for her." She took a deep breath. "She said an angel was taking care of her."

I shuddered. Not *an* angel. Angel. Angel Monzon. Kiddie pimp.

"Consolidated came up a complete blank?" I asked.

She pressed her lips into a thin line. "They said . . . ," she began, "they said they had information that she was . . ." She stopped again. Looking away this time. Shook her head.

"Turning tricks?" I prodded.

She gave the smallest of nods. I wasn't surprised. Pimps like Angel Monzon have a sixth sense when it comes to finding the broken ones. The secret is to find the ones who've already been to hell. Then the rest is easy. All that's left is to get them strung out on something they can't afford and then turn them out. I was betting Angel had been standing right by Misty's side while she talked to Grandma. Didn't like the heat from the posters. Especially not with one so young. They send your ass down for thirteen-year-olds, and nobody but nobody wants to do state time as a baby raper.

"Suppose I do find her," I said. "She's been on the streets for three months." She was stirring her tea. "Mrs. Hart," I said. Reluctantly, she raised her eyes to mine. "Have you given any thought to what I might bring back to you? Three months is an eternity on the streets for a kid that age."

"What you bring home will be my granddaughter." She said it with such immense dignity that, for a second, I almost believed it myself.

The words escaped my lips before I had a chance to think.

"I'll try to get a line on her," I said.

G's voice startled me. "What?" he barked.

I showed him my palms. "I didn't say anything."

"Yeah, but your big ass was thinkin'. I could hear it."

Two guys in yellow hard hats came out of the diner and got into an orange Parks Department pickup truck. The glare of the backup lights bathed the two women in stark black and white.

Funny how light works. In the spectral glare, Narva looked like the Vampire Princess. Tall, translucent, seeming to glow with a deep inner light, the midnight blue of her raincoat transmuted to black, lustrous and panther-rich. Darlene just looked old. Like you could lose your Visa card in the creases in her cheeks. She waved a long white cigarette as she spoke. About every third word, she'd jerk her chin over her shoulder, making sure the car hadn't moved, and then she'd go back to talking.

G noticed, too. He made a smacking noise with his lips. "That Narva girl."

"You said you guys work a straight percentage," I prodded.

"Strictly business," he said quickly. "Hell . . . she don't work but Friday and Saturday nights. Gross five, six grand a weekend. Goes to graduate school the rest of the time. Getting her a master's or some such shit."

"How much?"

"How much what?"

"How much does she get?"

He narrowed his eyes. "Lookin' for a little somethin' you can't git at home?"

"Just curious."

He eyed me closely. "The G man can be very discreet. No reason Rebecca got to know. You know me . . . hey, hey, I always say . . . a man's business is a man's business."

"How much?"

"Fifteen hundred. Straight half and half. Anything exotic is extra. Got her a small but real loyal following."

"That what she charges you?"

He scoffed as he adjusted his tie. "You crazy? I don't pay for no nappy dugout."

"So . . . you gettin' it for free, then?"

He didn't say a word, so I stayed in his face. "What? No freebies for the G man? I thought the G man always got freebies. You know . . . like one of the perks."

He rolled his eyes toward the headliner. "This one's different."

He sensed my astonishment.

"Shit, Leo. You know me." He twisted his lips into a wry grin and then laughed into the back of his hand. "She first come to me with the proposition." He made his astonished face. "I figured, you know . . . so who's this pushy ho tellin' the G man hisself what she's gonna do for him? So I grab a handful of her hair . . ." He reached out over the dashboard with his left hand. The handful of imaginary hair struggled mightily, but the G man held on with grim resolve. "And I tell her, you know, that ain't how it works down here, sweet cakes." He curled his lip as he began to force the hand down toward the floorboards. "I tell her, hey, baby . . . listen, what you do for me is get down on your pretty little knees and polish the G man's knob for a bit. That way, you and me get this arrangement off on a right and proper footing, so to speak."

"And?"

"And I do what I always do then, I pulled my joystick outta my pants." He held out his other hand, palm up. He now held an imaginary Narva in one hand and an imaginary dick in the other. "His Majesty's sitting right there in the palm of my hand; I'm tryin' to stick her face in it and you know what that crazy bitch says?"

"What?"

He looked down into his own palm as if confused. "She look down and say, she say . . ." He wiped the corner of his mouth on the shoulder of his suit. He was beginning to giggle. "She say . . . 'You know . . . that look just like a penis, but much, much smaller.' "

We burst out laughing together. I nodded.

"Your dick ought to have one of those warning labels about how maybe things appear to be bigger than they really are."

He waved me off. "Don't start that racial envy shit with me. I seen that pathetic little string of yours."

We kept bonding until Narva emerged from the shadows and began walking toward the car. She got in behind me, slid her way to the center and handed the picture back to G.

"Darlene says she saw the girl last night."

She kept her eyes glued on G as she spoke. "She says one of those little farm weekends is going on over in Bellevue. Says she went last night with a john. Says that's where she saw the girl."

"Farm?" I said. "What's a farm weekend?"

They passed meaningful looks before G took over. "It's like a little private something for the exotic trade, if you can dig it. Every once in a while, this rich motherfucker name of Spooner likes to stage what they call a 'power exchange weekend.' Very exclusive. You got to know Spooner or somebody who knows somebody. Got to call ahead and make arrangements, so's they can have whatever weird shit you want ready for you."

I must have looked blank.

"You know, man," he continued. "Like bondage, S and M, that sorta Gothic shit. You name it, the farm got it. They don't got it, they'll send out for it. You want a big mama in leather to stuff her panties in your mouth while she beats your ass wid a canoe paddle, you go to the farm. You want a prune juice enema from a transvestite wearing a red pig mask, you wangle youself an invite to the farm."

"Don't trivialize what those people do," Narva said quickly.

G began to sputter. "Don't what? What you say? Trivia. What kinda shit is—"

She ignored him, speaking instead to me. "They do all that Gothic scene stuff." She shot G a look that would have killed lesser men and then returned her eyes to mine. "What he's not telling you is that if you're on the guest list and what you happen to want is a twelve-year-old boy"—she made a gesture with her hand—"who, say, you want to bugger and then brand with your family crest . . . they'll get you one of those, too." She reached over the seat and snatched the picture from G's hand. "Or a thirteen-year-old girl who you maybe want to—"

I couldn't help myself; I interrupted. "How in God's name would a kid end up in a place like that?"

"Might have trolled her up off the streets," G suggested.

Narva sneered at the idea. "Darlene said the girl's tricking for Angel Monzon. Says Monzon leased her out for the weekend." She made a disgusted face. "He probably wasn't satisfied with her work. Maybe she wasn't making her quota, or maybe she wasn't coming across with what the customers wanted and he figured she could use a little attitude adjustment, so he sends her to spend the weekend at the farm.

Figures after a weekend in there, she'll be more of a happy and contented camper."

"Doan put me in wid those people," G protested. "I ain't never loaned one of my bitches to those folks. Never." He threw a hand at the windshield, at the back of Darlene wobbling her way out of the darkness and into the light out by the highway. "Not even that no-good ho there," he protested. "I turn 'em down every time."

"Yeah, G . . . you're a prince," Narva said.

"Who you—"

"Only reason you don't rent your girls is because you're too goddamn cheap to pay their medical bills afterward," Narva snapped.

"What?" G sputtered.

As they sniped at each other over the seat, I tuned them out and thought it over.

"How solid is Darlene's information?" I said finally.

"She a no-good, crack-smoking—" G began.

Narva cut him off. "If Darlene says the girl was there last night, then she was last night."

I turned to G. His face was a knot. He waved a finger in my face.

"Don't be givin' me that look."

"What look?"

"The 'you owe me' look. That's what fuckin' look."

"I'm not giving you any look," I protested.

"I'da beat that rap. With or without your help."

"You'da done fifteen to twenty-five," I countered.

"Arnold woulda done the right thing. He'da come around, told the cops I didn't have nothin' to do with that shit."

"Yeah . . . that's how come I found him hiding out in a roach motel in Sarasota, Florida. How come I had to take him across three states in the trunk of the rental car, so's he'd know I was serious. How come he sat in County for eighty-five days before he'd talk to the grand jury. Oh, yeah, old

Arnold was just dying to get your moldy ass off the hook for murder. Chomping at the bit, he was."

G looked like he was about to swallow his lips. We sat in silence.

"Ain't no problem either way," he finally declared. "You ain't got a reservation, you just flat don't get in that motherfuckin' place. Period. End of story."

"You could get us in," Narva said.

G peered over the seat at her. "You hear what you sayin' here, girl? This here ain't no college girl shit. Can you dig what I'm sayin'?"

"Can you?" I asked.

"Can I what?"

"Get me in there."

"No motherfuckin' way. You shittin' me?" He chuckled. "Trust me, Leo. You a badass motherfucker and all, but, you don't mind me sayin', you just don't come off as the Gothic scene type."

"I'll go in with him," Narva said from the backseat.

G's voice rose an octave. "What is it wid you and this thing, girl? This ain't no shit of yours."

She turned her green eyes my way. "If G can get us in, can you get us back out?"

"Depends on the layout of the place and what kind of security they've got inside." I looked over at G. First he tried to pretend he didn't see me; then he said, "Got this leg-breaker name a Gunter. Drives his car for Spooner. Big ugly motherfucker wid a funny lip. Handles the door. That's all the security I ever seen."

It made sense. That sort of scene, most anybody was gonna need was an occasional bouncer. Last thing in the world they wanted was any serious noise.

Narva thought it over and shrugged. "Get us in," she said to G.

First he claimed he couldn't. Said it would make him persona au gratin. Then he claimed he wouldn't. For our own good, you know. Finally, with a great show of reluctance, he pulled his cell phone from his jacket pocket, shouldered the door open and stepped outside. In three long strides he was ensconced under the wraparound eaves of the building, shaking his big head, dialing.

As G leaned against the diner with the cell phone pressed to his ear, the beads of water on the side window outlined Narva's profile like sequins as she stared impassively out into the darkness.

"G's right," I said. "This could be dangerous as hell."

"I heard him," she said.

I pressed. "I don't want you to think I don't appreciate your help here, but . . . you know . . . G owes me. You don't."

"I can take care of myself," she said.

"I wasn't suggesting you couldn't."

She turned her stony gaze my way. "What, then?" she demanded. "Should I make up some personalized sob story, so's the great big private eye will feel all warm and fuzzy?"

"Maybe," I said. "Let's give it a try."

She moved her attention back toward the window. "Let's just say I draw the line at consenting adults."

"I appreciate that," I said. "And I feel the same way, but . . . it's like G said. This is some serious shit."

"Listen to me," she began. "Leo . . . that's your name, isn't it?" I said it was. "You have any personal experience here?" she asked. "Ever been abused by anybody? Anybody in the family?"

When I told her no, her expression said that was what she'd figured.

"How many people do you trust, Leo?" she asked suddenly. "I mean implicitly, with no reservations."

I mulled it over. "Maybe three," I said.

"Not many, is it?" Before I could answer, she said, "Imagine what the number would be like if the people who were supposed to be protecting you when you were a kid turned out to be abusers."

"I try not to think about that," I said. "Finding kids is hard enough without putting myself inside their heads."

"You got lucky with Darlene here tonight," she said. "Most of the street girls are so zoned they wouldn't recognize their own mothers."

She picked up Misty McMahon's picture. I watched as her eyes traveled down the kid's face, from the outlandish radar bangs down over the freckles to the thick row of railroad tracks crossing her teeth.

"Could be it's already too late," I offered.

Narva didn't disagree. We sat listening to the sound of the rain on the car, as G pranced up and down under the diner's overhang, phone pressed to his ear, free hand flapping about like he had a nervous disorder.

"G said you're getting your master's degree."

"G talks too much," she said quickly.

"What in?"

I heard her take in a great breath and then let it out.

"Business."

The passenger door popped open. G held the phone tight against his chest. He took us both in. "Y'all are sure?" he asked. "You fools really wanna do this shit?"

When we said we were, he turned his back, spoke briefly into the receiver and then snapped the tiny phone shut. Nobody said anything as he got back into the Explorer and fastened his seatbelt. As a matter of fact, nobody said a word for the better part of twenty minutes. Until we were out in the middle of the 520 bridge and the silence had begun to wear on me, when I piped in with, "So . . . you guys never answered me . . . why do they call it a farm weekend?"

G coughed into his fist. I could feel Narva's gaze on the back of my neck.

"You don't want to know," she said.

Something in her tone told me she might be right, so I let it go.

2 "PULL OVER HERE," G ORDERED.

I slid the Explorer to the curb. The street was empty. Somewhere in Medina. Old-time Boeing money, no more than a couple of miles from where Bill Gates was building himself a little five-acre shack down on the shores of Lake Washington. Houses way back from the street. Massive oaks and maples forming a low arch, completely blocking the sky, creating the illusion of a tunnel.

"Kill the lights and the engine," G said. After I followed directions, he grabbed the door handle and limped out into the street. I followed him up to the front of the car.

He pointed. "See them lights up there in the middle of the block?" I said I did. "Spooner's house. Other side of the street is all this horsey shit he got. Pastures, barns, stables, that kind of crap. You park over there and walk across."

I walked around to the rear of the car. Opened the hatch and then the tailgate. Pulled out my old blue gym bag from high school. The ornate first letters had long since worn away. The bag read: RANKLIN IGH CHOOL.

Narva was out of the car now, standing to my left as I pulled the Glock .40-caliber from its plastic holster and stuck it in my pants at the small of my back. Next, I put one foot up on the bumper and strapped on an ankle holster. Just above the ankle bone. Tight. The little Beretta .765-caliber slipped right in. I snapped the safety strap in place and put my foot on the ground. Stomped it hard once. Still tight.

I reached into the bag, rummaged around, pulled out a police special .38 and offered it to Narva. "Just in case," I said.

She made a face. "I have a philosophical problem with guns," she said.

I knew better than to ask G. He didn't go to the bathroom without his little custom-made .32 auto.

"Wadda ya think?" I asked him.

"I think this is dumber than shit," he replied.

When I failed to respond, he pointed up the street. "I can't be going in there wid you two fools. You know that, don't you? Ruin my business. I'd be a piranha."

"Nobody's asking you to go in," didn't satisfy him.

He clapped me on the shoulder. "I could, I would, you know that, Leo."

Behind his back, Narva was bobbing her head up and down as if to say, *Oh yeah, sure you would.*

He reached into his inside jacket pocket, pulled out his cell phone, pushed a series of buttons and then listened. He handed the phone to Narva and then pulled a pager from his belt. More button-pushing. He handed me the pager. "You push that red button, I'll have the car outside the front door in thirty seconds." He snapped his long fingers. "You got the best camouflage on the planet, man. Standing next to Narva, here, most folks won't even know you in the fuckin' room."

It was sad but true. As if to emphasize the point, Narva unbuttoned her raincoat, slipped it from her shoulders and handed it to me.

Imagine my irritation when she reached down to the hem of the matching blue silk dress and pulled it completely over the top of her head. She handed the dress to G. Must have been blue night. Everything matched . . . little see-through panties, garter belt, half bra, stockings. Everything baby blue with little bows all over it.

"Leo," she said. It took me a second. She held her hand my way.

"What?"

"Could I have my coat back?"

"Oh yeah, sure." I fumbled as I helped her on with the coat. We got back into the car, G driving this time. I sat in back with Narva.

"So, who is it we're supposed to be?" Narva asked as G pulled to a stop. Two huge white barns at right angles. Out across the pasture, some other structure. Couldn't make it out through the gloom. Twenty-five, thirty cars. Mostly expensive and German.

"A couple of LA scene types. I imitated that maybe you all could reciprocate with some similar action old Spooner ever got down to LaLa Land. Said you all wanted a party and maybe do a little threesome with something female and springtime-fresh. Said you knew Angel from when he was down there. Figured what with him subcontracting and all, his name be good."

"What if he's in there?" I asked.

G hadn't thought of that. He mulled it over. "I guess, if that happen, you shoot the little bastard," he said, finally. "Ain't nobody likes that little razor-totin' motherfucker anyway." He grinned. "Aw hell, Leo. You a professional. You just got to remember that old saying."

"Which saying is that?"

He tapped his temple with his index finger.

"Discrepancy is the better part of valor."

I was still trying to figure out whether he was kidding when Narva took charge.

"Let's go." She shouldered the door open. I followed her out.

Halfway across the street, I took her elbow. We stood in the middle of the empty street. Mercury-vapor light filtering through the canopy of trees. Lavender. Above the sound of moving water, I could hear distant music. She put her hands on her hips. With the coat unbuttoned, the effect was stunning.

"Listen," I said. "One last time . . . you sure you want to do this?"

She cocked a hip. "You're beginning to bore me, Leo."

"Okay then, here's how this thing is going to come down. Last thing people like this want is a lot of noise. That's our hole card. Faced with a big messy scene, they're most likely to let us walk. If we play our hand right, we ought to be able to pull this off. No reason for them to have any more security than what G says they got. Maybe a drunk gets out of hand once in a while, but that ought to be the most trouble they're expecting. But . . ."—I hesitated—"when and if the action starts, we switch roles, right? You stay close and do like I do. We'll both do what we're good at."

She agreed, talking as we crossed the street and started up the driveway. "While we're looking for the girl and figuring out what to do, you do like G said. Just smile a lot and do the strong silent type." No problem.

She reached up and banged the brass knocker. Three times. The sound of muted music was louder here. Classical. Violins.

Bald guy about six-five at the door. Black-tie formal. Neck about the size of Narva's waist. Harelip scar. A Gunter all the way.

"We're up from LA," Narva said.

He took her in from head to toe. "And you know who?" He had a soft, almost childlike voice, a couple of octaves higher than I expected.

I thought about telling him it was *whom* but decided against it.

"Mr. Monzon," she said.

He pulled the door open and stepped aside.

We were in a narrow hall. Double doors left and right. Huge central staircase in front of us. I had to admit, it did kind of look like *Gone With the Wind*.

He gave Narva a leer. "Can I take your coat?"

"I'm a little chilly," she said.

"Yeah," he offered. " I can tell."

The drone of voices and the muted clinking of glasses became a dull roar as Gunter pulled open one of the doors on the left. Narva pulled me through the doorway. The first impression was that of a nineteenth century gentleman's club. Dark walls and drapes, big chandelier casting a yellow light over banquet tables and acres of overstuffed furniture lining the walls. Whatever sense of propriety the furnishings might have provided was immediately dispelled by the fact that the waiters weren't wearing pants. Or, more properly, that's all they were wearing. Black leather bow ties and tight latex briefs.

Gunter stepped into the room behind us and closed the door.

"Stay here," he said. "I'll find Mr. Spooner."

I heard a yelp of pain followed by scattered applause. The music changed to Chopin. Opus something-or-other. Gunter walked past us, back to the door.

Spooner wore a monocle.

"Our new friends from the south," Spooner said.

Narva offered her hand. Spooner took it and brought it to his lips.

"Oooh," Narva enthused. "And all these wonderful boy toys."

"We have a strap-on collection second to none," he assured her.

He was still slobbering on the back of her hand. She leaned over and spoke into his ear. "Tonight," she said. "We had in mind . . . how shall I say . . . something . . ."

"Pristine," he finished for her.

"Yes," she said. "Pristine."

"Of the female persuasion?" Spooner asked.

She nodded. Spooner leaned in and whispered in her ear.

I only caught the end of what Spooner was saying. ". . . shouldn't be much more than an hour or so. We'll have her fresh as the morning dew for you."

I moved to Narva's side. "In the meantime," Spooner was saying, "allow me to show you around our little gathering." He took Narva by the ass and started into the party.

I walked along the center of the room. The furniture had been moved off to the sides. Each grouping was afforded some measure of privacy by a series of antique screens that shielded the occupants from prying eyes.

No compilation or description of the carnal acts being performed within those walls could adequately describe the scene. My mistake was to let my curiosity get the best of me. Halfway down the room, I peeked around the corner of one of the screens. The woman wore a white gown, kneeling on a chair, dress thrown up over her head. Red shoes. I turned away. After that, I minded my own business.

Spooner had his hand down the back of her panties as he steered Narva around the corner toward what appeared to be the dining room. I took in a demonstration of Japanese rope bondage being given in the library. There were three schools. One, the artsy, was a triumph of style over substance, where it didn't matter what position the subject was in as long as the ropes and knots were pretty. A second was all about making the victim as uncomfortable as possible without obstructing entry. The third style involved trussing the victim up like a rib roast, while placing knots and braids at precisely those areas designed to produce the most long-term discomfort.

Narva jostled my elbow. She was alone. "Our host was called away," she said.

"A pity," I said. "You two seemed to be getting on famously."

Narva smirked. A black woman in a leather jumpsuit stopped by our sides. She put the tip of her finger in her mouth and then traced it around one of Narva's nipples.

"A ménage, perhaps," she said. "Something wet?"

When we allowed how we'd given up those very acts for Lent, she moved on.

"The exotic stuff is upstairs," Narva said.

I was horrified. "You mean this isn't it?"

"Hardly," she sniffed.

"How do you know?"

"He said we should enjoy ourselves. Introduce ourselves to people before Gunter takes us upstairs."

"Let's go," I said.

The house was laid out exactly like my parents' house before the renovation. Big central staircase leading down to the front door. Another, smaller set of stairs leading directly from the kitchen. Easier on the servants, you know. Bedrooms running the length of the back of the house. Assuming that the door at the end of the hall was the master bedroom, nine bedrooms in all.

We got lucky. I don't know how many more doors I could have forced myself to open. The first one was horrific. I pulled my head back through the crack and closed the door. I must have looked bad. Narva stepped over, peeked in and had the same reaction.

"Yuk," she said.

Door number two. An older blond woman in jodhpurs and riding clothes rode around the room on the back of a younger man, flailing a riding crop at his naked buns. "Jump, damn you," she yelled as she swung. "Jump."

Door number three was locked. Narva raised a finger. Walked back to the equestrian events, pulled open the door and took the old-fashioned key from the inside of the lock. When I pushed it into the lock, I heard another key fall to the floor on the inside.

He was struggling into a pair of blue silk boxers when I pushed open the door. Looked like the Monopoly man. Old, big white mustache. I'd have said distinguished if he hadn't been locked in a room with a naked thirteen-year-old girl.

"Now, see here," he sputtered. "I was assured—"

I gave him everything I had. Got a good hip turn and rolled my shoulder over, getting my weight behind the punch. Hadn't caught anybody that clean in years. He hit the wall on the fly and then slid to the floor in a pile.

Misty McMahon opened her mouth to scream, but Narva was on her in a flash, kneeling astride the girl, stifling the shout with her hand. "We're friends," she kept saying as the girl thrashed about. I knelt on the bed beside her struggling form. "Your grandmother sent me," I said. She stopped thrashing and turned her frightened eyes my way. I gave her the abridged version. "Do you want to go home?"

She nodded and began to cry. Narva removed her hand. "They won't let me go," she sniffled.

The Monopoly man flopped over onto his back, groaning. He rolled into the thick red puddle his broken mouth had left on the floor.

The only clothes she had were in something of a Catholic school motif. Our Mother of Hollywood. Plain white blouse. Knee socks, a plaid skirt barely long enough to cover her ass and a pair of patent leather shoes with the strap across the top.

While Narva got her dressed, I checked the hall. "We're going to march right down the front stairs and out the door," I said.

"Angel will never let me—"

I reached into my coat and brought out the automatic. Thumbed off the safety. Folded my arm across my chest so most of the gun was under my arm. "You let me worry about Angel or anybody else who gets in our way. You just stay close behind me and do what I tell you, okay?" I didn't like the look in her eyes. She was wired to the ears. Meth, probably. Wouldn't want to waste good drugs on a kid. "Okay?" She didn't answer. I looked over her to Narva. "Keep her between us and keep moving," I said.

I checked the hall again, still empty. "Let's go," I said. At the top of the stairs, I pushed the red button on G's pager and started down.

We almost made it clean. When the front door first came into view, it was unattended. I checked over my shoulder. Narva was close behind the girl, pushing her along. I took Misty's hand in mine and pulled her down the stairs behind me. Then the voice. "So where's dese players been usin' my name in vain?"

Gunter came into view. The sight of us standing on the stairs stopped him. He lifted a hand to his coat. I pointed the Glock at his forehead. The hand flopped back to his side. I slid the gun back under my arm.

Angel Monzon was barely five feet tall. He wore a stiff white shirt with a butterfly collar. Around his neck enough gold chain to tow a Metro bus. Little ballet slippers with bows across the arch.

He read Gunter's face and followed the frozen stare my way. Misty stopped moving her legs; I had to pull her down a step to keep her behind me.

"What we got heeeere?" Monzon said. "We got us a weasel. Think he gonna leave the coop wid a chicken."

"The three of us are going to walk out that door," I said.

Monzon laughed. "You think you walkin' outta here wid one of mine? You focking crazy or what?"

I left the gun hidden in my armpit. "Maybe you ought to back off like a nice boy," I said. "We don't want to get grease all over everything, do we, Monzon?"

He laughed again and put his right foot on the first stair. "We see about some grease dere, cholo," he sneered. I watched as he reached toward the back of his belt, and then I pulled out the automatic and shot him through the top of the shoe.

The foot exploded, sending a shower of shoe and blood all over the foyer. Gunter looked down at the red spots dotting his tuxedo shirt, pawed twice at his face and began to

back away. Monzon threw himself around the floor screaming, cursing in Spanish.

I reached behind me, grabbed Misty McMahon by the
waistband of her skirt and dragged her stiff-legged down the
stairs behind me. Gunter backed off. I pulled open the door
and pushed Narva and the girl out into the night.

Behind Gunter one of the double doors opened. Spooner's
head poked out. The sound of shouts filled the foyer. I picked
a spot about nine feet up the door and put two slugs through
the mahogany. The door slammed. I heard screams now and
the shuffling of many feet. Angel Monzon was groaning,
holding his foot, rocking on his spine. I pointed the gun at
Gunter. "You stick your head out this door and you're going
to have more than a funny name and a bad lip."

I yanked open the right-hand door and stepped outside.
G had both hands on his shiny little gun, sighting over the
top of the car. "Let's roll," I said.

3 | FROM THE WALKWAY ABOVE THE MAIN DECK, THE FERRY *Spokane* seemed to open its mouth and swallow the dark water running headlong toward its bow. The huge vessel slid so softly among the whitecaps that it seemed as if it were pulling the water deep into its innards and somehow using the flow as a silent means of propulsion. Despite the wind on my cheeks and the low throbbing of the diesels, when I looked left or right, we appeared to be standing still. Only by focusing my attention on the oncoming escalator of green water was I able to maintain any sense of forward motion whatsoever.

Rebecca kept one arm entwined with mine as she sipped a Starbucks latte through a red plastic straw. We had the upper deck to ourselves. The tourists had lasted all of five minutes in the wind before packing their cameras and scurrying inside for a cuppa joe and a prune Danish. Regular commuters stay in their cars for the twenty-minute passage between Edmonds and Kingston. They figure the six-dollar fare is bad enough without blowing any more hard-earned cash upstairs.

Rebecca used a gloved hand to point north.

"Look," she said.

Fifty yards to starboard, silhouetted against the pale yellow slope of south Whidbey Island, a sea lion poked his glistening head through a carpet of kelp. His thick neck twisted nearly in a circle as he sought whoever had disturbed his afternoon nap. I watched as his bright blue eye fixed us in space and, as he then rolled onto his side, he made what I took to be a dismissive gesture with his flipper and slid silently beneath the surface. I threw an arm around Rebecca's shoulder and pulled her close.

On the rusted car deck below, Misty McMahon stood clutching the yellow safety rope, her back to the forwardmost cars, staring out over the onrushing waters of Puget Sound as if she were expecting something familiar to come floating by at any moment. The stiff wind puffed the red ski jacket around her small frame and caused the new blue jeans to flap and snap in the breeze like pennants.

"The jeans are a little big," I commented.

"It's the style," Rebecca said. "Baggy's all the rage."

Misty had spent what was left of last night and most of this morning in our guest room. I say *spent* because I was certain she hadn't slept. Maybe I was afraid she was going to make a run for it, or maybe it was just a matter of having a stranger in the house. Either way, I spent the night with the sound of her shiny little shoes rolling through my head like claps of thunder.

Around ten A.M., while I was calling Constance Hart, Rebecca ran downtown to The Bon Marché and bought the kid some new duds. She was right. No way we could bring the girl home to grandma in the Lolita outfit.

While she was gone, I segued into domestic mode. I don't know why, but whenever I'm feeling bad, I like to feed people. God knows I'm no Julia Child, but stress me out and I start inviting people to dinner. People we haven't seen in years. Rebecca claims it's my twisted way of nurturing people. Way I see it, hassles make me hungry.

I warmed four poppyseed muffins, toasted a couple of cinnamon-raisin bagels, set out some butter and some raspberry preserves, sliced up a cantaloupe and some fresh strawberries. Crystal tumblers for the OJ. Place mats. Napkin rings. The whole nine yards. Eat your heart out, Martha Stewart.

It was eleven-fifteen before the three of us sat down at the kitchen table. After a dozen increasingly feeble attempts at conversation, I was forced to consider the possibility that the kid was still too stoned on whatever she'd been taking to make conversation. She'd answer yes and no if you asked her direct questions. She'd mumbled a thanks for the half a bagel she'd torn to pieces but hadn't eaten and at one point asked if it would be okay if she went to the bathroom, but that was about it.

When Misty finally left the breakfast table and went upstairs to get dressed for the trip, Rebecca crossed the kitchen to the sink where I was rinsing the dishes, spun me around toward her and put both arms around my neck.

She gazed deep into my eyes. I hate it when they do that.

"You can't fix it for her, Leo. I know how badly you want to, but you can't." She pulled me close and kissed me on the neck. "You've already done everything you're good at. Leave her alone."

She was right, but it didn't matter; something inside of me wanted to do something more. For whom? I don't know. At that point, I didn't much give a shit.

Rebecca let me go and took a step back.

"Know what she said when I brought her the new clothes?" she asked.

"What?" I growled.

I was being crabby, so she made me wait.

"She looked down into the bag"—Rebecca sighed—"and then she asked me if this meant she should take off all her clothes now."

Constance Hart stepped out onto the porch, closing the door behind her. The house looked more like a commercial hunting lodge than a single-family dwelling. A rambler. River rock and polished logs spread out for what seemed like a quarter mile along the rim of a small butte. Behind the house, the land sloped quickly away, pulling the eye down toward a five-acre mountain lake and the valley beyond, where an unbroken series of natural meadows and first-growth forest ran all the way to Puget Sound, shimmering like a black mirror some three or four miles in the distance.

I hadn't expected her to return so quickly. After the bizarre scene in the driveway, I figured we were going to be a while. Not once during the hour-and-a-half journey had Misty McMahon uttered a syllable. Just sat there staring out the side window, picking at her fingers and humming something under her breath . . . until we drove up to the back of Constance Hart's house, that is. I heard her stop humming. Suddenly she sat forward in the seat, and I saw a glimmer of recognition in her eyes. Before Rebecca managed to bring the Explorer to a complete stop, Misty had jumped out onto the pavement, pushed her way through her grandmother's outthrust arms and disappeared into the house without so much as a word. I stood, one foot on the asphalt, half in, half out of the passenger seat. Constance Hart shot me a puzzled look. When I merely shrugged, she followed the girl inside.

I'd figured getting Misty settled would take maybe a half hour, so I was stretching my legs around the yard; Rebecca sat in the Explorer, listening to Frank Sinatra pledge his love to Chicago while she read the *Seattle Weekly*.

Ten minutes later, however, I'd just gotten started checking out the spectacular scenery when Constance Hart reappeared. She walked slowly. Looking down at the flagstone path. A thick shock of gray hair had escaped the tortoise shell clip and now flitted about in the wind like a silver web. She lifted her chin as she spoke.

"Misty wants to be alone."

Her voice said it matter-of-factly, but her eyes frisked me for an explanation. I didn't have one, so I kept my mouth shut.

She looked back over her shoulder toward the house.

"I had hoped . . ." she tried again.

"I know," was the best I could manage.

Constance Hart folded her arms across her chest and paced in a small circle. A hundred feet above us, the wind rushed through the treetops like traffic.

"I'm not going to hurry her. About anything." She said the lines as if she'd rehearsed them. "I'm going to let her get settled into her new environment. Move at her own pace. After that . . ." She let it ride.

"Give it time," I offered.

"She's been through a great deal."

Despite all she knew, she wanted me to tell her I'd found the kid in church, but there was no way I could help her. Instead, I stood there in the driveway listening to the wind, shifting my weight from one foot to the other, hoping that Constance Hart wasn't reading me as easily as I was reading her.

I unzipped my jacket and pulled out the envelope that had been resting against my ribs. The paper was warm as I held it out.

"I wrote you up a report," I said.

She shook her head. Stiffened her spine. "No," she said. "I have no need to know what's in there. I already have everything I want. You found my granddaughter." She waved her hand. "As far as I'm concerned, Misty's life starts over today. Right here, right now." I returned the report to my ribs and zipped the jacket.

Her earlier words still rang in my ears. "After that . . ." she'd said. Yeah, what about after that? They sit down to a nice heart-to-heart talk? Some bizarre version of how I spent my summer vacation? What then? Then they go down to the school district and register Misty for the eighth grade? She tries out for cheerleading? Becomes Homecoming Queen? Marries Brad from Microsoft. Births Tyler and Courtney. Maybe I was having eye trouble, but I just couldn't see it working out that way.

She wasn't going to read my report. This meant I wasn't going to be able to appease my conscience by telling myself that my recommendations had been right there in black and white. No such luck. I was going to have to step up to the plate and come out with it. I was sorting through my mental euphemism file when she reached into the patch pocket of her red jacket. Two checks folded in half. She unfolded the checks, separated the two, held one of them out toward me.

"What we discussed on the phone for expenses and your fee," she said.

While I took it from her hand and put it into my jacket pocket, I used my other hand to wave off the other check. "There's no need—" I began. She cut me off.

"I insist," she said. "You did what others failed to do. You returned my granddaughter to my side."

Reluctantly, I stuck the check in with the other. I knew what was coming. Above us, the wind was building. Bits of tree debris ticked off the roof of the house. Behind me, one of the massive trunks groaned inside its silver bark. I shivered.

"Misty's probably going to need to—" I began.

She met my eyes with a granite stare. "Yes?" she interrupted. I'd seen the look before. Happens when you bring kids home. I'd done my duty. I'd been well paid. I was now supposed to show some class and get my act up the road. Preferably move away . . . say, to the planet Neptune. One minute Saint George. Next minute the dragon.

"She's probably going to need to see a doctor," I said.

For a moment, I saw hatred in her eyes. "If there's something—" she began.

Quickly I interrupted. "Nothing specific."

I kept my eyes on hers. They were black and filled with denial. The strained silence swallowed the sounds of trees and wind. I forced myself to maintain eye contact. No blinking allowed. It took a while. After what seemed like minutes, her eyes suddenly lost their luster and her face turned the color of custard.

"Oh . . . you mean . . ."

"Yeah. You ought to get her tested for AIDS," I said. "Just as a precaution."

She opened her mouth to deny that anything so unspeakable could possibly have entered her realm and then slowly closed it again.

"Yes," was all she said, before turning on her heel and starting back toward the house. I stood in the driveway until she disappeared.

4 | IN MY BOOK, THERE'S NOTHING WORSE THAN SOMEBODY trying to cheer you up when you're down. When I'm feeling bad, I want to roll in my sorrow like a pig. I want to hear Buddy Guy shout the blues or Tom Waits sing songs about old men in wheelchairs and waitresses with Maxwell House eyes, marmalade thighs and scrambled yellow hair. I want to drink bourbon till I spill a couple drinks on the carpet. Maybe shed a tear or two for the miserable state of the human condition. Then maybe, if nobody's looking, shed a few more about the state of my own miserable ass. Most of all, though, I want to be quiet . . . quiet and alone.

I kept telling myself it was one of those *Men are from Mars, Women are from Venus* kinda things. For the past twenty minutes, Rebecca had been rambling nonstop. Early on, it was about how I should be proud of my role in returning Misty McMahon to the bosom of her family. How there was nothing to be depressed about. After that . . . coulda been anything. I zoned her out.

She poked me in the arm. We were pulled over on the side of the road at the junction of Routes 20 and 101. Home was left.

"Well?"

"Well, what?"

"Do you want to?"

"To what?"

I heard her sigh. "Have you been listening to me?" she asked.

I figured I'd save myself Act One wherein our hero denies all.

"No," I said. " I was somewhere else."

She took one hand off the wheel and put it on my shoulder. "You okay?"

"Tired, I guess."

She made her "poor baby" face and asked, "Did she give you a bonus?"

"Yeah. I think so."

"How much?"

I shrugged. "Haven't looked."

I fished in my jacket pocket for the checks. First one made out for fifteen hundred and sixty dollars. My bill. Opened the other. Blinked. Counted zeros. Whistled.

"How much?" Rebecca asked.

"Ten grand."

Next thing I knew, she was enthusing again. About god knows what. Making a conscious effort not to sigh, I stuck both checks back in my jacket pocket and picked up the conversation the last place I could remember.

"Do I what?"

I should have known better.

"Never mind," she said.

God, how I hate the old "never mind." Always makes me feel like a circus animal. Cue the calliope music. Jump, Leo. Roll over. Good boy.

"No . . . really," I tried. "What is it you asked me if I wanted to do?"

She sighed, but cut me some slack. "Take the long way home. Maybe spend the night over at Ocean Shores or Grayland or someplace like that."

I thought it over. I'd wondered when she volunteered to come along today. Wondered more when she'd practically insisted. On her off weekend, too. Officially, her hours as a forensic pathologist for the King County medical examiner were nine to five, Monday through Friday. Three weekends a month, however, she was on call and seldom got all the way to Monday without having to make at least one guest appearance at the morgue. Way I figured it, after failing to cheer me up, she'd probably feel compelled to resort to gratuitous hotel sex. What could I do? Might as well go along with the program, huh? Wadda guy.

"Sure," I said. "Why not?"

She turned right onto 101 heading west toward the edge of the world. The long way back to Seattle meant circling the Olympic Peninsula, driving all the way down to Aberdeen, cutting across to Olympia and then driving the freeway for the last sixty miles home. Maybe eight hours of driving instead of an hour on the road and twenty minutes on the ferry. An odd choice for a woman who detests driving in general and freeway driving in particular. Like she explained to me years ago, you see enough folks who've extruded themselves through the windshield, you develop a terrific urge to walk.

Mercifully, she didn't make me figure it out. "I thought if we got to Stevens Falls early enough . . . maybe we could stop and visit J.D. and Claudia."

While pretending to check my watch, I searched my memory banks. J.D. and Claudia? J.D. and Claudia? I was pretty sure they weren't related to me. Yeah, definitely, her family, not mine. An image of a couple flashed on my inner screen, and I had it. Claudia O'Connor, Rebecca's goddaughter. Yeah. Daughter of the late Muriel O'Connor, Rebecca's long-ago med school friend from the East Coast. The one who was always going to come and visit but never quite made it. Since Muriel's death last year, Rebecca had been making a concerted effort to keep in touch with Claudia. Trading cards and calls. I felt better. At least now I had an explanation why the good Dr. Duvall would want to spend her off weekend traipsing about the wilderness. I hate it when she's more than three steps ahead of me.

In my mind's eye I could see a blurry image of Claudia. A pretty blond girl with long hair parted down the middle. Oversized brown sweater, long skirt and combat boots. And the wiry little guy who stood beside her. Very neat and preppy. All angles, cheekbones and wire-rim glasses.

"The fisherman," I said.

She nodded and smiled. I was awarded style points for remembering.

"You liked J.D.," she said.

She was right. I had liked the guy. The one time I'd met him—a Thanksgiving dinner, as I recalled, a couple of years ago—he'd seemed several cuts above most of the thirty-somethings I meet. I remember we were standing on somebody's back porch. Screaming kids had driven me outside. After the football game but before the dinner. It was raining like hell, and nobody had cleaned the gutters. A solid wall of water ran off the porch roof. Like standing behind a waterfall. He'd stuck out his hand. J.D. Springer. He'd handed me a business card. Neat little picture of a guy with a fish on the line, standing at the bow of a drift boat. Underneath J. D. SPRINGER, FISHING GUIDE.

As with most people who love what they do, he was more than willing to tell his story. Originally from the eastern part of the state. Tri-Cities area. Dad a high school English teacher. Mom the town librarian. Grew up fishing the Columbia and the Snake with his dad. Rainbow trout, cutthroat, salmon, sturgeon. All two quarters at Washington State taught him was that, architecture be damned, what he really wanted to do with his life was to fish. Used his savings to buy a used sled boat, got himself some business cards printed and went into the fishing guide business. I recalled what he said to me.

He said, "I figured, what the heck, I'm nineteen years old. If a nineteen-year-old can't take a chance, can't follow his bliss, who can? Got plenty of time to be Dilbert later." I remember how he'd laughed at the idea of life in a cubicle.

Within a couple of years he's the most popular guide in the area. Booked months in advance. Making a good living. Meets Claudia at an Outdoor Show in the Kingdome. Love at first sight. She moves over to Richland to be near him just about the time he applies to the state of Montana for a guide license on the Yellowstone River. The state, of course, informs him that they have a waiting list of six-thousand-some-odd souls who want the same thing and that his only chance would be to pay his five-hundred-dollar fee for the right to take part in the annual lottery. Seems one guide license per year is awarded to the lucky so and so whose name is drawn from the barrel. Proceeds go to fish habitat management. A good deal all around. He sends his dough.

First year, damned if he doesn't win. "God protects fools and drunks," he'd told me with a twinkle. He and Claudia get married. Move to Montana. Takes him a full year to learn the river. After that, same deal. Booked one hundred percent of the time. Two years in advance. Making more money following his dream than he ever imagined possible. Five years of guiding European royalty, pro athletes, Hollywood stars and, for a week in '95, former president George Bush. And . . .

Two kids change everything. J.D.'s mom and dad want to be able to see their grandkids more often. Start a low-key propaganda campaign. No way he's moving back to eastern Washington, so they compromise. Agree on western Washington. Parents retire and move to this side of the Cascades. Somewhere up by Marysville. J.D. and Claudia and the kids move back from Montana.

That's when I met him. That rainy Thanksgiving Day right after they'd moved back to Washington. When I asked him how he felt about giving up fishing heaven to come back and be nearer the family, he took off his glasses and began to polish the lenses with a tissue. "Never thought I'd hear myself say this," he mused, "but a man can only catch so many fish and use so much money, and you know . . . there's some things in life just more important than fishing." Said he was shopping for a piece of property over on the Olympic Peninsula. Something on one of the rivers where he could set up a destination fishing lodge. With more than a little envy, I'd wished him luck.

I was having trouble keeping my eyes open. Felt like fine sand under my eyelids. I checked the door to make sure it was locked and then leaned my head against the window. Closed my eyes and dreamed of the way the line stops and then the first tug and then pictures of enormous silver fish, tail-walking across broken water.

I woke up when she shut the engine off. By the time I'd blinked myself into focus, Rebecca was out of the car, standing in front of an orange-and-white-striped barrier. I got out, stretched, allowed myself a yawn and wandered her way.

"Problem?" I inquired.

"It says the bridge is closed for repairs until further notice."

"So?"

She turned to face me. "We're at the end of the road. My directions to Claudia and J.D.'s place say to go over this bridge."

She was right. We were indeed at the proverbial end of the road. You either turned left over the bridge or you turned around.

"How far back was the last town?"

"Five or six miles."

"Guess we'll have to go back and ask."

When she headed for the car, I got my first good look at the barrier. Not the usual sawhorse barrier made ominous by bright orange signs. No, no . . . this was a welded steel security gate, custom made to lock directly to the bridge abutments. Both sides. Top and bottom. Big stainless steel chains. They really didn't want anybody using that bridge. I didn't get much of a chance to think about it. The notice said the bridge had been declared unsafe by City Inspector Emmett Polster. Behind me the Explorer started. I hustled over, got in and fastened my seatbelt.

The road back to town was newly paved, still smelling of oil, with only an intermittent series of yellow dots to mark the center. The bullet-riddled sign at the west end of town claimed a population of sixty-seven hundred souls.

Stevens Falls used to be a lot bigger place. Twenty years ago, the better part of thirty thousand people had lived at this end of the valley. There'd been half a dozen lumber mills, a couple of plywood plants and enough work in the woods to keep everybody busy. Nowadays it was standard-issue Northwest rural. A mill town without a mill. A forest community without a forest. Five blocks on either side of the highway. Ten blocks long. Most of the inhabitants living off in the hills somewhere. One of everything except taverns. Those numbered three.

Trying like hell to draw tourists. Old West motif. The businesses along the main drag were connected by raised wooden walkways. Cute little hitching posts and horse-watering troughs used for parking barriers. Hanging baskets of flowers were evenly spaced along both sides of the main drag. Red-and-white-striped ice-cream parlor. Antiques. Espresso. Collectibles. Step right up.

The surrounding hills were painted with the browns, the reds and yellows of fall. Pretty this time of year, if you didn't know any better. Nothing but scrub oak, big-leaf maple and madrone. The money trees—the cedar and spruce, the Douglas fir, the pine—they were long gone. In the Pacific Northwest it's customary to leave fifty yards of tall trees immediately adjacent to all highways. That way the tourists were treated to the illusion of the unspoiled forest and the timber barons could then feel free to clear-cut every saleable stick of timber for the next fifty miles. Or until the next highway, of course. Whichever came first. Around here, they hadn't even bothered with the fifty-yard tourist barriers. They'd cut down everything that would bring a dime.

I pointed to a Texaco station at the far end of town. "Pull in there. I'll ask."

Urban renewal hadn't gotten this far. Behind the counter a skinny guy in filthy gray overalls. Bad teeth and the narrow eyes of a weasel. He was wiping the grease from his hands with a rough red rag. On the radio Buck Owens was cater-wauling about the streets of Bakersfield. "Hi," I said. A patch on his chest said *Linc*.

He nodded slightly, looking me over as if he were think-ing of cannibalizing me for spare parts. "What can I do for ya?" he asked.

I told him about our problem with the closed bridge.

"Ain't nothin' over there anyhow," was his response.

"Looking for a guy named J.D. Springer," I said.

He looked me over for a long moment and then turned his back and began fiddling with some carburetor parts on the counter. "Told ya, ain't nothin' over there," he said.

Ten years ago, I'd have jumped the counter and taught ferret face some manners. Sure it would have involved bail. Probably have to come all the way back for court, but god-dammit I'd have felt better. Today, I jammed my hands in my pocket and went back outside feeling old and ineffective. I walked around to the driver's window.

Rebecca lowered the window and raised her eyebrows. "So?"

"I think I may be losing my boyish charm," I said.

"So . . . what else is new?"

"So, I'm going to need to ask across the street. Stay here." I trotted out my best Arnie impression. "I'll be back," I in-toned.

I tried a different tack on the lady in the Laundromat. Not looking for a soul. Just tourists who wanted to get off the beaten path. She pointed with a three-inch purple finger-nail. Another bridge eight miles back. Just turn right and you could drive right back to the closed bridge. Longer, bumpier, but eventually you'd get there.

Eventually, we did. Forty minutes later, we rolled to a stop at the head of a paved driveway. Above the idling engine, I could hear the rush of water somewhere below. Twenty-four-oh-seven, it read. Three Rivers Lodge. Nice hand-crafted sign. A posted NO TRESPASSING sign every fifty feet along the fence.

Rebecca consulted the paper she'd been holding in her lap.

"This is it," she said, turning left down the narrow road.

A half a mile later we rolled out of the tunnel of trees onto an open five-acre plateau. Two cars. A battered Chevy Blazer and a shiny new Subaru wagon. To the left, eight new guest cabins were spaced along the top of the bank. Directly in front of us an asphalt ramp ran down to the river. To the right, a moss-encrusted log cabin. The cabin windows were filled with construction-paper ghosts and bats. On the small concrete porch, a thirty-pound pumpkin had been expertly carved into a fierce jack-o'-lantern.

First Claudia and then J.D. stepped out onto the porch. J.D. looked just like I remembered him, like he'd been chiseled out and left rough. Claudia had gained about twenty pounds and traded the long skirt and the combat boots for a bright yellow Nike jogging suit and a pair of sneakers. Two little blond heads poked out from around and between Claudia's legs. The minute Claudia saw Rebecca's face, the high-pitched noises began.

Claudia and Rebecca hugged and mewed and hugged and squealed and then hugged some more. Tears and tissues. J.D. and I shook hands and traded weather reports. The kids were introduced to their aunt Rebecca and uncle Leo. The boy's name was Adam. He'd turned two last week, and was quite proud of being nearly potty-trained. The girl was Alicia. Gonna be four on the day before Christmas. Mama's Christmas angel.

The place was small. Two bedrooms. No more than twelve hundred square feet. J.D. explained how when they were up and running, the family was going to live over in Sequim and how they were going to gut this place and turn it into a kitchen and dining room for the resort. Iced tea for Rebecca. A cold Moosehead for me.

We did what people do in those moments. We took turns trying to encapsulate a couple of years' worth of living into a hundred words or less. Sawing off the peaks and valleys so as to seem neither boastful nor weak, ending up with fictional renderings of our respective lives that hardly seemed worth the telling.

The children wormed their way between Claudia and the couch back. She leaned forward. "You'll have to stay for dinner," she said.

I inwardly groaned; Rebecca came to the rescue. "Oh Claudia, we'd love to but . . ." She looked my way for confirmation. I did my best. "But we're going to have to be leaving here pretty soon," she continued. She explained how we were trying to make it down to Ocean Shores before it got too late.

"You know how bad that road is," Rebecca said.

"Wicked at night," J.D. agreed quickly.

Claudia flicked a glance at her husband. "They can spend the night with us, can't they, J.D.? They can have our—"

"They said they needed to go, Claudia," he interrupted.

"I heard what they said, J.D. There's nothing wrong with my ears." Her tone had that singsong quality people develop when they spend too much time talking to children. I felt like I'd walked in on the last act of an art film.

The knotted muscles along his jawline suggested that he was about to tell her what parts of her anatomy did indeed have something wrong with them. He opened his mouth, thought better of it. "Hot in here," he said. "I'm gonna take a little walk."

He took two quick strides across the room, jerked open

the door and was gone. Screen door banged. Children stood still and silent. The air was magnetic with tension.

Amazing the kind of nonverbal communication you develop with a partner over time. I was already halfway out of my seat when Rebecca shot me look number forty-nine. The one that meant I should follow J.D. so's she could find out from Claudia what was really going on here. She didn't have to ask twice.

J.D. was walking in circles in the driveway, rubbing the back of his neck and looking up into the racing gray sky.

"How's fishing?" I tried. Seemed like a good bet. To fishermen, the only thing as good as wetting a line is talking about it. No go.

"Fishing," J.D. snorted. "What's that? Heck, Leo . . . I don't even remember the last time I went fishing." Behind him loomed the forest primeval. North America's only rainforest. A hundred-fifty-foot canopy of leaves and needles so deep-green thick that, in places, the sun never reaches the ground. Sodden and springy underfoot, a serpentine maze of fallen limbs and eight-foot sword ferns so thick and tangled you have to crawl. Perpetually wet and smelling of decay. Everything covered with thick iridescent moss. Everywhere the sound of moving water.

"Sorry about . . . in there," he said.

"You ought to hear Rebecca and me on a bad day."

He snorted again. "Lately, seems like that's the only kind me and Claudy have."

He laughed at himself. "Listen to me . . . sound like I ought to be on Oprah or something. Come on. I'll show you around."

I fell in beside him. We walked down the asphalt ramp. To my left, directly beneath the guest cabins, a pair of spanking-new jet boats sat beached on the rocky shore. Aluminum, twenty-footers. Probably thirty grand apiece. Same Three Rivers logo painted on the sides. At the bottom of the ramp, a gray Avon raft was pulled partway up onto the pavement. The wooden floor of the inflatable was littered with pop cans, candy wrappers and orange life jackets.

At the bottom, we turned right, picking our way along the bank for sixty yards, until we came to a rocky point. We stood at the crux of an inverted Y. A genuine confluence. Over one shoulder was the Bogachiel, over the other, the Hoh. In front was the two miles of tidal flow called the Quileute River. Beyond that . . . Tokyo.

Yesterday's rain had leached the red clay banks down into the water, leaving both rivers murky and out of fishing shape.

"There's the beauty of it," he said emphatically, as if he were trying to convince one of us of something. "You own this property, you own the last seven miles of the river before it empties into the ocean."

He turned and pointed upriver. "You can see there . . . see how steep the banks get?" I saw. No more that a half mile upstream, the river was the better part of thirty feet below the forest. He pointed out in front of us. "Half a mile downriver right at the end of this property, it becomes a big tidal mudflat. No way to get anything in there to pull a boat."

He pointed out toward the ocean. "Between us and the ocean there's something like a thousand acres of private land with the reservation on three sides and the ocean on the other. This was a homestead. It was here before the reservation. Old guy I bought it from, Ben Bendixon, his grandfather lost an arm to a Hoh musket ball."

"A lucky find," I commented.

He looked up at the leaden sky. "Yeah . . . that's what I thought," he said.

I didn't figure him for the type who'd readily tell his troubles to somebody he'd only met once before, and I sure as hell wasn't the type who particularly wanted to hear them, but something inside of me had the urge to draw him out.

"How's that?" I asked.

He picked up a stone and threw it out over the water, trying to skip it. Sunk like . . . yeah, you guessed it.

"It's the local yokels," he said. He threw another rock. Two skips. He slapped himself on top of the head. "Why am I boring you with this? You don't want to hear this stuff."

I sat on a smooth black boulder. Watched him pitch rocks at the river for a while. On the far side of the Hoh, two black-tail does bent low over the water for a drink.

"What about the locals?" I pressed.

"It started with vandalism," he said. "Had all the signs torn down several times. Then somebody hooked a truck to the fence and pulled out a couple of hundred feet. Left it just laying there in the road. Threatening phone calls all hours of the day and night.

"Got the numbers on my caller ID. Took 'em down to the sheriff. Nothing." Then, he told me how the family came home from a weekend with the grandparents and found their new station wagon missing. Glass all over the ground. Thought it was stolen until he noticed the glass on the boat ramp and the oil in the water. It took a Navy diver and three tow trucks to pull it out of the river. Totaled. Squashed nearly flat by the force of the water. Insurance had replaced it with the new Subaru in the driveway. He picked up a rock the size of a baseball and heaved it out into the river.

"Right there," he said. "There's a hole in the bedrock nearly twenty feet deep. Right off the end of the ramp. You can feel it in your feet when you're in the boat. Millions of years with two rivers beating on it. It's like a black hole. Anything you throw in there, it don't come out." He shook his head and continued the story.

When none of that worked, the road was suddenly under construction. Closed. Tore it down to bare rock and then just left it that way. Six months they had to come in the way we came in today. J.D.'s attorney complained to the state Highway Commission. Finally the state started nosing around and the powers that be had to get on with the project. Then, the bridge. Soon as the road was paved, they closed the bridge. Said it was unsafe.

"Is it?"

"Not one darn thing wrong with it. Heck, for a month or so after they closed it, I just pulled the barrier aside and drove right on over."

"Until they got serious about the gate."

He nodded. "You noticed."

I said I had. He picked up on what I was thinking.

"I know it sounds paranoid. Every time I say it out loud I wonder about myself, but I swear, Leo, it's the truth. They're trying to run me out of business." He skipped another rock across the surface. Three.

"Why would they want to do that?"

" 'Cause Ben sold me the property."

"So?"

Seems the county had been making a major effort to buy the property, but this Bendixon character had steadfastly rebuked all offers for the place. Said he was born there and, by cracky, he was gonna die there. When he suddenly reversed field and sold out to J.D, things turned ugly, 'cause first thing J.D. did was to post the place NO TRESPASSING, which meant that every other boater and fisherman had to pull out way upriver at the town boat ramp. Either that or learn Japanese. What had heretofore been one of the most heavily used boat launches and fishing holes in this neck of the woods was suddenly off limits. Needless to say, feelings ran high.

"How come he sold it to you?"

He told me about how he and the old man had met one day. Both of them out bank-fishing. Ben had invited him to the cabin for coffee. How they became friends. About how he used to stop and make an offer on the property whenever he was around this part of the peninsula. Trying to win out on pure persistence. How it got to be a joke between them and how one day, out of the blue, the old man left him a message on his voice mail. You want the property, get yourself over here.

"I'd given up. I was looking at eighty acres on the Dungeness. I think he was lonely. By the end, if you wanted to find him during the day you just went to the Timbertopper Tavern. He didn't drink much but . . . and then the dog . . ." he began. "I think that was the last straw."

"What dog?"

"Ben lived out here for the last fifteen years with this old springer spaniel named Chappy. His wife died back in the mid-eighties. Ever since then, it was just Ben and that old dog." He could tell I was lost. "Chappy died the day before Ben called me. I don't think Ben wanted to live out here all by himself. I think Chappy dying kind of put him over the edge, if you know what I mean."

I said I did. "Where's the old man now?"

"Moved in with his daughter in Port Townsend." He searched the ground, kicked up a flat stone and then sent it sailing. One skip.

"I guess he knew I'd take care of the place," he said finally.

I asked the obvious question. "No way to avoid posting it?"

"What was I going to do?" he asked me. "Let the locals do for free what I'm charging customers thousands of dollars to do?" He had a point, but I could see how that move could make J.D. more than a bit unpopular with the local sporting set.

"Besides that," he went on, "they've got no regard for the fishery. They ignore the catch limits. They gill net; they dynamite. Heck, I've seen 'em shoot fish. To them it's just a resource that's always been. No matter how many times you tell them, they just can't imagine that the fish won't always be there." He skipped another rock. Five skips. "Guy that owns the tackle shop in town, name of McGruder . . . that SOB likes to brag about how one time he and his brother-in-law wired two volleyball nets together, came down here and netted themselves up the better part of a ton of Chinook salmon in one night." He shook his head sadly. "You came through town, didn't you? You saw what they did to the land. How you going to be reasonable with people like that?"

When I told him I didn't know, he became even more animated.

"And the bridge and stuff was just the beginning. Suddenly the electrical wiring in the new cabins—which they'd preinspected and approved—all of a sudden, it was no good. Nope. They waited until I had all the finish work done and then told me they'd changed their mind and none of it passed inspection. Heck, I've had the interior finish work on some of those cabins done three separate times."

It went on and on. All that was missing was the CIA involvement. As he recounted his litany of conspiracy, I couldn't help but notice how different he seemed from the person I'd met a couple of years before. The guy with the twinkle in his eye and the very real sense that his life was charmed suddenly seemed mortal.

He threw up his hands. "I should have been open for business six, eight months ago. Took me ten years to build my client list and now I'm losin' 'em. One by one I'm losin' 'em. I don't know how much longer . . ." He caught himself. "You know, Leo, I almost called you a couple of times. I thought maybe . . . you know . . . a detective could find out what the heck is going on around here." He looked up at the sky. "Except, of course, I wouldn't be able to pay you, either."

I couldn't decide whether he was just letting off steam or whether, at this point, I was supposed to volunteer to help him out, so I chose my words carefully.

"If what you needed was a detective, the money wouldn't be a problem," I told him. "We could work that out."

Not carefully enough. I watched as his face took on that same knotted quality I'd seen back in the cabin. "You don't believe me, do you?" he said suddenly.

"If you're asking me whether I think you're lying, the answer is no."

"Oh . . . so what I need is a shrink instead of a private detective."

"If you're asking my opinion, I think you need an attorney."

"I don't have time for—"

Above the rushing of the river, Claudia's voice. "Jaaay Deee," she called. Then again. "Jaaay Deee."

He brushed his hands together and then wiped them on his back pockets.

"We better get back," he said.

He talked as we picked our way among the rocks. How he'd hired state-certified inspectors of his own. How he was taking it to court. Already won the wiring battle. Plumbing was next. How he'd been in contact with the state Attorney General's Office. He stopped at the bottom of the boat ramp and pulled the Avon farther up out of the water.

"Sorry," he said. "I didn't mean to lay a bunch of stuff on you. I'm just frustrated." He kicked a rock down into the water. I told him not to worry about it.

"Gotten so bad, Claudia's working at the daycare center over on the res. She and the kids putt over in this thing every morning."

The slap of little feet pulled my attention up the ramp. It was a race. Giggling madly, both children ran down the slope, nearly out of control, rushing headlong toward their father. J.D. met them halfway, scooping one up in each arm, swinging them around his head as they squealed with delight. He carried them the rest of the way to the top on his shoulders while they laughed and struggled to escape.

At the top, he set the kids back on their feet. Rebecca was wearing her coat, twirling her keys. The little boy ran to Claudia's side. Tugged on her dress. She scooped him up, resting him on her hip. He whispered in her ear.

"Adam needs to use the potty," she announced proudly. Adam swallowed his fist and kicked his feet. "Let me take him inside, then we can say goodbye." She turned and started for the house. The little girl ran over and grabbed Rebecca by the hand.

"Come on, Aunt Rebecca; let's go watch."

Rebecca left in tow. She looked back over her shoulder. Look number forty-two. Hang in there, baby. This won't take long. We be gone.

J.D. and I wandered up toward the cars. The cleared area at the far end was the helipad. Let 'em keep the darn bridge. Said he was only about twenty hours short of his commercial chopper license. He explained how he was going to fly customers directly from Seattle. Groups of four. Wine 'em, dine 'em, limit 'em out for a few days, back to the city for a new group. Eventually hire another guide, get both boats working. Eight cabins at a grand a day. Do the math.

The newly bulldozed edge of the forest seemed embarrassed by its silver nakedness. Several of the trunks showed the brown gouge of the blade. Halfway up the hill, the frail tops of the hemlock shivered in the breeze. J.D. pointed toward the back of the clearing. A new aluminum shed, maybe thirty by forty. A couple of big black storage tanks. A white U stenciled on one. A white D on the other. A dusty Honda ATV. Big grassy traffic circle in the center of the area. Big enough that boats on trailers could easily be backed up next to the fuel tanks. Some sort of crude stone marker adorned the center of the circle.

"See that pile of rocks?" J.D. asked.

"Yep."

"Chappy," he said. "I promised Ben we'd work around him."

We rode in silence. All the way back to the working bridge, back through Stevens Falls. Took the right fork over toward the coast, instead of the left toward J.D.'s and the end of the road before she broke the spell.

"Sorry," was what she said.

"Nothing to be sorry about. You had no way of knowing."

She made a rueful face. "Not exactly what I had in mind for cheering you up."

No argument there. The Olympics filled the windshield. Looming slate gray against a cantaloupe sky. Two miles later, she gave me the rundown from Claudia. How this whole thing with the business seemed to have driven a wedge between them. How Claudia felt they were slipping apart and didn't know what to do about it.

"You and J.D. talk?"

"A little."

"And?"

And I ruminated for a moment on how Claudia spoke exclusively of relationships, while J.D. had confined his talk to the business. Why wasn't I surprised?

Then I gave her the rundown. Conspiracy Theory 101.

"What was your take on it?" she asked when I'd finished.

All I knew was that the more I thought about it, the more unlikely it seemed. Sure . . . I could see a few redneck fisherman getting real upset about losing their boat ramp to some tree hugger. And Lord knows there's no telling what a crazed cracker will do behind half a gallon of Jim Beam. Yeah, I could see good old boys ripping out a fence and pushing a car in the river. No problem there. But town government? County government? They're all conspiring? Over a fishing hole? Please.

"That's quite an operation they're trying to put together there," I said finally. "I think it's most likely they just plain bit off more than they can chew."

She nodded in agreement.

"Claudia wants him to ask his parents for money, but he won't."

I didn't mean it, but I said it anyway. "He'll figure it out." I leaned my head against the window and closed my eyes.

Funny how people are. To keep our pain at bay, we create a hierarchy of suffering. For reasons I don't understand, it seems like we automatically place our own brand of agony at the bottom of the order. Relegating it nearly to the status of the mundane. At the other end of the pain chart are the sufferings of others, whose tribulations always seem so much more romantic, so much more dramatic, and, in the end, so much more life-threatening than our own. Go figure.

5 | FLOWING DOWN FOURTH AVENUE IN AN ADRENALINE MIST. The red bows on the lampposts whispering a reminder that Christmas isn't optional. *You will participate and you will have a good time. You will participate . . .* Seems like it never ends. Before the Halloween pumpkins have even begun to rot, the Christmas decorations are everywhere. No wonder it drives us nuts.

Rebecca had a list. A "Things to Be Buried with the Pharaoh" scroll. She worked it hard with a pencil. Crossing out, then erasing and then crossing out some more. I heard her rolling it back up and then heard the snap of her purse. "Done," she announced. My heart soared like a pigeon.

"Ready to head back to the car?" she asked, removing the other parcel I'd been squeezing with my forearms. That left me with one jammed under each arm and a shopping bag in each hand. She reached for another bag. I shook my head.

"I'm good," I said. "Let's go."

We surfed down Fourth Avenue on a wave of hustling humanity.

"I wanted to compliment you, Leo on how patient you've been."

Across the street, a four man steel drum band played a reggae version of "Deck the Halls." The sound of Salvation Army bells came from several directions at once and, although there wasn't a tree in sight, the air smelled of pine boughs.

"Must be middle age," I said.

Distressingly, she agreed with me.

We turned right down Olive, passing under the Monorail, then cut diagonally across Fifth Avenue and around the corner toward the Vance Hotel. The Explorer was parked about four blocks up Stewart. We were giving a scant nine bucks to park for the afternoon. In this neighborhood it's a buck a block. Every block closer to Third costs you another dollar, until it peaks at fifteen bucks a pop to leave your car for a couple of hours. Joni Mitchell was right. You want good advice. Put up a parking lot.

By the time we'd stuffed our second load of holiday cheer into the Explorer, rear visibility was a thing of the past. Hell, there was barely room for us as we bounced down Boren. "You ask the Boys to the party yet?" she asked.

"I can't find 'em. I asked around the square the other day and nobody'd seen 'em for a couple of weeks."

The Boys weren't exactly boys. As a matter of fact, with the exception of Nearly Normal Norman, they were all pushing seventy. The remains of my old man's political machine, Harold Green, George Paris and Ralph Batista had all managed to drink their way out of the middle class and into the streets. They'd been homeless since before there was such a thing as homeless. Back then, they'd just been bums.

What I discovered, however, was that, if I kept them relatively sober, they made excellent street operatives, because they could hang around places for hours and nobody noticed; they were invisible.

Nowadays, I try to find them a little work whenever I can. Between their meager monthly pension checks and what I throw their way, they manage to stay juiced nearly all of the time and out of the rain some of the time. Works for them.

Rebecca and I had been thinking about throwing a little Christmas party for them. Maybe the week before the holiday. Wasn't like you could have a big regular Christmas bash and just invite them along with the rest of the crowd.

"You mind swinging by the Zoo on the way home?" I asked, naming their favorite hangout. She said she didn't and took a hard left on Fairview.

The Eastlake Zoo had occupied the corner of Lynn and Eastlake for as long as I could recall. It hadn't always been called the Zoo, but it had always been a tavern. Fisher's back in the forties. Then Mac's and then Hank's. I remember my old man bringing me into Hank's and how I used to love to play the bowling machine. The one where you slid the little shuffleboard disks at the pins and how they folded up when you hit them. I could still hear the *kaa-ching* sound. That was back in the days when it was illegal to walk around with your beer and ladies were allowed to sit only in the booths.

Back in my heyday, the seventies, it was called the In and Out. A place where you could always find a cold beer and a good blues band on Friday and Saturday nights.

Rebecca pulled the car into a loading zone across the street and I hustled inside. Terry the bartender was polishing glasses behind the bar. I nodded on my way by. A dozen people were spread throughout the gloom, a couple of pool games in progress, a couple playing pinball, half a dozen smokers up in the balcony. But nobody I knew.

"Ain't been here in a couple of weeks," Terry shouted. "None of 'em," he added. Terry had bad feet. Always walked like he was barefoot in broken glass. He motioned me up to the far end of the bar. "They found a crib."

"Really? Where?"

He told me.

"You're shittin' me," I said.

He held his hand over his heart. "Swear to God," he said. "Stopped in last week to see for myself. Ya can't miss it, Leo. Gotta see it wid your own eyes."

"You go in?"

"Hell no. No way in hell you get me in there."

*   *   *

We parked way up the street so's not to blow their cover. Two square condos. Identical and ultramodern. Brown. Built on a highly questionable piece of ground between a freeway exit and the base of Capitol Hill. Everybody remembers when these two started sliding down the hill because they'd closed the whole northbound half of I-5 for three days while they figured out what to do next. What that did to traffic will live in commuter infamy for years.

Generally, any house that slides thirty feet downhill is firewood, and anybody who has the misfortune to be inside becomes the dear departed. What saved both the occupants and the structures was the sheer enormity of the piece of ground that moved. The entire section of hill upon which the structures stood, at least three acres square, had separated from the surrounding earth as if sliced by a spade, and slid the better part of thirty feet closer to the highway. Everything went in one piece. The concrete sidewalks showed no cracks. Hell, from what I could see from behind the police barrier, the shrubbery was still alive down there.

The original fear had been that any further slippage might result in the condo's sliding the rest of the way down the hill and landing on the interstate. That's why they shut it down. After surveying the scene and crunching some numbers, state and federal engineers, however, assured the city that were further slippage to occur, the hill and the houses would surely take the steeper line down the gully to the south and therefore posed no danger whatsoever to the highway. I remember reading in the paper that the reason the condos hadn't been razed was because the insurance companies were suing the county, claiming that building permits should never have been issued for such an unstable piece of property. The county was countersuing . . . yamma . . . yamma.

Rebecca peered down at the square roofs and laughed out

loud. "No way I'm going down there," she said. She held a hand to her throat and chuckled some more.

"I'll either be here or in the car. Give the lads my love."

I had a feeling that this was going to be something worth seeing, but Rebecca Duvall wasn't the type of person one talked into or out of anything, so I didn't bother trying. I said I'd tender her regards to the troops and set about looking for how it was they got down there.

Two things I knew for sure. First, the path wouldn't be hard to find. Stealth required just a bit too much attention to detail for this group. Second, it would not be hard to negotiate. These guys got way too drunk for anything even remotely athletic. If they could get there, Stephen Hawking could get there.

It was like I figured. A hundred yards up the sidewalk, I stepped over the cable guardrail onto a dirt path that meandered along the top of the freeway wall. Nice and wide. Chain-link fence to hold on to. Following the contour of the land downward until, eventually, I took a right through a grove of scrub oak and stepped onto the lawn of the nearest condo. Fine, unless you turned and looked back at the hill, where a wall of mud loomed overhead like a cresting brown tidal wave. I made a mental note not to look in that direction and started across the patch of grass separating me from the porch.

From the street above, the structures appeared to be sitting more or less on the level. From here it was obvious that they sloped away from the hill at a fairly substantial angle. I walked gingerly toward the door. I knocked hard. Silence. "Shhhhhhhhhhhh," I heard. "Shhhhhhhhhh." Then the sound of feet. I knocked harder and longer.

"Open up. It's Leo," I said. More scuffling feet and then a watery red eye at the peephole. A full thirty seconds of fumbling before the door finally swung open.

Ralph Batista had once mustered the longshoreman vote for my old man. Pound for pound he was the biggest lush of the lot and could, in any given day, put away more booze than anyone I'd ever met. He was full-scale hammered and having trouble with the slope, weaving and sliding back along the incline until his grip on the doorknob jerked him to a stop. "Leo," he slurred. "Whatcha . . . Hey hey hey . . ."

I checked my watch. Bad timing. Three-thirty-five. I'd caught them at the low point in their drinking day. Especially if they had a crib. Having a crib completely changed their drinking habits. While the average citizen would relish being able to sleep dry and warm, the boys saw the windfall in totally different terms. To them, having a place meant they didn't have to drink in bars, which, in turn, meant that the price of booze went radically down, which likewise meant they could drink even more than usual. Not only that, but a crib meant a place where they could pass out whenever they wanted without risking waking up at either the King County Jail or the Union Gospel Mission. Yeah, three-thirty was just about nap time for this crew.

I kept one hand on the wall as I stepped inside. The floor listed forward at a twenty-degree angle. I kept my butt back and my steps short as I worked my way past Ralph and tottered into the living room. The place was completely furnished. It hadn't occurred to me, but I guess if your house slides thirty feet down a hill with you in it, you don't call Bekins to come back for your furniture. You just take the insurance money and thank the fates.

At the far end of the room, a striped mattress had been thrown up against the double glass sliding doors. Kind of a safety barrier, I guessed. In case a guy worked up a head of steam on his way across the room and couldn't stop. Billy Bob Fung and Big Frank sat on the floor leaning back against the mattress, chins on chests and a bottle of gin on the carpet between them. In the high-rent district along the left wall, everybody had his own bottle. Gravity had pushed Norman, Harold and George down to the low end of a black leather sofa, where they sat pressed together hip to hip, heads lolling. In front of the sofa, a rosewood coffee table with a glass top. They'd nailed a two-by-four to the floor at the far end to keep it from sliding and cut five inches off the near legs to level it. At least three of them were snoring. The air smelled like wet dog.

"Heeeeeeeey," Ralph bellowed. Nobody moved, so he hollered again. Nothing. "Buncha damn drunks," he mumbled.

I saw George Paris twitch down at the far end of the couch and then crane his neck forward. With his gaunt face and slicked-back white hair, George looked like a defrocked boxing announcer. Years ago he'd been an important banker and a mover and shaker in the Downtown Businessman's Association. He blinked me into focus and then put the bottle to his lips for a quick pull. "Leo," he said. "Damn good to see you, boy."

I watched as he tried to lever himself off the couch. "Ugh," he grunted as he tried to sit forward. No go. The force of Harold and Norman pressing against his right shoulder was too great. He was stuck. I suppressed a giggle.

Undaunted, he tried again. And again. This time kicking his legs out in an attempt to create some forward momentum. When that didn't work, he completely lost it. Thrashing about like a stroke victim. Spewing spittle. Screaming. "Goddammit, get offa me. Ya hear me, here. Goddammit. Stop leanin' your big ass on me. I'll . . ." Neither Harold nor Norman batted an eye. Against the far wall, Frank broke wind and fell over on his left side. George redoubled his thrashing and swearing efforts. I couldn't help it. I started to laugh.

Behind me Ralph clung on to the doorknob for dear life, laughing hysterically. I turned back toward him. "You stay right where you are," I said. I don't know whether he heard me. By that time he was down on one knee, pounding the floor, his body wracked by uncontrollable whoops of laughter.

I kept my weight back like I was waterskiing and crossed

to George. He didn't look good. "Gemme outta here, Leo," he wheezed. I took the bottle of schnapps from his hand and set it on the coffee table. Taking both of his hands in mine, I leaned back and pulled him from the couch like a cork from a wine bottle. As I threw an arm around his narrow waist to prevent further slippage, Harold and Norman slid across the slick leather surface of the couch, filling in the area so recently occupied by George.

He snatched the bottle from the table and started up for Ralph. By the time he was halfway up the incline, he'd walked completely out of his baggy woolen socks and was now barefoot and waving the bottle in the manner of a drum major with a baton.

When it appeared he might falter and end up back on the couch, I grabbed him by the belt and propelled him the rest of the way. "What's so goddamn funny?" he demanded. Ralphie, of course, laughed harder. I decided to nip the bickering in the bud.

"George," I said. He was still glaring down at Ralph. "I came to invite you guys to a party."

"I don't see what's so goddamn—" He stopped shouting and looked over at me. "A party? What kinda party?"

"A Christmas party for you guys," I said. "Next Thursday night."

Ralphie staged a miraculous recovery. Regaining his feet, wiping his eyes.

"At your place?"

"Yeah."

George leaned in close. "Can . . . you know . . . some of the other . . ."

"Sure," I said. "As long as it's somebody I know."

When we'd hatched this scheme, Rebecca and I had made a list. By our reckoning, if you counted the fetid foursome, we knew about twenty of the domestically disadvantaged, sixteen of whom had worked for me at one time or another.

We figured we could handle it. With a little help from a caterer, of course.

I slipped George a twenty and told him to have the gang take the bus to the top of Queen Ann Hill and then walk over. Eight sharp. Spit and polish. No kneewalking drunks. Cops aren't going to like a pack of you in that neighborhood. Scout's honor.

They both followed me outside. Rebecca's voice rang from above. She was standing behind the barricade at the far edge of the cut, waving.

"Hi, Georgie," she trilled. George looked up too quickly and nearly swooned. He had to lean back against the doorframe or go down in a heap.

Ralph showed a couple of teeth and waved. "Miss Duvall," he shouted.

I could hear them shouting back and forth as I made my way back up to the road. She saw me coming, cupped her hands around her mouth. "See you at the party," she yelled. I looked down. George waved the bottle. I waved goodbye.

The little drummer boy was beating that friggin' drum on the car radio. That's another big player in the Christmas crazies . . . that damn music. Coming at ya twenty-four seven, from every channel like Red Chinese propaganda. Used to be just the standards. Bing crooning White Christmas. Gene and Rudolph. Burl and Frosty. Nat roasting those chestnuts. These days we've got everything from squads of beefy tenors Aveing so high even Maria can't hear it, to rednecks telling us how their grandma got snockered and was trampled by hooved creatures. What's next ? In twenty years . . . ? "Marilyn Manson—A Christmas to Remember." Yeah, the tunes are a killer.

As we rolled into the driveway, I punched the garage door opener. She slid the Explorer in next to the Fiat. Home again . . . home again . . .

Something about living together changes all the rules. It's

like when you move in together, you automatically become your parents. Our nearly twenty-year relationship had always been based on equality. Sort of a physical, spiritual and intellectual Dutch treat, so to speak. Sure, I'd always been in charge of the heavy lifting and anything that involved sewage. And you sure wouldn't want me out there buying baby shower gifts. Rebecca had always handled that sort of thing. But . . .

She stuck the Explorer into park and turned off the engine and the lights.

"Put the stuff up in the guest room," she said cheerily and headed for the house. I took a deep breath. I'd made a pact with myself. No matter what little annoyances I encountered this holiday season, I was going to remain Mr. Affable. Mr. Christmas Spirit himself. No more hanging out by myself. No more of those turkey dinners at the Yankee Diner, where everybody else in the place looks like they work for Ringling Brothers. No sir. Chalk it up to getting old and sentimental, but these days I'm prepared to gag down a piece of my aunt Hildy's truly execrable fruitcake in return for the joy of seeing four generations of my family, gussied up and gathered under a single roof. Something about time making cowards of us all, I guess.

Four trips between the car and the guest room had us back to where we'd started this morning, except way broker. When I came downstairs for the last time, Rebecca was sitting on the couch going through the mail. The doorbell rang. She was closer, but I said I'd get it. What a guy. The UPS person. Gender not immediately apparent. Two big parcels wrapped in brown paper. Sign here. And here. Thankyouverymuch.

Packages were, and always had been, Rebecca's domain, so I carried them over and set them down next to her leg. She pointed to the card in her hand. "From Jed and Sarah," she said, naming my attorney and his wife. It was one of those family portrait Christmas cards. Jed, Sarah, both girls and their hubbies, and this year . . . the first granddaughter.

All dressed to the teeth around Jed's massive dining room table. Crystal both overhead and at hand. The perfect turkey on the table. Very nice indeed.

"What's this?" she said while I was still studying the picture.

"Gifts," I said.

"No," she said emphatically enough to get my attention. "No, they're not. These are the packages I sent Claudia and J.D." She picked up the top box and held it up under the lamp. The purple stamp read, *Undeliverable. Party no longer at this address.*

I don't believe in ESP or any of that stuff. I think it's like the guy said: Inevitable is hindsight for random. But, I must admit, the instant I read that bright purple message, something inside of me went bump in the night. Something cold. I wandered out into the middle of the room and began to count my breathing. In . . . out . . . one . . .

I needn't have worried about passing on the vibe. Before I got to three, she was headed for the kitchen. A couple of drawers slammed and then I heard her banging the buttons on the phone. Then nothing.

She came back through the swinging door. "No answer. Just the machine."

I did my duty. I came up with a half a dozen well-reasoned explanations why there was nothing to be concerned about. Reluctantly, she allowed how I was probably right, and she was just being silly, but she didn't believe a word of it. I could tell.

Dinner was declared to be a "fake it," every person for himself, eat anything you can find in the house, no ordering takeout, except by prior agreement. I put together a procciutto and provalone sandwich on onion rye, sliced myself a kosher dill and washed it all down with a couple of ice-cold Mirror Pond Amber Ales.

Rebecca was down the hall in the den, working on some notes for a speech she was going to deliver to some pathologist gathering or another. I was sitting on the couch reading Stephen E. Ambrose's *Citizen Soldiers*. Every half hour or so, she'd pad into the kitchen and try Claudia's number. No go.

By ten-thirty, middle age caught up with me and I was beginning to yawn. She said to go ahead; she'd be right up. At two in the morning, I awoke to find her wrapped up in a green blanket, sitting in the rocking chair across from the bed with a cookbook in her lap.

I sat up. She'd combed her hair all the way out and was wearing one of her old flannel nightgowns. One I hadn't seen in years.

"Sorry if the light's bothering you," she said. "I'll—"

"We'll go in the morning," I said.

She nodded and turned out the light.

6 No BLOOD. WE'D BEEN OVER THE CABIN FROM THE SOOTY ceiling to the glass-covered floor and hadn't found a drop. Rebecca was down on one knee, using the screwdriver she'd found in the kitchen to pry another slug from the logs in the living room. She held it between her thumb and index finger and squinted at it, then placed it in her palm and hefted it. "They're all from high-powered rifles," she announced.

No way to tell exactly how many rounds had been fired into the cabin. By conservative reckoning, at least fifty. In the back of the house, not only were the windows completely blown out, but several of the window casings had been torn to splinters by the high-velocity slugs. The board for hanging keys on had taken a direct hit, but except for the one marked SUBARU, the keys remained. Out front, the big window overlooking the river was also gone, but with the majority of the glass on the outside, you had to figure it had been shattered by one of the rounds passing through the master bedroom door. Didn't take a forensic team to figure out that the gunfire had come from the woods behind the house.

Not much doubt about the source of the fire that had claimed two walls and most of the ceiling in the kids' bedroom, either. You don't set moss-covered logs to burning with a Bic lighter. Somebody'd used an accelerant. The heavy alligatoring around the exterior window frame said it had been started from the outside. Below the window a wide arc of burned grass. As if the firebug had tripped and spilled most of the gas on the ground. Overhead, the charred ends of rafters stuck out like ribs. On the tangled floor, a thick red fire extinguisher. Empty.

The old smoke had clogged my nostrils and painted a gritty, acrid taste on the back of my throat. While Rebecca was working another slug out of the wall, I stepped out into the yard and blew my nose down onto the grass. First one nostril, then the other. Then I hawked a couple of times and spit. Better, but I still felt filthy, so I walked down the launch ramp to the river. I squatted with my toes in the shallows, scooped up a double handful of water and rubbed it over my face. Then again. Slowly this time. Better.

A mantle of fog covered the rivers like a shroud, leaving the far banks sketchy, and indistinct, like a half-erased pencil drawing. Somewhere in the fog, a fish rolled. I listened intently for another, but the ripple never came. I shook the water from my hands, then dried them on my jeans. The jet boats bobbed quietly at moorage. The Avon inflatable was gone.

Rebecca was standing on the concrete porch, peeling off the pair of blue rubber gloves she'd found under the bathroom sink. "Well," she said.

"You want to know what I think?"

"You're the detective."

Normally I would have taken this as an invitation to banter. Not today. No point in beating around the bush, either. She was far more experienced in this kind of site investigation than I was ever going to be.

I beckoned her out onto the lawn with me and then pointed at the ghostly line of trees a hundred fifty yards behind the house. "The shooting came from up there in the trees," I said. "That explains why the impact points are so much higher up in the back of the house than in the front."

"At least three different calibers," she said. "Probably more."

I took her by the arm and led her around to the back of the house. Walked her down to the far end, to the gray electrical service box bolted to the back of the house. In modern homes the service panel is in the laundry room or the garage. On old handmade houses, they just cut a hole in a wall and nailed the box over it.

The rectangular steel box had been torn to pieces by gunfire. The door had been blown completely off and lay pretzeled in the high grass at our feet. The interior section where the plastic circuit breakers had been was completely gone, leaving only a dangerous-looking thicket of black and white wires sticking out like quills.

"I'm thinking the first salvo or three went right here," I said. "Knock the power out. Put 'em in the dark. Scare the hell out of them."

I saw her shiver. She'd done it a couple of times since we'd come sliding to a stop in the driveway, but she'd never lost her cool. Not when I'd noticed the shot-out windows. Not even as we'd crept from room to room looking for bodies.

She looked up the hill at the tree line. "Pretty good shooting."

She was used to more urban forms of mayhem. Up close and personal. Uzis and Saturday night specials, where hitting something at a distance greater than a hundred feet was pure dumb luck.

"Deer rifles," I said. "Telescopic sights. In a place like this, everybody over the age of ten can make that shot."

"So . . . you think they were home when it happened?"

I thought it over. "Hard to tell," I said. "If I had to guess, I'd say yes."

"There's no other explanation for the fire extinguisher," she said. "If J.D. or Claudia didn't put out the fire, who did? The shooters?"

Smart girl. Always was.

"Yeah," I said. "And because I think whoever did this was trying to scare the hell out of them rather than kill them. And if that's what you've got in mind, you make sure they're home before you start."

"Why just trying to scare them?"

I gestured toward the service panel. " 'Cause of that," I said. "I mean . . . what's the point of all the marksmanship? What does it matter whether or not they have lights? If you want 'em dead, you sneak down, kick the door in and shoot all four of them in their sleep."

I could see she wasn't convinced, so I kept at it. "Picture yourself in the cabin when the shooting starts. You've got two little kids sleeping in the next room. What do you do?"

"I go for the kids," she said immediately.

"What then?"

No hesitation. "I take the children and run for cover."

"Which is where?"

"I don't understand."

I bobbed my head at the cabin. "Where in there could you find shelter?"

She looked over her shoulder at the cabin; I saw the light bulb go on. She bobbed her eyebrows. "It's a log cabin. Nothing is going to penetrate the logs. Shelter is everywhere except right in front of the windows."

"That's how I see it," I said. "They take their time . . . pump a dozen rounds into the electric service, create a little chaos, give the folks inside time to hunker down and then they start laying down a field of gunfire while their buddy sets the other end on fire."

"The firebug must have had a lot of faith in his friends to come down here with all that lead flying around."

She had a point. If it came down as I was pretty sure it had, whoever had crept down to start the fire either had very big balls or a very small brain.

"I agree with you," she said. "I think they left on their

own. I checked the closets and the drawers and the bathroom. Everything personal is gone. There isn't so much as a toothbrush or a diaper anywhere in there. Adam's potty-training seat is gone. They may have left in a hurry, but I feel certain they left."

Part of me knew what we were saying made sense, but another part knew how badly we wanted the family to be okay and how having such a personal stake in something colors the judgment. I closed my eyes and thought it through again.

"What now?" she asked.

"I'd say we go talk to the local law."

"Great minds think alike," she said and headed for the car.

I hoped we were right. I hoped it had come down the way we imagined. That, scared stiff, they'd packed their tents in the dead of night and stolen away. Maybe over to his parents' place. Normally I could have sold myself the story, but I'd already seriously underestimated the situation once.

If I was wrong this time . . . Naaah . . . not twice in a row.

7 "MR. SPRINGER IS DEAD." HE SAID THE WORDS IN A NEUTRAL voice. No "I'm afraid to say" or "I'm sorry to report." Just the fact. Sheriff Nathan Hand was fifty maybe. Narrow shoulders and no gut. Shaven smooth, his narrow face looked like it'd fit through the mail slot. His uniform was perfectly pressed and fit him precisely.

Rebecca and I spoke simultaneously. She asked, "How?" I asked, "Where?"

He pretended to draw it from memory. "Let's see, if I recall . . . it was two weeks ago tomorrow that . . ." He turned to the deputy. "I am right about that, aren't I, Harlan? It was two weeks ago tomorrow that we had the big fire over on West River."

The deputy's name tag read: HARLAN R. SPOTS, DEPUTY, STEVENS FALLS, WASHINGTON. Spots had narrow little eyes, thick red lips and an ass so big it wobbled when he walked. I know because the minute we'd told him what we wanted, he'd said we'd need to talk to Sheriff Hand and had wobbled off to find him.

"Yes, sir, I believe you are correct," he said in a wheezing tenor.

I had the feeling that if Hand had asked Spots to verify the presence of aliens in our midst, he'd have gotten much the same response.

"Terrible car accident," Hand said. "Just terrible."

She frowned. "You said something about a fire?"

For a second I thought he was going to pat her hand. Instead, he gave her a patronizing smile and a tone of voice that said she shouldn't worry her pretty little head about something so tawdry. He put both elbows on the counter and leaned toward her.

"Yes ma'am," he said. "More terrible than a lady like you could possibly imagine." Bad move. She tossed a business card onto the desk between them.

"I wouldn't count on that, Sheriff," she said. "People in my line of work tend to lead rich fantasy lives."

Hand ran his eyes over the card once and then slid it over to Spots. His lips moved as he read. "Well, well . . . " Hand said.

"The fire?" she prodded.

He tried to keep the question casual, but something in his demeanor had changed. No more Mr. Nice Guy funnin' with the tourists. Suddenly the cop.

"So . . . you're here in an official capacity, then?"

"I'm here to find out what happened to Mr. Springer," she snapped.

Not liking what he was getting from Rebecca, he turned his attention my way.

"And you?"

"I'm a friend of the doc's." I scribbled my cell phone number on the back and then handed him my card. Same deal, a quick robo-scan and over to Spots. I watched as the deputy sounded out *Investigations*.

Hand stood up straight, took a hitch in his belt.

"Harlan, get me the yard keys," he said.

Hand walked to the far end of the counter, lifted the gate and came around toward us. Deputy Spots slapped a ring of keys into the sheriff's outstretched palm. Unlike his deputy, Nathan Hand walked with a martial economy of motion. He strode on past us and pulled open the door. "After you," he said.

He led us around the west side of the building, where a black gate on rubber wheels spanned the drive. Behind the gate, three police cruisers. Two five-year-old Chevy Citations. Stevens Falls logo on the doors. One brand-new Crown Victoria, same logo but with the word SHERIFF painted above it in gold.

Hand rolled back the gate. Behind us, a passing car tooted its horn. Hand waved without looking. He pulled the gate behind us but didn't bother with the chain and lock.

We followed him along the length of the building. Beige cinder block with a single ground-level window about halfway down. Blinds tightly drawn. Air conditioner. Sheriff Hand's office, I was willing to bet.

When he stopped and turned back our way, I sensed he'd regained some of his bravado. "Now, normally," he began, "I'd feel compelled to warn you all"—he stepped aside and beckoned us forward—"but with you all being in the law enforcement field and all . . ."

It was one of those wrecks that freezes your innards. Reminds you of those times when you've been stuck on the freeway for hours and hours, ranting, raving, cursing your fate and damning every other driver on the road, especially the nitwit son of a bitch who caused this particular logjam, and then finally you see the flashing lights up ahead, you're about to make your escape when you look over on the shoulder and see the wreck that caused all this, and instinctively something in your gut knows that nobody, no living creature could possibly have walked away alive. And you drive the rest of the way home wondering about yourself. Again.

What had once been a stylish Subaru Outback had been reduced to its metal parts, and most of those were mangled. The front end was pushed in so far the floorboards had buckled. The roof was peeled back, the edges jagged and uneven, like the track of an old-fashioned can opener. Not a shred of rubber or plastic, or fabric, or glass, or for that matter any of the god knows how many other substances it takes to make a car. Nothing remained but soot covered metal.

I don't know what Rebecca was thinking, but Sheriff Hand read my mind.

"No way of telling whether the gas tank exploded and then set off the ten gallons of unleaded he had in the car with him, or whether it was the other way around."

"Where exactly did this happen?" I asked.

He pointed east. "You know the bridge back there?" I said I did. "Three-point-nine miles from the bridge. A steep little gully leading down to Taylor Creek. You could see the smoke all the way to town."

"Why would he have ten gallons of gas in the car with him?" I asked.

Rebecca moved over to the side of the wreck and was moving around it slowly.

"No idea," Hand said. "His insurance company had that same question. We both asked his missus, but she didn't know, either."

Rebecca stopped. "Where's Mrs. Springer now?"

"Couldn't tell you," he said. "She and the kids came in to make the arrangements for the body, then a couple of days later I went out and served her." He rubbed his chin and shook his head. "I certainly hated to have to do that. What with her just losing her husband and it being the holiday season and all."

If he was looking for somebody to feel sorry for him, he'd fallen in with the wrong crowd. "Served her with what?" I asked.

"Eviction," he said. "Had thirty days to pack up and vacate."

"On what grounds?" Rebecca demanded.

"Taxes," he said. "Something to do with it being a homestead."

I walked over to the car carcass and looked into the black hole that had once been the hatchback. "To tell you the truth," Hand said, "I been kinda worried about the Springer family myself."

I felt Rebecca stiffen. "Why's that?" I asked.

He wiped his forehead with his sleeve. "About a week later, I sent two of my deputies out to remind her—Bobby and Roy, three weeks to go now—and they found the place all shot up and the family gone. They said it didn't seem like anyone was present when the shooting happened. Naturally I hustled out there myself." Naturally.

Sitting on top of the rim that used to hold the spare tire was the galvanized top of a five-gallon gas can. The part with the flip-up handle and the screw-off top.

"No sign of any injury to anyone—"

I interrupted him. "What kind of progress have you made at finding out who it was shot the place up?"

He bristled. Didn't like being questioned about his work. Probably couldn't remember the last time it had happened. Rebecca had finished her circumnavigation of the car and was back at my side. Hand folded his arms across his chest. "Mr. . . . er . . . a . . ."

I helped him. "Waterman."

"Mr. Waterman . . . I don't know how much you know about hunting and outdoorsy activities"—I tried to look rugged—"but we're right in the middle of deer season around here. At any given moment, I've got hundreds and hundreds of people walking around in the woods with rifles and, as if that isn't bad enough, it just so happens that bunches of those people with rifles have absolutely no use whatsoever for the late Mr. J.D. Springer."

I wanted to hear what he'd say. "Why was that?" I asked.

He ran it by me pretty much the way I'd heard it before. I only stopped him once, and that was early on. He was talking about how pissed off everybody was when Mr. Bendixon sold the property to an outsider. "Of course, feelings just magnified when it turned out he'd cheated the old man."

"Whoa," I said. "Cheated the old man how?"

"On the price," he said. "You can look it up down at the clerk's office. It's a matter of public record. Springer paid one hundred thousand dollars for thirty-five acres. The figures are right there in black and white."

Rebecca piped in. "So?"

"So . . . a year ago the county offered him the better part of three." He waved a hand. "Two hundred ninety-something anyway. That's also a matter of public record." I opened my mouth to speak, but he beat me to it. "I've been told that half a dozen private parties offered him even more than that over the past couple of years. Check with the realtors, they'll tell you."

"How is J.D. supposed to have pulled that off?"

"Nobody knows for certain," he said. "Most folks think he caught the old man when he wasn't rational and got him to sign the papers. Old guy *was* eighty-two or so. Drank like a fish. Down to Freddy's Timbertopper every day at nine. Back home at six. Regular as clockwork." The sheriff shook his head. "I kept telling myself that the first time he drove off the road or hit something, I was going to have to tell him to either quit drinking or quit driving. Kept my fingers crossed, I did."

"Your point is?" from Rebecca.

He sighed. She sighed back at him. Bigger. I was hoping they'd keep at it and maybe we could have a Bugs and Daffy moment. But it wasn't to be.

"My point . . . is that it didn't take a genius fly fisherman to figure out that if you showed up at old Ben's place 'long about six-thirty in the evening, you were very likely to find the old man snockered. Most people figure that's just what Springer did. And I'm telling you, they didn't like it one bit. That old man was kind of a landmark around here. Like he was their link with the past in some manner or another."

I thought it over. J.D.'d said that he'd stopped in to see the old guy all the time. He'd admitted to trying to wear him down. What had he called it? *Winning through persistence.*

Maybe J.D.'s definition of persistence included catching the old man at an unguarded moment, maybe even drunk, and taking advantage of him. Hell, I'd only met him twice, and god knows, with those kind of numbers, there's no shortage of people who would do the same thing in a heartbeat and called it good business.

"Anybody ask the old man about it?" I asked.

"He was packed up and gone before anyone had the opportunity."

"Who did the autopsy?" Rebecca asked.

Hand chuckled as he slid the gate shut and locked it. "First off, Miss—"

"Doctor," she corrected him.

"Yes . . . Doctor . . . like I was saying . . . we don't have a coroner or anything like that. If and when we need that kind of work done, we call the state police. Second . . . anyone who has seen that body isn't likely to have the slightest doubt about the cause of death, believe you me."

Apparently she didn't. "Who prepared the body for burial?" she asked.

"Dewitt Davis," he said. "Davis Funeral Home up on Third."

He eased over by the cop shop door and put his hand on the handle.

"Did he take any pictures of the body?" Rebecca asked.

"I believe he did," the cop said.

I wasn't sure whether I meant it or not, but I said, "Thanks," and turned to leave.

"Ah . . . listen," he said. We waited. "You seem like nice folks," he started again. "A word to the wise." I could smell what was coming. "A great many people around here aren't altogether sorry about what happened to Mr. J.D. Springer. As a matter of fact, the way most people around here see it, when it comes to Mr. J.D. Springer . . ." He hesitated. "The way most of them see it . . . the deader the better." He waited for it to sink in and then said, "So you be careful now." With that, he turned the handle and stepped from view.

8 | ONE OF THE REASONS WHY REBECCA DUVALL AND I HAVE
been friends for thirty-five years is because we
learned early on that our minds don't work the same way.
I'm a batch processor. You send me out for a goat, I'm coming back with a goddamn goat. No . . . I won't get the dry
cleaning on the way home. This is a goat trip. Next, I'll make
a dry cleaning trip. Rebecca is totally the other way. Inter-
active. Everything is connected to everything else is connected to everything else. What store we start out for has no
effect on where we end up. Whatever product we went there
to get has little or no bearing on what we walk out with. All
plans are subject to change without notice. You cope.

We were ensconced in a Naugahyde booth along the west
wall of the Chat and Chew Café. A pecky cedar palace half
a mile east of the police station on the opposite side of the
highway. We'd perused the lunch menu and ordered coffee.

Halfway through our second cup of brown water, she
rolled her eyes up out of the cup. "What did you make of
the sheriff?" she asked.

"Not what I expected."

She nodded. "Me neither."

"Seemed too . . . too something for a small-town cop."

"Urbane."

"You check out that uniform?"

"Hand-tailored."

"You think so?"

"Women know these things."

"I don't think he was used to uppity women."

"Uppity? . . . *Moi?*" She took a sip, made a face and put the cup on the table. "I'm worried about Claudia and the children," she said.

"J.D.'s parents probably picked them up," I said. "Which would also explain why the Blazer is still in the driveway."

She had to admit this made sense. For my part, I didn't believe a word of it. As a matter of fact, I thought I knew just exactly where Claudia and the kids were, but I couldn't be sure and I didn't want to get Rebecca's hopes up. So I downplayed it.

"I've got a plan," she said.

"Let's hear it."

She spread her hands. "We're here . . . right?"

I couldn't find any loopholes in the statement, so I agreed.

"As long as we're here, let's do everything we can." She looked to me for agreement and got it. Hell, I make my living running errands for people who know full well I can't solve their problem. They just want to feel like they've done everything possible. Makes it easier to live with themselves later.

"I want to talk to the undertaker. By state law, he has to have a set of pictures of the body. I want to see them."

I blew out a lungful of air. "If J.D. was in that car—"

She held up a hand. "I just want to be sure," she said. I said I understood.

"I also want to find out about these eviction proceedings."

Again, I agreed. Everything Claudia and the kids had was tied up in that property. No way we could let anybody walk off with it without a fight.

"You want me to do that?" I asked.

"You're no good with bureaucrats," she said.

She had a point. Sooner or later they'd say something about how they had a policy against something or other or about how they just worked here and weren't actually responsible for shit and then I'd start to get snotty and things would go down the toilet from there. "You want to handle that, too?"

She nodded. "The assessor or the city attorney or whoever handles things like evictions in a burg like this is probably in the same building with whoever keeps the records. While I'm checking on the eviction, I can see if what the sheriff said about J.D. getting the property cheap is true."

I liked the sound of that. I was uncomfortable with the possibility that J.D. might have stepped over the line. Color me with a cynical crayon, but if I'm forced to bet my body parts on the likelihood of whether, out of the goodness of his heart, one man chose to sell a piece of property at a fraction of its value or whether it is more likely that the other man screwed him out of it . . . well, damn . . . sort of asks which is more prevalent, generosity or greed, doesn't it?

"What do you want me to do?" I asked.

"What you do best," she said with a grin. "Do what you always do. Turn over some rocks. Make bad jokes at people. Be obnoxious. Piss somebody off."

It's nice to be appreciated. "Meet back here when?"

The time was twelve-thirty. We agreed on two hours, give or take. Two-thirty or three.

9 I READ A BOOK ONCE BY SOME SOCIOLOGIST NAMED OLDEN-burg. He called it *The Great Good Place*. His point was about bars, coffee shops, beauty parlors, health clubs . . . what he called "third places," those places between work and home that allowed the unrelated to relate to each other. He believed these places, rather than job and family, were the glue that held a community together. I don't know if that's true, but I do know that when you're in a shitburg town like this and you want to find out what's going on, you head for the local watering hole.

I'd counted three, so I knew a little trial and error was going to be involved. When you're on foot, whether you like it or not, life gets linear. First one I came to was Freddy's Timbertopper Tavern. Turned out to be the old man's bar. The place you gravitate to when you don't hear well enough to talk around the jukebox, and you don't mind if the old woman comes with you, 'cause you no longer do anything she'd object to. I pulled open the door to find a room full of giveaway baseball caps advertising heavy equipment, chain saws and the ever-present John Deere tractor. I ducked back outside and kept walking.

Downtown Stevens Falls was decked out in its holiday finery, the hanging flower baskets replaced by Santas and reindeer and holly and mistletoe. Light posts were wound with red ribbon to simulate candy canes. Colored lights in the store windows. As I moved from store to store, I tried to work up a little holiday cheer, but I couldn't push that burned-out car from my mind. Some perverse instinct kept asking me to imagine what J.D.'s last moments must have been like. The loudspeakers were having a "Holly Jolly Christmas." I hummed along, but my heart wasn't in it.

Smack in the middle of town was the Stevens Falls Bar and Grille. Yeah, with an *e* at the end. Dead giveaway. A quick peek in the door confirmed my suspicion that the place had been urban-renewed. The butcher paper and the jars of crayons on the tables said it all. No . . . this wasn't the place, either.

The bartender told me the Steelhead Tavern was the last building inside the town limits. Took me the better part of fifteen minutes to walk it from downtown. What they didn't tell me was that the next-to-last building in town was a small white church with a round steeple that looked a whole lot more like a grain silo than a finger pointing to heaven. The sign out front read, CLOSED.

I trudged along the shoulder, traffic whizzing by, my sneakers crunching around in the gravel, contemplating whether or not a church could rightly be closed. The more I thought about it, the more sacrilegious it seemed. Even if it was true, they should have thought of a better way to phrase it. Maybe something like MOVED ON TO A BETTER PLACE or something like that, but not CLOSED.

Right away, I knew the Steelhead Tavern was the joint I'd been looking for. Set down below the road, it was a squat rectangle made of a little river rock and a lot of mortar, with a rusted corrugated metal roof thrown over the top. Beer signs blinking in every window. Three acres of muddy parking lot, half full at one-twenty-five in the afternoon. The National Beater Pickup Finals. Seldom, if ever, have I seen such an assemblage of dusty, dented, tailpipe-draggin', chicken-wing-box-for-a-window pickup trucks collected in one place. None of that Jap crap neither. No. These old boys bought strictly American. About every third generation, whether they needed a new rig or not.

I stood to the right of the doorway and waited for my eyes to adjust. On the jukebox, Travis Tritt was offering somebody a quarter, suggesting they use it to call somebody who cared. I heard the crack of pool balls and then the sound of a ball hitting the floor. Whoops and laughter, pinball machine bells and the drone of conversation.

I was at the short end of a big L-shaped bar. All the way at the back, the kitchen and a five-door cooler. The wall behind the bar was dedicated to pull tabs . . . the 401K plan of the terminally unemployed. Taped up high, bright iridescent scorecards with winning stickers pasted here and there. Down below, fifteen bright plastic bins overflowed with tabs. Thirty-six-inch TVs in every corner. A Pepsi can clock.

A low wall divided the bar area from the rest of the place. On this side, six two-person tables were squeezed against the wall. Then two stairs down into the big part of the place. A ten-by-twenty stage occupied the center of the far wall. Restrooms on either side. Ladies and Gents. Four pool tables, three pinball machines, an old-fashioned shuffleboard setup and about a dozen tables filled the remaining space. One waitress with big hair was moving from table to table at light speed.

The jukebox changed its tune. None of that nouveau country shit here, no sir . . . 'round here they played the real deal. Merle Haggard tellin' the big city to cut him loose and set him free . . . somewhere in the middle of Montana.

As I started down the bar, Merle was tellin' 'em just what they could do with their welfare and their so-called Social Security. A third of the way down I found an empty stool and squeezed myself in between an old woman in a bad wig and a skinny kid who was talking to his buddy and had his back to me.

"He's right, you know," the woman said. She was somewhere between sixty and eighty, with a face like a satchel and an auburn wig she wore on the top of her head like a hat.

"Who's right?" I asked.

"Why, Merle Haggard . . . that's who." She waved her cigarette at the bartender. "Ain't gonna be no damn Social Security."

"Yes ma'am," I said.

This seemed to satisfy her. She went back to chewing her gums and smoking.

The bartender poured her a fresh shot of Canadian Club with a water back.

"What can I get ya?" he asked me.

He was my vision of the perfect WWII sergeant. Square face, thick neck, flattop haircut and an expression that said nothing you ran by him was going to be new.

"What have you got on tap?"

"Bud, Bud Lite, Rainier, Rainier Light." He expected me to demand some sissy microbrew. I fooled him. I ordered a Bud and a cheeseburger.

"Up for the season?" he asked. Around here, that meant "deer" season.

"No," I said. "I came up to see a friend of mine. Turned out he was dead." Nothing like a little death and mayhem to spice up a conversation. Like I figured, it wasn't possible to walk away from a lead-in like that.

"Somebody local?"

"Fella named J.D. Springer."

His eyes checked the immediate area. He leaned over, his face in mine.

"I'll tell you, mister," he said in a low growl. "I don't have much of a stake in it one way or the other. I don't fish, and I never met this Springer guy." A bell rang down by the food service window. He straightened up, checked the shelf and then leaned back over. "But I'm tellin' you, lotta people around here got strong feelings regarding this Springer guy. Real strong."

"So it seems."

"If I were you, I'd keep his name under my hat."

He straightened up. "Thanks for the advice," I said as he walked off.

I turned my stool around and nursed a beer while I waited for the burger. About a dozen state highway workers in their orange overalls had pushed three tables together over by the ladies' room. They were beginning to clean up after themselves, so lunch break must be just about over. A pair of heavyset women wearing black stretch pants and voluminous flowered blouses played pool at the center table. After each missed a shot, they heckled each other in shrill voices. The older woman drew back a large loose arm and sent the cue ball rocketing the length of the table. Missed.

"Too hard," the younger one squeaked.

"Ain't no such thing, honey," trilled the other.

Their laughter could only be heard by dogs.

The action was over in the far corner, where a game of partners for pitchers had drawn a crowd. Maybe a dozen. Twice as many men as women. Half as many tattoos as teeth. A skinny guy in a Megadeth T-shirt stalked the table looking for a shot. He'd just called and made a long rail shot but had left himself stymied behind a trio of stripes. His partner was trying to get him to play safe, but Megaman just kept chalking his cue and circling the table. They were paired against a pair of brothers. Twins. Every Anglo-Saxon mother's bullet-headed sons. They were under six feet, but thick all over, with mean little eyes and the kind of Popeye forearms you get from repetitive manual labor. If the mill were still open, I'd have bet they pulled green chain—and it doesn't get worse than that.

"You gonna shoot or what, man?" the nearest twin demanded.

Megaman curled his lip and said, "When I'm ready, man. When I'm ready."

"I come over there, you'll be ready."

A couple of uneasy giggles rose from the spectators.

"Take it easy, Dexter," his brother said.

The counter over by Megaman's partner held four pitchers of beer, three of them full. The brothers were nursing foam. Megaman called a bank shot. "Six ball in the corner, cue ball off the rail." He sighted down the cue and rolled the ball slowly toward the other end of the table, where it eased behind the twelve ball, which seemed to be blocking the pocket, bounced softly off the cushion and deposited the six ball in the corner pocket, leaving the cue ball positioned so that the eight was child's play. The crowd stomped and whistled. "Bad hit," Dexter said.

"What?" yelled Megaman's partner.

"You heard me. It hit the twelve. I seen it."

"Bullshit," said Megaman, lining up the eight ball.

Dexter stepped over and jerked the cue from his hands.

"It's Mickey's shot."

"Cut it out, Dex," his brother said.

Megaman must have seen the act before, because he got his hands out of the way before Dexter slammed the cue back down on the table, shattering it, sending shards of wood flying in all directions. The crowd covered their beers and ducked their heads.

From behind the bar, a shout. "Goddammit, Dexter, quit it."

"I'm tellin' ya," he persisted. "I seen it."

When the crowd hooted him down, Dexter moved several paces from the table and stood there tapping the bottom of his cue on the floor, talking to himself under his breath. Megaman picked the splinters from the table, got another cue from the wall and made the eight ball in the corner. The applause was spotty.

"Make these two Rainier," crowed the partner.

Mickey bumped himself off the wall and walked over to Dexter. Dexter's cheeks were cherry red. They huddled and swapped money. Dexter leaned his stick against the wall and headed to the bar for beer. The brother fished in his pockets for quarters and then went over to rack the balls.

When Mickey stepped out of the way, for the first time I saw the counter against the back wall. Standing there, with a burger in one hand and a paper cup in the other, was the weasel from the gas station. Linc, as I recalled.

I looked down the bar to the serving window. My burger was nowhere in sight, so I grabbed my beer and walked across the room.

"Hey, Linc," I said. "Remember me?"

He stopped midchew. "Can't say as I do," he said.

"Remember, I stopped in a couple of months ago and asked you how to get over the river so I could visit the Springers. You told me there wasn't anything over there."

"I might recall," he hedged.

I heard the slide go in and then the unmistakable sound of pool balls dropping and then rolling and finally being racked.

"Mind if I ask you a few questions?"

He waved the burger. "I got to get back to the—"

"Mr. Springer buy that gas from you?"

"Wha—"

"You remember Mr. Springer, don't you? Guy that bought the Bendixon place. Died in that car accident on West River a couple of weeks ago."

He took a sip of his drink. "What gas would that be?"

"The gas he was carrying in the car with him."

"Why'd you think a thing like that? Like I sold it to 'im."

"As far as I can tell, you're the only gas station in town. Kinda figures if he bought gas, he must have bought it from you." I took a chance. "Could be I misunderstood Sheriff Hand."

You could practically see the gears turning in his narrow head.

"Sheriff Hand says I sold it to 'im, then I musta," he said.

"So then—" I started.

From behind me: "What about that Springer asshole?" Dexter.

I ignored him. "He get the cans from you, too?" I asked.

A hand dug into my shoulder. I grabbed it by the wrist, took it off and turned to face him. He had his nose stuck in my throat. "I asked you a question," he said.

"This is a private conversation."

His brother: "Dex . . . cut it out."

I looked back over my left shoulder. Linc was missing. The bar was about half as noisy as it was a minute ago. "Dexter, goddammit," yelled the bartender.

"You a friend of that Springer asshole?" He wasn't talking to me anymore; he was talking to the bar. We were having an E. F. Hutton moment.

"As a matter of fact, I am," I said with a smile.

It wasn't the answer he expected. I was supposed to wheedle. Not be standing there looking down at him grinning.

"Well . . . you the only one," he said. He thought it was a great punch line and looked around the bar for a laugh. Silence.

I raised my voice. "He had another friend in town."

Dexter played to the crowd. "Yeah, who's that?" he demanded.

"Probably shouldn't count her, though," I went on, " 'cause, you know"—I gave him a filthy wink—"she's everybody's friend, if you know what I mean."

I had him going now. "Yeah, who's that?"

"Your mother," I said.

His brother stopped fiddling with the rack and stood up straight. Deep-space silence, then somebody coughed. In my peripheral vision, I was aware of people clearing the area. He grinned and made like he was going to turn away and say something to his brother. "Hey, Mickey," he yelled. "Did you hear—"

I kept my eyes on his hands. When he shifted his grip on

the cue stick, I started to move. He brought the cue straight over the top like I was a nail and he was going to drive me into the floor. I ducked down, took two strides forward and brought my head up between his descending arms, using the power of my legs to drive the top of my head into his chin. I heard his jaw snap shut, heard the cue shatter somewhere behind me and then felt the sharp pain at the top of my head. I kept my head wedged under his chin and my legs driving until he went over backward onto the floor, with me on top of him.

After that, it was standard barroom brawl. Within five seconds, ten people were piled on top of Dexter and me. On the way down, I'd gotten my right hand up under his chin and was still pushing for all I was worth. Other than that, neither of us could move a muscle. Dexter was whimpering and making gargling noises. The air was filled with shouts and screams and curses. I kept trying to bench-press Dexter's lower jaw.

After a while, the pile began to lighten and then suddenly strong hands had me by the ankles, dragging me from the writhing mass of humanity. I came out rolling, shielding my head, ready to fight, but it was the bartender. I showed him my palms, got to my feet and backed over against the wall. He stood there facing me, making sure I wasn't going to start again. "What did I tell you?" he said. "Didn't I just tell you?"

"That cheeseburger ready yet?" I asked.

He couldn't help it; he smiled.

Dexter was still down. Several people knelt at his sides. I couldn't see the top half of him, but his legs moved on the floor like he was marching in place. He seemed to be mumbling something. The waitress trotted down from the kitchen with a white towel. Mickey was yelling at one of the spectators, a heavyset girl with braces on her teeth.

"Well, get a dish or something, goddammit," he yelled.

She scrunched up her face. "I'm not touchin' that thing."

He tried to backhand her, but she saw it coming and rolled out of range.

"Get it," he bellowed.

The waitress accompanied the girl up toward the kitchen. Mickey got to his feet. He had blood on his hands. "You son of a bitch," he growled at me.

The bartender moved his way, keeping his bulk between us.

"You best be getting Dexter to the clinic," he said.

Mickey leaned out around him. "I'm gonna find you," he said. "Soon as I take care a my brother. Don't think I won't."

A rough voice said, "You're dead, motherfucker."

The girl came trotting back, carrying a small white dish. Mickey jerked the dish from her hands and knelt by his brother. Megaman pulled several napkins from a dispenser and handed them down. The bartender wandered back my way.

"Bit off the end of his tongue," he said.

When they helped him to his feet, Dexter made a noise like he was gargling oatmeal. His eyes were squeezed shut. He held the towel to his mouth with both hands and seemed to be humming something through his nose as half a dozen men got him moving toward the door. His legs were bent. His toes dragged on the floor.

Mickey pulled their jackets from the pegs by the pool table and started after them. As he mounted the pair of stairs, he pointed back my way. "We're comin' for you," he shouted. Halfway to the door, he stopped and turned back toward the girl, who stood stupefied, her back to the wall, holding the dish out at arm's length like she had a weasel in a bag. "Come on, Melody," he screamed. "Hustle it up."

Melody took two steps in his direction and turned back my way with a malevolent gleam in her eyes. She dropped the dish to waist level and tilted it toward me. The little plate was bloody around the rim. At the bottom rested what looked like a piece of raw beef liver about the size of my thumbnail. She grinned a dull metal grin and started for the stairs, holding the dish high, like a waiter with a tray.

When the door banged shut behind her, people started moving. The air was filled with excited conversation and the sound of scraping chairs. The road crew paid up and filed out. The women went back to playing pool. The jukebox started again. Jim Croce. "Time in a Bottle." I headed for the bar.

Amazing what spilling a little blood will do. Ten minutes ago, when I'd ordered the cheeseburger, I'd barely had room to sit on the stool. All of a sudden, I had the whole center of the bar to myself. Except for the woman in the wig. She'd waited for me.

"They say you're a friend of that Springer fella."

"Yes ma'am."

She chewed a couple of times. "He's no damn good," she said.

"He's dead."

She grabbed a package of Kents and a Zippo lighter from the bar.

"Any man cheat an old man like Ben . . ." She stopped and chewed some more. "No damn good," she repeated before she waddled off.

The burger wasn't bad. A bit on the cold side, but I was hardly in a position to complain. About halfway through, the bartender slapped a fresh Bud down in front of me. "Slick move," he said.

"I was lucky," I said.

"Bullshit," he said. "Luck had nothing to do with that."

When the door opened, every head in the place swiveled. Who could blame them? These days you can't pick a fight with a twelve-year-old altar boy for fear he's got an AK-47 in his backpack. You could almost hear the collective sigh of relief when it turned out to be a woman of about forty. Stunning. Short curly hair worn close to her head. Tall as Rebecca but not as willowy. Put together more like one of those old-time pinup girls from the fifties and sixties. *Lush* would be the word. A Vargas girl.

"Hiya, Glen," she said to the bartender. Glen sucked in his gut and walked her way. "Hi, Ramona, how's it going?" he said in a voice two octaves lower than the one he'd been using on me.

"Got your ad ready?"

He reached under the bar and produced a videotape in a black plastic case.

"Right here," he said.

"What's the posse doing outside?" she asked.

He didn't answer. Instead he walked past her, lifted the gate and let himself out from behind the bar. He had everyone's attention as he opened the door and stepped outside. "Can I get you something, Miss Haynes?" the waitress inquired.

"I'm fine, Charlotte," she said.

The waitress shook her head. "You're always in such a hurry," she said.

"No rest for the wicked."

The door opened and Glen reappeared. "Charlotte," he called. "Call Nathan Hand. Tell him to come on down here." Charlotte picked up the black phone and dialed.

"What's the story?" the Haynes woman asked.

He leaned over the bar. I couldn't hear what he said, but as he spoke, she kept turning her head and looking at me. "Oh . . . that's nice," she said when he finished. "That's great. Just the image we want to project."

Glen shrugged. "You know Dexter," he said.

She walked the length of the bar and stuck out her hand. "Ramona Haynes," she said.

I took her hand. "Pleased to meet you," I said.

"I'm the president of the Chamber of Commerce and I want to apologize to you for any trouble those idiots may have caused you. I'd hate to have you go away from here thinking that's the kind of town we are."

"No problem," I said. I drained the last of my beer and got to my feet. "Everything's under control."

She went on about what a nice place Stevens Falls was, but I was having trouble paying attention. All I could think about was rubbing my face in her.

"If you'll excuse me," she said, "I think I better have a few words with that bunch before the sheriff gets here." Heads turned like radar dishes as she walked to the door. Didn't look a bit like Deputy Spots in motion. No siree.

I tried to keep it adult and professional. "Attractive woman," I commented.

"I get a chubby when she walks in the door," Glen said.

"Least you got the bar to stand behind."

"Had that effect on me since grade school," he said wistfully.

"So you're a native?"

"Sure. Both of us. Her family owned the mill. My old man drove forklift for her old man for thirty years."

He pried his eyes off the door and looked at me. "Anybody told you about old man Haynes?" I said they hadn't. "About how the day the bankruptcy court padlocked the building. Took his house, his land. How he walked all the way from his office down to the park in the middle of town. Apologized to every person he passed and then blew his brains out, sitting on one of the picnic tables."

"When was this?"

"Few years ago. That's when Ramona came back."

I threw a ten on the counter. Glen picked it up and handed it back to me. "Hell," he said. "By the time Dexter heals up, I'll have saved twice that in pool sticks."

"Thanks," I said.

"You better stay inside till the sheriff gets here."

"Why's that?"

"Dexter's friends got a little welcoming committee for you out there."

I feigned astonishment. "And we've allowed the fair damsel to go unescorted?"

He chuckled. "The fair damsel can flat-out take care of herself."

"Me, too," I said with a grin.

He stayed behind the bar, matching me step for step.

"Now, come on. Just when I was takin' a liking to you, you're gonna have me thinkin' you're a troublemaker."

When I pulled open the door, she was yelling at a group of five guys. Four I remembered from inside. The fifth was an albino guy about my size. He wore a confederate flag cap, a pair of striped coveralls and workboots. No shirt of any kind.

". . . as if we don't have enough problems and things to overcome around here without you fools . . ." She reached out and pushed on the forehead of the nearest guy until she had eye contact. "I'm up here, Noah," she said. "No matter how hard you stare at them, they aren't going to talk to you." She got the laugh she was looking for.

The pool partner, from the back of the crowd: "They talk to me, Miz Haynes."

She stopped talking when I stepped onto the porch.

"O-oh," she stammered. "You better—"

"That's him, Whitey," somebody said. "The one suckered Dexter."

Whitey showed me a mouthful of green teeth. I walked right up to him.

"They been doing this to you for years, haven't they, Whitey?" I said.

Everything got quiet. I could hear cars passing on the highway.

I'd say Whitey looked dumbfounded, but that would be redundant.

"What's that?" he asked.

"Using you for a trial horse. Taking advantage of you."

His forehead looked like a washboard. "Nobody takes advantage . . ."

"You know what I mean, man. They want to know if the water is deep enough, they talk you into jumping off the bridge. They want to know if the dog bites, they get you to try to pet him. They don't know how tough some guy is, they get you to try him out. I'd bet dollars to doughnuts they been doing that stuff to you for years. They have, haven't they?"

Somebody yelled, "Don't listen to that shit, Whitey, kick his ass."

Ramona Haynes shook a finger at him. "Don't you dare," she said.

The area around his eyes was so pink it looked like he had a disease, and his pupils were nearly colorless. "Dex is my friend," he said.

"Dex isn't anybody's friend," I countered. "As a matter of fact, I'd be willing to bet that most of the time when your so-called buddies here get you to do something stupid, I'll bet Dexter's the one who starts it." I thought I saw a glimmer, so I stayed at it. "He is. Isn't he?" I pressed.

"Bust him up, Whitey," a voice came. Partner again.

Without turning, Whitey said, "Shut your mouth, Monk, 'fore I come back there and bust you up."

The Crown Victoria with SHERIFF painted in gold came sliding to a stop about ten feet behind the crowd. Nathan Hand and a deputy I hadn't seen before got out, leaving the car doors open. Hand sauntered up onto the porch, while the younger cop leaned back against the hood of the car. The crowd parted. He tipped his hat. "Miss Haynes," he said.

He looked over at Whitey. "You still fighting their battles for them, Clarence?"

Clarence took off his hat and checked his shoes. His scalp was iridescent pink.

"Yessir . . . I mean, ah . . . no sir."

"Bobby," Hand called.

"Right here, Sheriff."

Bobby was a good-looking kid of about twenty-five. He had a long neck and a loose, easy way of moving that suggested competence. The gold tag read DEPUTY BOBBY RUSSELL. Like his boss, he'd had his uniform tailored. Except that the job wasn't nearly as good. Along the inside of his right leg one of the seams was coming loose.

"Check your watch."

"Yessir."

"In exactly two minutes, I want you to begin checking the licenses and registrations of every vehicle still in this parking lot. I believe I see some expired tabs out there."

"Believe I do, too, sir."

"And Bobby . . ."

"Uh-huh?"

"Make sure you check for current insurance. Make 'em show you the paperwork. What's that citation up to these days?"

"Seven hundred seventy dollars, Sheriff."

Hand whistled. "A tidy sum."

By this time, Hand was playing for the deputy, the Haynes woman and me. The rest of them were long gone. We stood and listened to the sounds of grinding engines and pickups bouncing out into the road in a hail of gravel.

The sheriff wagged a finger my way. "I knew you were going to get yourself in trouble." He checked his wrist. "Thought it might take you more than an hour, though."

"I didn't start it," I said.

He gave a hearty chuckle. "Hell, with Dexter Davis involved, I don't even have to ask. Neither of those Davis twins has got brains enough to blow his nose, but Dexter . . ." he shook his head. "They tell me he fell off his bike when he was nine, you know. Landed on his head. Hit the curb out in front of Mrs. Fontaine's house. Never been the same, they say. Last sheriff told me for years after that, wherever the family lived in the valley, all the neighborhood cats would turn up missin'. Neighbors would call . . . they'd come out . . . find a little tabby foot here . . . a little tabby tail there . . . never could quite catch him at it, though."

"And Dexter and Mickey are a step up from the parents," Haynes added.

"Oh hell . . . two, at least," said the Sheriff.

"That's a frightening thought," I said.

"I'm glad you think so," she said.

"Well . . . ," Hand began, "much as it pains me to break up this merriment, duty calls." He cocked an eyebrow at me. "Now, you think maybe I can leave the big-city private eye alone for a couple of hours without him getting in any trouble?"

I held up two fingers. He smirked.

"Where you parked?" he asked.

"I'm on foot," I said.

He shook his head. "No . . . no . . . that won't work here, now, will it Bobby?"

"No sir."

"You get to walking around out there, you're just surer than heck gonna end up tied over the front of somebody's truck. You better get in the car."

"You arresting me?" I asked.

He looked hurt. "Now, why would you ask a thing like that?"

"Because that's the only way I'm getting in the car," I said.

Bobby bumped himself off the fender. Hand thought it over.

"He can ride with me," said the Haynes woman. She looked over at me. "Or am I going to have to place you under arrest?"

"I'll come quietly," I promised.

10 "WHERE ARE YOU STAYING?" SHE ASKED.

"I'm not," I replied. "I'm just here for the day."

She stepped down off the porch and started around the side of the bar, talking as she walked. I hustled after her. "That's what I figured," she said. "You don't look outdoorsy enough for most of what we've got to offer."

I don't know why, but I thoroughly resented this aspersion of my rurality. Before I could take issue, however, she wanted to know where she should take me.

"Anyplace in town. I'm meeting a friend at three. I'll just wander around till then. Do a little Christmas shopping."

She popped the locks on a blue Dodge Dakota pickup and we got in. The seatbelt harness did wonders for her. "Did you tell me your name? You must not have. I'm usually good with names." She dropped the tape into an upright paper bag on the seat.

"It's Leo," I said. "Leo Waterman."

"So then you've got an hour to kill, Mr. Leo Waterman?" Her voice held the hint of a challenge, as if somehow I were being tested.

"Yep."

"So why don't you come along with me? I've got a few errands to run. It'll give me a chance to convince you that we're not all a bunch of crazed rednecks around here. Maybe even send you on your way with a positive feeling about the place. Wadda ya say?"

"Probably keep me out of trouble, too."

She grinned. "Yeah . . . there's that."

"Okay," I said.

"Gotta stop at the office first," she said, throwing the truck into gear.

She drove like a disaster movie, like molten lava was nipping at the rear tires. Fortunately, the truck was equipped with one of those "oh shit" handles up by my right ear, so I was able to look confident while holding on for dear life. In a roar, we headed back toward town.

"Did I understand Nathan to say that you were a private detective?"

I allowed how that was indeed the case as she fishtailed around a corner.

"And you're investigating what happened to J.D.?"

"Nope," I said. "I—we—just came out to visit some friends." I told her of getting the packages back and of being unable to raise them by phone. "And come to find out he's dead . . . somebody shot up his place . . . his wife and kids are nowhere to be found. I'm just trying to get some sort of personal handle on the thing."

"Poor J.D.," she said.

"You knew him?"

"Oh sure," she said. "By the time he . . . by the time it was over, I guess I was pretty much the only person in town still talking to him."

From this direction, the downtown area was backlit by a long line of poplars whose golden leaves shimmied in the breeze like a beaded curtain.

"Why was that?" I asked.

She told me the by now familiar tale. As much as it pained me, the story of the outsider taking advantage of an old-timer and then offending the whole town by closing off the river made more sense than the notion that town and county government were conspiring to put J.D. Springer out of the fishing guide business.

We whizzed by the police station, rolling toward the east end of town.

"He didn't understand," she said finally.

"What?"

"Oh . . . the culture, I guess. The people. How things are done in a place like this." She took one hand off the wheel and waved it about. "Everything . . . poor J.D. just didn't understand any of it."

A flush that had started below her throat had now reached her cheeks.

"For instance," I said.

"Oh . . . for instance, he didn't understand the ramifications of posting his property. I'll bet there's close to fifty men in this community who rent themselves out as fishing guides at one time or another during the season. That's a couple of hundred people whose livelihoods are affected by his actions." She was waving the hand again. "In a town like this that's just holding on, mostly what they do is provide services to one another. That's how they stay alive after the industry is gone. Most of the men in this town do four or five different things for a living. They cut some firewood. They drive school buses, hire out as mechanics, guides, handymen. Work part-time for the county. They do whatever it takes. I don't think J.D. ever really got a sense of what he was doing to that system."

She stomped the brakes and crimped the wheel into a U-turn. I hadn't noticed it before, but at the junction east of town, where you either go right and drive out to the ocean or you continue on ahead into Stevens Falls, a sparkling new A-frame sat on the triangle of property between the two roads. The sign read, VISITOR INFORMATION CENTER. WELCOME TO STEVENS FALLS: GATEWAY TO *YOUR* MOUNTAIN EXPERIENCE.

She slid to a stop in front of the building, turned off the engine and grabbed the bag of tapes. "In the summer, we hire college kids to run the Visitor Center. This time of year, I do it myself, but only on weekends." She yanked the door handle. "You can stay in the truck if you want; I'm only going to be a minute."

I got out and followed her inside. She walked around the counter and let herself into the cramped back room. Boxes full of brochures, a small battered desk with an old Macintosh computer, a video recorder and a big black electronic device I didn't recognize.

"What's that?" I asked.

"A combination videotape editor and converter." She pointed to the bag of tapes. "I spend all of every Wednesday editing and changing the format. If I screw up, it sometimes takes me till the wee hours. I take all of those and put them on one tape. And then I convert a half-inch video into a three-quarter-inch video tape loop." She could tell I was lost.

"We have our own TV station," she said. "It used to be an electronic monitoring station for the Strategic Air Command. They gave it to us when they didn't want it anymore. It was cheaper than tearing it down. We use it to run ads for local merchants, the community bulletin board, sports schedules, the church calendars. That kind of thing. Here in town it plays on Channel Fourteen all the time. Friday afternoons we broadcast to most of the peninsula for an hour." Her eyes were bright. "It's been a heck of a boost for business. Something like fifteen percent, we figure."

She picked up the phone, dialed her access code and listened to her messages. She made a few notes in a battered day planner and then got to her feet. "Ready?"

When I said I was, she grabbed a red videotape box from the center desk drawer.

"After you," she said.

She locked up behind us and got behind the wheel. I was already belted and hanging on. "Nobody likes my driving," she said.

As we were racing back toward town, I asked, "How come you're . . . I mean . . ."

A smile twisted the corners of her mouth. "You're working up your version of what's a nice girl like me doing in a place like this?"

"Something like that," I admitted. "I mean, I'm sure this particularly bucolic hamlet has its charms . . ."

She knitted her brow and narrowed her eyes. "Careful what you say, now. I was born and raised here."

"And you can still speak in complete sentences."

She had a rich, muscular laugh.

"That's because I went away for a while."

When I didn't say anything, she went on. "Chicago . . . fifteen years."

"What brought you back?"

"Oh, a bunch of things. A divorce. A job I was good at but didn't really like." She shrugged. "Just a general sense of disconnectedness."

"So are you cured? Are you connected now?"

She mulled it over. "I'm cured of some of it, I suppose." She threw me a sharp look. "You ask a lot of questions, you know that?"

"I'm a detective," I said. "We're allowed to do that."

"It was just so sad," she said after a moment. "The town," she said without me asking. "Lots of people were talking about leaving, they were talking about closing the school and busing the kids to Sequim. I don't know. The whole way of life just seemed to me like something worth saving."

"What did you do in Chicago?"

"Real estate development."

"Ah . . . so it was a natural."

She gave another laugh and launched into the prepared part of the program.

"Nothing about Stevens Falls is natural. It's like I keep telling anybody who'll listen. This is a town and a way of life on the brink. We either bootstrap ourselves into the new century or we go the way of all those hundreds and hundreds of other Northwest towns that just dried up and blew away when they ran out of whatever it was they were selling. Coal, tin, lead, lumber, it doesn't matter. One ending is another beginning. One man's loss is another man's opportunity."

She was right; it could be done. Up in the Cascades, the mountain town of Leavenworth had transformed itself into an alpine village, Octoberfest, lederhosen, dirndls and all. Farther over the mountains, Winchester had turned itself into the wild wild West, with saloons and staged gunfights in the streets. Vast tracts of eastern Washington, once considered unusable, were now covered by trendy vincyards.

She caught me looking at her. "I was doing my spiel, wasn't I?"

"You've got my vote," I said.

"I'm afraid I am something of a fanatic on the subject."

"It usually takes a fanatic to get anything worthwhile started."

"Who said that?"

"I was hoping it was me."

"No," she said. "I've heard some variation of that before."

We rolled back past the Steelhead, out the west end of town, toward J.D.'s place and the damaged bridge. "You know that bridge that's coming up in a few miles?" I began.

"The Fox Creek Bridge."

"The one to J.D.'s place."

"Yeah."

"What's wrong with it?"

She kept her eyes on the road. "Actually . . . nothing. We've just had it closed all this time so we could drive J.D. crazy."

She put her right hand across her chest, Pledge of Allegiance position.

"I swear, Leo. That's what J.D. thought was going on.

That man honest to God thought the whole thing was a conspiracy to drive him out of business."

"So then, it is damaged."

She looked at me as if for the first time. "Of course it's
damaged. Why else would it be closed? He's not the only
one who uses that bridge. It's a heck of an inconvenience for
a lot of people, not just Mr. J.D. Springer."

She went on. "Last winter we had nearly double our average rainfall. You remember how bad it got out here?"

I said I did. I recalled pictures of people rowing boats
through downtown.

"We had rocks the size of houses rolling down the Hoh.
It's a seventy-year-old wood frame bridge. It took quite a
beating."

"How long is it going to take to fix?"

She barked out a dry laugh. "Ha," she said. "With or
without money?"

"I thought the state—" I began.

"The state comes up with half of it. The feds come up
with half of that. The rest is our responsibility."

"And you don't have it."

"Touchdown," she said. "Things like the road we can do.
But we don't have the engineering expertise to do anything
about the bridge."

"What about the road?"

She took her eyes off the road for a moment. "You're
doing that detective thing again, aren't you?" she chided.

I resisted a strange desire to confess all. "It's in the
blood," I said.

"The road was easy. We had Tonkin Construction go out
of business. He had all his construction equipment up for
sale. He was getting offers of five cents on the dollar because
the equipment was so old. The stuff just sat there in the rain,
month after month. When the river washed out this part of
the road . . ." She made a rueful face. "As usual, we couldn't
come up with our share."

"Yeah?"

"I had an idea. What if we did it ourselves? Lord knows we've got enough people who know how to operate heavy equipment and have the time. I sat down and did the math. The way I calculated it, if we paid old man Tonkin twenty cents on the dollar and paid operators ten bucks an hour, adding in the cost of materials, it was still seventy percent cheaper than having an outside contractor do the job. So . . . I went to Mr. Tonkin and put it to him."

I was thinking the old guy never had a chance. "And he went for it," I said.

"Oh heck. He was thrilled. He helped us put the stuff back into shape and then taught everybody how to run the machines."

She anticipated my next question. "It was slow going. There was a pretty steep learning curve. Especially with some of the people we had doing the learning." She grinned over at me. "You remember Whitey from back at the tavern?

"Sure," I said.

"Well, just to give you some idea of what we were working with, Whitey drives the dump truck on the road crew."

She could tell I was suitably impressed. "We made a lot of mistakes, but we learned from them. We did it as soon as we could pay for it. That's something else J.D. had a problem understanding."

"What's that?"

"That he was the only one living out this far, and that, you know . . . that we were going to get around to this end of the road when we got around to it. He seemed to think that we should aim all our resources at his problem, and when we didn't, when we took care of the most first, he seemed to think it was personal or something." She took a deep breath and went on. "In the end, we got it done for about half the cost, and now we collect the state and federal money, do the work ourselves and pocket the difference. This fall, we put a new roof on the school with the leftover money."

About a mile before the Fox Creek bridge, we skidded to a stop in front of a galvanized cattle gate. Ramona got out, unfastened the lock and chain and then tied the gate open. When she got back in, she said, "Wait till you see this thing. The Air Force guy they sent out when we took it over said it was designed to survive anything short of a direct nuclear hit."

We went bouncing up a well-worn dirt track, winding our way up the side of a steep clear-cut mountain. Ten minutes of gunning it up the straights and then sliding around the switchbacks. The scenery never changed. All the way to the top, the unbroken ranks of huge gray stumps sat among the scrub brush like tombstones.

We arrived at the top on two wheels, a combination of too much speed and a steep final grade that gave way a little too quickly to the man-made plateau at the summit.

To my left, in a large fenced-in yard, a dump truck, a road grader, an asphalt spreader and a steamroller. In front of me, something that looked like it should be defending the Siegfried Line. A squat concrete bunker with a massive antenna on top. At least two hundred feet of welded steel and dull red paint.

I chuckled. "You could broadcast to Rangoon on that thing."

"We could send pictures into space, if the FCC would let us," she said. "All we had to buy was the rig you saw in the office and a commercial VCR. Everything else was already here."

She turned off the truck and checked her watch. "Gotta hurry," she said, grabbing the red tape box, popping the door and hustling toward the bunker. I pried my fingers from the overhead handle and followed along at a leisurely pace.

She looked back over her shoulder. "You always walk

this slow, Mr. Leo Waterman, or do you just like being behind me?"

"A little of both," I admitted.

She laughed and walked faster. Over to the thick steel door. She unlocked it and pulled it open, blocking my view of the interior. "Come on," she said. "The tape loop recycles at two-thirty. If it's going to be nice and neat and I'm not going to stop something midstream, that's when I need to change the tape."

The interior was tiny, one table, one chair, still smelled of fresh concrete. Two overhead lights cast a dim glow over the low room. The feeling was one of being squeezed. Of dampness. Of an oppressive weight coming at you in all directions. I felt trapped and had to overcome the urge to back out the door. On the wall to the right of the door, someone had drilled into the concrete and hung a piece of plywood with a series of hooks. On the hooks hung keys labeled TRUCK, SPREADER, ROLLER, GRADER. A bead of sweat rolled down my spine and I shuddered at the dampness.

"It's a weird feeling, isn't it?" she said. "I used to feel the same way, like the whole thing was going to come down around me." She checked her watch. "Here we go," she said. She pulled this week's tape from the red box. We waited in the damp silence until the three-quarter-inch video player on the table beeped twice and then made a loud clicking noise. She pushed the eject button. The tape slid out. In went the new. Buttons were adjusted and knobs turned. "It's completely automatic," she said. She pointed to a red toggle switch on the VCR. "I come up first thing on Friday, flip that switch up, and we're on the air all over the peninsula."

"I'll be outside," I said. I stood in the clearing taking deep breaths, feeling disassociated from myself. I heard the whoosh of the door being closed and the crunching sound of her feet on the gravel. "You okay?" she asked.

"Like you said," I replied. "It's a weird feeling in there."

She took off for the car. I ambled along behind, taking in the scenery.

"Just when I was wondering if there was *anything* that made you uneasy."

"What do you mean?"

She pulled open the truck door and stood there. One arm over the open door, one arm on the roof, her hair moving slightly in the breeze. "Well, you slew the town bully. You faced down a whole pack of his friends."

"I had you on my side."

She waved me off. "You weren't one bit afraid of that motley crew. Don't tell me you were." I tried to protest, but she gave me the raspberry. "And then you very nearly get into it with Nathan Hand about whether or not you're going to get in the police car." She shook her beautiful head. "Just when I was beginning to think you were Superman." She snapped her fingers. "Another illusion shattered." She got in the truck and started the engine.

"Better now than later," I said. I hopped in beside her and fastened myself down as she did a doughnut in the gravel and then went ripping back down the narrow road.

11 Rebecca was seated at the same table where we'd had coffee a couple of hours before. "How'd you do?" I asked as I sat down.

"Where do you want me to start?"

"The eviction," I said, "seems like the most pressing."

She agreed. "I talked with the city attorney—a man named Mark Tressman. A dedicated letch of the first order."

"Really?"

"Mark, as he insisted I call him, assured me that he and his wife had"—she made quotation marks with her fingers—"an 'arrangement' about such things. I asked if he'd mind if I called her and chatted and all of a sudden he got all professional on me."

"Do tell?"

"Anyway . . . according to Mark"—she bobbed her eyebrows up and down—"the tax rules for homesteads differ radically from those which cover regular property." She waved a hand. "Did you know that a homestead reverts to the county if it's not continuously occupied by the owner or his agent?"

"Really?"

"According to Casanova. He went into all this legal mumbo jumbo, but the deal is this: There's an old law, still on the books, that allows cities or counties to foreclose on homesteads after the taxes are more than ninety days in arrears."

"How long do regular property owners have?"

"According to Tressman, virtually indefinitely. All they have to do is occasionally make some sort of token payment on the back taxes and the city or the county is required to start the eviction process all over again."

"How long has she got?"

"Eleven days."

"What if the taxes are paid?"

"Tressman claims it's too late for that. He said J.D. challenged the order and the edict was upheld by a county judge."

"If the law were that cut-and-dried there wouldn't be more lawyers than white rats," I said. "We better get Jed on this right away."

"Amen," she sighed. "I stopped at the clerk's office."

"What's he like?"

"She. Nancy Weston. And . . . pretty much what you'd expect. Fifty or so. Struggling to stay in single-digit dress sizes. A bit full of herself. A little officious, maybe." She took a sip of coffee. "Their records show that this year's taxes were due on March fifteenth and had technically been in arrears for several months before the county took action."

"Why aren't the taxes part of the payment on the note? That's what everybody else does."

"Because there is no note. J.D. paid cash. She also confirms that the county did indeed make Mr. Bendixon a number of offers for his property and . . ."—she bent over the table and made a scrunched-up face—"and although she was not at liberty to divulge the exact figures, she thought she could safely say that the figures I had mentioned were by no means far from the mark."

"Not that she's one to gossip," I said.

"Perish the thought."

"What else?"

"The body."

She pulled a handful of photographs from the bench beside her.

"Do I want to see those?"

She held the photos against her chest and leafed through them. "You know . . . when the flesh is rendered this far asunder . . ." She looked up at me. "Just think of it as E.T."

She pushed the stack across the table. I picked up the top picture, turned it right side up. Not E.T. What it looked like was a mummy. One of those Egyptian mummies I'd seen on the Discovery Channel a while back. All black like tarred leather and clenched up, its mouth agape and eyeless sockets somehow seeming to bulge. The face was gone from the nose down.

"What happened to the head?"

"It exploded," she said. "Look at the last picture."

It was a view from the back, with the mummy lying on its side. The back of the head had a hole in it. "In a very hot fire, the brain and the fluid surrounding it begin to boil. If the fire lasts long enough and the temperature inside the skull gets hot enough, the skull literally explodes." I must have looked dubious. "Think of those self-contained popcorn things you buy. The ones where the tinfoil top swells up until it breaks open."

I made a mental note to buy chips for a while.

I worked my way back through the photos until I got to the one I'd started on.

"Anything catch your eye?" I asked her.

"What catches the eye here is that, from a forensic standpoint, we don't know anything. J.D. could have died from bubonic plague for all we know. The undertaker never even took an X-ray." She pulled the photos from my hands and rifled through them. "If you are asking me what I'd get on the stand and swear to . . . From the pelvis, it's a male . . . by the table ruler, the cadaver measures sixty-four inches, so even allowing for double the normal amount of tissue shrinkage, he was probably under six feet in life. That and the cadaver was badly burned in a fire that, in all probability, included an accelarant." She turned the photos facedown. "Any more is speculation. What about you?"

"I discovered that just about everybody in town had an active dislike for our former friend Mr. J.D. Springer."

"Like Sheriff Hand told us."

"Worse. I'm telling you, Rebecca, six to sixty, blind, crippled or crazy, they uniformly despise the guy."

"Isn't it odd," she said, "that you and I should have a vision of a man that is so completely at odds with what everyone else seems to think?"

"It's eerie, is what it is," I said. "Kind of makes me wonder what else we might be missing."

"What else?" she pressed.

I told her about my brief conversation with Linc.

"Am I missing some profundity here, too?" she asked.

"Just an odd little exchange, is all. I mean, why hem and haw about it? Either he did or he didn't sell J.D. the gas. Either way, he's not responsible."

She wasn't impressed. "Anything else?"

"Then I ran into the Chamber of Commerce person."

"Bubbles with the blue truck?"

I knew there was no way it had gone unnoticed, Ramona Haynes had gotten out of the truck with me. Before we got a chance to shake hands and offer farewells, she gave herself a good stretch, lacing her fingers together behind her, arching her back and rotating her shoulders. I'd made it a point to check the clouds for rain.

"Yeah," seemed like the right answer.

"Did she do those sort of contortions the whole time you were with her?"

I did it well. Face like a rock. "What contortions were those?"

"That skywriting-with-my-nipples act she was doing out there in the parking lot. The one that caused that old geezer at the front table to drop his fork in his lemonade."

Mount Rushmore. "I musta missed it," I said.

"Hmmmm," was her reply.

"Now, Miss Haynes—" I began.

"Bubbles?"

"Yeah . . . Miss Haynes, as far as I could tell, sort of liked J.D. She just thought he was an insensitive, paranoid loser who had no idea what he was doing."

"Good thing she liked him."

"Around here, that's as good as it gets."

"What now?"

"So . . . let's go back to J.D. and Claudia's place."

"Why?"

"There's something I need to check."

She started to speak. I jumped in. "I don't want to say anything until I check back at the homestead, okay?"

"I hate it when you do this."

I changed the subject. "Is that why you told me about this Tressman character being such a letch and coming on to you?"

"What?"

"Because you were jealous of Miss Haynes?"

Flabbergasted, then disgusted: "Is that what you think? Don't flatter yourself."

"It was, wasn't it?"

She put on her conspiratorial face. "Let me ask you something."

"Go ahead," I said.

"Do you ever . . ." She wagged a finger in my face. "Tell the truth. Do you ever wish that I had a set like that?"

I tried, "A set of what?" But it didn't float. She cupped her hands and held them about a foot from her chest.

"Arthritic hands?"

"Answer the question."

"You mean knockers?"

She nodded. I gave her my best shit-eating grin and my

best southern drawl. "Hell, darlin', you had you a pair a hooters like that, I'd never leave the house."

She got to her feet and put two bucks on the table. "You're an evil man," she said.

12 | THREE-POINT-NINE MILES PAST THE BRIDGE, I PULLED THE car into a turnout. Two hundred yards ahead, the dirt road turned sharply to the right. "This is about where the sheriff said the accident took place. Let's see if we can find the spot."

On the left, the road cut rose ten feet into the dark trees above. On the right the ground fell away in a hurry. The absence of reliable light persuaded the vegetation to experiment. No two trees or bushes or vines grew from the earth at precisely the same angle. Dark shoulders of granite loomed among the sword fern and bracken.

Rebecca said what I was thinking. "Sheriff Hand said you could see it all the way in town, so it shouldn't be too hard to find."

Ahead the ground grew steeper, and the plants fewer. Mostly native scrub oak. The boulders ran in lines like knuckles across the slopes. "There," she said.

Must have been two hundred feet down the ravine. Looked like it had been hit with a meteor. A thirty-by-thirty boulder blackened nearly to the top. A quarter acre of black, scorched earth.

"Went over right here," I said, pointing to a broken piece of embankment right in front of my feet. Thirty feet ahead, the tow trucks had plowed a path with the burned-out chassis. Rebecca walked over, looked down the chute and said, "Let's go."

It took us ten minutes to get down to the wreck site and half an hour to climb back out. Not because the climb was so arduous, but because it was on the way back out when we finally got smart and stopped obsessing on the destination and started paying attention to the journey. Actually, she, not we.

The site itself was nothing special. We tramped around on the sooty vegetation for a few minutes, as if we were going to learn something through osmosis, and then started back up, this time taking the elliptical route the car had taken, rather than the nearly straight up-and-down section we'd descended. We were halfway back up the hill, sitting on a boulder for a breather, when Rebecca looked at her hands. "Did I touch anything when we were down at the scene?"

"Not that I recall."

"Then why are my hands all dirty?"

I checked mine. Same deal. All black.

"Must be coming from the bushes," I said, referring to the omnipresent scrub oak that we'd both been using to pull ourselves back up the ravine.

"I thought the scenario was that the car hit the rock and then, for reasons unknown, burst into flames."

I reckoned how that was likewise my conception.

We continued up, paying attention now, getting down on our knees to rummage among the leaves. No doubt about it. Halfway down the hill the car had been on fire. The wiry oak stalks were singed. Here and there, half-burned leaves lay among their freshly fallen brethren. By the time we reached the top, we were certain. When J.D. Springer's car had left the road, it had been fully engulfed in flames.

"Maybe he lit a cigarette or something?" I tried.

"What with . . . a blow torch?"

We started for the car. "I want to drive," I said.

I took it easy, nosing my way around the blind corners all the way to J.D.'s place.

"I need to use the bathroom," Rebecca announced.

I started up the incline toward the shop. I didn't like what I was thinking at all. When I opened the spigot on the tank marked U, I liked it even less. U for unleaded. D for diesel. I tried to shake the tanks but they wouldn't budge. I stooped down and put my back under the unleaded tank as if I were going to dead-lift it. No way.

I searched the perimeter of the building and came up with a weathered piece of one-by-two about five feet long. I climbed the makeshift stairs at the back of the tanks, unscrewed the bung on the unleaded tank and stuck the one-by-two down inside.

The tank was nearly full. My high school math had deserted me even before high school, so I was forced to look at the tank and ask myself how many fifty-five-gallon drums it would hold. Four, I figured. Something like two hundred gallons of gas.

"Leo," Rebecca yelled.

I hustled down the hill. Her face was in a knot.

"I called J.D.'s parents. They're frantic. They haven't heard from Claudia and the kids, either. Not since she shipped the body back."

"How'd you get the number?"

"They were autodial number one," she said.

I told you. A smart girl. Her face forced me to play my hand.

"Okay, listen . . . this isn't for sure or anything, but I think maybe Claudia and the kids are over on the reservation. Probably at the daycare center where she works."

"Why do you think that?"

"Because the inflatable boat she's been using to go to work is missing."

She put her hands on her hips. "Well, why in bloody hell didn't you say so?"

"Because it was a lot more likely she was with J.D.'s folks. And because I didn't want to get your hopes up and then turn out to be wrong."

She poked me in the chest with her finger. Once for every word. "Tell you what . . . from now on, I want you to feel free to get my hopes up . . . okay?"

I checked my shirt for holes and said I would.

"Why would she go over there?" she asked.

"Maybe because it's safe," I said.

I jogged inside and pulled the keys to both jet boats from their hooks in the kitchen. Each had a blue floating key chain with the Three Rivers logo.

I got the right key in the right boat on the first try. Set it neutral, quarter throttle, turned the key . . . started right up with a deep throbbing sound. I let it idle.

"What were you doing up there on the hill?" she asked.

"Checking those tanks."

"And?"

"And the one marked 'U' has about two hundred gallons of unleaded gas in it. Which begs the question—"

She finished for me. "Why a man with that much fuel at home would be riding around with ten gallons of gas in his car?"

"If he'd been traveling toward town," I began, "then maybe—"

"But he wasn't," she said. "He clearly was on his way home."

Implications hung above us like cannon smoke. I pushed the red handle forward a notch, increasing the rpms. "I don't like it," I said after a minute. "I don't like it that the guy who owns the only gas station in town can't answer a simple question about whether or not he sold J.D. some gas. I don't like it that J.D. needed ten gallons of gasoline like a fish needs a bicycle, and I really don't like it that the car was fully engulfed in flame when it left the road. Something stinks here."

"Great minds think alike," she said.

As Rebecca cast off the bow line, I eased the boat out into the current. J.D. had been right: As we moved downstream over the mouth of the boat ramp, I could feel the deep rumbling of the hole in the bedrock beneath my feet. I gave it some gas and sent us sliding over the water toward the far shore. I worked the bank upstream for the better part of a mile and didn't see a thing, so I turned around. Six hundred yards downstream from the homestead, I saw the Avon, tied to a little floating dock set back in a recess in the bank. I eased the sled over to the downstream side and tied us up.

We followed the power lines into the settlement and then the signs that said DAYCARE CENTER—with an arrow, no less—to the daycare center. Modern woodsmanship.

Northwest Indian tribes learned a great deal from the mistakes of their eastern brothers. They hired first-rate lawyers and ended up with the choice real estate instead of the land nobody wanted.

The building sat on an outcrop of rock overlooking the Pacific Ocean. Painted in traditional red and black and white, a stylized eagle adorned the area above the door. To the north, forty or so houses looked out on a narrow bay and ramshackle marina. To the left, a stone breakwater stretched nearly all the way across to the nearest island. North and south for as far as the eye could see, the ocean was studded with rocky outcrops, some big enough to have trees growing on top, others barren and sharp as teeth.

Daycare occupied the landward end of the building. Two women and about eight kids were playing a board game at a table. The shrill sound of children echoed from elsewhere in the building. One of the women rose from her chair and crossed the room. She was short and stout and had probably never in her life cut her hair. It hung to the backs of her knees like a shiny black curtain. "Help you folks?"

"We're looking for Claudia Springer," Rebecca said.

The woman's face closed like a trap. "Don't have anybody by that name." Before either Rebecca or I could respond, she asked, "You folks know where you are?"

"Excuse me?" I said.

"No," she said quickly. "I do not excuse you. This land

belongs to the Hoh people. They said it in court and on a paper. You have no place here. Go back to the United States where you came from."

"Please—" Rebecca began.

"Would you rather I called the tribal police?"

And it probably would have ended right there, except at that moment two more women entered the room from a doorway to our left. They led a column of about a dozen chattering children into the room. Why, I don't know—it's not like I'm any good with kids; maybe he missed his father and somehow, in his little mind, had us connected—but Adam Springer broke from the ranks and ran to my side, holding out his arms and shouting my name. I picked him up and kissed him on the cheek. He stuck his face into my neck and hugged me. The little guy was a bit ripe. I guess getting shot at will wreak havoc on a guy's potty training.

The woman smiled. "Children don't lie," she said. "You come with me."

13 "LET ME GET THIS STRAIGHT," I SAID. "THE NIGHT AFTER J.D.'s death. After his body . . . after he was already on his way to his parents . . . that's when the house got shot up?" Claudia nodded.

"And you didn't use the fire extinguisher to put out the fire?" I asked.

She shook her head. "I was so scared. I just grabbed the kids and ran for the boat. I knew they couldn't follow me here," she said.

Since the night of the fire, Claudia and the kids had been living in two rooms over the tribal offices. Sheriff Hand had brought the news of J.D.'s death late on a Wednesday afternoon. Knowing that Claudia and the kids were out there alone, he'd brought along a trio of local church ladies, who'd made tea, fussed with the kids and done all the things that well-meaning souls do in a moment like that. They'd provided everything from shoulders to cry on to helping with the delicate business of telling J.D.'s elderly parents the news. They'd called the Springers' car insurance company. They'd called J.D.'s life insurance provider. Two of the women had stayed overnight. As she spoke, I remembered what Ramona Haynes had said about small towns and a sense of belonging.

First thing in the morning, right after Deputy Spots drove off with the church ladies, Claudia had begun to pack. What she wasn't planning to take, she carted up and locked in the shop. About three o'clock that afternoon, a gray Ford Taurus pulled to a stop in the driveway. Claudia'd given me his business card. J. Morris Thompson, Senior Adjuster, Prudential of North America. Seattle address and numbers.

"How much was he insured for?"

"Three hundred thousand dollars."

"Good service," I'd commented.

Her eyes filled with tears. "They're not going to pay," she said.

Rebecca beat me to it. "What?"

"He said they had some questions regarding J.D.'s death and were withholding payment of the claim until they were satisfied about how he died." Rebecca and I eyed each other. She took the lead. "We had some questions, too," she said. We took turns. She told Claudia how we knew the car had been fully engulfed when it left the road. Claudia just shook her head; she seemed numb, as if unable to process the ramifications of the news.

When I started with the unneeded gasoline, however, Claudia perked up.

"That's exactly what I told him," Claudia said. "And he'd never have carried gas in the Subaru, anyway. That was the family car. We had an agreement about not carrying messy things in the station wagon." She pounded the table in front of her with the flat of her hand. "That's even more ridiculous than J.D. not paying the taxes."

"You're saying he paid them?"

"Of course he paid them. It's right there in our checkbook."

Checkbook notations only prove you had a pen that worked, so I asked, "Do you have a receipt?"

She nodded. "The county says it's not one of theirs."

"It's not on letterhead or anything like that?" Rebecca asked.

"It's just a plain receipt. It's not even signed," she said. I thought she was going to bawl, but she kept it together.

"What did we know? It was the first time we'd ever paid them. We had no idea what an official receipt looked like."

"What about the check?" I tried.

"It's never been cashed," she said.

I felt like I was lost in the Twilight Zone, so I backtracked. "Tell me again what the insurance guy said."

She started to sob, so it was hard to understand. "He . . . he . . . didn't quite come out and say it . . . he . . . ." She balled her hands. "He said that . . . considering J.D.'s position and all, they weren't satisfied that it was an accident."

"Neither are we," I said.

Now she began to bawl. "You don't understand," she said, struggling to get it out. "They think J.D. killed himself so the kids and I could have the insurance money." A dam broke somewhere inside. Her body was wracked with sobs. Rebecca went to her side and held her as they rocked slowly back and forth on the sofa.

Rebecca's arms were around Claudia, but her eyes were locked on mine. We'd never even considered suicide, and yet, if you looked at it that way, suicide explained everything. Faced with bankruptcy and ruin, J.D. doesn't see any way out for his family except to stage an accident. That way no matter what happens with the property, his family has a nice little nest egg.

What didn't make sense was the timing of the attack on the house. In a town the size of Stevens Falls, everyone knew what had happened to J.D. Springer within an hour of when he went over that embankment. I mean, who's going to sneak out in the dead of night to terrorize his widow and children? To what end?

"What happened after the insurance guy left?" I asked. She blew her nose, swallowed most of a Dr Pepper and told me the story. Naturally, she'd been upset. She'd been telling herself that no matter what, at least she'd be getting the insurance money. "I guess I kind of went to pieces," she said. By the time she had regained some measure of composure, it was just about dark. She'd called J.D.'s parents to say there had been a change of plans and that she and the children would be over tomorrow afternoon.

The shooting had started at about ten-thirty that night. The kids were asleep. Claudia was lying in bed looking at pictures of their life in Montana. Like I'd figured, the first barrage took out the lights. By the time shots had started tearing through the windows, she and the kids were hunkered down in the living room, with two log walls between themselves and the shooters. By the time she worked up the courage to do something about the fire, smoke had filled the upper half of the cabin.

"I waited till after the firing stopped," she said. "It got really smoky. I was afraid if I left by car, they'd be waiting for me up on the road, so I put the kids in the Avon and came over here." She looked from Rebecca to me and back. "I didn't know what to do," she said and began bawling again. Rebecca held her while we both assured her that she'd done exactly the right thing.

She separated herself from Rebecca and ran both hands over her face. "I've got to get myself together," she said. She looked at me.

"Do you think J.D. killed himself?" she asked.

I answered truthfully. "I don't know," I said. "From what I know, I'd have to say it was a possibility."

Rebecca jumped in. "It's also possible it was an accident."

"Or that . . . ," Claudia began, "that somebody did that to him."

"Equally possible," I agreed.

"We could try to narrow it down," Rebecca said.

"How?" I asked.

"The body was neither embalmed nor autopsied. No telling what it might be able to tell us." She turned to Claudia. "He wasn't cremated, was he?"

She shook her head no. I thought she was going to cry again, but instead she wiped her nose and said, "That was

his wish. He wanted his ashes sprinkled on the Yellowstone."
She dropped her hands to her sides. "But after what happened . . . how he looked . . . I couldn't. I just couldn't burn
him up the rest of the way." She turned to Rebecca. "Are you
saying that you want to . . ."

Rebecca stopped her. "I want to do whatever you want
to do," she said. "And I want to be honest with you, Claudia.
I've seen pictures. With the tissue in that condition, it's going
to be quite a challenge."

Claudia paced the room. "Do his parents have to know?"

"The matter is totally in your hands," Rebecca said.
"You're the only one with the power to exhume."

She paced some more, talking more to herself than to us.
"I don't know what to do. I've never had to decide anything.
I've always deferred to J.D. J.D. always knew what to do."
After a while, she stopped pacing and seemed to steel herself.

"If it's possible to know what happened, I've got to
know."

"Then we'll do it," Rebecca said.

Making the decision to exhume her husband seemed to
give her strength. We put together a plan. Claudia and the
kids were leaving tonight with Rebecca. Going over to stay
with J.D.'s parents. I was going to hold down the fort at Claudia's place, at least until the autopsy was completed. After
that, we'd play it by ear.

Claudia and Rebecca began to pack. All she had was the
two green garbage bags she'd fled the house with, so it
wasn't going to take long. They sent me downstairs. Told me
to send the kids up so they could get them dressed.

The other children were gone. It was dark and quiet
downstairs. A single bulb in the kitchen area cast a dim yellow glow over the room. The woman we'd met earlier was
named Juanita. She was closing up the center for the night.
"It's good they are going to their people," she said as she
locked a window. "Bad times like these . . . you got to be with
your people." I told her I agreed. "Us Indians, we know that,

you see, 'cause one another is all we got." She pulled a white plastic liner from the trash can and tied it with a twist tie.

"You think it's like the insurance guy says?" she asked me. "You think maybe J.D. killed himself?"

I told her there was no way to tell. "You know J.D.?" I asked.

"Oh sure," she said. "He come over all the time. Sometimes for lunch with the kids. Sometimes just to visit."

"What do you think?" I asked.

"You never know about people," she said. "I know white people are crazy about land. They came out here last year . . . want to make us rich, they say. Fifty grand for every member of the tribe. People say, hey, those Lummi people want to give us fifty thousand a head, I better find my old lady and make me some children." She laughed. "I say, hey, we already gave them a bunch of land . . . so look what they did to that." She laughed again. I was lost. The Lummi were another Northwest Indian tribe. How they qualified as "crazy white people" was beyond me. I never got a chance to ask.

"Leo," Rebecca called from upstairs.

It was full dark. I carried Adam and one of the bags. The two women carried the other bag between them while the little girl walked out in front of us all. Our pathfinder. We loaded the bags into the Avon and the people into the jet boat. With the little boat in tow, we cruised downstream to the confluence and then over to the homestead.

I'd have bet the farm that Claudia would have found some reason she had to go into the house. Some memento or something that she needed. But no. All Claudia wanted was for her and her children to be someplace else. I don't think she even looked at the cabin on the way by.

We don't have kiddy car seats and the Springers' had been in the Subaru. So we buckled the kids in as best we could. Claudia rode in between them, an arm around each. Rebecca was behind the wheel. I leaned in the window and asked, "What's the best motel in town?"

"The Black Bear," Claudia said. "They redid it last year."

"That's right next to that little downtown park, isn't it?" Rebecca asked. Claudia said it was. I started up the Springers' Blazer and followed them to town. I saw the big bruin sign from two blocks away. It was lit up like an airfield. I blinked my lights and stuck my arm out the window, pointing to a dark area across the street from where we were now. Powers Saw Shop.

She turned hard; I followed. Rebecca got out with me. "No point letting anybody see who's in the car," I said. She hugged me, told me to be careful, not to run with scissors and to eat my vegetables. She handed me her cell phone, walked around the Explorer's passenger side and opened the glove box, pulled something out and returned to my side.

"Here's the charger," she said. "If you're going to leave it on all the time, then you'll have to charge it whenever you get the chance. It charges better if you run the battery all the way down." She hugged me again. For a long time.

"You know, we work pretty well together," I said.

She nodded. "I just wish it were something else we were working on."

I watched until the taillights disappeared and then drove the block and a half up to the Black Bear. A TV was blaring from another room. *The X-Files*. The sign said to ring the bell, so I did. An old man limped around the corner on a leg so stiff it had to be artificial. "I'm right here, dammit," he said. He wore a Hawaiian shirt outside of his pants in the Philippine dictator mode and a pair of chinos. Seventy-five if he was a day. Last combed his hair sometime in early spring. Still owned every other tooth, which stood spaced like pickets in his retreating gums. He looked me over and then looked over me out into the parking lot. I confirmed his worst fears.

"Just what you were hoping for," I said. "No luggage . . . one night."

"Cash or major credit card?"

"Which do you prefer?" I asked.

"Cash," he said. "Forty bucks even."

He picked up a registration card. "You want to—"

"Not unless you insist," I said. The card disappeared.

"Goddamn government . . . rob you blind," he muttered. From the next room, sound effects rose toward a crescendo. The old man limped over to the doorway and peered intently around the corner. He stayed that way until it went to commercial.

"You watch *The X-Files*?"

"Sometimes," I said.

"It's true, you know."

"You think so?"

He waved with his hand. "Hell yeah. They had 'em for years."

"Ah . . . you mean like paranormal . . ." I hedged.

"Aliens. They had one since '47."

"You mean like Area Fifty-one and all that."

"Damn right. Roswell, New Mexico, July eighth, 1947. Bastards covered it all up. But I seen the pictures on the Fox Network."

"Oh yeah," I said. I'd seen them, too, and at first thought I was on the Comedy Channel.

"They're watchin' us right now," he said.

"We better look busy, then."

"Spend two weeks every year down in Roswell, working at the museum and research center. Been doin' it for eighteen years." He gave me a sly wink. "Earnin' my points for when they come back."

"Smart," I said, tapping my temple.

"Damn right."

We spent a full five minutes commiserating on the evils of big government, the failure of the welfare state and the brilliance of Rush Limbaugh. I kept a straight face.

In the next room, a short electronic fanfare announced

that *The X-Files* was back from commercial. He clapped me on the shoulder and slid a key across the counter.

"Room nine," he said. "It's the best one we got."

When I turned for the door, he said, "I'm up early. I make coffee."

Nine was at the east end. I grabbed a couple of Pepsis from one machine and two packs of cheese and crackers from another. Standard-issue roadside motel. Decent-sized room. Itsy-bitsy bathroom. I pulled the cord and the drapes slid back to reveal what appeared to be half a dozen RV hookups scattered among the trees behind the building.

I turned on the tube and made a lap of the dial. Sure enough, Channel Fourteen was SFTV, your ticket to scenic Stevens Falls. Got bad brakes . . . see Junior at Martin's Muffler and Brake. Looking for that piece of retirement property, Harv Leonard will fix you right up. I switched to ESPN, then sat down on the bed, dialed eight for an outside line and called my attorney at home. The maid answered.

"Marie, it's Leo Waterman."

Marie was a substantial Norwegian grandmother of eight and the true power behind the throne. "You want the mister, I better hurry, he's on his way out."

"Please," I said. The phone banged in my ear. It was a couple of minutes before Jed came on the phone. "Leo, you just caught me. I was—"

I interrupted him. "I need five minutes," I said.

He read my tone of voice. "Go," he said. I ran the whole scene down for him. He interrupted me once to tell me that, quotation marks, in the long run, evictions never hold up in court. In Jed's parlance, this meant that the cost of winning the case would, however, approximate the national debt of Bosnia.

"What can I do for you?" he asked when I'd finished.

"I want to start fighting the eviction."

"You want my best advice, find a local attorney. Those rural counties don't like it when city sharpies show up in their courtrooms. I once went two weeks without having an objection sustained. If you want, I'll make some calls. See if I can't find you a good man. Somebody who's familiar with the judges."

"See what you can find out," I said.

Then, somewhere in the extinct crater of my mind, a smoldering ember suddenly flared. I'd have told him to forget about it, that I'd had a better idea, but by that time he was gone.

14 PENINSULA COUNTY SUPERIOR COURT JUDGE WAYNE Bigelow frowned as he laced his fingers across his ample middle and leaned back in his chair. He had a round pink face and a serious set of jowls. "I am *not* being difficult, Constance. You simply must realize the gravity of what it is that this young man is asking me to do. He's asking me to overrule a decision by a colleague." He pointed to his right. "The man who occupies the chambers at the other end of this very hall. A man with whom I've played golf every Thursday for the past eleven years."

"Frank always said he cheated on his score," Constance Hart said.

When the judge chuckled, he shook all over like Jell-O.

"Let us say that Milton often renders somewhat liberal interpretations of the rules of golf," the judge corrected. "A habit much in keeping with his general judicial proclivities."

"Do you necessarily have to reverse the decision?" I said.

"What would you suggest?" he asked affably.

"Just delay the eviction?"

"The insult to my esteemed colleague would be the same in either instance."

Constance Hart chided him like a schoolboy. "Wayne, if you can't or won't do it, just say so," she said. "But for gosh sake, let's skip the song and dance."

The judge pursed his lips and then sat forward with a

twinkle in his eye. "Constance . . . your choice of words reminds me . . ." He looked over at me. "I hope you'll forgive me, Mr. Waterman, if I conduct a bit of private business. It's a rare day indeed when Mrs. Hart graces my chambers."

"By all means," I said.

He turned his attention her way. "As to the aforementioned matter of song and dance . . ." He began to redden.

Her eyes narrowed. "Yes," she said.

The judge began to sweat. "The country club is having its . . . the, ah . . . annual New Year's Gala," he said. He spread his hands. "As a board member . . . it is somewhat de rigueur that I attend. I was wondering if you . . . perhaps would do me the honor of . . ."

She bailed him out. "Why, Wayne," she said. "Are you asking me for a date?"

He sat forward quickly, harrumphed twice and said, "Yes, I believe I am." He was the color of a beet, working his way toward a concord grape.

She shot me a look I didn't care to interpret. Wayne slumped slightly.

"Under no circumstances will I occupy a table with that Macdonald woman," she said finally. She looked my way. "You have never heard such prattling."

The judge perked up like a terrier. "She shall be banished to the farthest reaches of the building," he assured her.

"Well, in that case . . . it would be my pleasure, Wayne," she said.

He sputtered a bit, but for the most part managed to look like he knew all along she was going to say yes. They agreed he'd call later in the week to work out the specifics.

He got to his feet and began to pace. His color was down to a good sunburn. "Legally, they're within their rights," he said. "I looked up the case and the citation when Connie called me this morning. The action conforms to the letter, if not the spirit of the law. That particular statute was intended to allow municipalities to recover property from homesteaders who found the rigors of Northwest life too taxing and deserted their claims."

"So what do we do?" I asked.

"You do understand, don't you, that any competent law firm, given, say, a year and a half and several hundred thousand dollars, could undoubtedly overturn this or any other eviction order?"

"The widow doesn't have either," I said.

He stroked his chin. "Yes . . . I gathered that from your tale."

I'd laid the whole thing out for him in detail. Everything I knew. How, at this point, accident, suicide or murder all seemed about equally likely.

He rubbed his hands together. "Well . . . in that case"—he gave Constance an impish grin—"we fight fire with fire. One old law deserves another."

He crossed to a bleached oak table on the far side of the room, picked up a lawbook and opened it to the page indicated by a red leather bookmark. He read. "Washington statute number twenty-seven-forty-three, dated June nineteen and seventeen, otherwise known as the Widows and Orphans Act of 1917." He snapped the book shut. "Shorn of its arcane legal trappings, the act says that widows and orphans shall be given special consideration when it comes to such things as delinquent taxes or even legitimate suits from third-party creditors."

"Sounds awfully sensible, for the law," I said.

The judge agreed. "That's because it's bad law. One of the spur-of-the-moment Band-Aid statutes that, in all probability, should have been dealt with at some level other than the law. The intent was to protect widows of the First World War. As I understand it, there was a rash of carpetbaggers buying up paper, preying upon the unfortunate survivors to the extent that some oaf felt a statute should be enacted."

He crossed to his desk and sat. "I'm going to ask the state Supreme Court to rule on the obvious conflict between the

Homestead Act and the Widows and Orphans Act of 1917. In the meantime, I am going to issue a restraining order forbidding further action against the property until such time as our state's highest court can see fit to rule on the matter." He pushed a button on his desk. "The widow or her authorized agent must, of course, immediately pay the taxes."

"I have her power of attorney," I said.

He held out his hand. I passed it over. A light knock and then the door opened. Young guy, under thirty, with bad skin and wiry black hair. The judge introduced him as his clerk, Robert Downs. They huddled at the judge's desk; Robert took notes on a small spiral-bound pad. Constance Hart was leafing through an old *Arizona Highways*.

As Robert started for the door, the judge got to his feet. "I certainly hope I can persuade you two to join me for lunch. Robert will have your paperwork ready by the time we've finished."

"That would be lovely," she said.

I guess judges are like baseball umpires; they're always right. An hour and a half later I stood in the courthouse parking lot with Constance Hart. I had in my possession a restraining order forbidding any and all legal action on the property. A Peninsula County authorization to pay delinquent taxes, which demanded the signature of the city clerk herself, and a county document declaring that I was the registered agent for one Claudia Teresa Springer. Six copies of everything. All of it on file with the county.

"I don't know how to thank you," I said to Constance.

"No need," she replied. "You made Wayne's day."

"His year," I corrected. We shared a strained laugh.

When I'd called her early this morning and told her I needed her help, she hadn't hesitated, but had merely asked for my number and said that she'd call me back. I hadn't mentioned Misty. I figured if she had something she wanted to share with me, she would.

When she pushed the button on her electronic key ring

and popped the Caddy's door locks, I thought the subject was dead. I opened the door for her. Thanked her again. She started to slide into the seat but stopped, regained her balance and met my eyes with her predator gaze. "I'm on my way to see Misty," she said.

"How's she doing?"

She searched the clouds for a moment. "A little better, I think," she said finally. "I . . . she's living in a residential center in Edmonds. She has full-time counseling there . . . young people her own age . . . some of whom have had similar . . ." She let it ride. She put her hand on my arm. "When last we met, Mr. Waterman, I'm afraid our parting was somewhat less than pleasant." I assured her it came with the territory, but she wasn't through. "You tried to tell me . . . but I wasn't willing to listen. All the way along the line, you tried to tell me." Her grip was powerful on my arm. The diamond as big as the Ritz was gone. "She needed so much more than I could give her," she said.

"You made a wise choice," I said, choosing my words carefully. "The situation she's in now is probably her best chance."

She made a rueful face. "Does this mean that love really won't conquer all?"

"Better not tell Wayne," I said. This time we shared a real laugh.

She released my arm and dropped her purse inside the car. She had a gleam in her eye that I hadn't seen before. "And I don't want you to think you sold me into bondage or anything," she said. "I knew perfectly well what Biggy Bigelow was going to want in return. Lord knows he's been clogging up my phone lines for months." She looked down at the pale streak on her finger. "I had been refusing all social invitations. I thought Misty and I would . . ."

"She's where she belongs," I said.

She took a deep breath. "Yes, she is." I held the door as she seated herself in the car. "I was thinking this morning, after you called, and I'd heard Wayne panting on the phone. This is my first date in thirty-nine years. I believe I'll buy myself a new dress."

I allowed how it was a girl's right, closed the door and watched as she drove off.

15 | THE STEVENS FALLS CITY BUILDING SPOKE OF A MORE prosperous time, back when nearly thirty thousand people had used the town as the hub of their daily lives. The kind of public edifice that spawned a sense of pride and solidarity in those whose labors had made it possible. Designwise, it was more or less a brick mockup of Monticello, complete with the classical portico, the columns and the dome on top. The sign in the lobby said the city attorney's office was down the hall to the left. Beneath the sign, a tray of brochures. *Your City Government.* I took one and stuffed it in my pocket.

One-twenty-four was the office at the end of the hall. Big gold letters outlined in black. MARK TRESSMAN. Underneath, CITY ATTORNEY.

I'd started the day early. A six-thirty cup of sludge with Monty, the guy who owned the Black Bear Motel. Monty now saw me as a coconspirator, another citizen-soldier demanding that his government come clean about alien lifeforms. Monty and I parted with the secret handshake, and then I drove the Blazer down to the Chat and Chew for a slab of ham and pile of flapjacks, which could be expected to linger in my colon well into the next millennium. By nine-thirty, I'd shanghaied an electrical contractor by the name of Jensen and dragged him out to the homestead, so he'd be sure to know what he needed for parts. Then back to town and Beaver Building Supply, where I'd bought what I figured I'd need to clean up the cabin. About the time I got back to the homestead, Constance Hart called back to say we had an appointment with the judge at noon, and I'd had to drop everything and start on the two-hour drive to Port Townsend.

I checked my watch now. Three-thirty. Too late for the Kiwanas lunch. Too early to go home for the day. I liked my chances.

He kept me waiting for twenty minutes and then came out into the receptionist's office rather than inviting me back into his. He was about forty or so. Dressed Nordstrom from head to toe. The hair along the front of his head seemed to grow in rows, like the hair on an old-fashioned doll. Transplants, I guessed. He was trim but losing the battle of the love handles anyway. From the way he held his mouth, you could tell his pride and joy was the thick mustache, which he wore waxed and curled up at the ends. "So," he said without introducing himself, "what is of such import as to require my personal attention?"

I held out my hand. "Leo Waterman," I said. He took my hand, gave it a single perfunctory shake and then stuck his hand in his pants pocket as if it were now diseased and would require sterilization before being used again.

I handed him a copy of the restraining order and watched as a line of white started at the front rank of his grafted-on hair and worked its way down his face until he was the color of the paper he was holding. "Is this some kind of joke?" he asked.

"I don't see anything funny about it," I said.

"He can't do this," Tressman said with a sneer. "No judge would ever—"

"He can and he did," I interrupted. I reached over and tapped the last paragraph with my fingertip. "You'll notice that I'm required to get a signed receipt."

I thought I saw a slight tremor in his hand as he read the order again. Top to bottom. "Where do you come into this?"

I handed him a copy of my power of attorney. "I'm Mrs. Springer's duly certified agent," I said. "If you'll read carefully, you'll find I'll be needing a receipt for that document as well."

He wore a gold Rolex watch and a diamond ring on his left hand. "I hope you won't mind if I call the county before I begin issuing receipts?" He turned and disappeared through the door. The receptionist was about thirty or so, with a wide expressionless face as open and bland as a cabbage. A nameplate on her desk read June. She pretended to shuffle papers, all the while watching me from the corner of her eye as if someone had left a baboon in the reception area.

Tressman was gone for exactly eighteen minutes. When he came back, his color was bad again. He huddled in the corner with June. Right away, their mutual body language caught my eye. Something about sex changes the manner in which adults share space. They stood a little too close together, at times touching at the hip, and on two occasions, as he whispered in her ear, his hand drifted to the shoulder of her brown flowered dress. I'd have bet a finger they were boinking one another.

I stayed in the baboon section twirling the Blazer's ring of keys while they worked it out. When he came over to the counter, I set the keys down and ambled over.

"I don't know what you think you're doing here," he said calmly, "but this Widows and Orphans tripe is never going to hold up."

"We'll see," I said. "And what I'm doing here is looking for a little equity for a grieving widow and two small children. Which, if you don't mind me saying, seems to be an issue that's lacking around here."

"This office was perfectly within its legal rights."

"Maybe it was. But what about the human issue? What about a woman who just lost her husband? Who's left with two small children to care for? What about that end of it? I mean, I know it sounds corny, but doesn't anybody care?"

"That property should have been returned to the public trust years ago. Homesteads are a relic of another age."

"And that makes evicting widows and orphans acceptable to you?"

He rearranged himself inside his suit coat. "Leadership often requires that one distance oneself from individual concerns for the good of the community as a whole."

It was everything I could do not to reach over the counter and pop him in the mouth. Instead I put my elbows on the counter, getting as close to him as I could. I strained to maintain control of my voice. "Well then, Sparky," I said. "How's about you get me those receipts . . . for the good of the community as a whole."

Now, generally, if you lean in on a guy and start calling him Sparky or Scooter, you're going to get some kind of physical reaction. He's at least going to step back and retrieve some space. Not this guy. He just stood there for a moment and then eased himself back through the nifty glass door, with June in hot pursuit.

Ten minutes later, June reemerged. Her eyes were puffy and lined with pink. Red finger marks nearly encircled her left arm. She slid me the documents and then quickly turned away, taking her seat, swiveling around to face the wall while she wiped her nose with a tissue. I took a moment to satisfy myself about the documents and then I stepped out into the hall.

If I'd stopped for long enough to scratch an itch, I would have missed her. As I stepped onto the second-floor landing, an elderly couple crossed in front of me and started down the stairs; behind them, a woman walked quickly down the hall in my direction. Her purse hung from one arm, her coat from the other. She had a narrow face and a severe shortage of chin. She wore her brown hair long, in the manner of much younger women. Something about the way she tugged at her dress while she walked reminded me of what Rebecca had said about Nancy Weston trying to stay in single-digit dress sizes.

"Excuse me," I said, when she reached the stairs. I made it a statement. "You're Nancy Weston, aren't you."

Her face said she didn't know whether to be flustered or flattered.

"Yes, I am," she said. "But you'll have to excuse me, I—"

I went into my Jimmy Olsen, cub reporter, routine. "Boy, it's a good thing I caught you," I said with as much teenage earnestness as I could muster. "I have some Peninsula County legal papers to deliver to you. Just another second and . . ." I managed not to say, *Gee whiz.*

She started down the stairs. "If you have business, Carmen can help you."

"I'm afraid that won't be possible," I said.

She turned back with an annoyed grammar-school teacher look. "And why would that be?" I skipped down several stairs to get closer to her. I could make out a line that ran down her cheek where her foundation makeup ended and her neck began. She sniffed and pulled at the waist of her dress.

"Because you're specifically named as the person to whom they should be delivered. And because we're well within the official hours of the city clerk."

First she tried outrage. "Do you presume to tell me—"

I cut her off. "And because we wouldn't want Judge Bigelow to think that an elected official had willfully disregarded a restraining order."

Then her feelings were hurt. "How can you say such a thing?" Apparently she could make her lower lip tremble on demand. "I would never—"

I pulled one of the Authorization to Pay Delinquent Taxes forms from the folder I was carrying and held it under her nose. "I know you wouldn't," I said in a soothing voice. I pointed to the bottom of the page. "See . . . down in the last paragraph."

She looked down for long enough to see her own name. Whatever Tressman had said when he'd called her wasn't enough to overcome her unwillingness to cross a superior court judge. We marched in lockstep back up to the clerk's office. Five minutes later, my checking account was fifteen hundred and fifty-five dollars lighter and I was back at the head of the stairs with an official-looking receipt resting in my sweaty palm.

Four-twenty and it was nearly dark. I had one of those disassociated moments in the parking lot. My brain had not yet logged that I was driving J.D.'s Blazer. For about a minute and a half, I ran around like Chicken Little, sure my car had been stolen. Then it hit me. I looked around to see if anyone had noticed my panic and then hurried toward the car. Imagine my consternation when I realized I'd left the keys on the magazine table in Tressman's office.

I gave the stairs another workout. In the second-floor hallway, June was feeding quarters into the candy machine as I walked by. She flashed me a wan smile. As if anybody who could cause Tressman that much anxiety deserved a grin, however tentative.

"I knew you wouldn't get far," she said. "They're on the counter."

As I picked up the keys from the table, I heard voices from Tressman's office. The connecting door was closed. They were yelling back and forth, and unless I was mistaken, I recognized both voices. I pocketed the keys, stepped around the counter, opened the door a foot and peeked. A ten-foot hall, a couple of bathrooms on the left and then Tressman's open door. Nancy Weston stood in Tressman's office with her hands on her hips. "I told you, Mark. What was I going to do? I couldn't just leave. I had the Dickinsons in my office. They wouldn't go. What was I going to do, just get up and walk out on them? You know how—" She looked over and saw me standing there. She clapped her hands on her sides and gestured toward the door. Tressman's head poked around the corner. His eyes were wide and his mouth open.

I jiggled the keys. "Came back for my keys," I said. "Thanks a lot for looking out for them." I turned and left in a hurry.

June was still loitering in the hall as I scurried past. My guess was that Tressman had told her to get lost while he and Weston talked. I had a thought and stopped.

"What's a good place for lunch around here?" I asked.

She didn't hesitate. "The Country Corner down on the highway," she said. "The courthouse cafeteria is . . ." She poked a finger at her throat.

I thanked her and started down the stairs for the third time.

I dropped some more paperwork by Sheriff Hand. I didn't bother about receipts; I'd annoyed enough people for one day. Hand seemed genuinely pleased that Claudia and the kids were safe and generally amused about what I was doing. He shook his head.

"I'll bet you've even got Mark Tressman's bloomers in a bunch," he said with a laugh. "Ain't that right, Bobby?"

His deputy laughed and said, "Heck, Sheriff, I'd pay good money to see that."

I gestured toward the door with my head. "Can I speak to you outside for a minute, Sheriff?" I turned to the deputy. "Just something personal," I said. He seemed like a nice kid, and I didn't want to annoy him. He waved me off. "That's how come he's the sheriff and I'm not," he said with a smile.

I followed Nathan Hand out the door. "Listen," I said, "I don't want it to sound like I'm questioning either your methods or your results . . ." I hesitated.

"But," he said.

And I told him about how I was sure the car had been fully engulfed in flame before it hit anything and about the two hundred gallons of gas back at the cabin.

He was surprised, but not like I figured. "You and the doctor are pretty darn good," he said with a smile. "I missed that the car was on fire, but heck, when I was out there it was pitch-black and it seemed like everything was on fire. I'll get out there and have a look for myself first thing tomorrow. But the gas . . ." He ran a hand over the stubble on his cheek. "Now, the gas always bothered me. Bothered that insurance guy, too. I didn't say anything to him—heck, insurance companies got most of the money already—and I sure as heck didn't want to say a thing to the widow . . . but if you were to ask me how that man died, I'd have to bet he took it over the edge on purpose."

I didn't realize it until that moment, but the voice inside of me that had been pressuring me to imagine J.D.'s last moments had known what it was doing.

"Sheriff," I said. "You know, I just had a thought. About ways to die."

"What's that?"

"Well. Let's assume you're right and leaving his family with the insurance money was the only way out that J.D. could see."

"Okay," he said.

"Now, you and I are in the kind of business where, I think it's safe to say, we're probably as brave as the next guy. Maybe we're not heroes or anything, but I figure the truly timid find something to do in life that doesn't involve sticking their nose in other people's business like we do."

"All right," he said.

"So, I'm asking you . . . kind of like man to man. You think you've got the stones for it? Think you could do what he did?"

Hand whistled softly. "You mean to . . . like Mr. Springer?"

"Yeah," I said. He rubbed his chin but didn't speak, so I went on. " 'Cause I'll tell you, Sheriff, last couple of days I've searched my soul, and I know damn well I don't. No way, no how do I have what it takes to pour ten gallons of un-leaded all over myself and then flick my Bic. Period. End of story."

Hand was still mulling it over when I waved goodbye and began walking to my car. For the first time in twelve hours, my to-do list was empty. Got in, buckled up and gave her the gas.

I kept driving, past the motel, down to the Steelhead. I took the stool at the end of the bar, keeping as far away from the Davis brothers as possible. Glen fetched the waitress from the kitchen, straightened his apron and walked down to me.

"You gonna behave?" he asked.

"Depends," I said. "Can you put me together a couple of cheeseburgers and an order of fries?"

He glanced over his shoulder at the dozen or so degen-erates who were milling around, taking notice of my pres-ence. "To go." A statement.

"Fine," I said.

"In that case"—he held out a hand—"good to see you." I shook it and watched as he motioned to the waitress, gave her my order and then turned back my way. "Didn't figure I'd see you again."

"I had a few questions and I thought you might be the guy to answer them."

"About?"

"Some of your local luminaries."

"Like?"

"What do you know about Mark Tressman?" I asked.

He thought it over. "Just about everything, I guess."

"Except who he's sleeping with this week."

"Hell, he's always been like that. Wanted to screw now and talk later."

"Kiss and tell?"

He laughed. "With Mark, it always seemed to me that the telling was more important to him than the kissing was."

"You know his parents?"

"Just a mama. Fran worked for the mill about the same time as my old man. Ramona's daddy's secretary for something like thirty years. Died a couple of years back."

Turned out they were all lifers. Tressman, Weston and Polster. Small-town kids who'd gone off to other places and then returned to their rural roots. Polster about ten years ago. The rest of them in the past three or four years.

"What about Sheriff Hand?"

He shook his head. "Nah. He's not from these parts. Hand's from back in the Midwest someplace. Used to be a corporate security guy of some sort."

"Doesn't seem like the small-town sheriff type," I said.

"Probably why most folks can't stand his ass."

"How's that?"

Over his shoulder, Mickey Davis strained to make eye contact with me as he carried a pair of empty pitchers up to the bar to be refilled. The vibe pulled Glen's head around. He pointed a thick finger at Mickey. "You just get your beer and go on about your business," he said. "You start any more trouble in here, you all are gonna need to find a new place to do your drinking." I resisted the urge to smile and wave.

"You were saying folks weren't fond of the sheriff."

"Yeah . . . some because of the way he took over from Buddy Brown, the old sheriff. Some cause he's a hard-ass. He busts drunk drivers. He enforces the speed limit. He makes sure you've got fresh tags and insurance." He chuckled. "We had guys who hadn't renewed their registrations in fifteen years until Nathan Hand took over. Hadn't ever had insurance, most of them."

"What about this Sheriff Brown?"

"Buddy Brown was sheriff around here since maybe the late fifties. He and the town kind of fit each another like an old pair of jeans."

"And?"

"And one day . . . what, two years back . . . the City Council just up and fired him. Next thing anybody knew, they'd appointed Nathan Hand. And then Hand decided he didn't like his chief deputy, Sam Williams—the guy most folks thought would replace Buddy Brown—so Hand pushed Sam into early retirement and hired that crazy Russell kid, whose only law enforcement experience was from the other side of the bars."

"Do tell."

"Hell yes . . ." He pointed over at the pool players. "Three years ago, you'd have found Bobby Russell right over there with the rest of those lamebrains. Hell, he was the worst of the lot. At least Dexter and Mickey are stupid."

The waitress was headed our way with a bag.

"Nice seeing you again," I said to him. I reached into my pocket.

He handed me the bag. "On the house," he said. I started to argue, but he cut me off.

"It's like training a dog," he said. "This is your treat for not busting up the place today." I thanked him and pushed my way out the door, heading for another scintillating night of ESPN at the Black Bear Motel.

16 BY NOON I'D WORKED UP A SERIOUS SWEAT AT THE cabin. In the grand scheme of things, it probably didn't matter whether the place was shipshape or not, but it made me feel better, as if restoring a little order to the universe would in some way help my mind to sort out the strange passing of J.D. Springer.

As the fog rose from the rivers and morning bled into afternoon, it occurred to me that, in spite of my having met him only a couple of times, J.D. Springer had attained a symbolic status in my life. As if the manner of his success and the insistence of his vision had somehow validated many of the odd choices I'd made throughout my own life and thus in some small way lessened that collection of roads-not-taken regrets that seem to visit me more regularly with each passing year.

I'd hauled everything but the bed out into the yard. Shook everything out and left it there, hoping the damp air might dilute the odor of fire. Then I swept up the glass and the splinters and used the old-fashioned mop to wash the walls and the floors. Used up half a million staples covering the broken windows with plastic sheeting, inside and out, and then dragged all the furniture back inside. Got a ladder from the shop, climbed up on the roof and covered the burned-out rafter ends with plastic. It wasn't much of a job, but unless we had some big wind, I figured it would keep the water from getting up under the roof.

Jensen the electrician had done a good job. He'd shortened the mast coming down through the roof and tucked the new service panel back up under the eaves and out of the line of fire. And for a scant four hundred seventy-nine dollars, everything worked.

Same could be said for the eight guest cabins, too. Everything worked. Heat, lights, toilets, refrigerators. I went from cabin to cabin, testing things and pulling the red tags off of everything. Each and every failed inspection notice was signed by one Emmett Polster, City Building Inspector. Apparently a very fussy man, this Mr. Polster.

I figured I'd spend the night here instead of the Black Bear. Maybe run into town, buy myself a clean shirt, do a little grocery shopping and cook myself up something good.

By two, I had the radio blasting from the house, and was on my way up to the shop to look for some fishing gear. George Thorogood playing sloppy slide and growling about being the big dog. The rivers were clear. I'd been watching fish roll all day and thought maybe I'd wet a line and then . . . bang. Rebecca's Explorer came barreling down into the yard. From sixty yards, I knew that look from grammar school. Her "I know all the answers on the test and you don't" look. She waited for me to walk down. Made a face at how dusty and dirty I was. Didn't want a hug.

"What's up?" I said. "I didn't expect you back so soon."

"Somebody shot J.D. in the face," she said. "With a shotgun."

I rescued my tongue from the gravel. "Tell me about it," I said. And she did.

Hadn't even required an exhumation order, because they hadn't gotten around to burying the poor soul yet. Seems the cemetery that J.D.'s parents had chosen was having a water table problem. An unusual amount of fall rain in the Skagit Valley had made it impractical to inter anyone at this time. Seems newly buried caskets kept floating to the surface and bobbing about in an unseemly manner. They'd had J.D. in a cold storage warehouse full of apples.

"Tommy timed the autopsy at fourteen seconds," she said. "That's how long it took the X-ray machine to warm up." She was referring to Tommy Matsukawa, another pathologist with the King County ME.

She pulled a glass vial from her pants pocket. Held it for me to see. Shotgun pellets. About half a dozen. Some round, some flattened. "He had thirty-two of these in his head. Tommy said it looked like he was using his head to store nuts for the winter." Tommy, like many people in the dead body business, had an unusual sense of humor.

"You do realize how odd this is, don't you?" I asked.

"How so?"

"How many times are you likely to arrive with the message that a friend has been murdered and have it be *good* news?"

"It is, isn't it?"

"At least the insurance company will have to pay Claudia."

She nodded. "What now?" she asked.

I was sweaty and covered with dust. I'd planned on jumping in the river after I was through fishing. "Let me get cleaned up a little. Then we'll go to town and see Sheriff Hand."

"I brought you some clothes," she said.

Nathan Hand paced the area behind his desk like a tiger in a cage. "I'll be honest with you," he said. "I'm embarrassed about this. For me, for my department, for all of us. Worst kind of sloppy police work. Makes us look like a bunch of hicks who can't look after their own business." He plunged his hands into his pockets. "And I don't mean it as an excuse or anything, but you spend enough years handling nothing but drunks and domestic violence and you forget. You get to thinking that if it walks like a duck and quacks like a duck, it's bound to be a duck."

Rebecca cut him some slack. "With the condition of the remains and the facilities available to you, you reached the obvious conclusion."

"I appreciate the help, Doctor, but none of that's an excuse for sloppy."

He rested one cheek on the corner of his desk. "Hell, I had to have you two tell me that the car was on fire before it went down the hill." He slowly shook his head.

"What are you going to do now?" I asked.

"I'll do what I should have done to begin with. I'll see if I can't put together what his last day looked like and go from there."

"You like your chances?" Rebecca asked.

His face loosened. "You know the answer to that as well as I do, Doctor. Case this cold, with this many suspects, the chance of successful apprehension and prosecution is miserable," he said. "But I'll tell you one thing: As God is my witness, that case will be open and will be actively investigated for as long as I'm in office."

"J.D. told me he'd received threatening phone calls. He said he recorded the number from his caller ID and gave it to you."

He made a disgusted face. "Pay phone at the Steelhead. Could have been any of them nimrods you met the other day."

"Sheriff," Rebecca said. "I don't want you to feel like I'm creeping around behind your back, so I think you should know that when I get home this evening, I'm going to call a friend of mine in the state police. I'm going to see if I can't get them to commit a couple of people to an investigation. Nothing personal . . . but I believe they're far better equipped to handle something of this nature."

"I don't blame ya a bit," he said. "The way we've handled

it so far don't exactly inspire confidence. You can be sure I'll cooperate in any way I can."

We got to our feet. I handed him another business card. "I hope you'll keep us posted on the status of the investigation." Hand said he'd consider it his duty. "And I'd appreciate it if you'd keep a close eye on the property. I'm going to stop down at Beaver Building Supplies and buy a lock and chain for the gate," I said. "Then I'm gonna run out and put it on. I'll drop a key off on our way out to the place."

"I'll have the boys make it a regular patrol stop on every shift," he said.

"You know what Claudia told me about the price of the property?"

We were at the east edge of town, on our way to lock the place up. I'd spent thirty-two bucks on a serious lock and chain and had left one of the keys in the care of Deputy Spots. Rebecca was filling me in on her time with Claudia.

"What?"

"She said the old man asked J.D. what he could afford to pay for it in cash and when J.D. told him how he wouldn't be able to come up with anything like its value, the old man said he didn't care; he wanted cash, and he wanted it right then."

"Maybe he's one of those old codgers who doesn't trust banks," I offered.

I put on my signal, waited for an oncoming Budweiser truck to pass and turned right over the bridge. The tires snapped and popped on the rough wooden surface. I turned right, back toward the homestead. The first mile of West River Road was scenic. After that, the river looped out to the south and you were in that open high ground where J.D. had gone over the edge.

On the left, a deep, nearly vertical notch cut into the side of the mountain; on the right, the rocky canyon of the Bogachiel River. The road was about a lane and a half wide. Every so often, turnouts had been cut into the steep bank.

"So . . . let me tell you about your paramour Mr. Tressman and the Case of the Recalcitrant Clerk," I said. Ahead, the Bogachiel gleamed like a black ribbon.

"Do tell," she said.

"So anyway, he keeps me cooling my butt for twenty minutes and then . . ." A log truck was parked in the road, facing our direction. "Oops," she said. I slowed down and, when he made no move of any kind, stopped. The rig was filthy. The only places on the cab not covered by an inch of dried mud were the twin crescents the wipers had cleared. I wasn't sure of the local protocol, but I knew I'd passed a turnout not too far back, and figured it was going to be a lot easier for me to back up than it would be for him. I rolled down the window, threw my arm out, and followed it with my head. My turn to say, "Oops." Another log truck, this one behind us. I could see gray diesel smoke rising from the pipes and hear the rapping of his engine. "Oh goody," sighed Rebecca. "Rush hour."

They must have been talking on the CB radio or whatever truckers talk on these days, because they started for us at precisely the same time. The truck to our rear nearly pulled a wheelie when the driver popped the clutch at full throttle. Rebecca was still looking forward; she screamed, "Leo!" I snapped my head around. The mudmobile was bouncing over the dips at us like a rhinoceros. As it charged our way, clumps of mud shook loose from the fenders and splattered in the road. The last image I had of Rebecca was of her throwing her arms up in front of her face and turning to look at me. Then we were hit from behind by what seemed like a freight train. The force blasted me forward. My lap belt kept most of me in the cockpit, but I'm several inches taller than the average American, so the force tried to pitch me up and out. My forehead collided with the top of the windshield and my world went red. Blind, I groped to the right, reaching toward Rebecca, when suddenly we were hit from the front, pile-driving the air from my lungs, snapping my head back into the headrest; I remember the feeling of being pelted by stones, and then I was floating forward again into the white, and the crumbling dashboard and something pushing sharp on my leg, and then the roar and the scraping and the dim sensation of moving forward, and the unmistakable teeter-totter moment of equilibrium as the backseat started to rise and the car went into free fall straight down, landed on its nose, rested for a moment and then flopped over onto its top.

The roaring stayed in my head long after the real sounds departed. I never heard the forest grow silent around us: that moment when the wheels stop turning and the fluids cease to flow, as the last piece of debris settles into place and the first bird sings.

Next thing I knew, my hands were at my face. I pawed at the red mud until suddenly I could see the deflated air bag in my lap. I could make out that the roof had buckled in the center. Couldn't see Rebecca. I tried to call her name, but nothing came out, so I swallowed several times, tried unsuccessfully to work up some spit and then tried again. "Hey," I croaked. No response.

And then, out of the blue, I started to sob. First one little hiccup, then a rhythmic succession of spasms shook my chest and lasted for several minutes. Turned out to be a good thing because, by the time I regained control of myself, I knew for sure that if either of us was getting out of here alive, I was going to have to get my shit together in a hurry.

I wiped my nose on my shoulder. Concentrated on my breathing as I looked around. Even in my muddled state, there was little question that I was hanging upside down in my seatbelt, and that not much was going to happen until I wasn't, so I groped around until I found the release, braced a hand on the headliner and pushed the button. I dropped about a foot. Though the windshield was buckled in the center, there looked to be enough room for me to crawl out.

Problem was the steering wheel was pushed up under my chin, so there was no way I could move in that direction. I looked to the left. The window was bent into a trapezoid, but mercifully it was open. When I pulled my feet around so I could go out head first, I realized that my right shin hurt like hell and the foot was warm and wet. I ignored it, reached out and grabbed the window frame with both hands and began worming myself out, until my hands were in the leaves and I could pull my feet down to join them.

When I tried to stand, my stomach hurled its contents up my throat. I dropped back to all fours, began to retch and stayed at it until my mouth was filled with the taste of bile and my lower lip was connected to the ground by a silver string of spittle.

And as I knelt there staring at a pile of my own puke, I had one of those thoughts that separates man from the beasts. I thought, You should have killed me, motherfucker. You should have come down here with a gun and popped a cap on both of us, because, as of this moment, I am coming for you. Maybe not today, but you should make it a point to rest a bit more lightly, because I'm coming.

The car had fallen nearly thirty feet straight down into the canyon and was now about two-thirds the size it had been earlier. In the darkness, I could make out pieces of chrome and plastic scattered here and there. Most of the shattered windshield lay twisted on the ground behind the car. I pulled my left leg up so the foot was on the ground and then got to my feet. From the knee down, the right leg of my jeans was thick with blood. Gritting my teeth, I eased the pants up and had a look. From ankle to knee, a strip of flesh four inches wide had been peeled from my leg. Despite the seeping blood, the shin bone was visible. I eased the pants back down. I could feel blood squishing between my toes as I struggled for balance. Gingerly, I made my way around the back of the car.

Rebecca's door had sprung open on impact and I could

see her arm hanging out the door. The pain from my leg had my ears roaring again as I limped to her side. Her head was thrown back. She had a bruise the size and color of an eggplant across her forehead and blood coming from the corner of her mouth. I put my finger on her throat. Her pulse was strong and regular.

I pushed the button and slid the seat back as far as it would go. When I popped her seatbelt, she fell out into my lap. That's when I saw her other arm, and the bone sticking out, and the blood all over the place. Compound fracture. Shock. Stop the bleeding. Keep her warm. I laid her carefully on the hillside and went to the back of the car where I'd thrown my dirty clothes. The blue work shirt was draped over my old gym bag and covered with glass. I reached in through the twisted frame and pulled it out and then made my way back to her side.

The break was six inches below her elbow, and there was no way I was going to try to poke the bone back inside or set it or anything like that. I tore the shirt into strips and did the best I could with a bandage. She groaned and thrashed when I tied the last strip tight around the others and then groaned again when I picked her up in my arms.

I began to traverse the hill, walking like Boris Karloff in _The Mummy_. The cliff down into the river canyon got smaller as you got closer to the bridge, so I kept moving in that direction, laying Rebecca down when my arms could no longer bear her weight. The third time I picked her up and started on, something in my head broke loose and I began to bleed heavily from the nose. Time and distance got real fuzzy. If you'd asked me then, I would have spoken in terms of hours and miles. Later it turned out I'd carried her a little over six hundred feet and that from the time I left the key with Deputy Spots to the time help arrived had been a mere fifty-five minutes.

I left her in a dark recess between two boulders. The roadbed was no more than three feet above her head. She had a big snotty red stain on her chest from where my nose had been dripping on her and she'd begun to bleed through the makeshift bandage on her arm. Her lips moved slightly, as if she were trying to whisper, but no sound came out.

"Rebecca," I said. Her lips stopped. "I'll be back. I've gotta go now, but I'll be back." I think maybe I told her a bunch of times, but I can't be sure.

I climbed up to the road and took off my bloody shirt. I tied it around the nearest bush and started for the bridge in a stiff, labored gait. From that point on, there's a lot of it that I don't remember. I don't, for instance, remember crossing the bridge, but I must have because I got as far as the highway, where, for the first time since coming to Stevens Falls, I got lucky. Forty yards from where I staggered bare-chested out onto Route 101, two cars were pulled over on the shoulder of the eastbound lane. The car in front showed only parking lights, which was okay because the one behind had a rack of red and blue lights blazing into the night. The cop was handing the guy something through the window.

I must have been a sight. At first he didn't know who I was.

"What in hell . . . ," he said as I came staggering toward him.

It was Deputy Bobby Russell. He tossed the guy in the car his license and registration and began to jog my way. "Sir . . . ," he started to say. Then he figured it out.

"Jesus . . . is that you, Mr. Waterman?"

"Get an ambulance on the way," I said.

"Come on. Get in the car. I'll take you to the hospital myself."

"For my friend," I said with as much volume as I could muster. "Maybe a mile up West River."

He turned and sprinted for the radio in the patrol car.

17 REBECCA GRIMACED AT ME, GOT UP WITH THAT AIR OF dramatic slowness and crossed to turn the stereo off. The room was still. She stood with her back to me and took a final sip from her coffee cup, and as she turned slowly, she attempted to set the cup on the glass shelf beside the stereo, but she missed the shelf. In the first hasty action I had seen her make in weeks, she reached for the falling cup, which shattered on the oak planks, sending a starburst of coffee out in all directions. She took a deep breath and backed through the swinging door into the kitchen and then returned with a paper sack and roll of paper towels and dropped the scattered pieces of the cup into the bag and then began to wipe the floor clean of coffee, rubbing hard, going over and over the same area, continuing to scrub until long after the need was over. When she got to her feet and turned back my way, I knew we were through sparring.

"You can't be serious," she said.

"Why's that?"

"You're going back there?"

"I've got a client."

"All you had to do was say no."

"I didn't want to say no."

"Claudia I can understand. She's about to come into a great deal of money. She wants to know what happened to her husband. But you? You've still got over two hundred stitches in your leg. The front of your head looks like the Frankenstein monster . . . and you're thinking of going back there. For what? You heard what Billy said about the case. There's nothing to investigate."

Billy was Captain William Heffernen of the Washington State Police, a twenty-year veteran of the force and a close friend of Rebecca's. Whenever he needed better pathology work than the state provided, he called Rebecca. Over the past ten years, she had become the forensic witness of choice for the Washington State Police. At her request, he'd sent a pair of investigators to Stevens Falls. Two days and they were back. They reported that the likelihood that J.D. Springer's killer could be brought to justice was about nil.

"Why?" she demanded.

"It's what I do."

"It's more than that. It's more like who you are."

"Thank you, Dr. Laura."

"What you do is dabble at being a private detective until you come into your trust fund. What you are is a perpetual adolescent."

"What? This is suddenly news to you?" I said in mock surprise. "I've never made any bones about not being either the most ambitious or the most mature guy in the world. Excuse me, but I always figured that was more or less a given."

She waved her good arm around. "There are no givens," she yelled. To the best of my recollection that was the first time she'd ever raised her voice to me, and she wasn't through. "Whatever givens there were went over that damn cliff with us." She put her hand to her throat, as if to contain her voice. When she opened her mouth, her tone was tight, but under control. "I don't know whether you'll understand this or not, Leo . . . maybe you're so used to that kind of thing that what happened to us doesn't have an effect on you, but . . ."

"But what?"

She thought it over. "But everything's different now," she said finally. "This thing you do that's so important to you . . ." She took a deep breath. "I'm not sure it's okay with me anymore."

"What's that supposed to mean?"

"Just what it says." She searched for a phrase. "It's not a job . . . it's like some sort of quest with you. Some game you play at so you don't have to get a real job."

"Like yours."

"Yes, dammit, like mine." Yelling again.

"I'll pass, thanks."

She threw the wet towels into the bag and then rifled the roll in on top. When you only have one usable arm, you consolidate. Moving quickly now, she picked up the bag, strode to the door and disappeared into the kitchen. The air in the room was heavy and still. So what else was new?

Things had been heavy ever since we got back from Stevens Falls. Instead of staging a party for the boys, we'd suffered through nine days of doctor appointments, hospitals, and surgery. At first I attributed the air of tension to the severity of our injuries. Rebecca's arm had required three hours of surgery and four steel pins and was now encased in plaster from shoulder to wrist. Not only was she still in considerable pain from the arm, but she'd been having migraine headaches from the blow she took to the head.

As for me, I was never going to look good in shorts again. I'd left a big hunk of shin meat somewhere on the floor of the Explorer. They'd taken two-hundred-some-odd stitches, and done the best they could, but there was no way to replace the divot. They said I'd probably have the scab for a year. My head . . . well, it was like she said. I had another forty stitches about an inch back in my hairline. At least in what used to be my hairline before they shaved it back into its present mental-patient cut. So as not to scare small children, I'd taken to wearing a baseball cap at all times.

Funny how people respond to things. I hadn't necessarily

expected Rebecca to treat me like a hero or anything. I'm a firm believer that people do what they have to, but I sure as hell hadn't expected her to blame me for the incident, either. Go figure.

I can practically smell something unsaid. I grew up on it. It was my pabulum. Whatever had torn my parents apart had hung like Spanish moss in this house for most of my childhood, so I knew what was going on between Rebecca and me. It's just that I didn't have any idea what to do about it. So we'd canceled all of our holiday plans and limped our way through the last week and a half, making and keeping our separate appointments and allowing the curtain of antagonism that hung between us to go unacknowledged. And then Claudia Springer showed up this morning, on the day before Christmas, with some good news, an armload of presents and the straw that broke the camel's back.

"Guess what? I got an attorney," she said. "And the city of Stevens Falls has made me the same offer for the property that they made Mr. Bendixon. It closes the seventeenth of January."

I was happy for her. It not only cleaned up her legal problems, it made her a wealthy young woman. She jumped to her feet to administer hugs. We ooohed and aaahed and directed her to those portions of our anatomies that could safely be fondled.

Rebecca, of course, immediately began to tender investment advice, which inadvertently segued into the subject of today's escalation of hostilities. When Rebecca mentioned the need to be conservative and not go hog wild just because you've come into the better part of eight large, Claudia'd agreed wholeheartedly.

"Right now, there's only one thing I'm going to spend some money on."

"What's that?" Rebecca asked.

I figured a new car. A house in the 'burbs. Nope.

"I want to hire Leo to find out who killed J.D."

Rebecca's first reaction was to laugh. "Oh . . . Leo can't possibly—"

"Why?" I asked Claudia.

"Why do I want to hire you?" she asked.

"Yeah."

She sat back on the couch and ran it through her circuits.

"What am I going to tell the kids?" she asked after a moment. "When they ask me what happened to their daddy, what am I going to say? That he was killed by person or persons unknown? That I don't know what happened to him? And that I just, like . . . let it go at that?"

"Four out of ten homicides are never solved," I said.

She wasn't going for it. "Somebody knows," she said. "Somewhere in that valley, somebody knows who did that to J.D."

Rebecca moved slowly toward the stairs. "If you'll excuse me," was all she said, but the vibe hung in the air like the smell of blood. Claudia picked up on it.

"Oh . . . ," she stammered "I'm sorry; I didn't mean to—"

I held up a hand, and we watched in silence as, with great deliberation, Rebecca mounted the stairs and disappeared from sight.

"Have you thought this through?" I asked Claudia, before she got a chance to start apologizing again. "Neither the local law nor the state police think there's any chance of apprehending J.D.'s killer. You could end up spending a lot of money and not know any more than you know now."

Her jaw was set. "Is that what you think?" she asked.

"I think that from their standpoint that's probably true. I don't think conventional investigation techniques will do a darn thing," I said.

"I thought you of all people would—"

"I didn't say it couldn't be done," I interrupted.

"You just said—"

"I said it couldn't be done by conventional means."

"But you think it could be done . . . I guess, then, by unconventional means."

"Yes, I do."

"Like what?"

I shook my head. "From your standpoint as the client, it's better that you don't know the specifics. If what I've got in mind somehow goes haywire, you're going to need to be able to say that you merely hired me to do the job and that the specifics were a complete mystery to you."

"I can live with that," she said. "I don't suppose this is very nice, but I really don't care how you do it."

Something about the last line sounded a bit too cavalier for the earnest girl I'd known, so I pressed her. "What else?"

Her first instinct was to go ditzy. "I don't understand . . . whatever do you . . . ?"

I waited patiently until she was finished. "You through?" I asked.

Her big blue eyes filled with tears. "At the end . . . the last few months . . . J.D. was distant . . . it was like he wasn't there."

"He had a lot going on," I said.

She closed her eyes and nodded. I used my thumb to wipe at a tear that ran down her cheek. "I didn't want to say anything," she whispered. She squeezed her eyes harder and spit it out like a chicken bone. "I thought there . . . for a while I thought that . . . maybe he had . . . he was seeing another woman. Something in me just knew it." She swallowed a sob and began to shake.

I stifled the urge to say something.

"I don't know where to hold him in my heart, Leo," she said. "I'm not sure what to feel." She put her head in her lap and began to cry like she was never going to stop. I mentally auditioned a couple dozen soothing phrases but settled for rubbing her shoulder while she worked it out of her system.

After that, we'd cut a deal. My fee plus expenses. I told her the truth: It was likely to cost quite a bit. She made it a point not to ask what for, just wrote me a check for ten grand and hugged me Merry Christmas in the doorway. I told her to give Adam a hug for me, and she said she would.

"I'm sorry if I . . . I mean you and Rebecca . . . ," she said before leaving.

"This doesn't have anything to do with you," I assured her.

It was true. Rebecca and I had been living alone together ever since we got back from the peninsula, so the rest of the afternoon was pretty much status quo. I made the obligatory attempts at conversation and was rewarded with a couple of amazingly unresponsive monosyllables. So I unplugged the downstairs phones and settled into the den with a six-pack of Rolling Rock, a large can of cashews and an unending succession of college football games.

Around seven, I heard a horn in the driveway. Got up to check. A cab. She was going to her mother's for Christmas Eve. Yeah, Merry Christmas to you, too. On the way back to the den, I snagged the afghan from the couch.

18 JED HELD A BOTTLE OF RÉMY MARTIN LOUIS XIII. COMES in a crystal decanter at a mere thirteen hundred bucks a fifth. "A drink?" he asked.

"Sure," I said. "Why not?"

He crossed the room to the built-in bar and poured us each a hundred bucks worth.

Around ten, I'd gone for a drive. The streets had been deserted. Nobody out but me and the losers with no place to go. Around eleven-thirty, without consciously willing it so, I'd found myself parked in Jed's driveway, so I'd figured, what the hell . . . might as well knock on the door. The maid answered. "Oh," was all she'd said. Jed appeared over her shoulder. "Leo," he said, taking the door from her hand. "Come in."

Sarah, the girls, the hubbys and the new granddaughter were all tucked in their beds, presumably experiencing those visionary sugar plums of song and story. Jed ushered me into the den, while Marie headed back for the kitchen.

I stuck my nose in the oversized snifter and took a ten-dollar whiff. A golden chain pulsed across the surface of the rich amber liquid. I looked around. The table on my right held one of those clocks in a glass dome. The golden balls twirling silently in one direction and then stopping and twirling back the other.

The den was Jed's domain and, as such, had been spared

the holiday treatment. He used the long butane lighter to get the gas fireplace going. We all used gas these days. Hell, these days, you had to drive seventy-five miles to get somewhere you could cut wood. Not to mention that none of us even knew anybody with a pickup truck anymore. He retrieved his brandy from the mantel.

"Everything okay?" he asked.

"Oh yeah," I said. "I just happened to be in the neighborhood." I checked my watch. "At eleven-forty-five on Christmas Eve."

"That's what I figured. Nice to see you getting out, though, by the way."

"Wouldn't want to get mansion fever."

"Certainly not," he agreed.

I took a sip of the cognac and looked around the sumptuous room. "You ever wonder about all of this?" I asked. "I mean, like who we were when we first met and who we are now, and like how in hell we got here?"

"No more than a dozen times a day," he said.

"I mean, you and I are sitting here drinking liquor that costs more than the cars we were driving when we first met."

He raised his glass in salute. *"Viva la France,"* he said.

We'd known each other for more than twenty years. When I'd first met him, he was fresh from New York and a job as the ACLU's top litigator. We'd met in jail, where he was cooling his heels on a contempt charge and I was looking at an assault rap, for defending myself against an irate transit cop on whom I'd served a subpoena. In those days, Jed drove a beige Gremlin and worked out of a ratty little office on Third Avenue, right where the new symphony hall stands today. He'd taken on every lost cause that walked in the door and won most of them, until he'd become the bane of the DA's office. Well-known judges took unexpected fishing vacations when Jed James's name appeared on their dockets.

Now, James, Junkin, Rose and Smith occupied the whole thirty-eighth floor of the Rainier Building, which in Seattle was about as uptown as things get. It costs five grand to sit down and discuss fees with him, and he was talking with the local Democratic party about running for King County judge whenever Wendel Woods either stepped down or dropped dead. He sat in the brown leather chair opposite me and began rolling the snifter between his palms. "So . . . Leo, I'm going to draw upon my years of legal training and go out on a limb here and figure that, it being Christmas Eve and all, this is probably about you and Rebecca?"

I thought about telling him that was how come he was making the big bucks, but swallowed it instead. "I don't think living together is turning out to be what either of us imagined."

"How long has it been?"

"Just over a year."

"That would sound just about right for having some second thoughts."

"It's not the little things, either. It's deeper than that."

"Like what?"

"It's like all of a sudden, she wishes I was a CPA."

"Instead of . . ."

"What did she say I do? . . . Oh yeah . . . I dabble at being a private detective until my trust fund comes due." I threw up my hand. "I always thought she liked what I did. Now all of a sudden—"

"That's the cliché isn't it?"

"What?

"The same stuff they used to love about you ends up being exactly what drives them crazy?"

"Yeah. I guess it is."

Jed retrieved the cognac, gave me one more finger than he'd given me the first time and then did the same for himself. "In your defense, Leo . . ."

"I was hoping we'd get to that part."

"I don't think you've ever been shy about your plan to move directly from adolescence to retirement. And I don't think you dabble. I don't know anyone more committed to what they're doing than you are, but that's not the point, now, is it?"

"What do you mean?"

"You really think whatever is going on between you two is about what you do for a living?"

"No," I admitted. It was more than that. I told him about how it wasn't even a question of where we were going but more of how we were going to get there. How, lately, I kept finding myself at dinner with other couples our age whose exclusive subject of conversation was the state of the stock market in general and their own 401(k) plans in particular. I raved about how it seems like you can't turn on the tube without some mutual fund reminding you that sleeping under a bridge is just around the corner, and about how all of it absolutely bored the shit out of me.

"That's the rub, then, isn't it?"

"What?"

"You're not traveling the same path as most of your peers."

"Have I ever been?"

"Not to my knowledge."

"I feel like when I married my first wife Annette. I married into this huge Sicilian family. First non-Italian to marry in. Her father always called me *desgratiado*. It means the disgrace."

"Because you weren't Italian."

"No . . . not really. Actually he and I got along pretty good. What he held against me was that I didn't wish I was Italian. Heredity, he was willing to forgive me. My attitude about it, he was not."

"So you're saying . . ."

I thought it over. "Let me ask you a question. Suppose I didn't have my trust fund looming on the horizon. You think I'd be doing what everybody else is doing and planning for my retirement?"

No hesitation. "Absolutely not," he said. "You'd be doing exactly what you're doing now. It's what I love about you."

"Me, too," I said.

We worked our brandies. Except for the hissing of the fire, the room was silent.

"That was quite a trauma you two had."

I hadn't thought of it before, but I said, "I don't think she's ever been scared like that."

"Most people haven't."

"I don't think she knows how to handle it."

"Most people wouldn't."

"Stop being sensible, will you?"

"Have you thought that this may not be the best time in your life to be making decisions?" he said. When I didn't answer, he continued. "Like when a spouse dies, they say not to do anything drastic for a year. Don't quit your job, don't sell your house, that kind of thing. The suggestion being that trauma quite often does not for wise choices make."

"What happened to us in Stevens Falls just amplified what was already going on," I said.

"Which was?"

"I think that would depend upon which one of us you asked."

"If I asked you?"

"If you asked me, I'd say . . . maybe I'm feeling a little chafed. Like my relationship isn't so much part of my life as much as it's becoming my life, and I don't know how I feel about that. It's like for the first time in my life, I pretty much know what next week is going to look like." Before he could say anything, I held up my hand. "But I don't want it to sound like it's something Rebecca's doing to me, because it's not. Lots of it is internal."

I got to my feet and walked over to the fire and turned my back to the flames.

"I'm feeling like an old fart. There's nothing on the radio I like anymore. It's like I've been banished to either the jazz channel or the oldies station. I watch these TV shows and they've got kids who don't shave yet playing grizzled homicide dicks, on programs I can't remember the names of. The only programs that sell anything I might even remotely want to buy are golf tournaments, and I'm telling you, man, that just scares the hell out of me."

"What is it you're afraid of . . . ending up like everybody else?"

I wouldn't have put it that way, but, "Yeah, I guess it's something like that."

"Notice how we keep getting back to the things about you that I love."

"You lost me."

"That's where we were a while back, on the question of why you'll never be one of those guys calling his broker at six in the morning. It's the same answer. It's because you've got your own thing going on, your own set of standards, your own set of goals about which . . ."—I started to speak, but he raised his voice—"about which—and this is the crux of the issue—about which you do . . . not . . . compromise, Leo. And that, my old friend, while a noble and romantic stance, will get you old and alone."

I could feel the blood rising to my cheeks.

"So what, then? I take a job for one of the big outfits? Wear a tie? Spend my days tracking skip traces by computer?"

"Certainly not. Not only would it kill you, but you'd be lousy at it."

"Being a PI is all I've ever done."

"You'd be useless at anything else. A clockwork orange."

As usual, Jed had hit it right on the head. At this point in my life, whenever I pictured myself in another career, the image I saw always seemed as unnatural and unnecessary as a piece of mechanical fruit. I tried to lighten things up.

"Well, of course, there's playing lead guitar for the Stones, but you know Keith's already got the gig."

"Dreams die hard," he said. I took a sip of the cognac and let it roll around on my palate before swallowing. For the first time in weeks, the burnt smell was missing from my nostrils. I swirled the liquor and took another sip.

"About a month ago, I'm having lunch with Charlie Cook. You remember Charlie?" Jed nodded. "At the Two Bells Tavern on Fourth. Anyway . . . before I start this story, I should give you a little history. Charlie's about three years older than I am. I used to look up to him like the big brother I didn't have. We used to do a lot of crazy things together." I took another sip of my cognac.

Jed raised his glass in a toast. "Ah, youth."

"The one that comes to mind is the time he had a date with this Italian girl. Name of Carlotta Somethingorothera. Very strict old-school parents. They wouldn't let Charlie take Carlotta out unless he got a date for her little sister Rosie, which, of course, is where I come into it. So we show up on Friday night. The family had this delicatessen down in Garlic Gulch. Parents have gone home for the day. The only one there is this brother Mario, who, while the girls are on their way down, tells us all the things he and the family are going to do to us if we put so much as a hand on their girls."

"Sarah's father threatened to put my scrotal sac through an offset press."

For the first time in weeks, I laughed. "So the girls show up and they're both gorgeous and nice and we take 'em out to a movie—A Shot in the Dark, I think it was the first Pink Panther flick. Anyway, we're bringin' 'em home when they say they want to stop at the deli. So we stop. They drag us inside, where they snag a couple of bottles of chianti from the shelves and lead us up onto the roof, where, much to my and Charlie's amazement, they turn out to be the horniest creatures either of us had ever encountered. Within minutes I'm naked and doing all the things I always thought I wanted to be doing. Charlie's over on the far side of the roof with the sister, but, you know, I can hear that the same thing is going on over there."

"Your first time?" Jed asked.

"No . . . but pretty close. It was the first time it wasn't pitch-black and there wasn't a gear-shift lever involved."

"Go on."

"Okay . . . to make a long story short, about the time we're halfway to paradise, the brother Mario shows up and can hear what's going on up on the roof. Thank God one of the sisters locked the door to the roof. So Mario goes ballistic. He's throwing himself at the door, screaming in Italian. By then we'd put away the wine, so we're all laughing our asses off while we're trying to get it down, but you know . . . I'm young and I'll be damned if I'm going to stop until I get some relief . . . but I'm laughing my ass off, which is not helping the matter at all."

"A dilemma."

"Well, anyway, about the time the fire axe starts to come through our side of the door, Charlie and I figure it's time for our withdrawal."

"Literally and figuratively."

"Except there's no way down. Not even a drainpipe to climb down, so, in order not to become geldings, we end up having to jump two stories into a dumpster full of spoiled fruit."

Jed gave me another toast. I did my end.

"So . . . thirty years later, I'm sitting in a tavern with this same guy and he's got his glasses on and he's studying the menu like there's going to be a test, when he looks over at me and he says, 'I'm gonna be really bad today. I'm gonna have the chicken.' "

Jed burst out laughing.

"I mean, it was like a moment of epiphany for me. What the hell has happened to us? How'd we get to where being 'really bad' involves ordering the chicken instead of the fruit plate? What happened to those kids on the roof? To the spontaneity . . . the joy?"

"Same dilemma you're faced with now."

"How's that?"

"Whether to follow your instincts and get the hell off the roof, or stay with the girl and risk being neutered."

"*Neutered* is too strong a word."

"What would you prefer?"

I thought it over. "*Diminished,* maybe."

"Or maybe *tamed.*"

"Something like that," I admitted.

"I'm sure it won't be news to you if I say that life is a system of trade-offs."

I started to speak, but thought better of it. I could think of thirty more things to say, but in the end, all of them, in some manner or another, validated my feelings and trivialized Rebecca's. So I shut up and finished my cognac in silence. I set the empty glass on the mantel and said, "Hey, man . . . thanks for putting up with me."

He got up and gave me a hug. We were embracing and patting one another on the back when Maria poked her head in the door to say she was going home for the evening. I gave her a salacious wink over Jed's shoulder.

She closed the door. "Maria's going to think we're gay," I said.

"Who cares?" he said and hugged me tighter.

Used to be I could count on Jed to come to my aid at a moment's notice. These days it's not that simple. "Hey," I said as we patted ourselves back into shape. "First week after the new year, I've got a little something going on . . . I was wondering if you could maybe lawyer for the crew if necessary."

"Are you anticipating problems?"

"No," I said honestly. "Just as a failsafe."

"This wouldn't include a little fishing vacation, would it?"

"It might," I said.

He motioned toward the half-empty cognac bottle. "Care to tell me about it?"

I shook my head. "Couldn't possibly do it," I said. "Not with you being an officer of the court and all."

19 SOME PEOPLE YOU PICTURE IN YOUR MIND'S EYE AS A smile or a unique tilt of the head. Others are most readily recalled by the ear as a hearty laugh or a breathy tone of voice. Floyd was the only person in the world whom I associated with a smell. On three prior occasions, I'd hired Floyd to protect me. In each case, someone had died violently. The last one heaved his final breath in the front seat of my former car. It had probably been my imagination, but after that night in west Seattle, I'd never been able to get behind the wheel of that car without the sweet smell of brains tickling my nostrils, and to this day, the mention of his name carries that faintly metallic odor to my nose like a breeze.

Even now, the smell loitered in the air around me as I dialed the number you started with, if you were looking for Floyd. "Windjammer," the rough voice answered.

"I'd like to talk to Floyd," I said.

His routine never varied. "Got nobody here with a name like that," he growled.

"In case you do," I said. "Have him call Leo Waterman." I left the cell phone number.

"Whatever floats your boat, buddy," he said and hung up.

I snapped the phone closed, turned the ringer all the way up and put it in my jacket pocket. Floyd would get back to me when he could. Time to find Kurtis Ryder III.

Kurtis was the black sheep of the socially prominent Ryder clan. A solitary stain on an otherwise pristine landscape of old money and privilege that for four generations had occupied the very apex of Seattle society. And what a black sheep he was.

Kurtis came out before most people were aware there was a closet. He was neither flamboyant nor apologetic about his preferences, but merely went about his life in the manner he saw fit. Despite the narrow-minded attitudes of the time, the family, to its credit, closed ranks around Kurtis, and for a while became ardent financial supporters of the burgeoning gay and lesbian rights movement. Interestingly enough, Kurtis's problems had nothing to do with his sexual preferences. Kurtis liked to gamble.

By the time he'd graduated from Stanford with an electrical engineering degree, he was over three hundred thousand dollars in debt to a pair of Oakland bookies. He claimed he was so naive he figured he'd just move home to Seattle and that would be the end of it. Predictably, the bookies didn't see it that way. A week after graduation, two gentleman in bad suits pulled him from his car, dragged him into the alley behind what was then the Green Parrot Lounge and beat the living crap out of him with iron rods. They told him they hadn't broken his knees only because they wanted their money and breaking his legs would have delayed that process. They gave him ten days to get even or, as they put it, get measured for a creeper. Kurtis, naturally, went to his father.

His father, naturally, said no. Not only no, but he forbade anyone else in the family, on pain of disinheritance, to assist his irresponsible and ungrateful son in any way. Kurtis made the rounds of the relatives, but it was no go. By the time the family dust settled, Kurtis had six days left until he became differently abled. He spent a day and a half considering everything from suicide to the Alaskan wilderness and then came up with the plan that was to change his life forever.

He remembered a party he'd been to a couple of months before, during spring break. A friend of a friend of a friend. Some people with a big new house up on the Magnolia Bluffs. He remembered his amusement at how eager they had been to show off their newfound wealth in an obvious and ostentatious way that would have appalled the bluenose members of his own family. Money and jewelry strewn about. How she'd insisted he look in her jewelry collection, and how the husband had dragged him around by the elbow showing off his new burglar alarm setup, and how he'd stood there thinking that anyone with even a rudimentary knowledge of electronics could walk right through something like that.

I still remember when he told me about that night, and the look he had in his eyes while he recounted the story of bypassing the alarm with a piece of tinfoil, creeping around the house, with his heart pounding out of his chest, and then finding what he was looking for right there in the bedroom with the couple. "And when I was standing there in the dark," he told me, "I've got all this stuff in my arms, and it's deadly quiet and both of them are laying there snoring . . . man, I'm telling you, I had a religious experience. I felt like electricity was running through my body, and in that moment I knew that all that money I'd pissed away gambling had just been for the risk . . . I didn't like gambling. I like risk. I knew right then that burglary was my calling."

At forty cents on the dollar from a fence, he hadn't pulled enough jewelry out of the Magnolia house to pay his whole debt, but he had bought himself some time. Time that he used to get himself reestablished on the local highbrow party scene, where his scandalous presence brought an air of insubordination to what might otherwise have been a series of opulent but dull gatherings. Like clockwork, however, a couple of weeks after the party, the hosts would brush the sleep from their eyes to find their family's most treasured baubles missing and presumed fenced.

To this day Kurtis claims that, having paid off his debt and socked a little away for himself besides, the burglary he was caught committing was to have been his last. It was ugly. They not only got him for the hotel room he was caught in, but his fence rolled over on him and then it turned out that they were already hip to him on the society burglaries, so, in spite of being a first-time offender, Kurtis ended up doing the three of a three-to-five on McNeil Island, where he went to burglary college.

The difference between Kurtis and your average convicted felon is that Kurtis is highly intelligent, while most of them are dumber than dirt. He'd picked the brain of every thief, second-story man and cat burglar in the institution and returned to Seattle a true master of his trade. He still spent quite a bit of time in police stations, because anytime anything of great value was missing, he was number one on the "usual suspects" list, but, to my knowledge, he had never done any more serious time.

Kurtis lived in the Ravenna area, up on the hill behind the university. He rented the upstairs of a blue and white Edwardian house from a pair of married attorneys who just happened to be his attorneys of record. Interesting arrangement, I'd always thought.

I pushed his button on the door. Voice-over speaker.

"Be right down."

Kurtis is a handsome fellow with a thick shock of what used to be called strawberry-blond hair, beginning to grow slightly gray at the temples and worn long. He was what I'd call willowy rather than thin, as if he weren't connected quite as tightly at the joints as the rest of us. He gave the impression of flowing from point to point.

We shook hands. "There was buzz that you came home on your shield, Leo," he said with a perfect smile. "So glad to see the rumor was unfounded."

"That makes two of us," I assured him.

We walked down to the Queen Mary Tea Room, ordered

coffee and traded recent life stories for a few minutes. Seems the Bellevue police were making his life miserable over a burglary-related shooting. "Hayseeds," he was saying. "As if . . . like I'm going in armed." As far as Kurtis was concerned, any thief who went out armed was lower than whale shit. You did your homework. You made your entry. Took what you came for. And then made your exit. Period. If something went wrong, you kept your mouth shut until your lawyer arrived. He claimed to have talked his way out of darkened rooms on more than twenty occasions, and I believed him.

Kurtis had even less patience with small talk than I did. Before we got our first refill he said, "On the phone, you didn't say much."

"Cell phone."

He held up a hand to say he understood.

"I need a man of your talents."

He raised his eyebrows. "Which ones?"

"Breaking and entering."

"Ooooh."

"To get in and out of places." I pointed a finger. "Don't," I said.

First he looked hurt, then bored. "Any competent lock-smith—"

"Under adverse conditions."

"Aaah," he said. "Why me?"

"Because I need somebody who Carl Cradduck will work with, and you know what an incredible pain in the ass he is."

"When you're as good at what you do as Uncle Carl is, you get to be as eccentric as you want to be," he said.

"I've heard several buzzes that said you've worked to-gether before."

"I don't think it would be telling tales to say that the horrific Mr. Cradduck and I have on several occasions con-sulted."

"That's why I'm coming to you first."

"You and him are tight," he scoffed. "He wouldn't turn you down." His eyebrows went up a notch. "This wouldn't perchance be pro bono, would it?" he inquired.

"No," I said. "I'll pay you for your time, but there isn't going to be any score at the end of it. I want to let you know that right now."

"Talk to me."

I did. I gave him the abridged version. "Interesting," was all he said.

"So . . . what do you say?" I asked.

He steepled his fingers. "I've been in remission lately . . . what with those Bellevue hicks and all."

"So . . . a week out of town." I knew better than start in on the fresh air and sunshine shit with him. Kurtis was strictly indoorsey.

"In the event of mishap?"

"In the event of mishap, I personally guarantee to bail you out for any bailable offense and James, Junkin, Rose and Smith are riding legal shotgun for us until your attorneys arrive."

"I'm in," he said.

I left the café feeling like Lee Marvin, as Captain John Reisman, in the beginning of *The Dirty Dozen*, when he's going from cell to cell deciding exactly which raving lunatic to take on the mission. I tried to remember the theme so I could hum it.

Carl Cradduck and I went back to the days before no-fault divorce, when I earned my living kicking in doors, taking pictures and running for my life. They weren't the kind of pictures you could take down to the local drugstore, so every PI had to have some guy who did his developing. Carl was mine. He'd had a one-man shop south of the city. Before losing his legs in an auto accident, he'd been a photographer for the AP. He'd been in Seattle visiting his sister when a teenage driver lost control and put him in a wheelchair for life. The way he saw it, where a cripple lived didn't much matter, so he'd stayed.

Over a twenty-year span, the camera shop had mutated into an electronics and stereo store, then into the first place I could remember that sold car alarms and those portable phones in a bag and satellite dishes, and then eventually turned into Advanced Electronics, Inc., a high-tech security firm specializing in the detection of audio/visual electronic monitoring devices. In other words, if you thought maybe the competition had you bugged, you called Advanced Electronics.

He still ran an outlet for used electronic gear in Lake City. He claimed it was just a way to get some return on last year's gear, but I knew better. He liked working the store, though he'll never admit it. He was a guy who could pay cash for any house in the greater Seattle area but lived in four small rooms behind the store, because, like I said before, he figured where a cripple lived didn't much matter.

The front door buzzed as I stepped into the shop. He came rolling out from behind the counter.

"Merry Christmas," I said.

"Yeah," he said. "I got so excited about the festivities I'm just now taking solid food again."

The walls of the shop were covered with Carl's old AP photographs. Vietnam. Kent State. Altamont. And here and there Carl with this guy or other. When you looked at him in the photos, you could tell he was about six feet tall, yet when you saw him sitting there in the chair, it didn't seem possible that he'd ever been that big. He wore a red plaid Pendelton blanket across his lap and, unless he'd turned over a new leaf, a Beretta automatic rested somewhere within the folds of the blanket.

We shook hands. "I heard you were going to be laid up for months," he said. I pulled up my pants leg and gave him a look.

Carl asked the professional's question. "So . . . you got careless, or what?"

I thought it over. "No," I said. "Not really. Even when I look at it now, there wasn't anything to get careless about."

I told him the story from beginning to end, leaving out only the personal shit between Rebecca and me. When I finished he said, "Well, don't mind me saying, Leo, you look pretty fuckin' bad for a guy who was careful."

"That's not what I meant. What I got wasn't careless; it was more like fixated. I had this mind-set that said nobody gets that upset over a fishing hole. And another one that said J.D. Springer was financially in over his head and that maybe he'd pushed an old man a bit too hard, and that people had noticed and that he was just doing that thing that people do when they're ashamed of themselves. How they get paranoid and blame everybody else for the situation they're in."

"And now?"

"Now I'm asking myself, 'What if?' What if this doesn't have anything to do with boat launches or fishing holes? What if J.D. was right? What if all these forces were conspiring against him for some reason or other?"

"That's a mouthful of 'what ifs,'" he said.

"Think about the overreaction," I said. "Rebecca and I are closing up the place. We're leaving town. If everything goes according to plan, they're never going to see our asses again. Sure, we've bent a few noses by getting their eviction order postponed and by finding J.D.'s cause of death, but, you know, when it comes to finding out why or who killed J.D. Springer, we haven't accomplished a damn thing. If anything, we're more confused than when we started. And they try to punch our tickets. Why?"

"So, other than my own special brand of Yuletide cheer, what do you want from me?"

"Depends on how busy you are."

"Depends on how much money you've got."

"I can pay my way."

He pushed the button on his chair, rolled over to the door and turned the sign to CLOSED. "Come on in the back," he said. He talked as he drove. "You know what my business has come to?"

"What?"

"Cameras in the women's restroom. Yep . . . a big problem for big business. You just let one honey find out somebody's been taking pictures of her wiping her twitchit and you've got a lawsuit to put the fear of god in you. They sue the business, the building, the city, everybody."

"No kidding?"

"Oh no. Not only are we growing perverts in record crops, but there's a big market for hidden camera shots out on the Internet. We find cameras all the time. It's cheaper to pay us to check the place than to pay lawyers and judgments."

"What's the world coming to?"

"I'll show you the tapes sometime. Got one girl, looks Armenian—"

When I reckoned on how maybe I'd pass on that honor, he motioned for me to have a seat at the ancient kitchen table. "You got something more interesting than fat girls in the crapper?"

"I think so . . . yeah."

"Lay it on me."

I told him what I had in mind. "I take it you've got no paperwork on this thing."

"You mean, like court orders for electronic surveillance . . . that sort of thing?"

"Yeah, Sherlock . . . those little details that will keep us out of the lockup."

" 'Fraid not," I said.

I expected a hard time. Instead, he said, "Good. What's the layout?"

He found an old blueprint; I used the back to draw a makeshift map of beautiful downtown Stevens Falls, Washington. He kept checking me for distances. How far was this from that, and that from the next thing. When I'd finished, he sneered at the drawing.

"Christ . . . place like that, you give me a couple of days and we'll be able to tell when and if anybody in that burg takes a dump. Here's what I've got in mind . . ."

When he finished outlining his plans, I stood open-mouthed.

"You can do that?"

"Shit yes," he said. "That's why I started Advanced. So I could do stuff like this. I figured if we were going to keep running wires on people, we better know what we were up against in the way of detection systems. So I started a detection company. Anytime anybody invents anything new, they send it to me to see if I can detect it. I end up with everything. I've got stuff the FBI won't have for another five years. But"—he held up a bony finger—"when it comes to the phones, you're living in the past. Phones are a bitch these days. Fiber-optics make it almost impossible to isolate lines from the outside."

"I've got Kurtis Ryder to do inside work."

"And I've got Robby to handle the technical end, but that don't help the phone problem. Problem with the phones is that most of the shit that's been manufactured in the last ten years isn't intended to be repaired. You're supposed to use it till it falls apart and then just shitcan it and buy another one. So, for the most part, phones don't come apart any more. They're all just molded plastic. Which means you'd need Robby to go inside with Kurtis." He shrugged. "Even with somebody as good as Robby, you figure fifteen minutes a phone, so that makes, what? An hour, hour and a half."

Carl was right. No way we could be inside anything for that long.

"So what are we going to do?" I asked.

"We'll wire the offices instead of the phones. Then we wire their rides so's we can keep track of what they do next.

Where they go. That is what you have in mind, isn't it? Stirring up the whole crock of shit to see which turds float."

"Nicely put," I said.

"So . . . what are you going to do to stir the pot?"

"Depends on whether or not you can still get Social Security numbers."

"Went up to fifty bucks a pop." His eyes narrowed. "You gonna steal Charlie Boxer's old tax number, aren't you?"

"Sure stresses folks out," I said. "Lenny Duke's still in business, isn't he?"

Carl said he was. "Lenny's got the same friggin' problem I do. We both spent so many years creating a front business that the damn thing eventually took over and made more dough than the scams we were using it to cover for. I mean, the only reason I started the damn business was to cover the kind of thing I was doing for guys like you." He shrugged. "You think that's what they meant when they said crime doesn't pay?"

I allowed how I thought maybe they had something else in mind.

"Who's gonna answer the phone?"

"I figured George could handle it."

He rolled over to the kitchen sink, opened the small drawer on the left and pulled out a small wire-bound notepad. "Write down the names of the people you need numbers for and where they work. I'll call Buster when he gets home from work today."

"This means you're in."

He waved a finger at me. "You know me, Leo . . . what's that song say about being caught between the yearning for love and the struggle for the legal tender?"

"I'll pay you—" I started.

He cut me off. "Me you can have for free. I'm so fucking bored, I was thinking about taking a cruise. Can you picture that?" Frankly, I couldn't. "I'm gonna need Robby to do my legwork, and the van. You're going to have to take care of him and pay expenses for the van and for the cherry picker and . . ."—he hesitated for effect—"any equipment we can't retrieve is on you." I agreed to his terms.

"What else are you going to need?" I asked.

"Someplace in that downtown area where we can park the van without attracting unwanted attention. We can monitor for up to four miles, but it'd be better if we were right there."

"I'll work on it."

"We're going to need to do the pole work on a Sunday. Nothing worse than having the real fucking phone company show up while you're up one of their poles."

"I'll plan around it," I said.

"When?" he asked.

"It's the twenty-seventh," I said. "Thursday is the first. What say you plan on doing the pole work on Sunday the fourth? I'll get in on Friday and have things set up."

He nodded. "What else have you got in mind for raising their blood pressure?"

I told him. He actually smiled.

"You've got a mean streak, you know that?" Coming from Carl, I took that as the highest form of praise.

I turned the sign on the door back to OPEN on my way out. Not that long ago, Lake City Way had been a viable means of getting from Seattle to the eastside without driving on the bridges. Six or seven miles of car dealerships, muffler shops, crummy strip malls and bad Chinese restaurants that wound around the northern edge of Lake Washington all the way to the eastside's interstate parking lot, I-405. No more. You know traffic is bad when you pass the same guy on a bicycle six or seven different times in the same half hour. I'd have been better off stuck on the bridge. At least the view would have been nice.

Unlike Carl, Lenny Duke had evolved backward. As I understood it, he'd started out as a successful small-time counterfeiter. He made tens, they say. And good ones. When technological innovations made counterfeiting impossible, he'd moved into counterfeit documents. Driver's licenses. Social Security cards. Passports. Whatever you were looking for, Lenny could put you together a facsimile that would pass muster. By the time computer technology made false documents a thing of the past, the printing shop he'd started as a cover for the document business was flourishing. Lenny, being an agreeable soul, rolled with the punches and went legitimate. More or less. Mostly less.

The printing plant looked like an IBM showroom. The clattering noises had been replaced by the snap of paper and the whoosh of air, and Lenny's two sons now ran the shop. Although he no longer toiled at the business he'd created, Lenny still kept a small office against the back wall. They stored paper on the roof.

I should have been suspicious when the receptionist refused to open the door for me. The way she smirked and hurried back across the floor. When I yanked open the door, Lenny Duke was right there in front of me. Sitting behind a battered steel desk staring at a computer screen with his pants around his ankles. The screen was filled with a full-color picture of a blond woman in a red headband and a light coat of machine oil, engaged in what can most charitably be described as out-of-species dating.

"You ever see anything like that?" he asked without taking his eyes from the flickering screen.

"I never imagined you could train a dog to do that," I said.

"Dog, hell . . . ," he growled. "It's a chimp."

I'll never know for sure. My psyche was too battered for animal husbandry. I sat down on a folding chair at the end of the desk, where the screen was pointed the other way. I watched as he pushed some keys. He looked up at me. "Hey, Leo, Merry Christmas," he said.

"Hey, Lenny. Merry Christmas to you, too."

"Wait till you see this next one," he said.

"You still have those letters Charlie Boxer used to send out?"

"The tax stuff?" He sat back in the seat. "Yeah, I've got 'em. Why?"

" I want to put together a set."

He snorted, and started to swing the screen my way.

"Can you do it for me?"

He pushed some more keys. "Sure. By when?"

"Middle of next week."

"Sure. Leave the info on the desk."

I told him to call Carl later tonight for the names and numbers. He stopped me on my way out the door. "You want the 'we were wondering about this or that' letter or you want the 'you'll like federal prison' special? You want the fear of god, you got to have somebody working the phone. With that one, they call the number."

I told him I'd take the latter.

"You remember how Charlie ran it?" I asked.

His eyes stayed glued to the screen. Mine to the ceiling. "Sure . . . he'd be just nasty as hell on the phone, and then he'd always give 'em an appointment a couple of weeks down the road. He liked for 'em to sweat it out. After everybody called, he'd fix the phone so's anybody called, they went on to perpetual hold. Used to play the same Lennon Sisters song at 'em, over and over. Thought it was funny as hell."

I pulled out a business card and scribbled on it. "Use this for the phone number for the letters," I said. He leered at the screen.

I let myself out. I shot the receptionist a dirty look on the way by. She gave an exaggerated shrug. "They put him on the Net last Christmas, when he retired, " she said. "He only goes home to eat."

20 ON NEW YEAR'S EVE, I THOUGHT OF CONSTANCE Hart and Wayne Bigelow. I pictured them wearing pointed hats in a conga line, blowing noisemakers and drinking champagne. Wondered whether Wayne got lucky, but had my doubts. Worse yet, I wondered about me getting lucky and had even more doubts.

I sat up and switched off the TV. The ball had dropped in Times Square an hour ago. After that, I'd alternated between checking the local festivities down at the Space Needle and an old Randolph Scott western on Channel Twenty-two. It was 1999. The Fop Formerly Known as Prince was going to make another fortune.

I stood in the dark by the side of the bed, dropped my jeans and shirt into a pile and crawled into the sack. "Happy New Year," she said.

"Happy New Year."

"I'm going back to work on Monday," she said. "Tommy's going to pick me up and drive me home." Neither fact was surprising. She couldn't drive because of the angle of the cast on her left arm, but she was going crazy hanging around the house. And Tommy Matsukawa had spent the past twenty years or so hoping I'd fall in a hole and disappear so he could bowl in Rebecca's pagoda. It made complete sense.

"I can second on autopsies and do paperwork. Who knows . . . I might even catch up with my paper-shuffling."

"Sounds good," I said.

Over the past four days we'd both made serious attempts to talk our way through our problem, but the same thing happened every time. We're both clever, caring, educated people, with gifts of gab and enough social awareness to know that making the other party wrong is not the way to fame and fortune when it comes to conflict resolution. So we'd backed off, softened our stances and analyzed and wheedled and analogized and taken our feelings to whole new levels of abstraction, and yet every time, when I lay there at night unraveling the serpentine paths of our conversations, I could see that we never really got past the original question of who was right and who was wrong. Even yesterday, when we'd reasoned ourselves all the way to the very high state of agreeing to disagree, somewhere inside each of us, a voice whispered that we were right and the other poor misguided soul was wrong.

"What about you?" she asked from the darkness.

"You want to do this now?"

She turned over and levered herself up on her good arm. "Is there a better time?"

"No," I said. "I don't think so."

I sat up and flicked on my light. She was wearing that ratty old flannel nightgown again. "I'm not trying to be a pain in the ass about this," I said.

She made a "so what?" face but said, "I know."

"Friday, I'm going back over to J.D.'s place. The county's offer on the place closes the fifteenth. I'm going to use the time in the middle to do what Claudia's paying me to do, which is to get a line on who killed her husband."

She hooded her eyes, looking down at the bed. "I'm going to have to work on that agreeing to disagree stuff," she said. "I'm not very good at it."

"Me neither," I admitted.

In the basement the furnace turned on. I could feel the warm air from the register in the ceiling. "You know, Leo . . .

in the past several months I've been making an effort to push our lives together more into the . . . into a more traditional pattern."

Hence all the dinners with couples, the opera, her sudden insistence that I attend pathologist and medical examiner functions with her.

"More into the mainstream," I said.

"Is there something wrong with that?"

"Nope. I've been doing my end, haven't I? I showed up. I was polite."

"That's all you did."

"Most of the people you're talking about—I mean, what can I say?—I just don't have much in common with them. It's all investment strategies or office politics or how they're in therapy together and learning so much or their next cross-country skiing trip." I sighed. Same old, same old. "Maybe it's me," I said.

"Doesn't it seem odd to you that you're middle-aged and half the people you know are criminals?"

"I'm in the crime business."

"What you're in is denial."

"Should I go over and lie down on the couch, Doctor?"

I shouldn't have said it, but there's something about being psychoanalyzed by amateurs that brings out the worst in me. I always figure that since I don't have the faintest idea why I do some of the things I do, it's a good bet that nobody else does, either.

"Sorry," I said.

She flopped down onto her back and stared at the ceiling. After a while, she said, "This isn't getting us anywhere." I told her I agreed. She said, "Didn't I hear you on the phone with George yesterday?"

"Yes."

"Don't tell me you're getting that bunch of drunks and do-nothings involved in this?"

When I didn't answer, she pressed, "Well?"

"You told me not to tell you."

She rolled away from me. "Turn off the light," she said.

I had the urge to laugh boldly and call out, *Drunks and do-nothings, my ass; hell, girl, I've got a gay burglar, a pervert forger, a crippled wireman, a couple professional thugs and a who—* Nah . . . not even in my dreams do I tell her about that one.

Floyd lived directly across the street from the Kingdome, in an ancient building without doors or windows on either of the first two floors. I know how that sounds, but trust me, I've walked all the way around and looked. More than once. The only hint as to how such a building might have come to be is found on the north and west sides, where patches of darker bricks betray a pair of windows on the north and, on the west, what at one time must have been a wide loading door, before it, too, was bricked in. All I could think of was that the place must have once been some sort of warehouse from which you then entered the floors above. Floyd gets in and out, so obviously, somewhere belowground, it's connected to one of the nearby buildings, which, as it happens, in this part of the city is not nearly as unlikely as it might seem.

In 1889, when much of the city burnt to the ground, city officials decided to cure an old mistake and raise the level of Pioneer Square a bit higher above the tide line, so that the newly fashionable flush toilets would stop becoming sewage fountains during high water. Many of the brick buildings in Pioneer Square that had survived the fire were then buried alive up to their second stories, which became ground level, leaving a five-square-block area of the city with a town beneath its feet. For a mere six bucks you can take a tour. Maybe even have a commemorative rat named after you.

What you did was push the buzzer that was mounted directly into the brick on the King Street side. Then you walk across the street and stand in front of the parking lot fence. Floyd will be along in a few minutes. You screw around and push the button for fun, and Floyd will be down even quicker, but you won't be standing for long.

I'd heard street talk about Floyd for years. Nothing solid, just a few murmurings to the effect that this guy was a serious shooter for hire. I'd originally gotten the Windjammer number from an old enforcer friend of my father's named Frankie Ortega. Since Frankie himself had occupied the "baddest motherfucker in the valley" seat for the better part of twenty years, I was impressed when he told me to keep my mouth shut about where the number came from, because, as he put it, "I'm too old for the likes of that crazy motherfucker."

When Floyd and I spoke a few days ago, we'd settled on a price. Talked it over and decided that we needed another hand. Floyd said he had a guy he'd worked with before. A Russian. That he'd had occasion to see the guy in action and had been suitably impressed. I said okay, but I wanted to meet him. We'd agreed that I'd come by the building, push the button and then meet them over at the Red White and Blue Café, a greasy spoon on Second Avenue.

Floyd was a big guy, six-four or so, with the biggest wrists I've ever seen. He had curly hair, little close-set eyes and thick lips, under a nose that had seen a lot of wear and was flat at the tip. All that was left off his right ear was a withered flap of skin that stuck straight out from his head like a dried apricot.

We shook hands. "Long time no see," he said.

"Nothing personal, man, but I'd just as soon not see you at all."

"I'm kind of like the dentist that way," he said.

He tilted his head toward the nondescript-looking guy who was wedged up against the wall on his right. "This is the Russian." He was about forty, five-ten or so and narrow all the way down. He sported a hair helmet that I suspected he dyed and a pair of those Moscow snow-cutter eyebrows that Russian men seem to sprout in middle age.

"Does the Russian have a name?" I asked.

"Peek one," the Russian said.

"How about Boris?" I suggested.

"Vhy you Americans tink ve are all named Boris?"

His English wasn't any worse than, say, a drunken Canadian's.

"It was a cartoon we all watched when we were kids."

Floyd snapped his fingers. "That's right . . . Boris Badenov," he said.

"Oh . . ." The Russian nodded. "Propaganda."

He'd been a major in the Russian Army and was a veteran of the Afghan war. Been in the country for a year and a half. He had a résumé of villages sacked, livestock slaughtered and crops burned that was second to none. Seemed like just the guy I needed, so I took him on.

"Seriously though," I said. "It's got to be real names on this one. Valid ID. The whole ball of wax. No weapons without permits."

"How come?" Inquiring Floyds want to know.

"Because we're going to be taking on the powers that be, and the powers that be can instantly check on those kind of things."

"The cops?"

"Yeah," I said. For a second, my answer surprised me. I guess it was because I'd never verbalized it before. I'd spent a lot of time thinking about the night Rebecca and I were pushed over that cliff, and every time I ended up with the same question about the timing of the thing. How had they known we were coming? No way they could have been sitting there with the road blocked for very long. A couple of dozen families used that road. No . . . they knew just when we were going to arrive. Really, it was simple. I'd made two stops before starting back to J.D.'s. First one at Beaver Building Supply for a new lock and chain. Second one to leave a gate key with Deputy Spots. The former had no idea where

I was going from there. Spots knew exactly where I was headed next. Pretty much a no-brainer.

I went over everything I had on my list. Used a napkin to draw a crude map of the cabin and the surrounding terrain. They were coming up on their own. Shooting for three or four tomorrow afternoon. They loved the river at our backs but hated the forest at our throats. I gave Floyd directions to the homestead and twenty-five hundred bucks for up-front expenses. He slipped a thousand to the Russian and pocketed the rest. He slid out of the booth so that the Russian could get out. I stood up and shook his hand.

"Seriously," I said, "what's your name?"

"Boris," he said with a smile. "Vould I lie?"

I laughed. "Okay, Boris. See you tomorrow."

Floyd and I stood next to the booth and watched him leave.

"What about you?" Floyd asked.

"What about me?"

"You capable of taking care of yourself or are we gonna need to wet-nurse you, too?" I pulled up my pants leg and then took off my cap. I was used to sympathy. Floyd looked at my wounds like they were mosquito bites.

"I can't be duking it out with anybody," I said. "Other than that I'm okay."

"Tomorrow," he said.

I made a show of pulling five hundred-dollar bills from my pocket and then flourished the cash in hand as I approached the receptionist's desk.

"Lenny's got some work ready for me," I said boldly.

She didn't look up from her typing. "You know the way."

"I'll give you twenty bucks to go get it for me."

She chuckled. "No way."

"Fifty."

"Forget it."

Suffice it to say that Lenny was as I'd left him. "Over there," he said.

Sure enough, five official-looking envelopes, Seattle postmarks, canceled postage. Perfect. Beneath the envelopes, two typed pages.

"What's this?" I asked.

"The one on top is Charlie's phone spiel. He wrote it down so he wouldn't forget. I thought maybe your phone guy could use it. The other one is directions to the addresses on the envelopes."

"You know Stevens Falls?"

He made a disgusted face. "It's on the web, Leo. Maps of every damn place in the world. If you want to waste your time on that crap." He slapped the computer on its top. "Goddamn phone lines are so friggin' slow during the day. Got every little bastard in every school clogging up the airways. Ought to keep the little bastards off—"

I pointed at the screen. "Can you print that?" I asked.

"Sure," he said. "You want one?"

"Please."

A minute later he held a piece of paper by his fingertips. "It's wet," he said.

I took the picture, left the money in place of the work and scrambled for the door.

"Thanks, Lenny," I said on the way out.

"Wait . . . wait, you gotta see," was the last thing I heard him say.

On my way by the receptionist's desk, I slipped the picture onto the counter. She was reaching for it as I hit the door.

I'd have walked right by her on the street. The blond hair was gone. So were the green contact lenses and the slinky raincoat. The woman who slid into the booth opposite me was the All-American Girl. Drop-dead cute. Curly brown hair worn close to the head, blue eyes and the kind of makeup job that makes you wonder if she's wearing any.

"G said you wanted to talk." She waved at the waitress, who seemed to know what the gesture meant. We were sitting in a booth at the Five Spot. A trendy café at the top of Queen Anne Hill. She read my eyes. "I'm a chameleon," she said.

"Is Narva your real name?" I asked.

"Nobody's named Narva."

I told her what I knew about Constance Hart and Misty McMahon.

"The kid's lucky to have her," she said when I'd finished.

The waitress showed up with a double tall latte of some sort, something brown sprinkled on top. "Hazelnut," she said and took a sip. Ended up with a milk mustache, which looked great on her. "So?" she said.

"I have need of your services."

She frowned, which also looked good on her. "Really?"

"Not for myself. For somebody else."

Her brow smoothed out. "Good," she said. "I'm glad to hear that."

I wasn't exactly sure how to take that, so I shut up.

"Not like that," she said. "I meant good because I like to think I'm a good judge of people, and I didn't make you for the type."

I wasn't sure how to take that, either, so I said, "Thanks. I didn't make you for the type, either."

Her blue eyes narrowed. "Are you still fishing for a story?"

"Not me."

"Let me ask you a question, Leo."

"Shoot."

"Are you involved with a woman?"

"Yes," I said and gave her the abridged version.

"So you guys . . . you know . . . get it down once in a

while . . ." She held up a hand. "I don't mean to be personal. I'm merely making a point."

"I understand."

"So, Leo . . . Is it free?"

"Is what free?"

"The sex." Before I could speak, she went on. "I'm not asking whether you leave money on the nightstand. I'm asking you as a man who's involved in a long-term, committed relationship. I'm asking whether psychologically, emotionally . . . or even financially whether you'd characterize the service as being free."

"Relationships have other benefits," I hedged.

"I didn't say otherwise." She raised her eyebrows. "Is it?"

I thought it over. "Not strictly speaking," I admitted.

"My point exactly. It's not a question of whether you pay. It's a question of what the price is and over what period of time the payments are made."

"It's like that joke about the difference between a pigeon and a dove."

"Which is?"

"The dove has a better agent."

She laughed and said, "So what is it you've got in mind?"

I told her. When I finished, she said, "That's not very nice."

"You abuse the public trust, you take your chances," I said.

She looked at me over the coffee. "My, my," she chided. "Indignation. And from the son of the legendary Wild Bill Waterman?"

"That was sharks bilking other sharks. The public didn't enter into it."

"Hmmm," she said. "I guess we all have our stories, now, don't we?"

If this were a boxing match, I'd be stopped on cuts, so I changed the subject.

"So what do you think?"

"I've never done anything like this before. I'm concerned for my safety."

"I'll be right there. Less than a hundred feet away."

"Watching."

"In a purely clinical fashion," I said.

"No doubt."

"Be a chameleon."

She leaned back in the booth, hugging the coffee cup to her chest as she thought it over. "You were pretty impressive that night in Bellevue."

"So were you," I said.

"No . . . I mean it."

"So do I."

"I was terrified."

"Me, too."

"Bullshit. You were having fun. I could feel it." She raised an eyebrow. "Trust me. I'm in the fun business. I knows it when I sees it."

"So . . . we've got a deal."

"My rate, plus expenses, plus you'll owe me."

"You drive a hard bargain."

"We both know you can get this done a lot cheaper, Leo. I'd be glad to give you some names and numbers."

I'd made up my mind. If I was going to do this, I was determined to give it my best shot. "No," I said. "I need you."

"It would have to be Monday or Tuesday. Wednesday and Thursday nights I have class."

Monday was perfect. As Carl had so lyrically said, by then some of the turds ought to be floating. And by then I'd be a better judge of the tide.

"Monday, then," I said. "Gives you, like, two whole days for . . . you know, in case he turns out to be hard to get."

She laughed. "Sure," she said.

She finished her coffee while we worked out the details. I threw a five on the table as we got to our feet. "A pleasure doing business with you," I said.

"That's the idea," she said.

21 HAROLD AND RALPH DON'T GET OUT IN THE COUNTRY much. Passing out in Volunteer Park was their idea of confronting the unspoiled wilderness. I wish I'd had a camera when they first got out of the car at the Springer place. Ten-thirty on a Friday morning. About the time they usually get out of bed. Hazy sunshine. Bright blue sky to the west. Fifty degrees. The rivers wearing a layer of fog like a mantle. Absolutely gorgeous. I don't know whether it was the scale of the wilderness or whether it had dawned on them how far they were from the nearest liquor store, but they were blown away.

"Jesus," Harold said. "You mean people lived here?"

"On purpose?" asked Ralph.

"What the hell do you do in a place like this?" Harold asked.

"Commune with nature," I said.

"I could commune with a drink," Ralph said.

"No shit," said Harold.

They were getting sullen. It was understandable. After all, it was going on eleven in the morning and they were still sober.

"I'm going to drop you guys off at a tavern," I said.

Eventually, the cheering subsided.

"You've got the right men for the job," Ralph declared.

"What do you need us to do?" Harold asked.

I told them everything I knew about Ben Bendixon. How he used to be a regular at the Timbertopper. How he moved to Port Townsend to live with his daughter. How I needed somebody who knew the daughter's name, or maybe somebody who'd kept in touch and had a number or an address. Anything. I wanted to talk to Ben Bendixon.

"I know you guys can do this," I said. "Just go in there and do what you do best. Don't mention me. Don't mention J.D. Springer or this place. Tell 'em whatever you want. And promise me, if anybody gives you a hard time or takes offense at you wanting to know about Ben, back off. Play it cool. Just asking. No big deal, right?"

"What is the big deal?" asked Harold.

"The big deal is that I don't know what the big deal is. Things keep happening around here that I don't understand. I just want you to be careful. Okay?"

They said it was. I gave them Cabin Number One. To those two it was the Taj Majal. A real bed, a kitchen and bathroom that worked. A front porch overlooking the river. It was like Ralphie said. "Nice place. Too bad it ain't somewhere."

I packed them into the rental car and started back for town. I must have missed it on the way in. Probably so intent on getting off West River Road alive that I had tunnel vision. I turned right out of the driveway as Harold groped the dial for a radio station; my eyes drifted to the left and the Fox Creek Bridge.

I slid the car to a stop, backed up, turned left over the bridge. Drove out to the middle and stopped. The Bogachiel was running hard but clear, one of those blue-green colors for which women have a specific name. Teal, maybe. I rolled over to the far end and looked around. Everything was gone. The gate, the barriers, the signs, everything. "Is this the way we come?" asked Ralph.

"No," I said.

The bridge changed the trip to town from twenty-five

minutes of curves and dips to ten minutes of smooth pavement. Whitey and the crew had finished painting the yellow line. It wavered in a few places. But, all in all, looked pretty darn good.

Monty was sweeping up in front of the Black Bear when I drove by. I tooted the horn. Without looking up, he waved with the broom.

Another mile up the road, I pulled the Malibu into an alley behind the Stevens Falls Veterinary Clinic, hidden from view, diagonally across the street from Freddy's Timbertopper Tavern. "This is where we'll meet," I said. "I can't have anybody seeing you with me." I gave them twenty-five bucks apiece. "Right here," I said. "Three o'clock." It's not often you see them jog.

With a little help from his secretary, I found Emmett Polster just as he was leaving a construction site on Fifth Avenue. He was about sixty, thin with pointed features and rimless eyeglasses. He carried a rolled blueprint under his left arm and wore a yellow hard hat. "Mr. Polster," I called.

He stopped and turned, so I figured I had the right guy. "Yes." His nose twitched as if he were testing the wind. I stuck my hand out. "Leo Waterman," I enthused. "You're a hard man to catch up to," I said. Always tell public employees how hard they're working. It matches their inner dialogue.

"Lotta work to do," he said. "What can I do for you, Mr. Waterman?"

When he brought a hand up to wipe the corners of his mouth, I noticed his fingernails were bitten to the quick. I went into my good old boy friendly act.

"I'm staying out at the Springer place. Got a bunch of friends coming out this weekend. Gonna do a little fishing before the run is over, and I was wondering if you could help me out with what it is that might be the matter with the electric and the plumbing in those guest cabins, 'cause I went around and tried everything and damned if it don't all work, and I noticed your name on all those red tags and I sure don't want to endanger anybody if there's something, you know, like dangerous about them."

"To the untrained eyes, flaws in electrical or sewage systems are not always obvious." He said it like he'd been rehearsing it, so I went over the top and lied.

That's exactly what I was thinking," I enthused. "I said to myself . . . I said self . . . what do you know about this stuff? You better get somebody who's expert in these matters before you go making any accusations. That's why I've got a State Building Inspector coming Friday to have a look at the systems."

The longer I talked, the tighter his lips got. And unless I was mistaken, some of his color had drained out at the mention of the name *Springer*.

"You can't be out there," he said. "The place has been sold to—"

"Yeah, the city, I know, but you know, the deal don't close till the fifteenth and we kinda figured we'd take this last opportunity to do a little fishing." I gave him a lewd wink. "You know, get away from the little women for a week or so." When I dug a playful elbow into his ribs, he jumped a foot and stepped back away from me. "Those structures have been banned from commercial use."

"Good thing we're just a bunch of friends, then, huh?"

I saw the light bulb go on as it dawned on him who I was. He started to put the corner of his index finger into his mouth, but caught himself and stuck the hand in his jacket pocket. "I don't have to talk to you about this," he announced.

I tried to look hurt. "That's not very polite," I whined. "I was just trying—" He walked briskly over to a new Honda Accord, got in and locked the door.

I pulled my notepad from my pocket and wrote down his plate number as he drove off. His face was tight as a fist in the rearview mirror. I gave him my best smile. Time to deliver the mail. Charlie would be proud of me.

Charlie Boxer had been a part-time PI and full-time con man around the Pacific Northwest for forty years. Whenever he was scamming anybody and it didn't seem like things were moving along quick enough for Charlie's taste, he'd turn the screw a couple of notches. The mark would wake to find a city of Seattle assessment for thirty-two thousand dollars for sewer repairs. Or a threatening letter from a collection agency. Or he'd come home to find that someone had delivered six tons of coal in his driveway, exactly as he'd been so carefully instructed over the phone. Or all of the above.

He tried a bunch of them, but eventually found that, pound for pound, the IRS audit packed more stress than any of the others. Always on a Friday. Something about coming home after a week of work to find a notification of audit that uses the bothersome clause "considerable amounts of undeclared income" and then quotes the federal statute for tax evasion, which uses the even more unfortunate phrase "for a period of three to five years in a Federal Correctional Facility." It's all a mistake, of course. Silly, really. You'll just make a call and straighten the whole thing out. Except it's Friday and the line's busy. So you sweat for the weekend, only to call on Monday and have this supposed auditor absolutely ream you out like the filthy criminal you are and then give you an appointment for your audit about two weeks hence. Now you're nervous. So you call your accountant and your attorney. Of course, by the time they get around to your little problem, the phone line is set on perpetual Lennon Sisters. So they call the real IRS, who quite naturally claim they don't know anything about it. But having worked with these slugs before, the attorneys and accountants take cold comfort in this claim and demand a thorough search of IRS records before notifying their clients. You get the picture.

Lenny's directions started from the little park in the center of town. Tressman and his wife filed separate returns so they got one apiece. Weston was single. I saved Polster for last, so I could end the job with a nice fuzzy sense of satisfaction.

The number they'd all soon be calling was that of a stolen cell phone I'd borrowed from Carl, plugged into the wall in my kitchen back in Seattle and rigged to forward all calls to the office in the Zoo. That way nobody was going to be able to run a caller ID number on us. Not coincidentally, the number was going to be busy for the rest of the afternoon. Friday, you know. That gave them the whole weekend to stew. Starting Monday, George was going to man the phone at the Zoo during regular business hours. I'd given him Charlie Boxer's script, fifty bucks in cash and a twenty-dollar-a-day bar tab. Terry promised to do the best he could to keep George sober while he was working. I was keeping my fingers crossed.

Harold and Ralph were a couple of minutes early, juiced and sloppy. They piled in the back together, leaving me up front like the chauffeur. I eased along the back of the stores, out into the street, turned left, then right onto the highway.

As soon as I was up to speed, I asked, "How'd it go?"

"Not a daughter," Ralph slurred. "A granddaughter."

"Put on some music, will ya, Leo?" Harold said.

"Name of Pamela," Ralph said.

"No last name?"

"Nobody knew."

"Find somethin' with a beat, will ya, Leo?"

"What else?"

"None of that hip hop shit, neither."

"Like you said, he was a regular. Come in every day about nine, went home six or seven. Nobody knew for how long. Longer than any of them anyway."

"Leo, will ya please—"

"Harold," I said sharply.

"Yeah?"

"Don't make me come back there and kill you."

"Sheeesh . . . what a grouch," he mumbled.

"What else, Ralph?"

"Just tryin' to have a little . . ."

"It's all anybody knew. Nobody heard from him since he left. One guy name of Swede says he heard the granddaughter don't let him drive no more."

". . . cause some people got no goddamned . . ."

The church was still closed and empty. The Steelhead Tavern open and full.

On the surface, it wasn't much. No help on a name or a number. There was, however, the fact that the guy had been a daytime regular at Freddie's Timbertopper since before the beginning of time. Which in this case probably meant since the mid-seventies when his wife died. I already knew the answer, but I asked anyway. "So . . . Harold."

A sullen, "What?"

"Put yourself in Ben's place. You're getting way along in years and you've got no choice, you're moving in with your granddaughter."

"Yeah?"

"What do you do next? You're in a new town. You know nothing about the place, and she won't let you drive anymore."

He thought it over. "Have I got any money?"

"Plenty."

"Find a new gin mill," he said.

"Someplace I can walk to," Ralph added.

"Better be close. He's old," I said. "What are his other options?"

"If I got money, I can take a cab," Harold reasoned.

"It's either that or get religion," Ralph added solemnly.

I must have thought out loud. "How many gin mills can there be in Port Townsend?" because otherwise Harold read my mind and said, "Lots, I hope."

"Tomorrow I'm going to send you two to Port Townsend. First thing I want you to do is go to all the cab companies.

See if anybody's got an old guy coming and going from some bar every day. If that doesn't work, start in on the taverns."

They reckoned how it was a filthy job, but since they felt so highly about me personally, they'd put aside a rash of objections and muddle through the best they could.

When the Malibu emerged from the tunnel of trees into the light of the driveway, I could sense there was a problem. Deputy Harlan Spots was standing behind the door of the squad car, his service revolver in his right hand and pointing straight down at the ground. From forty feet away I could see his hand shaking. Thirty feet in front of him, Floyd and Boris lounged against the trunk of a blue Buick. Floyd was cleaning his nails with a pocketknife. Boris was watching Deputy Spots with a bemused expression. The deputy heard the sound of the tires on the gravel. He turned and his face fell. Whoever he was expecting, we weren't it.

I parked next to the Blazer. "Get down and stay down," I said to Harold and Ralph and got out. "Is there a problem?"

"Damn right there's a problem," Spots wheezed. "I'm arresting these two."

"What for?"

"For not doing what I told 'em to."

"That's not a crime."

"Is too. Interfering with an officer in the performance of his duties."

"What duties were those?"

"Patrolling this place."

"And they interfered with you doing that?"

"They wouldn't get in the car."

"That's not a crime, either."

His cheek was beginning to twitch. "Maybe you ought to get over there with those two," he said, "until the sheriff—"

"No," I said. "I'll stay right where I am, thanks."

I heard Boris chuckle. "Dat's vhat ve told him."

Our little party was interrupted by the sound of tires and the roar of an engine. Nathan Hand and Bobby Russell were out of the Sheriff's Crown Victoria before it stopped rocking on the springs. Russell held a black riot gun across his chest. Hand slowly surveyed the scene and said, "Harlan, put the gun away." Spots looked like he was going to cry. "Sheriff, these men—"

"Put it away," Hand said again, softly this time.

Deputy Spots did as he was told.

"What happened here?" Hand asked. He kept asking Spots questions. "Did they give you their identification?" Spots said yes. "Where is it now?" Turned out to be on the driver's seat of the patrol car. Hand picked it up and motioned to Deputy Russell, who came over and took the driver's licenses back to Hand's car. I watched as he brought the microphone to his mouth.

"And then you told them to get in the car."

"Uh-huh."

Spots looked around like one of us was going to help him with the answers.

"They said they'd rather not."

Hand looked over at me.

"He could tell 'em to paint the patrol car yellow," I said ". . . and they wouldn't have to do that, either. He asked for ID. They gave it to him."

"Harlan," the sheriff said. "Go back to the station."

Deputy Spots wanted to argue, but restrained himself. It took him three tries to maneuver his car between the sheriff's and the edge of the cabin. We stood and watched as he chugged back up the driveway and out of sight.

Deputy Russell returned from the car. "No wants on either of them. The big one rented the car with a Visa card in his own name."

The sheriff motioned with his head. Deputy Russell crossed the gravel to Floyd and Boris and returned their driver's licenses. He lingered for a moment, casting what he imagined to be a hard look at the pair, who returned the favor by looking him up and down in the manner of tolerant parents toward a precocious child. He rested his hand on the butt of his gun as he walked back toward Sheriff Hand.

Hand again turned his attention to me. "Didn't figure to see you again."

"Thought I'd do a little fishing," I said.

He looked over at Floyd and Boris. "And these two?"

"They're my fishing buddies," I said.

"Don't much look like fishermen to me," Hand said. "What about you, Bobby? These two look like outdoor enthusiasts to you?"

"No sir, they don't," he replied. "Not sure what they look like to me, but it sure ain't fishermen."

"Can the fishing buddies talk?" Hand inquired.

"Yes, ve can," said Boris.

"It's true," added Floyd.

Hand stuck his tongue in his cheek and looked from one to the other.

"What say I have a look in that car," he said.

"What say you don't," said Floyd.

"Are you refusing me permission?"

"Big as life," Floyd said, without looking up from his nails.

"Probable cause ees a vonderful ting," said Boris.

Hand stiffened his spine even more and then turned to me.

"You know Mr. Waterman, considering what happened to you the last time you visited our fair city, I would have thought you would have taken your vacation plans elsewhere."

"I'm sorry, Sheriff, if I gave you the impression that I was here on vacation," I said. "I am planning on doing a little fishing, but mostly I'm going to be investigating the murder of J.D. Springer."

"For a client?"

"I'm afraid I'm not at liberty to discuss that," I said.

Nathan Hand walked around in a small circle. "I've been

patient with you. Hell, my deputy here probably saved your lady friend's life out there on West River Road last month. But . . . you just don't seem to get the message, do you?"

"I'm renowned for my hard head." I pulled off the Sonics cap and showed him my stitches. "Literally and figuratively," I added.

Our eyes locked and stayed that way. All the good old boy pretense was gone now. "I hope you know what you're doing," he said. "You could end up with something they can't sew back together."

"I'll keep that in mind," I assured him.

He turned around and sauntered toward his car. "Sheriff," I called. I used my sweetest tone. "We won't be needing that extra patrol anymore. Thanks for the help."

His eyes flicked over at Floyd and the Russian. "Figure you got all the help you gonna need, do you?" When he smirked, his eyes nearly closed.

I couldn't resist. "We can't all have Deputy Spots on our side, Sheriff."

It didn't ruin his day, but it sure opened his eyes. He expelled another whale breath, gave me a little two-fingered salute on the brim of his hat and then took his sweet-ass time getting in the car, buckling up and getting on the road.

I turned to the pair leaning on the car. "When cops point guns at you, you really ought to try to look scared. It makes them nervous if you don't."

"Bubble Butt didn't need any help being nervous," Floyd said.

He bumped himself off the trunk, slipped the key into the lock and lifted the lid.

"Take Cabin Three," I said and then turned back toward the driveway. "Hey," I yelled. The rented Chevy remained still. I yelled again. "Okay." Nothing.

In my peripheral vision, I saw Floyd and Boris exchange puzzled glances. I gestured toward the car. "Harold and Ralph," I said.

"The Booze Brothers," Floyd said without enthusiasm.

Boris and Floyd each carried a long blue athletic bag with a white swoosh and a black rifle case sans swoosh. I walked across the gravel toward the car. I should have known. They were crapped out. Ralph snored. Harold drooled onto his arm. They seemed peaceful, so I left them alone.

Floyd and Boris emerged from the cabin carrying identical rifles. Floyd read my face. "Perfectly legal," he said. ".222 semiautomatics. Varmint guns. Reworked clips that hold forty-eight rounds. Virtually flat trajectory inside four hundred yards." He gave me what passed for a smile. "Tend to put nice clean holes in things. Keeps the complications to a minimum." He slipped one of the clips into the bottom of the gun and then leaned the gun low against the porch.

I checked my watch. Three-thirty. An hour of daylight. At ground level, the afternoon was still, only the ripple of breaking water cutting intervals into the silence. Above us, boxcar clouds, dark around the edges and dangerous-looking, rolled in hard from the west carrying moisture and the smell of the sea.

Boris used the sling and carried his rifle over his shoulder in the manner of a soldier as they sauntered about the property together, pointing, talking out loud, occasionally putting their heads together and whispering back and forth.

I walked over to the far end of the yard and looked down the Quileute toward the ocean. At the end of my vision, out where the final glare of the sun transformed the river into black ice, the heads of three seals poked above the surface like periscopes as they followed the salmon as far as they dared into the fresh water.

Floyd and Boris walked a complete circuit of the clearing and made their way back to me. Floyd said, "Everything but the cars goes behind the cabin." He gestured with his hand. "Out here on the lawn. That way the cabin's between everything and the hill."

I said it made sense to me.

"You said the wire man is going to have a van."

"It's a motor home," I said. "He just calls it a van."

"Back eet een so the rear is against the kitchen vall," Boris said.

Reduce the profile and get it where there are no windows. Simple enough.

Floyd looked around. "I presume we can pop a few and it's not going to be a problem. No close neighbors."

"No neighbors at all," I assured him. "Pop away."

Pop away they did, but first Boris went back into the cabin and came out with a roll of duct tape and then they rounded up half a dozen cans from the garbage bin and carried them up to the tree line at the back of the clearing, where they taped them to branches all along the edge. Then they came back, retrieved their rifles. Boris took a shot. Nothing moved. Then Floyd. Same result. Boris worked on the rear sight with a small screwdriver. Floyd fired three times. In the descending gloom I saw the bullet hit the ground at the base of the tree. Floyd, likewise, produced a screwdriver. You could tell it was a contest between them. Like the Thug Olympics. Rifle fire. Standing. Prone. And Drive-By. I couldn't tell who got off the first good round, but suddenly they had it zoned in. They both changed clips, took aim and started again. Tracers this time. The rifles made a soft popping sound as the yellow-green streams of fire lit up the yard. And I could hear the soft *tink* as the slugs pierced the cans up at the edge of the clearing and they began to dance around. When Floyd stopped firing, Boris made one last run down the cans. Left to right, as fast as he could pull the trigger. Six shots, six *tinks*, six dancing cans.

Even Floyd looked impressed. "A killer," he mouthed.

22 AT RIVER LEVEL, THIS TIME OF YEAR, THE HILLS BLOCK the sun until nearly ten in the morning, leaving the terrain laced with frost, everything silent and silver and slick to the touch. And when the yellow light finally slanted down the hill toward us, it was as if the earth suddenly caught fire, as plumes of steam and fog rose from the frigid ground to join the haze that floated upward and finally disappeared, leaving an acrylic blue sky that made you feel like you could reach up and run your fingers through it.

We had coffee, sugar, rice, three cans of peaches and a bottle of nondairy creamer. Last night we'd devoured every other edible morsel in the cabin. Other than a pair of lemons in the vegetable drawer, the stuff in the refrigerator was history. The kind of history where you throw the container out, too. In the cupboards we'd found half a dozen boxes of Kraft macaroni and cheese, five packets of Top Ramen noodles, a can of evaporated milk, one garlic bulb and a collection of canned vegetables. Floyd and I had opted for a box of macaroni and a Top Ramen each. Boris had eaten three cans of beets and, with a purple tongue, had professed to be as happy as a man could be.

Around nine last night, Harold and Ralph had stumbled in and eaten everything that remained. In one of those moments that speaks well for the theory of evolution, Ralph, while satisfying himself that the refrigerator was indeed empty, went boldly where no man had gone before. He jerked open the crisper drawer at the bottom of the refrigerator and found four bottles of Rainier Ale resting atop a blackened head of lettuce. He showed class and offered them around. Harold reckoned how he might be willing to swallow one or two, but Boris, Floyd and I refused. Such unbridled joy is seldom seen in adults.

By ten-thirty this morning, everybody had managed coffee and a shower. I slid the keys to J.D.'s Blazer and a hundred bucks across the table to Boris and told him how I wanted him to take the Boys to Port Townsend. To start with the cab companies and then with the taverns and, if that failed, with the bars. Told him to keep track of all expenses.

As Harold and Ralph squeezed out the door together, I put my hand on Boris's arm. He stopped. I leaned in close. "Don't give them too much money at once. Make sure they eat before they start on the taverns. Whatever you do, don't let either of them drive, and if they start getting too drunk to function, pack them in the car and drive them back here."

"Vat time?"

"They'll be hammered by five," I assured him.

Boris followed the fellas out the door and around the corner. I turned to Floyd, who was leaning back against the kitchen counter, slurping coffee from a red plastic cup.

"You and I are going to town to see a guy about a flying saucer," I said.

"I can't wait," was his reply.

Ten minutes later, we were halfway to town. Floyd found the Oldies channel. Del was singing a little "Runaway." For about two minutes, I forgot where I was and why I was here and just cruised behind the music. Rounded a sweeping right turn. The sun flickering through the bare branches like a strobe light and a quarter mile ahead, parked on the right shoulder, was an old Studebaker pickup truck. Hood up. Even if I hadn't remembered the Confederate cap, the lack of a shirt would have been a dead giveaway. Whitey's head peeked around the hood as I pulled the Malibu to a stop behind the wooden tailgate. He wore those same gray and white coveralls and a big pair of wraparound sunglasses.

"Come on," I said to Floyd as I reached for the door handle.

The old truck had been lovingly restored. The cab and the sides of the hood were fire-engine red. The rest of the body jet-black. Thick whitewall tires on spoked wheels. The tailgate was oak, sanded and then varnished to a sheen. Professionally painted Studebaker logo. Floyd walked up the shoulder; I stayed in the road.

Whitey looked from Floyd to me and then began to back up, his boots scraping on the pavement as he backpedaled. "Need some help?" I asked.

He stopped. His skin wasn't so much white as it was transparent. He gave the impression that if one were to pull down the bib on his overalls, his internal organs would be visible. Floyd leaned over and stuck his head under the hood. Whitey frowned.

"Great rig," I said.

"If it'd run."

"What year?"

"It's a '37 Coupe Express."

Behind the glasses, his eyes darted about.

"What's the problem?" asked Floyd.

"Just quit," said Whitey. "The battery's not charging."

"You tested the regulator?" Floyd asked, jiggling one of the battery connections. Whitey couldn't stand it. He walked around me and stuck his head under the other side of the hood. "New regulator, new battery," he said.

"That only leaves the generator or a short somewhere," Floyd offered.

"Better be a damn short," Whitey said, to himself more than to Floyd. "Shorts I can find. I'll have to go all the way to Seattle to find a generator."

"Can we give you a lift somewhere?" I asked.

"Nah," he said quickly. "I'll be okay."

Floyd pulled his head out from under the hood and started for the car.

"Good luck," I said and turned and followed Floyd.

"Hey . . . ah," Whitey said to my back.

I turned around. "Yeah?"

"The other day . . . you know, a while back there at the Steelhead?"

"Dexter," I said.

He nodded. "Yeah."

"No hard feelings."

"Yeah," he said. "Me neither."

"Sure we can't take you somewhere?"

He mulled it over. "Come to think of it, I'd 'preciate it if you would," he said. "Lemme close things up here."

I stuck out my hand. "Leo Waterman," I said.

His hand swallowed mine. His palm had the texture of a cinder block.

"Clarence Hunley," he said. "I'll just be a second."

I got back in the car and started the engine.

"Kid looked pretty spooked when you first got out of the car," Floyd commented. While the kid closed the hood and locked the doors, I gave Floyd a thumbnail sketch of our last meeting.

"Good move," Floyd said. "You see the arms on that sucker? Comes down to you and him throwing punches . . . my money's on the kid."

"Mine, too," I said.

Whitey got in behind me. "Hate to leave her like this," he said.

"Don't blame you," said Floyd. "That's a sweet unit."

I pulled back onto the road, heading for town.

"Just got her on the road last week," Whitey said. "This is the third time she just plain quit on me."

"How long you been working on her?" I asked.

"Better part of two years. Belonged to my grandfather.

Been out in the barn for longer than I been around. Did everything but the paint and the upholstery myself. Didn't have no idea how hard it was gonna be when I started out. If Idda known . . ."

"It was worth the effort," Floyd said.

"Thanks," he said with obvious pride.

"Where can we take you?" I asked.

"Steelhead's as gooda place as any."

We were about a mile from the tavern when he leaned forward. In the mirror, his eyes looked like dimes behind the glasses. "Hey . . . you suppose that instead of the Steelhead, maybe you could drop me . . . you know, someplace close instead?" I guess taking a ride was one thing, but being seen with me was another.

"No problem," I assured him.

I pulled into an abandoned log scaling station about a half mile past the tavern. Weeds nearly as tall as the hood grew from the maze of cracks and fissures in the greasy cement. Whitey jumped out. Checked the empty highway in both directions.

"Thanks," he said. I wished him luck. His heavy boots slapped the road as he ran to the other side of the highway.

I went into my voice-of-doom narration. "Now . . . to explore strange new worlds."

"You mean this isn't it," Floyd quipped. "It gets better than bubble-butt deputies and giant albinos wearing nothing but bib overalls?"

"You have no idea."

As I drove the mile and a half, I filled him in on Monty and the government conspiracy to keep the truth from us. He nodded solemnly. "My mom believed in all that shit." He twirled his index finger around his temple. "Crazy as a shithouse rat," he said.

Nature or nurture. On one hand, it was a good bet that whoever had nurtured a guy like Floyd was quite likely to have been more than a few degrees off center themselves. On the other hand, Kurtis Ryder's family was about as main-stream as you can get, and he's not just light in the fingers but in the loafers, as well. So I guess you never know. It's like the Algerian said, "After a certain age, a man becomes responsible for his face."

23 I HUSTLED ACROSS THE LOBBY OF THE BLACK BEAR AND rang the hell out of the bell.

"Goddammit," he growled from the other room. "I'm right here. No damn need..." He stopped. His mouth popped open. Monty was so surprised to see me, he had to grab the doorframe to keep from collapsing. "I heard they got ya," he whispered. "I thought you was a goner."

"You know how they are," I said.

"Goddamn liars," he spat. He looked over at Floyd. "Is he..."

"He's with us," I said gravely.

Monty started to apologize, but Floyd cut him off.

"Can't be too careful," he said.

Monty put his bony hand on my shoulder. "He's right. You gotta be careful. They damn near got ya once. They're sure to make another try."

I leaned over and whispered in his ear, "We're not waiting for them to make another try," I said. "We're taking the offensive."

"About damn time," Monty said.

"We've been lied to long enough," Floyd added.

I threw an arm around Monty's shoulders and pulled him close. He smelled of old wool and fried food.

"We need your help," I said.

He checked the room, paying particular attention to the ceiling.

"What can I do?"

"We need to use one of those RV hookups you've got out back."

His eyes took on a gleam. "Gonna do a little surveillance of our own, huh?"

Interestingly enough, that was precisely what we were about to do. And against the goddamn government, too. Amazing how things work out sometimes. I'm down here running a number on a guy who believes in flying saucers and it turns out I don't even have to lie to him. Made me wonder if maybe there wasn't a message here someplace.

"We've gotta be the only ones back there."

"Ain't open this time a year anyway."

"Nobody can know."

"Course not."

"Deniability is everything," Floyd said. "We learned that from them."

"Damn right," Monty said tentatively.

I described Carl and Robby and the van. Told him they'd be around sometime tomorrow to do a little setup work. After that they'd be camped out mostly during the daylight hours. He limped back inside his apartment and came back with a gold key on a floating key chain. Mercury outboard motors. "Gate's way up this end. Lock might be a little rusty, but I don't figure no rusty lock is gonna stop the likes of these guys."

I allowed how that was ever so true. "You just lemme know where they want to hook up and I'll turn the juice on for 'em," he said.

On my way out the door, I stopped and looked back over my shoulder.

"Lotta points for you here, Monty," I said in my most serious voice.

"I'm a shoo-in now," he said with a gapped grin.

As I slid back into the car, Floyd was singing. "Doo doo, doo doo, Doo doo, doo doo." *Twilight Zone.*

"Told ya," I said.

Nelson's Olympic Market was at the corner of Highway 101 and Fourth Avenue, a quarter mile closer to downtown than the Black Bear. The kind of old-fashioned, family-operated market that I remembered from childhood. Narrow, wood-planked aisles and the smells of sawdust and aging meat. Signs. Several offering to butcher and store game. Meat lockers for rent. Another proclaiming: PRICES WERE BORN HERE BUT RAISED ELSEWHERE. Behind the meat and deli counter at the back of the store, a trio of fly strips coiled their way down from the ceiling, their yellow spiraled faces littered with winged remains, like sprinkles on an ice-cream cone. Ya hadda like it.

Floyd was leaning back against the orange juice, hoping like hell nobody would notice that he was pushing the cart. I was pawing my way through the tomatoes when I looked up and found myself eyeball to eyeball with one of the Steelhead Tavern pool shooters. Not the guy in the Megadeth T-shirt. His partner. The one Whitey had called Monk. A beat-up thirty. Gonna be bald as a bowling ball before he was forty. His face was masked by three days' growth and a sour expression.

Monk may have been a decent pool player, but he'd never make a living at poker. I watched as his slot-machine eyes clicked on to who I was. He tried to look casual and cool as he returned a cantaloupe to its brethren, stuck his hands in his back pockets and then walked slowly up the center aisle in a loose-jointed and exaggerated manner, which I imagined he thought of as something of a manly swagger, but which, because of his bowed legs and the worn heels of his cowboy boots, suggested prostate problems more than latent testicularity.

Floyd walked over to me. "Is there something you're not telling me?" he asked.

"What do you mean?"

"I mean like how come anytime anybody sees your face, suddenly they look like they just crapped in their pants?"

"I've always had that effect on people. It's a gift."

"Is that guy going to be trouble?"

"Maybe," I said. "But it's not something we've got to deal with now."

We worked our way up and down the aisles. Disposable everything. Towels, toilet, paper plates, napkins. Two cases of beer. Ketchup, mustard and mayo. Pickles. Cookies. Crackers and three kinds of chips. Floyd requested Goldfish crackers and Fig Newtons—which had to be Nabisco. Add that to the four loaves of bread, the two pounds of roast beef, turkey and ham that I'd gotten from the deli, and I figured we had enough food to munch our way through Tuesday. After that, we could play it by ear.

One hundred thirty dollars and sixteen cents. Eight bags full. I gave Floyd a break and told the cute little blond bagger—Samantha, if her name tag was to be believed—that yes, as a matter of fact, she could help us out to the car.

Floyd and I followed along as Samantha threaded her way among the yawning mud puddles, expertly balancing the cart on the rims of the craters as she moved steadily toward the car. Suddenly Floyd's fingers gripped my arm like a vise; he jerked me backward and shouted, "Hey!" I heard the roar of the engine and realized the Ford insignia on the front of the truck was way too high.

Samantha turned her head toward the sound. I watched as her eyes expanded, as she abandoned the cart and ran headlong through the puddles, galloping toward the safety of the parked cars ten feet in front of her. At the same instant, Floyd pushed me between two cars; the truck hit the shopping cart, sending it airborne, dumping the contents in a line like carpet bombs.

Floyd looked my way. "You figure we should deal with this now?" he asked with a smirk.

"What the hell," I said.

Monk was driving. It figured. Only a short guy would have a truck so tall. Mickey and Dexter Davis rode in front. In back, two older guys I'd never seen before. Fortysomethings. Too much chin and not enough forehead. Beer bellies, baseball caps, red necks, white socks and Blue Ribbon beer. Each man carried a five-foot length of heavy chain in his hands. Mickey Davis rocked side to side on his feet. He shifted a big box end wrench from hand to hand. "I told you, man. I told you it wasn't over."

"How's the mouth, Dexter?" I asked his brother.

"Oooo fud me up, oooo modafuuuder."

"Sounds like he's got a mouthful of mashed potatoes," said Floyd, easing his right hand casually toward his jacket.

In the background, I heard shouts and could sense people scurrying around. Monk waved an aluminum softball bat like a flag. He was feeling bold now. One of those assholes who stays in the back until the fight is decided. Unless, of course, there's five of him and two of you, and him got weapons and you all don't, and suddenly sphincter boy starts thinking he's Bruce Lee. That's why he darted out from the safety of the pack and began shaking the bat in Floyd's face.

"This your girlfriend?" he demanded of me in a shrill voice. "That how come he was pushing the wagon?" He laughed at his own joke and darted away.

Floyd looked my way. His face said, *I told you so*. Mickey started for me, with the new guys bringing up the rear. Twirling their chains now, like mutant majorettes. Dexter held his ground. I guess he was just along as a symbol.

I pretty much thought it was over. Not for us . . . for them. Floyd's hand was inside his coat. The odds were stacked against us. I had no illusions. No way Floyd was going to take any kind of a beating. Somebody was about to get shot, and then things were going to get ugly. Monk saved the day by skittering forward and jabbing the bat at Floyd's face.

"Huh . . . are ya . . . huh?" he screeched.

In a single fluid motion, Floyd snatched the bat from

Monk's grip, flipped it end for end like a juggler and then backhanded him across the mouth with the business end, sending a spray of blood, spittle and broken teeth arching out into the air. Monk dropped to his knees. Sounded like he was humming Beethoven underwater.

Floyd flipped the bat across the car to me. I caught it in both hands. With a disgusted look, he pulled his hand from inside his coat and reached down into the side pocket, but I didn't get a chance to see what he was reaching for.

The sight of his buddy communing with mud enraged the chain-swinger on the left. With a bellow, he shouldered Mickey aside and came at me, twirling the chain at head level, grunting now as the chain began to whoosh like a propeller. I had no doubts. If he caught me with the chain, I was never going to play the piccolo again.

Mickey was using him like armor. Keeping away from the chain, moving forward in the wake. From the corner of my eye, I caught a glimpse of Floyd moving toward the other chain swinger. I stepped out from between the cars and faked a lunge at Chainman's groin and then quickly stepped back. He grunted and gave it everything he had, swinging from the heels, trying to wrap the chain around my neck. I dropped to my working knee. The chain bounced off the car on my left, shattering the rear window. I covered my head and retracted my neck like a turtle. I felt the metallic breeze as the rusted metal passed about a foot over my head and then heard the crash as it plowed into the car on my right.

Fortunately for Mickey, the cars had taken most of the bone-crushing velocity out of the chain. Unfortunately for Mickey, Chainman seriously underestimated the physics of force, which sent him spinning, lurching backward as if he'd reached out and grabbed hold of a speeding bus. In an attempt to maintain his balance, he did what every other primate on the planet would have done. He let go.

The middle of the chain hit Mickey just above the knee. Leaving three feet of corroded links to wind up Mickey's leg.

I hadn't noticed it before, but a heavy U-bolt was attached to one end of the chain. I noticed it now, because it hit Mickey in the nuts, sending the wrench clattering to the ground a nanosecond ahead of Mickey. The wrench just lay there. Mickey, on the other hand, clutched his crotch and kicked his feet, his breath coming in gasps, his eyes screwed shut.

I heard a series of sounds like somebody was playing pot roast tetherball. Floyd had his right foot on a piece of chain. The guy at the other end of it was sitting in a puddle. Nose bent way over, like he was trying to sniff his own ear. Spitting blood into his cupped palm, as if the fluids could be saved and used later.

Floyd shrugged and opened his hands. Couple of rolls of quarters. Nasty. If you've got the sinew to swing them, not only does it save your hands, but the other guy feels like he's being hit with a hammer.

Chainman put up his hands, as if to say, *Enough.* Looked just dumb enough to be dangerous, so I drew the bat back and waited. Never got a chance to find out, though.

The Sheriff's Crown Victoria slid to a stop about a foot from the guy sitting in the puddle. I exhaled for the first time in about three minutes. My body had that lighter-than-air adrenaline rush going through it. Fear is a focuser. Allowing into the senses only those items vital to short-term survival and eliminating the rest.

When I forced my eyes off Chainman and looked toward the cruiser, I found myself looking down the barrel of Nathan Hand's revolver.

"Not me," I said. "Them."

"Hands on your head," he screamed.

I dropped the bat, but kept my hands at my sides. Bobby Russell was a lot closer to Floyd than Hand was to me. The barrel of the riot gun must have looked like a sewer pipe. From forty feet I could see the kid's finger twitching on the trigger, and I didn't like it a bit. Floyd must have noticed. He stood absolutely still with his hands held out to his sides.

"Hands on your head," the sheriff screamed.

"Do it!" the deputy yelled.

Floyd looked at me with a bemused expression.

"Why do they always scream? Do they teach 'em that in cop school?"

"They must," I said.

"Hands on your heads," Hand bellowed again.

Floyd flicked his head toward the rear. As if choreographed, we both turned and put our hands on the tops of the cars directly behind us. I could hear the scraping of their shoes as they moved carefully toward us and then, as I was about to turn my head to see what was taking so long, a gun barrel was jammed hard under my right ear, as if trying to lift me from the ground.

"The criminals are behind you, Sheriff, " I said.

"Shut the hell up," he growled. "Put your right hand behind your head."

I followed directions. He slapped a bracelet on my wrist and then dragged it down behind my back, where he attached it to the other one. He grabbed me by the collar and turned me around. "I warned you," he said. "Now we're going to see."

"Well, looky looky," Deputy Russell said, holding Floyd's silver-plated .44 between his thumb and forefinger.

"It's licensed. There's a copy of my carry permit in my wallet," Floyd said calmly. Russell stuck his shotgun under Floyd's chin, forcing his head back. "I want to hear from you I'll say so," the deputy said. "Till then you keep your smart mouth shut. You hear me?" When he jerked the gun away, Floyd grinned and rolled his neck a couple of times, then hawked up a little phlegm from his throat and spit a thick green glob onto Deputy Bobby's shirt. Good shot. Half on, half off the badge.

The deputy went postal. He began to shake. For a brief moment, I thought he was going to blow Floyd's head off. Instead, he drew back the butt of the riot gun, his eyes ablaze, aiming to bash Floyd's brains in, but by then the sheriff had covered the distance between them and grabbed him by the wrist.

"That's enough," he said.

"Do you . . . did you see . . ." Russell sputtered.

He tried to kick Floyd, but Hand held him off.

"We'll add your shirt to the charges."

Mickey had stopped break dancing and now rocked rhythmically on his spine, breathing heavily through his mouth. Dexter knelt by his brother's side. He looked up at me. "Oooo on o a itch," he mumbled.

"You really ought to consider speech therapy," I said. "You sound like Scooby Doo on quaaludes." Drugs and cartoons. I figured he'd get it.

Mickey was panting like a spaniel and kneading his groin with both hands. Dexter reached out and, in a touching display of sibling support, patted his brother's arm.

"Why doncha kiss it and make it better," I suggested.

He sprang to his feet and started for me. I heard the sheriff shout, "Dexter," and begin moving our way. Slowly. At an amble. He figured to let Dexter have at me for a few minutes before he intervened. As for me . . . I figured I could whip a cretin like Dexter with or without hands.

I waited until Dexter was six feet away and then threw myself back along the trunk of the car, pulled my knees to my chin and planted both feet in the middle of his chest. The impact sent him staggering backward, sucking for breath. He fell over his brother and landed on his back in a puddle, next to a bloated bag of Doritos and a box of Wheat Thins that bobbed on the brown water like barges. Mickey caressed himself and whimpered. Dexter sucked air in ragged gasps. Tough day all around for the Davis twins.

From the other side of the parking lot a small voice sounded. "Those aren't the ones, Sheriff Hand." It was Samantha. "It's the other guys."

"You just stay out of the way, now, and let us handle this."

She pointed to Dexter and Chainman. "It was those moron Davis brothers and those others. They started it. Ask anybody. They almost ran me over."

An elderly woman in a bright purple ski jacket stepped out from between some cars.

"The girl is right," she said. "These fellas were just defending themselves. They very nearly ran that young woman down." She waved a hand. "Made all this mess."

"S'true," slurred an old geezer in a red plaid hat with earflaps.

They came out of the woodwork to support our side of the story, probably ten people in all, but Hand didn't give a shit. He began to drag me across the lot by my handcuffed hands. In the distance a siren wailed.

"Keep back and out the way, now," he said.

"But they didn't do anything," Samantha insisted.

"Dey bufted my teef," Monk gargled.

"We'll sort this out down at the station," Hand said.

"They got what was comin' to 'em," said the woman in purple. She pointed over at Dexter and Mickey. "Those two Davis boys ain't got the sense God gave a gopher. You know that well as I do, Mr. Hand."

Hand didn't like it. He had the beginnings of an insurrection on his hands. "Let 'em go," somebody hollered.

"Have another doughnut," a shrill voice suggested.

Hand turned to Russell. "Put him in the car," he said, and began dragging me along behind him. I played to the crowd.

"Dey bufted my teef." Monk again.

I knew the voice right away. "Why aren't you listening to these people?" she said. Hand stiffened and stopped yanking at me. He took a deep breath and turned us both around. Ramona Haynes stood with her hands on her hips.

"What's your problem?" she demanded. "These folks

here are telling you what happened. Open your ears." Her cheeks and chin were bright red.

Hand seemed to choose his words carefully. "You witnessed it, did you, Miss Haynes? Seen it all. Beginning to end."

"From beginning to end," she said. She pointed to her left, where her truck blocked the end of the aisle, motor running, door open. He let go of the cuffs. Put his hands on his hips and looked around at the crowd.

"Do you want us to sign something or what?" Ramona asked.

Hand ignored her. Instead, addressing the crowd: "I don't know whether you folks noticed or not, but several of your fellow citizens have been seriously injured here."

As if to punctuate the point, a red and white aid car with a fire department logo slid to a stop behind Monk's truck.

"Dey bufted my teef." Right on cue.

"They got what was comin' to 'em," the old woman repeated.

"That may be well and good, Mrs. Franklin, but don't none of that bears on the assault on Deputy Russell."

"Only assaulting I seen was you on them," said Earflaps. "Dinna have no cause to be wavin' a scattergun around."

"Why dontcha shoot 'em with your goddamn radar gun, Sheriff?" somebody yelled from behind me. The line got laughs and scattered applause.

Ramona Haynes stepped over next to the old woman. "Tell you what, Sheriff, we'll all forget about your use of excessive force, and you forget about a little spit."

A trio of EMTs started in on the wounded. To my right several store employees were picking our groceries from the mud and water.

Hand removed his hat and wiped his brow with his sleeve. He wagged a finger at his deputy. "Turn him loose," he said. "And check that permit he says he got."

For a second, I thought Deputy Russell was going to refuse. His face was the color of Boris's beets. His hand shook
slightly as he pulled the key out of his watch pocket.

"Turn around," he said. Sounded like he was being stran-
gled.

Floyd obliged.

"You, too," Hand said to me. I turned and offered my
manacled wrists for liberation. He grabbed the chain and
jerked me close. Whispered in my ear. "I were you, I'd make
sure I was somewhere far away. There's more where these
old boys came from. Do you hear me?"

I did horrified. "Are you threatening me?" I asked in a
stage whisper.

He did incredulous. "Threat? Heh, heh. What are you
talkin' about?"

I rubbed my wrists. Something about being restrained always makes me feel dirty and less human. As if the way the
metal bruises and disregards my flesh somehow carries over
into the realm of the spirit and injures me there as well.

I turned my back so he couldn't watch as I tried to massage away the feeling. I worked at calming my breathing,
counting my breaths until my senses began to widen and I
could hear voices and the rush of tires. The booming of rap
on a stereo. And then the shrill *kaak* of a gull. I looked up to
a pair of herring gulls gliding above our heads, air surfers,
swooping low toward the litter, gliding close enough for me
to make out the black and white polka-dot tails and the perfect red circles decorating the sides of their bills.

Dexter and Mickey were on their feet, both bent at the
waist, looking a little green but otherwise seemingly intact.
Chainman shuffled over to their sides. They formed a tight
whispering knot as they watched Monk and his remaining
teef get wheeled off on a gurney, along with redneck number
two, who walked himself to the aid car with his face pressed
into a towel. The deputy got out of the squad car.

"Permit's valid," he announced.

The sheriff tilted his head. With a childish show of disgust, Bobby dragged his heels over to Floyd and returned both the permit and the automatic, both of which quickly disappeared into Floyd's coat. Floyd reached into his pants and pulled out a roll of bills. Opened it up. Took out a couple of singles and held them out.

"For your dry cleaning there, sport."

The kid's eyes bulged. He slapped the bills to the ground, turned and strode to the far side of the patrol car, stood there with his arms folded, looking out toward the highway. A cough. People began to move off. Cars started. The Davis brothers and redneck number one left in Monk's truck. Watching Mickey and Dexter struggle up onto the seat brightened my spirits considerably.

I crossed the lot to Samantha. Gave her my thanks and twenty bucks that I eventually had to stick in her apron pocket. Next thing I knew, the store manager was at my elbow saying they felt terrible about what happened and were going to replace our whole order for us. I started to protest, but he didn't want to hear about it. When I turned back looking for Floyd, Ramona Haynes was standing about three feet from me.

"See," she said. "I told you. You're just too dangerous to be at large in this town without supervision."

Something adolescent in me wanted to ask her if she was volunteering, but I had an unexpected flash of lucidity and said, "Thanks for the testimonial," instead.

"Seems like every time I run into you it's some kind of disaster."

"Chaos is my medium."

Floyd appeared at my elbow. "Store says they're going to replace our stuff," he said.

"I know."

"Back home they'd drop a littering charge on you."

"That's the beauty of small-town life," Ramona said.

"And here I was thinking it was you," said Floyd.

The smile she gave him reminded me of that line from Voltaire when he was asked what he thought of the so-called Enlightenment and he'd answered, "I used to be disgusted, now I'm just amused."

"Thank you . . . Mr . . ."

"Floyd," he said with an enigmatic smile of his own.

Sheriff Hand's cruiser splashed by, both cops throwing their hardest looks our way. Floyd waved bye-bye. "Ta-ta," he hollered. He took a step backward. "Nice to meet you," he said to Ramona and then looked at me and jerked his thumb over his shoulder. "I'll see to the provisions there, boss," he said. We watched as he skirted a cavernous puddle, hopped another and disappeared inside.

"Interesting guy," she said.

"He'd be glad you thought so."

"Does he always carry a gun?"

"Even when he sleeps."

She searched my eyes with that back-and-forth, up-and-down thing women do.

"You're serious."

"Absolutely."

"Is Floyd his first or his last name?"

I shook my head. "Not a clue."

"He's your friend and you don't know his whole name?"

I shrugged. I'd never thought to ask. Silly me.

"I've heard that men friends don't talk, but . . ."

"Who said he was my friend?"

"What is he, then?"

Good question. "My bodyguard, I guess."

"*Pfui*," she scoffed. "You need a bodyguard like this town needs more out-of-work idiots with too much time on their hands."

"I'm a little banged up." I lifted the Yankees cap from the front of my head.

She ooohed and aaahed and gently touched my stitches

with the tips of her fingers. "That's right. You were in that accident over on West River."

"Is that what you heard? That it was an accident?"

She said it was. I don't know why I was surprised, but the notion that people had tried to kill me and nothing official was being done about it offended the hell out of me. Must be that public trust hang-up of mine again.

"Did anybody ever tell you your chin gets red when you're pissed off?"

"My ex," she said. Her lips wanted to bend into a smile, but she wouldn't let them. "According to Donald it also happens during . . ." She shot me a coy look. "At other times," she finished. I went shopping for a snappy rejoinder, but the sudden redistribution of my blood supply seemed to have left my cranial cupboards bare.

She began to back up. "Better get my rig out of the way," she said. "You think you can manage to stay out of trouble without me?"

"Probably not," I said.

She stopped. "Every time I see you I feel like I owe you an apology for the way those idiots act."

"You didn't do anything."

"You know what I mean."

I made the sign of the cross. *"Domini domini.* You're now officially excused from being the goodwill ambassador for those guys."

She put her hand to her throat. "Well, since it's official, I guess I have no choice but to lay my burden down, do I?" she joked.

"None."

"Gotta go. 'Bye."

"See ya," I said. "Thanks again."

Halfway to the truck she turned back my way. "You gonna be around for a while?" she asked.

"Probably," I said.

"As my last ambassadorial duty, why don't you let me make you dinner?"

"I'd like to," I hedged, "but I'm not sure of my schedule yet. You know, maybe if . . ." I felt like I was talking with rented lips.

"If you change your mind, I'm in the book," she said with a smile.

Samantha crossed between us, pushing a cart full of groceries.

"Did I hear that correctly?" Floyd was by my side.

"What?"

"Did she just invite you to dinner at her place and you turned her down?"

Ramona Haynes rolled down the window and waved goodbye and then went roaring off down the road. I listened as the sound faded.

"Yeah," I said with as much enthusiasm as I could muster.

He reached up and picked the cap carefully from my head. "They X-ray your head while they had you in there?" I snatched the cap and put it back on.

I started toward the car, where Samantha waited patiently for one of us to unlock the trunk. "Cut it out," I growled.

"Really, man, I'm serious. I'm concerned here."

Although I never would have admitted it to Floyd, I knew exactly what he meant. Hell, I was a little concerned myself.

24 THE STROLL WAS BORIS'S IDEA. HE'D COME ROLLING in at about three. Seems the deadly duo had not only come up empty again, but had been so shamed by their failure to produce results that they were forced to get drunker than usual. According to Boris, their last stop had ended when they were escorted out the door by a large and rather unfriendly looking African-American bartender, who'd waved them about like dolls before depositing them in a pile on the sidewalk. Time to go home, he'd figured.

We'd marched them by the elbows down to their cabin and left them happily snoring their little hearts out. "How far is dee ocean?" he asked me.

"A mile or so," I said. "At least I think so. I've never walked down."

"I neber seen de Pacifeec Ocean," he said.

I checked my watch. Three-ten. Looked at Floyd. "You mind holding down the fort?" He said it would be no problem. Said he'd seen the ocean and thought he could probably live without the hike.

We went out to the front of the yard and turned right, following the Quileute west toward the Pacific. J.D.'d owned the last of the trees. The minute we breached the tree line at the far end of the clearing we found ourselves in a series of lowland pastures with only a thin evening fog standing between us and the Pacific Ocean. Boris wanted to know about the plants, so I told him everything I knew. Lots of Scotch broom, its wiry limbs gray and desolate in winter, giving no hint whatsoever of the brilliant yellow blossoms that signal the arrival of spring on the Northwest coast. Marsh grass and sword fern and bracken. A collapsed corral and loading chute. And old fences, bent and crumbling now. North and south, east and west, dividing the valley into an irregular checkerboard of what must have at one time been pastures. Robert Frost came to mind with that poem about good fences making good neighbors.

Boris was amazed that land such as this was not being used.

"Who owns dees?" he asked.

"I don't know," I confessed. "The guy who was killed—"

"Spreenger?"

"Yeah. He told me there were a thousand private acres in here that were surrounded by the Indian reservation."

"I doan understand dees reservation beesnus."

I did my best to explain the concept of a reservation.

"So dey vas here first."

"Yeah."

"So how come dey doan own eet all?"

"We had more and better weapons."

This was a concept he understood. "Ah," he said. "Veectors and spoils."

It took forty minutes before we stood on a bluff overlooking the Pacific. Everything that wasn't Indian reservation sat on a narrow plateau between the Quileute and what I figured was Fox Creek, which rolled over a mossy crag down into the ocean about a half a mile from where I stood. Twenty feet below us, the Pacific roiled muddy green, crashing white foam over and around the black rocks offshore. Pretty much the same kind of property I'd seen on the Hoh reservation. Only a man-made breakwater away from having a nice little protected bay, safe from the murderous Pacific storms that rake this part of the coast for six months a year.

It was full dark before we picked our way among the hillocks and fences and back to the homestead. Floyd was sitting in a lawn chair with his rifle across his lap.

"Phone in the cabin's been ringing," he said.

Turned out to be a message from George. He'd checked the answering machine this afternoon and was reporting that all five tax criminals had tried to call yesterday afternoon. Said they sounded a mite upset. Especially the Polster guy. Said he's been practicing his spiel on Nearly Normal and was ready to, what he called "ream some ass" come Monday morning.

I tried Rebecca at home, listened as my voice apologized for neither of us being there and then the clicks as voice mail forwarded my call somewhere else, only to be told by Rebecca's voice that Dr. Duvall was unable to answer my call at this time, but that if I were to leave a message she would be sure to get back to me as soon as possible.

Over sandwiches and beer, we decided it would be wise to sleep in shifts. No telling what the manly types were going to do after today. Lord knows there was no shortage of assholes in this town, and if there's one thing a redneck can't abide, it's getting his ass kicked in public. We figured there was no sense in taking any chances. Four-hour shifts. First Floyd, then Boris, then me.

Around nine, Boris excused himself and headed to his cabin for a siesta. Floyd got his rifle from the corner and went out into the yard. I turned out the lights and lay in the dark for a moment before snapping on the bedside light and dialing home. She answered on the first ring. "Hello."

"Hey," I said.

"Hey yourself," she answered.

I could hear the strain in the spaces between the words as we traded news of the past two days. She said she stopped at the office on Friday and that everybody'd made a big fuss over her and that she'd spent most of today getting her clothes together for the week. Doing laundry and taking stuff to the cleaners in a cab. How everything took three times as long with one arm. As for me . . . I kept it vague. Said I felt like I was making some progress, a statement that, although not altogether true, seemed somehow to validate my presence here. I left out the fight in the parking lot. Couldn't for the life of me see how telling her that was going to improve the situation. When we ran out of news, we found ourselves listening to one another breathe over the line, as if we shared some terrible secret that neither of us wanted to be the first to utter.

"I feel us drifting apart, Leo," she said after a while.

"Doesn't seem like drift to me," I answered. "Seems to me it's you doing the paddling, not the tide."

"I'm just telling you how I feel."

"And I feel like nothing in my life is ever going to be the same again unless I say or do whatever it is you want me to say or do. Which, no matter how much my heart wants to agree, seems like some kind of betrayal."

"Compromise is betrayal? Is that what you're saying?"

"Compromise is the art of nobody getting what they want."

"Stop being cute. Answer the question."

"If you don't believe in what you're saying, it is a betrayal. If you just agree so your partner will get off your case, well, what's that? Not only don't the two of you agree, but now the other person can't even rely on you to tell them the truth."

"I see, then. You're in charge of defending the truth."

I kept cool and didn't rise to the bait. "Truth be told, Rebecca . . . I don't even know what it is you want. Honest to god. I don't have the foggiest."

The phone company was right. You can hear a pin drop.

"I want a regular life. I want to go to parties with somebody who wants to be there with me. I want somebody to strive with. Somebody who I know is going to come home alive every night. Who's not sitting in some alley staking out some drug-crazed something or other for a week at a time. A guy who doesn't have to shoot his way out of sex parties and then deliver broken little girls back to their families. I just want a life, Leo. A life like everybody else's."

When she put it that way, I knew Jed was right. Ending up like everybody else was my greatest horror. "I don't know what to say," I said.

"Me either," she sighed. "Goodnight."

"Goodnight."

I snapped off the light.

25 | JUST AFTER NOON, KURTIS ARRIVED IN A RENTED JEEP Cherokee. "Saw Uncle Carl and his beast on the ferry," he announced. "They should be right along. He said they were stopping in PT for some rental equipment." He looked around. "How bucolic," he enthused. "I feel positively ruddy."

I told him to take Cabin Number Five. The sight of Kurtis sashaying toward the cabin, singing "Oh what a beautiful morning . . ." in an operatic tenor caused Floyd to raise an eyebrow my way. "Best B and E guy in the business," I assured him.

The look on Floyd's face said he'd better be if he was going to walk that way.

At ten, I'd sent Boris and the Boys off to make one last run at finding Ben Bendixon in Port Townsend. Having passed out in the middle of the afternoon, Ralph and Harold had been up since before the crack of dawn. Knowing their habits as I did, I'd locked them out. They work on the assumption that people are passed out rather than sleeping. To them, this means they can make all the noise they want, regardless of the hour. I'd heard 'em rattling the door around three A.M., trying to get to something to eat, but I ignored them. You snooze, you lose.

When Boris woke me for my shift at five, they were sitting on the porch in the dark. Sullen and surly, they grumbled all the way to the refrigerator and their first cold one of the day. They cheered up a bit as they put together and then devoured scrambled eggs and toast. Washed down, of course, by a couple more beers. They got surly again, though, when I told them to wash their dishes and leave the kitchen like they found it. I guess nomads don't usually do housework.

They were still grousing when Boris packed them in the Blazer and went bouncing up the driveway. Just after one o'clock, Carl Cradduck's motor home rolled into the driveway, followed by Robby and the rented cherry picker. I introduced Floyd to Carl and Robby.

Floyd showed Carl where to park the RV. "Out of the field of fire," Floyd said, gesturing at the tree line behind the house.

"I got something to help out with that," Carl said. He craned his neck and yelled into the RV. "Robby . . . we still got those sensors we took off those Nazi bastards?"

"Yeah . . . somewhere," Robby yelled back.

"We did this wire job for the Pocatello, Idaho, police department. They had the paperwork to wire this white separatist group that they suspected of a couple of synagogue bombings, but they couldn't get anybody inside to plant the bugs. Seems like every time they got anywhere near the place, the skinheads knew they were there. Fuckers lived in this compound thing, like a frontier fort, way the fuck out in the middle of nowhere. So they came to us. Wanted us to see if we could figure out how they were surveilling the woods around their fucking fort."

"Motion sensors?" Kurtis asked.

Carl nodded. "First thing we did was run a sweep. Before we ever got out of the van. The board lit up like Christmas. We sent out a fucking signal that jammed every TV and radio within a ten-square-mile area and then backtracked on the sensor signals. I don't know where the hell they got 'em, but they'd gotten their hands on a dozen East German motion sensors. Same kind they used to patrol the Berlin wall."

As if on cue, Robby appeared at the RV door. He handed a cardboard box out the door to Floyd, who walked over and set the box in Carl's lap. "Ya gotta see these suckers," Carl said, pulling open the box and rummaging around inside.

He pulled out a bird. A sparrow, it appeared to be. With incredibly long, skinny legs. "Is this a pisser or what?" he asked. "Ya just put the little fucker up in a tree, wrap the wire legs around a branch and the little things are virtually undetectable. Good for a hundred yards in every direction, long as you've got line of sight, of course." He laughed. "Robby was nose to nose with the fucker before he figured it out."

Robby poked his head out the door. "I kept waiting for it to fly off. I'm way the hell up this tree, following the sensor signal, and this little bird is just hunkered down staring at me. I couldn't figure out for the life of me why he didn't get the hell out of there. At first I thought he was, like, too terrified to fly off. Like he'd never seen some idiot human climbing up his tree in the dead of night. So I wave the signal reader at him and not only doesn't he fly away, he turns out to be the damn signal."

He dropped the bird back into the bag and held the bag out to Floyd. "We got six, which is probably more than we need. Space them out." He turned to me. "How deep is that tree stand?"

"It varies . . . but maybe fifty yards until you get up to the road."

"Take them about twenty yards in and put them up above eye level. About as high as you can reach," Carl instructed.

"Aye aye, Captain," said Floyd.

"Take a radio with you so you can talk with Robby."

Floyd stopped at the RV for a handheld radio and then he started up the hill toward the tree line. Carl turned to

Kurtis. "You have a look at the City Building on the way here?"

Kurtis nodded. "I did a drive-by. Stopped at both the front and back doors. Standard-issue contact alarms. I'll have to get up on the roof to know if they've got anything other than that, but the system's pretty new, so I'm betting they've got a direct line down to the cop shop."

"You find me a pole?"

"Back of the lot. Perfect. When you drive up the street, it's right there in front of you. From the top, you should be able to see all the way down to the highway."

"Good."

"Somebody wire the cars already?"

"First thing in the morning," I said. "I got the makes, models and plate numbers. One of us can do it right there in the lot when they show up for work on Monday morning."

"Sounds together," Kurtis said. "What am I taking in?"

"Robby," Carl bellowed. "Bring me the hard goods."

"What are you, crippled?" Robby shouted back.

Carl pushed the button on his chair and backed over to the door. Robby's arm appeared, holding a ziplock freezer bag half full of electronics. Carl reached up and took it from his hand and then drove over to Kurtis. "Got both magnetic and adhesive mikes."

He reached into the bag and pulled out a bronze disk about the size and thickness of a silver dollar. He placed it against the bottom of the aluminum arm on his wheelchair. It stayed there. "Depends on how old the cheap-shit furniture is. Old stuff is all metal. Use these. The magnet makes the battery last longer. New shit is all plastic." He dropped the disk back into the bag and came out with another. This one bronze on one side, white on the other. Carl showed Kurtis, who took it in his hands and held it close to his face. "You just peel off the paper and stick it where you want it. Doesn't even have to be dry."

"What else?" Kurtis asked. "I don't much like carrying things in."

Carl held up his hand. "Got you covered." He pulled out a dull metal tube about the size of a Magic Marker. "Problem with cameras has always been power. Never could get any parity between the size of the camera and the size of the batteries you needed to run the goddamn things. Got cameras the size of your thumbnail, for chrissakes, but you wanted to run the damn thing for a week you needed something the size of a car battery."

"That's what I've been picturing," Kurtis said.

"Nah," Carl said. "As usual, some Jap got his head out of his ass first. Asked himself the obvious question." He looked from Kurtis to me. We were supposed to guess. "I give up," Kurtis said.

"What item can be found screwed to the ceiling in every public space in the civilized world?"

Kurtis and I engaged in a spirited round of synchronized shrugging.

"A smoke detector," Carl said derisively. "Gotta have 'em. It's the law." He held up a chrome tube. "Japanese," he said. "Use 'em to check up on their employees. Transmits up to four miles, variable remote focus." He pulled two wires from the end. "Low voltage. Same as the smoke detector. Made to fit right into all the standard models." He jiggled the wires. "You just twist white to white and black to black, aim the thing wherever the hell you want it . . . got holes all around to let the smoke in . . . snap the cover back on and you're on your way. Two minutes tops. Thing runs forever."

He turned to me. "No way Kurtis goes back in. Whatever we use is probably gone forever. Fortunately for you, this is all shit we got while doing inspections. We find good shit, we keep it and give the client something not so good. If it's traceable, it's not to us."

"How can I be sure they're pointing where we want them?" Kurtis asked.

"I've got an earpiece radio for you. You hook 'em up, turn 'em on and Robby and I will help you with the final adjustments."

"I'm looking for in and out twenty minutes tops."

"Shouldn't be a problem," Carl said. "When you want to go in?"

"Eight or so," Kurtis said. "As long as it's dark. It's a lot easier to explain what you're doing around someplace at eight-thirty than it is at four A.M."

Robby came out of the RV carrying a handheld radio and a black electronic device about the size of a ghetto blaster. He was talking into the radio. "Keep turning it that way . . . more . . . more . . . stop. Right there." As he spoke, a series of red lights flickered across the face of the gizmo. "Okay, next one needs to go to the left . . . yeah, toward the ocean . . . more . . . more . . ."

"They're overlapping the fields," Carl said. "Ya get 'em up high so ya don' have rabbits setting the damn things off."

Twenty minutes later, we had an electronic perimeter set up. For a final test, Floyd started at one end and walked the length of the cut. As he moved through the trees, the red lights began to glow in series. Robby fiddled with a knob. The next light was accompanied by a loud chirp, and then the next. Robby chuckled. "Ya gotta like it," he said. Robby pushed the button and spoke into the radio. "That's it. We're done."

Robby and Kurtis disappeared inside the motor home. They came back out wearing white coveralls with Pacific Power logos on the chest. White sky, green trees and blue water. Underneath, WORKING TOGETHER FOR WASHINGTON. Each man carried a yellow hard hat under one arm.

"Ready when you are," Robby said to Carl.

"You got your phone?" I asked Kurtis. He nodded.

Carl spoke to Robby. "Careful with the juice, huh? Power company don't exactly send its stars out to bumfuck like this. Everything may not be where it belongs."

"I won't run with scissors, either," Robby assured him.

Carl and I watched in silence as they walked over to the cherry picker. Robby walked around to the back, opened one of the storage compartments and pulled out a pair of magnetic signs. Pacific Power. Same logo. Same slogan. Stuck them on the doors, stepped back to check the alignment. Made an adjustment. Got in and left.

"Feels good to be fucking with folks again," Carl said.

I turned to Floyd, who sat on the lawn, leaning back against the barbecue grill, catching some early afternoon sunshine. "You might as well come with me," I said. "Way things are going, if I leave you here, I'll be battered and bitten by an old lady and her dog."

26 IF YOU'LL PERMIT ME THE PHRASE, MONTY'S EYES WERE as big as saucers as he looked around the inside of the motor home. A dozen small TV monitors, each with its own audio and video recorder, completely covered one inside wall. The collection of equipment, dials, lights, knobs and handles made an airline cockpit look user-friendly. From the outside it appeared that the lovely flowered curtains were closed, which in the strictest sense was true. What you couldn't tell from the outside was that the curtains had been stiffened with epoxy resin and were permanently screwed in place and that the interior had been gutted and turned into a mobile electronic surveillance command post. Like every other vehicle Carl owned, the RV was fitted with a hydraulic lift for his chair and had been completely retrofitted so it could be operated from the chair using hand controls.

"A little of their own medicine," Monty enthused.

The sight of Carl in his wheelchair rolling around inside the RV seemed to confirm his worst fears. "Almost got you, huh? Like they did Leo," he said.

"They'll stop at nothing," Carl told him. He turned to me. A flick of his eyes told me he wanted me to get rid of Monty, who for the past half hour had shown no inclination to leave. Floyd was down at the far end of the bank of monitors, wearing a set of headphones, tuned into regular TV, watching a cooking show.

I put my hand on Monty's bony shoulder. "Come on," I said. "Time to let these guys do what they've been trained to do."

He didn't like it. He'd waited a long time for the counterattack and wanted to be among the first rank. "Deniability is crucial," I insisted. "What you don't know, you can't give up under the truth drugs."

"Oh yeah," he said tentatively.

I began to steer him toward the door. "They'll pump you so full of truth drugs you'll think you're Roseanne Arnold. You won't be able to help yourself." I kept talking and steering until I had him back inside, behind the motel desk. I slapped the counter. Gave it the voice-of-doom narration. "This is the front line," I said. "Right here. We're counting on you."

When I got back to the RV, Carl was talking to Robby on the radio. The monitor in front of Carl flickered with blue static. "Anything yet?" Robby's voice.

"Nada," Carl said. "Check the ground."

A moment later, the screen lit into a street scene and then, just as suddenly, reverted to static. "You had it for a second there," Carl said.

"Hang on," Robby replied.

I tapped Carl. "I'm going to do a drive-by," I said. He nodded and adjusted two green dials. I hopped down from the RV and walked across the thick carpet of leaves toward the Malibu. Suddenly it was Indian summer in the middle of January. One of those Pacific Northwest days when the complex weather systems collide and momentarily seem to forget the season. Bright blue sky. Not a cloud in sight. Must be fifty-five, pushing sixty degrees. No breeze to speak of.

I drove with the window down. The minute I turned left off the highway and headed for the City Building, I could see Robby, way the hell up in the air. Damn near as high as the hydraulic arm would lift the bucket. Maybe forty feet in the air.

I followed the arrows around the parking lot. The cherry picker was braced against the street, its four hydraulic legs spread for balance, inside a perimeter of orange traffic cones. Robby was working at the very top of the pole. He wore a headset. I could see his lips moving as he talked to Carl back in the RV. Kurtis waved a bright yellow flag with a flair seldom seen in roadwork. I rolled down the passenger window and pulled to a stop next to Kurtis. "So far, so good," he said.

"You guys go right back to the ranch," I said. "Soon as we see you go by, we'll pack it up and follow."

"You got it," he said.

The lower section of the hydraulic arm whined and began to fold itself back into the bed. I jammed the car in park and got out. Robby manipulated the three colored handles in the bucket as he lowered himself back into the truck. "One down. One to go," he said.

Kurtis pointed to a mercury vapor light along the curb. The light nearest the back door of the City Building. "As long as we've got this erection set, we're going to fix that light so it doesn't work. Robby says it will just take a minute. Discretion, valor and all that."

"Good idea."

I got back in and headed to the Black Bear. Monty was sweeping up out front when I rolled back into the lot. He came limping over to the window.

"Next half hour or so a white cherry picker with Pacific Power signs on the side is going to come down the road heading west," I told him. "I need you to keep an eye out for it and come and report when it passes. Can you do that?"

"Damn right I can."

"Also, we're going to need room nine for the next few nights."

"When?"

"Monday, Tuesday and Wednesday."

He held out his hand. "Hundred twenty bucks," he said. I dug in my pocket, came up with six twenties and handed them over. I guess, as far as Monty was concerned, service to the cause was one thing, but commerce was another.

Floyd had turned one of the picnic tables right side up and was lying on it basking in the afternoon sun. "Hell of a day," he said. "First camera works like a charm," he said. He sat up. "I can't believe the shit this guy's got. It's fuckin' scary, man. You got somebody like Carl on your ass, you can't fart without him knowing it from across town. Personal privacy is a thing of the past, man, a thing of the past." He shook his head.

Disabling the streetlight must have been as easy as Robby had said. By the time I got through discussing privacy in peril with Floyd, he already had the second camera secured on top of the pole and was testing its field of vision under Carl's direction. I stood and watched as they tested it left and right, up and down, zoom and back.

"That's it," Carl said. "Button it up and get out of there." He turned to me. "That's it until Kurtis goes in tonight," he said.

"Monty's going to tell us when they go by."

"That fucker worries me, Leo."

"He'll be all right," I said with more confidence than I felt.

Carl began shutting the consoles down. Flipping switches, turning dials and toggling toggles. "Might as well leave this beast here until tonight," he said.

Floyd stuck his head in the door. "Buck Rogers says the truck just went by."

"Let's get out of here," I said.

27 "HE'S GOING UP A PIPE..." I COULD HEAR FLOYD breathing into the phone. "Fucker's like a monkey," he said. "He's on the roof and moving. In the shadows now; I can't see him anymore."

It was eight-thirty-five. Perfect night for a burglary. Outright balmy and no moon. Boris, Robby and the Boys were holding down the homestead. The fellas struck out in Port Townsend, but had a hell of a time doing it. Maybe it was like Ralphie said. Maybe the old guy found religion.

Carl and I waited in silence. Four minutes until Floyd spoke again.

"Coming back down from the roof. Okay. Doing the door. Still at the door. He's inside."

"Hang on and keep the line open," I said.

Two minutes later, Kurtis's voice crackled from the speaker. "Number one," he said. "City attorney's office. Got number one?" Carl said he heard him loud and clear.

So clear, in fact, that I could make out the sound of Kurtis setting a chair under the smoke detector and then the snap as he pried off the plastic cover. Bingo. The first monitor blinked twice and then stayed on. Looking nearly straight down onto Mark Tressman's desk. The plastic slats segmented the view as if we were looking through iron bars. "How's the view?" Kurtis asked. Carl told him it was fine. We watched on the monitor as Kurtis returned the chair somewhere out of camera range and then walked back through the picture on his way to the mayor's office.

The process was repeated two more times without incident. Three monitors were now lit. Tressman, the mayor and Nancy Weston were well on their way to having their fifteen minutes of fame. Kurtis had been inside for eighteen minutes.

Kurtis had just entered the engineering and inspections office when Floyd's voice broke the spell. "Got me a police cruiser," he said. "No hurry. Looks like routine patrol. Not to worry . . . not to worry."

"Steady," I said.

"It's fat-ass. Getting out. He's out checking the fucking streetlight. Dumb fuck's pounding on the pole. Dork."

We waited an agonizing minute.

"Back in the car . . . driving . . . stopped again. Fuck," Floyd said. "He's getting out again. Heading for the door."

"Has he been on the radio?" I asked.

"No."

No backup. After his embarrassing debacle with Floyd and Boris the other day, Harlan Spots was going to handle this one himself. Get back a little face.

Kurtis was on the speaker. "Audio four," he said.

Carl raised an eyebrow. "Keep going," I mouthed.

"Loud and clear," Carl replied. "Let's get this last one and get the hell out of there," Carl said.

"He's found the door open. Reaching for his piece. Got it out. Starting inside."

"Stop him," I said into the phone. The sound of the cell phone hitting the car seat resounded from the earpiece.

"Tell Kurtis to stay where he is," I whispered to Carl.

"Hang tight for a minute, Kurtis."

"Problem?"

"Maybe. Stay still and quiet."

Carl covered his mike with his hand. I paced up and down the narrow aisle. Seemed like an hour before Floyd's voice stopped me dead.

He was out of breath. "Get the kid out of there," he said. I heard the Blazer start. Floyd breathing hard as he turned the wheel and the squeal of tires.

"Let's go, Kurt, move your ass," Carl growled into the headset.

Another minute passed. Kurtis over the speaker. "Oh, man . . ."

Floyd sounded far away. "Get in. Let's go."

"What are we looking at with the cop?" Kurtis asked. We could now hear them both over the cell phone and from Kurtis's mike.

"He was breathing when I threw him in the back of the car," Floyd said.

"They're gonna find their alarm monkeyed."

"Can't be helped," Floyd said.

"He see you?"

"If he'd seen me, he'd be dead," said Floyd.

28 ROBBY WAS TRYING TO BREAK THE TENSION. READING from yesterday's newspaper, while we waited for our friends in city government to show up for work on Monday morning. Hoping like hell that Deputy Spots was okay and that we hadn't left anything behind that pointed our way. "Says here the Gillette razor company offered ZZ Top six million bucks to get a shave on television."

"No sheet," said Boris.

"Says they turned it down."

"It's their look," Kurtis said. "They couldn't."

"For six million bucks, I'd let Katharine Hepburn shave my ass with a bolo knife," Carl declared. I was still working on that image when Robby dropped the paper and sat forward. "Number one," he said.

MONDAY 8:46 A.M.   CAMERA 1—TRESSMAN

The lower half of Nathan Hand paced in and out of camera range. "I don't like it," he said. Mark Tressman sat at his desk and began rolling a paper clip around in his fingers. "It's just a burglary," Tressman said.

"You haven't been up on the roof."

"Don't start any conspiracy theory with me," Tressman said.

"No conspiracy. It's that Waterman and those hardcases he's got out there with him. I think they're trying to queer the deal."

"He admits as much. So what? He's got nothing. And there's nothing in this building that would advance his cause in any way. If I was going to worry about anybody, I'd be more inclined to worry about Loomis."

Hand leaned down and put both hands on the desk. "I don't get it. Loomis wants the deal to go through as bad as we do."

"Maybe they're getting nervous. Maybe they're checking up on us. We blew it once before. Maybe they don't trust us to get it done."

Eight-fifty-four A.M. Another voice. June the secretary. "Is Sheriff Hand back there?"

"Be right out," Hand called.

"Ten days," Tressman intoned. "Just ten days."

I wrote the word *Loomis* in my notebook, followed by three question marks. I knew I'd heard it before, but I couldn't remember where.

MONDAY 9:11 A.M.   CAMERA 3—WESTON

Nancy Weston drummed her fingers on the desk as she spoke. "I assure you, Mr. Wade," she said, "this is all some terrible mistake." Her face was twisted into a knot. "You have no right to speak to me that way. I want to talk to your supervisor." She listened briefly. "A criminal . . . a criminal . . . why . . . what? Attorney. I don't need an attorney. I keep telling you . . . what date?" She pulled a pencil from the desk drawer and wrote directly on the blotter. "Friday the twenty-third. One P.M. Now, just a moment," she began indignantly. "I will not be . . . hello . . . hello . . ." She returned the phone to its cradle and began to massage the bridge of her nose.

I turned to Carl. "George's doing good with his IRS agent routine," I said.

"Sure got her panties in a wad."

All the chickens were in the coop. Polster was in his office going through his mail. Her honor the mayor was dictating letters. Time for the vehicle transmitters.

I tore a page from my notebook and handed it to Kurtis. "Those are the makes, models and license numbers. The parking slots are labeled. Take Robby with you. Nobody's seen either of you guys."

"Make sure you get the numbers right," Carl growled.

"I'll use my fingers," Robby assured him.

MONDAY 10:06 A.M.   CAMERA 4—POLSTER

Polster had been dialing and redialing the phone for ten minutes before he finally got through. "Yes . . . hello. Yes. I've been having trouble getting through." He listened for a moment. "What do you mean, I don't know what trouble is? What kind of attitude is that? I'm calling to report a mistake." Listening again. "Of course it's a mistake, we don't . . . what did you call me? Why, I don't believe . . . what kind of language is that for a public servant to . . ." He groped for a pen and a small white notepad. "I want your name. Do you . . . January twenty-fifth, eleven-thirty A.M.," he recited. "I'll tell you what I think. I think you've been drinking. I can hear it in your voice. I'm going to report . . . Oh . . . a stroke, you say. No. No . . . I didn't mean. Of course I wouldn't . . . not a person with a disability . . . hello . . . hello." He hung up the phone.

I dialed the Zoo and got Terry.

"Terry, it's Leo. How drunk is he?"

"Twisted," he answered without hesitation.

"Get him for me, will you?"

He dropped the phone once before getting it up to his head. " 'Lo."

"George. You hangin' in there?"

"Course," he slurred. "Reamed 'em all good. 'Ceptin' the mayor lady. Her lawyer he called. Said he was comin' to the office."

"Good job," I said. "I think we best fix the phone to hold now."

"I dunno how, Leo I—"

"Give me Terry, will you?"

"Whatsamatter, you doan wanna talk to ol' Georgie anymore?"

"Just give me Terry, will ya?"

"Ya think you're too good for—"

On the other end, Terry must have been listening. I heard him say, "Here, gimme that." Followed by some grunting, and then he was on the line. "Leo."

"Shut him down," I said.

"Just rings or the recording and on hold?"

"On hold."

"Will do."

MONDAY 11:09 A.M.   CAMERA 1—TRESSMAN

He'd been on the phone for twenty minutes discussing an easement over city property for a driveway when his secretary popped her head in the door.

"Someone to see you, Mr. Tressman."

He waved her off. "Not today," he said. "Hold everything."

She seemed pleased when she turned and headed back out to the anteroom. A minute later, however, she reappeared. "She says it's important."

Tressman held the phone tight against his chest. "What

did I just tell you? Didn't I just this minute tell you—" Another voice now.

"I'm sorry to be such an inconvenience," Narva said.

Tressman looked up from his desk. If sharks smiled, that's what they'd look like.

"Come in," he said. "Come in."

He spoke into the phone. "I'll get back with you this afternoon, Herman. No, no . . . something's come up. Yes . . . yes . . ." He returned the phone to its cradle.

He scurried out from behind the desk, and for a second was lost from view. He reappeared with a red leather chair, which he set close to the desk. "Please," he said.

Narva looked as good from the top down as she did from any other angle. She looked like she had in the Five Spot. All-American, drop-dead gorgeous.

Tressman looked to his right. "That's all, June," he said. "Close the door, would you, please? Thanks." The door clicked shut.

Although it had never occurred to me before, as I watched her work, it became obvious that acting must be a major part of what she did for a living. The girl was too smooth for it to be any other way. She put it on him just the way we'd discussed it.

Here in town at the behest of a major corporation. Not at liberty to drop names. Just doing a little research on property. The Springer property and adjoining non-Indian land at the west end of the county. He told her about the sale. She nodded knowingly. "Just in case," she said with a Mona Lisa smile.

The more Tressman tried to convince her that he had a done deal with Claudia Springer, the more often she said, "You never know," and gave him that little I-know-something-you-don't smile. It drove him nuts.

Twenty minutes after she'd walked in his door, Tressman volunteered to take her down to the clerk's office and help her find the records she needed. She blushed and told him she didn't want to be a bother. He reckoned how he'd muddle through.

The cell phone at Carl's elbow rang. He picked it up. "Okay. Lemme see." He reached to his left and switched on a monitor. The rear of the mayor's Cadillac was visible as it rolled toward the highway. Just as the image began to get fuzzy, the view shifted. The picture was now coming from the front. We watched as the car stopped at the sign and then turned left. The lens followed as the mayor gave it some gas and disappeared around the nearest bend in the road. "Works great," Carl said into the phone. As Robby talked into his ear, Carl motioned for me to turn around. I did. I slipped my head into the earphones for camera four.

MONDAY 11:36 A.M.   CAMERA 4—POLSTER

Even in black and white, Emmett Polster's face was bright red. "It's not esoteric like bridges or sewer systems. They're going to know right away."

"You really think he's got state inspectors coming in on Friday?"

"Damn right I do."

"I think he's bluffing."

Polster paced the room, biting on his thumb. "It's pretty goddamned easy for you to think that. It's not your ass in the wringer."

"Will you relax?"

Polster raised his voice. "No, goddammit, I won't."

Nancy Weston put a finger to her lips and nodded toward the secretary in the other room.

Polster wasn't impressed. "I could lose everything."

"You're not going to lose anything."

"I'm not going down alone," Polster insisted.

"Nobody's going anywhere," Weston insisted.

"I've got a lot going on. I don't need this shit."

Weston raised a hand from the desk. "Believe me, Emmett. We've all got a lot going on today." Before Polster could respond, Weston changed the subject. "You hear about the burglary?" Polster said he hadn't, so she filled him in.

MONDAY 11:54 A.M.   CAMERA 1—TRESSMAN

Seated behind his desk again with a small smile twitching on his lips. The phone rang. "Yeah," he said. "I know. I took her down there."

Carl rolled past me, swung around and handed me the earphones for Camera Three. I checked the monitor. Nancy Weston on the phone. I had one voice in each ear. I was moving my head back and forth like I was watching a tennis match.

"I don't understand what she's doing here," Weston said.

"I think the Springer woman has received a counter-offer. I think they'd like to find some way out of the deal with us."

"How could they do that?" Weston demanded.

"They can't," he said.

"You're sure?"

"Absolutely."

"Because I've got my ass covered," she said.

Long silence.

"Oh?"

"That's all I'm going to say."

"Relax," Tressman advised. "Really, Nancy. Nine and a half days. That's it. Period. The rest won't matter."

Nancy Weston sat at her desk, her arms folded across her chest, staring at the wall. Tressman pushed one of the buttons on his phone and a moment later, June came in through the door. "Yes?"

"I'm going to have to cancel for tomorrow night," he said quietly.

When she came into camera range, her hands were on her hips. "I got a sitter."

"Can't be helped," Tressman said.

She backed up out of range. "You think it's easy?"

"I didn't say—" he began.

"Do you have any idea how hard it is for me to arrange to be away? For me to get a sitter? To make excuses to my mother?"

Tressman took the offensive. "Perhaps you haven't noticed, but there's quite a bit going on around here this morning."

His phone rang once and then again.

Tressman looked up at June. "I need to take this call," he said. The door banged hard enough for me to hear the glass shake in the frame.

Suddenly, his office door banged open.

"I'm going to lunch," June announced.

I listened to the sound of her heels receding and then grabbed my car keys.

"Where you going?" asked Carl.

"Think I'll join her for lunch," I said.

29 THE COUNTRY CORNER WAS HOPPING. WIDE-HIPPED waitresses in light green uniforms crisscrossed the room with platters of food, water pitchers and coffeepots. The clash of silverware rang above the low roar of conversation and shouts from the kitchen area. A veil of smoke hung above the room at about eyebrow level.

June had managed to find a booth at the rear of the restaurant, near the arch that led into the lounge. She looked up from her french fries as I slid into the booth across from her. "Oh . . . hi," she said around a mouthful of fries. She swallowed, washed it down with a gulp of strawberry milkshake and then wiped her lip.

"What are you doing here?"

"You told me this was a good lunch spot, so I was in the neighborhood . . . you know, up at the City building . . . and I thought I'd check it out."

She smiled the same tentative smile I'd seen before. Up close, she was younger than I'd imagined. Twenty-six or -seven. Pretty but blank in the amorphous manner of young girls. At this point in her life, she could safely be referred to as ample. Literally and figuratively a handful. Ten years down the road and we were talking heavy equipment.

"Saw your boss in the records office," I said. Half hidden behind a hamburger, her face clouded. "Going over platt maps with a . . . if I might be so bold as to say . . . a very attractive woman."

"I suppose," she said grudgingly. "If you like that type." She took it out on the burger, tearing off a chunk and grinding it between her teeth.

A waitress appeared at my elbow. Name tag read Betty. "Whatcha need, honey?"

"What's good?"

"Burgers ain't bad," she said.

I ordered a cheeseburger and a Coke. Hold the fries.

I leaned over the table toward June. "I thought I heard that Tressman was married ." Her eyes widened, so I kept at it. "Because if you don't mind me saying . . . when I saw him today, he surely had the look of a man on the prowl." Eyes wider. Chewing faster. "I could be wrong, of course . . . and you know . . . woman like that . . . who could blame him?"

Her expression suggested that she might grab me by the ears and take the next bite out of my face. "In name only," she said through her teeth.

"Excuse me?"

"They're married in name only." She checked the booth for spies. "She mostly lives in Seattle with her sister. Mark goes there on weekends."

"Not very romantic," I commented.

"He can't leave her. It's all hers."

"What's all hers?"

"The big house. The money. Everything. It all belongs to his wife. If Mar . . . Mr. Tressman leaves her, he's left with nothing but some worthless property his parents left him."

She filled me in on what a manipulative bitch Barbara Tressman was. How she'd never allowed poor Mark Tressman to mingle his meager resources with hers and thus create a "community property situation," as she called it. I kept sympathizing and looking for a button to push. I should have just shut up and listened instead.

I shook my head sadly. "Shame to have to live that way."

She went from angry to the verge of tears in about seven seconds. "Yes . . . it is." She dropped her half-eaten burger into her plate and looked away from me. She brought her napkin up to her face, changed her mind and flung it on top of the burger.

Before I could come up with something soothing, she began to slide out of the booth. "Excuse me," she choked. "I've got to get back to work." Oops. Wrong button.

She never looked back my way as she paid her bill at the register and pushed her way out through the glass doors. I was still going back over the conversation, looking for hints as to where I'd screwed up, when Betty strolled over.

"You always have that effect on women?" she inquired casually.

"It's a cross to bear," I told her.

She dropped a cheeseburger onto the table in front of me. "Hereya go, honey," she said. "The all-American meal."

"If God didn't intend us to eat animals, they wouldn't be made of meat," I assured her. She started to agree and then pointed a segmented finger my way.

"Good," she said. "That's real good. I'll haveta remember that."

Her lips rehearsed the syllables as she ambled back toward the kitchen.

I had just finished my burger and was fishing for money in my pocket when a shrill voice attracted my attention. Emmett Polster. Standing at the counter talking to a satchel-faced woman with prematurely purple hair. He smiled at her, said something and started my way. I pulled myself into the recesses of the booth and turned my face toward the wall as if I were studying the wallpaper. I felt the bump as he sat down directly behind me. Only the partition between us.

When the waitress appeared, he ordered a grilled cheese sandwich, a cup of chicken noodle soup and a beer. I wondered if he always had a beer with his lunch or whether maybe he wasn't feeling a bit more stressed out than usual. I handed Betty a ten on her way by, then got up and followed her to the counter, collected my change and walked out the front door into the sunlight.

I turned left, going around in front of the lunch counter, so as not to risk Polster seeing me through the big window that ran the length of the dining room. As I walked, I pulled the cell phone from my pocket. Dialed Carl and then asked for Harold.

"Round up Ralphie," I said. "Get Boris to drive you. Meet me in that park in the center of town. Hurry. Ten minutes." I hung up and hustled for the car.

It took thirteen. I left the Malibu parked and got in the back of the Blazer with Ralph. "Park over there by the ice-cream parlor," I told Boris. "Back it in."

I turned to Ralph. "I want you to flop on somebody."

He gave me a great big grin. "Been years," he said.

"You're the master," I told him.

"The best," echoed Harold.

"Vat ees flop?"

"Who?" Ralphie asked.

I went over it slowly. Exactly how I wanted it done. Had Harold explain to him how to watch for the signal about where to pick them up. How he had to be close when they got to the emergency entrance so he could see Harold.

I gave Harold a handful of change. I pointed to a phone kiosk immediately to the right of the restaurant's front doors. "Go call somebody. He drives that new gray Honda..." I counted. "Six cars this side of the door."

"By the orange truck?" Ralph asked.

"Yeah."

I was too far away to read the plate, so I reached for my notebook. Tore out the page with Polster's number and handed it to Ralph. "Check, but I think that's it."

As soon as they'd checked the plate and were in place, I told Boris that I'd be back. To stay where he was until I got here.

Emmett Polster's back was toward the door, so he never

had a clue until I slid into the booth across from him. "Hey there, Mr. Polster," I said. "You give any more thought to what was wrong with Mr. Springer's cabins, or are you just waiting around to be embarrassed on Friday?" He tried to stay calm and was doing okay at it until he missed his mouth with the spoonful of soup, sending a rivulet of thin liquid rolling over his chin, down onto his lap. "Get the hell away from me," he squeaked.

He was shaky. His body vibrated as if an electric current coursed through his veins. "I thought small-town folks were renowned for being hospitable," I said.

He groped for his napkin and then wiped his chin.

"Get away from me."

"First one who comes forward usually gets the best deal."

His narrow eyes darted around like flies.

"Forward?"

"Yeah . . . and tells how certain members of city government conspired to drive J.D. Springer out of business."

"You're crazy."

"Might even save your ass as part of the deal."

He moved so fast he scared me. In a second, he slid to the end of the booth, jumped to his feet and then turned and sprinted for the front door. He'd have made it, too, if the busboy hadn't had the aisle blocked with a silver cart.

Polster bowled through the cart like an NFL running back, pitching it over onto its side, spreading three shelves of cups and glasses, ashtrays, egg-stained plates and lipstick-smeared napkins out over the floor like a tidal wave.

For a second, it looked like Polster might maintain his balance and make his escape, but, alas, it wasn't to be. As he struggled for equilibrium, his right foot slipped on a half-eaten stack of pancakes, throwing him forward and down, until he came to rest with the upper half of his torso crammed under a table occupied by a pair of elderly women.

From there on, things got pretty hectic. Polster wiggled

out from under the old women and struggled to his feet. He had a ketchup stain on the front of his jacket and a paper napkin attached to the sole of his left shoe when he started for the door, pointing at me and screaming. "You stay the hell away from me, you hear? The hell away."

His voice rang in the air for quite a while after he was gone. A great many eyes seemed to be pointed my way, so I tried to look nonchalant and unhurried in my exit. I was halfway to the door when I ran into Betty. "You're hell on business," she said.

"Many are called, but few are chosen," I said cheerily.

At that moment, Harold came bursting in through the front doors.

"Jesus . . . somebody call 911. There's been an accident."

I stepped aside and let the crowd beat me out the door. By the time I pushed my way to where I could see, Ralph and Harold were well into the routine. Ralph was on his back, his face a mask of agony, his limbs shaking and contorted. Harold was lamenting at full volume. ". . . and this guy here just run 'im down like a dog . . ." He pointed at Emmett Polster, who sat white-faced on a concrete parking divider, his chin buried in his hands. "Just goin' like hell, not paying any attention . . . oh god, look at 'im . . . where the hell is that ambulance?" Somebody said, "It's on the way. Merla called 'em." Ralphie was flopping around like a trout on a riverbank, his nearly toothless mouth bellowing to the heavens.

Ralph's got a trick hip. Double-jointed or something. He can turn it out to the side at an ungodly angle. Used to make a decent living getting hit by tourists in rental cars. Many the traveler to the Emerald City has thanked his stars that the old geezer took the two hundred bucks and limped off into the sunset. As the sound of a siren became audible above the buzz of the crowd, Harold went into the finale. He crawled across the pavement, pulled back Ralph's coat and pointed at the impossibly aligned hip.

"Jesus . . . look," he cried. The crowd sucked air.

A woman's voice said, "I'm gonna be sick."

I skirted the crowd, crossing the highway half a minute before a red and white aid car came rocketing up the road.

I stopped by Boris. "Just stay close and meet them wherever Harold tells you. Then get them back to the ranch in a hurry."

"Amazeeeing," he said with a smile.

30 "YOU WERE RIGHT," NARVA SAID. "A CLASSIC PENCIL dick. Thinks he's God's gift to women." She pulled a black leather day planner from her purse. "I felt bad about what you wanted me to do until I met the guy. What a sleaze. Trying to tell me he and his wife have an arrangement. We're having dinner tomorrow night."

I told her about how Tressman had canceled his date with June.

"What an asshole," she said.

She leafed through the day planner. "The non-Indian property is owned by four parties." Turned another page. "Rough and Ready, Inc., owns the five hundred acres that adjoin the ocean. The estate of Frau Tressman two hundred. Gretchen Peabody owns a hundred sixty-five acres. And Nancy Weston the other hundred. That adds up to . . . nine hundred sixty-five acres."

"Plus the thirty-five for the homestead."

"A round thousand, then."

"What's Rough and Ready, Inc., and who's Gretchen Peabody?"

"Rough and Ready . . ." She licked her index finger and turned the page. "That one's interesting. That's the original name of the town. Back in the 1870s. Used to be . . . that same thousand acres was the land that was originally incorporated as the city of Rough and Ready, Washington. Lasted two

years, then they gave it up and moved the town to its present
location."

"So who owns it?"

"The estate of Hattie Sparks," she said.

"Who is?"

"No way to tell. Nobody has ever filed for the estate. As
a matter of fact . . ."—she flipped the page—"four months
from now—May tenth—if still unclaimed, the estate reverts
to the state of Washington."

"Gretchen Peabody?"

"I didn't have time. They close the office at four o'clock.
But"—she held up a finger—"it's also interesting that two
years ago a total of eleven people, not four, owned that block
of property. The four present players purchased three of the
plots for cash and foreclosed on three others." She read me
a list of names and the number of acres they'd owned. She
explained how the four remaining principals had each ap-
proximately doubled their holdings in a period of twenty-
seven months. "Looks like they ran the same delinquent tax
number on those people that they did on your friend," she
said.

"Until the last holdout was Ben Bendixon and his thirty-
five-acre homestead," I said. Which led right back to the
question of why Bendixon would repeatedly refuse offers in
the three-hundred-thousand-dollar range and then, out of the
blue, sell out to J.D. for a third of the price.

She closed the book. "Question is, why bother?" she said.
"This town barely has real estate values, Leo. You can buy
anything in this valley for ten cents on the dollar. Compa-
rable undeveloped property, no utilities, no access, is going
for three hundred an acre. Tops. The only valuable piece is
this one, because it's so unique and it has access and recre-
ational possibilities."

Shouting from outside in the yard: "Leo. Leo, ya gotta see
this," Ralph yelled.

Boris, the Boys and the Blazer had come rolling down the

driveway about a half hour after I'd arrived. Boris wearing an insane grin. Ralph wearing nothing but an ancient pair of argyle socks and a hospital gown. I dug through J.D.'s stuff and came up with a set of clothes that fit. I didn't figure J.D.'d mind. And as for Ralph, secondhand was about four hands sooner than he usually came into clothes, so he was as happy as a clam.

I could just see the top of Harold's head as he moved across the bottom of the boat ramp. Narva and I crossed the lawn. Boris had a fish on, or more accurately, the fish had Boris. He stood with his knees flexed, leaning back against the singing line, the pole bent nearly double. The pitch of the stretching line got higher.

"Loosen the drag," I shouted. He turned my way.

"Vat?"

I jogged down the ramp. Boris was moving away from me, giving ground as the big salmon tried to get around the corner and head back for the ocean. I worked my way among the rocks until I was in front of him, steadied the rod for a second and turned the silver knob on the side of the reel until the fish began to ratchet off some line. The rod straightened a bit and began to bounce at the tip as the fish shook his head. The line stopped singing. Only the rasp of the drag scratching above the sound of the water.

"When he runs, let him," I said to Boris. "The minute he stops, start pulling him in. Don't let him rest."

"Vat I got here?" he asked.

"Dinner," I said.

Twenty minutes later, he had whatever it was about half-way in when the RV showed up, Carl at the wheel, easing it slowly along the side of the house and then backing it up against the kitchen wall. Floyd, Kurtis and Robby piled out and joined the cheering section down on the riverbank. Carl used the hydraulic lift to lower himself onto the grass and then came purring over. I introduced him to Narva.

"What's he got on there?" he demanded.

"Probably a big king salmon," I said.

About thirty pounds. So fresh from the ocean, it still had a trio of sea lice attached to its sides. Boris knew how to clean fish, so I let him have at it. Carl and Robby were giving Narva the two-dollar tour of the RV. Kurtis was in his cabin taking a shower.

Floyd nudged me. "You on a roll with women, Leo. This one here's an even tighter-looking unit than the other one."

"Yeah," I said. "I'm having to beat 'em off with a stick."

Without charcoal, we had to burn wood in the barbecue for the better part of two hours before we worked up a bed of coals we could work with. I sliced the lemons, diced the garlic and then stuffed it all into the cleaned salmon, wrapped the whole thing in foil and stuck it on the grill. Twenty-five minutes a side. Robby cooked a batch of rice. Kurtis made a salad. The Boys commandeered the white plastic chairs from the front porches of the cabins. Just like regular folks.

We sat in a rough circle on the lawn. A perpetually adolescent private eye, two drunks, two thugs, two wiremen, a burglar and a call girl, eating salmon and salad and rice from paper plates and loving it. Drinking beer and talking about how you forget about the heavens when you live in the city. Pointing out stars and constellations to one another until Carl pulled a thick bone from his plate. Held it up for all to see.

"Good thing I didn't trust you," he said to me.

"Yeah . . . you're such a trusting soul," Robby said.

"Another illusion shattered," I added.

Floyd speared a forkful of salad. "Nobody in their right mind trusts anybody else."

"I do," said Ralph.

"My point exactly," said Floyd.

"Floyd's right," Kurtis offered. "As long as love is conditional, true trust isn't possible."

Floyd looked confused. "Did I say that?"

"You learn to trust your instincts," Narva said. "If you

learn to pay attention to your intuitions, the rest takes care of itself."

Floyd said, "I meant that what you do is to arrange your life so it's not an issue."

Kurtis shuddered. "How barren. What kind of life is that?"

"The kind where you stay alive," Floyd said.

"Family," Boris said around a mouthful. "You can only trust your family."

I was thinking of that old B. B. King line about how nobody loved him but his mama, and how she could be jivin', too, when Narva pointed her fork at me.

"What about you, Leo? You trust people?"

"I guess I'm in the middle somewhere. I figure you can trust the people you know to act like themselves."

"But people change," she said.

"Not fundamentally," Kurtis said. "They may cope more effectively, but they don't change in any real sense."

"Even when they cope worse, they're still the same," said Harold.

"See?" said Kurtis.

"Shit," said Carl. "I—"

An electronic cheep stopped him midphrase. Then another. Robby dropped his plate and hustled to the RV. Two more loud bird sounds. Narva looked confused. I held a finger to my lips. Robby's head poked out the door. "We've got company," he said in a hoarse whisper. "Five, maybe six targets."

Boris and Floyd sprinted for the corners of the cabin where they'd left their rifles. I took Narva, the Boys and Kurtis and stuffed then into the RV and then went into the house, got my automatic and doused the lights. I heard Robby's voice. "Six for sure."

I saw the blue muzzle flash before I heard the shot. The first slug ripped though the plastic covering the bedroom window and then slammed into an interior wall. I duck-walked into the bathroom, where I steadied my arm on the window ledge and let loose two rounds in the general direction of the woods. And then blue dots danced all along the edge of the cut amid the sounds of high-powered ammo tearing into wood, and then all hell broke out as Floyd and Boris cut loose, firing tracers in a deadly stream of green light, filling the air with the sharp sounds of their fire. I took aim and let go with two more rounds. Boris moved his fire along the tree line like a hose. I heard a scream, high-pitched and shrill like a woman's and then the shooting from the woods stopped, the claps of gunfire replaced by a series of shouts and the sound of broken branches and the guttural grunts of strain as our would-be attackers fought their way uphill through the forest. Floyd emptied another clip. This time well over their heads. Boris reloaded and sprayed the tree line again. When he finished, and the air settled back into place, the sounds of slamming doors and racing engines could be vaguely heard from up on the road. Boris had that crazy smile again. "I doan teenk dey coming back," he said.

31 |

MARK TRESSMAN HELD THE PHONE CLOSE TO HIS MOUTH, HIS knuckles tight and white on the receiver. "Get a hold of yourself, Emmett. Nobody dragged you into this." He listened intently for a moment. "Don't even talk that way," he said quickly. "You listen to me . . . no . . . I said no." Listening. "Of course you can . . . now you listen to me . . ." Took a deep breath and set the receiver back in the cradle. Picked it up again. Put it back down. It rang.

"Yeah. I just spoke to him."

Robby handed me another set of earphones and pointed to Nancy Weston on the screen. "He's out of control, Mark. You know he had an accident. Hit some man out in front of the Country Corner."

"I heard."

"Something has to be done."

"What's that supposed to mean?"

She put a hand to her throat; her voice rose. "What it means is that I've spent some of my prime years here. Doing my end. Putting this together."

"As have we all," Tressman said.

"Which is why something has to be done. I'm not getting stuck here, Mark. Loomis is my ticket out of here and I'm taking it."

On one screen, Nancy Weston banged the phone down hard. On the other monitor, Mark Tressman winced, depressed the button and dialed. Robby zoomed the camera in. Last four numbers were 9595.

"We need to talk," Tressman said.

Carl rolled back from the control console. "I hear sphincters tightening."

"First call was Polster."

"You always had him made for the weak link."

"Question is, will he blow up before Friday?" I said.

I walked to the back of the RV, popped open the door and stepped outside. Deep gray clouds rolled in from the west. The air was thick with moisture, which collected on the cheeks like dew. Floyd, Boris and the Boys were back at the homestead. After the scene yesterday, the Boys were used up. No way I could let anybody catch sight of them again. Kurtis was down in room nine watching television. Narva was back at the Records office, trying to get a line on Rough and Ready, Inc., and Gretchen Peabody.

TUESDAY 9:53 A.M.   CAMERA 1—TRESSMAN

Tressman leaned back in his chair. Folding and unfolding his fingers over his chest. Nathan Hand was parked in the same chair Narva had occupied yesterday.

"I think Emmett's going to be a problem," Tressman said.

"Coming from you, that makes me nervous," Hand said.

"He said something this morning to the effect that whoever comes clean first can expect the best treatment from the law."

Hand pulled his hat from his head and put it over his knee. "He said that?"

"Unfortunately, he did."

"You know he had an accident yesterday."

"I heard."

"Old guy he hit disappeared from the hospital," Hand said.

Tressman sat forward. "We don't have any liability, do we?"

Nathan Hand reached into his shirt pocket and pulled out a small piece of paper. "Not unless you consider this a liability," he said.

"What's that?"

"It was in the pocket of the old guy's pants."

"The one Emmett hit?"

Hand nodded and tossed the paper onto the desk. Tressman read out loud. "New gray Honda Civic. Nine eight two. Dee dee gee."

"That's Emmett's car," Hand said.

"Why would he be carrying this?"

"You tell me," Hand said.

They sat staring at one another for a minute. Tressman began to nod his head.

"The possibilities here aren't good," he said finally.

Hand thought it over and then reached for the phone. Robby zoomed in. Hand turned the phone his way. "Shit," muttered Robby.

"We're going to have to play our hand," the sheriff said into the phone.

I looked over at Robby and Carl. Head-shaking. Not the mayor. Not Weston. They were all accounted for on screen. Sure as hell not Polster.

"Because Emmett's coming apart." He listened with a disgusted expression on his face. "And don't you know I'm pretty darn tired of hearing about it, too." He didn't listen long. "Yeah and maybe some damn fools just put way too much stock in their damn pets. You act like I was supposed to know." Silence. "You're right," he said after a moment. "Let's stay in the present." He listened again. "Just the way we talked about yesterday. It takes care of both problems at the same time." Silence, as Hand listened intently.

"I'd sure like to know who's on the other end," Carl said.

"Got movement on car five. That's Polster," Robby said.

The camera at the top of the parking lot followed Polster's Honda a third of the way down the street. He signaled and turned right. Out of sight.

"He lives about three blocks west of there," I said.

"I was him, I'd lock the doors," said Robby.

"While I was calling for airline tickets," Carl added.

No matter how I massaged it, Polster wasn't my problem. As far as I was concerned, no matter what happened, he wouldn't be getting anything he didn't deserve. You betray a trust and you put yourself into a world where you can't expect to rely on anything more tangible than your own animal cunning.

I got to my feet. "Anybody want coffee?" Robby belched a no. Carl rubbed his diaphragm. "That shit Monty makes . . . ," he said, "I'll pass."

Wetter outside now. Hard to tell whether it was misting or whether the water was part of the air. Either way you ended up wet without the sensation of something falling from above. I kicked through the carpet of leaves and let myself into the back door of the motel. Monty was in his red leather lounger, playing machine gun TV, flipping through the channels so fast I wasn't able to identify anything except a snippet of the Home Shopping Network. He settled on *Baywatch*.

"Have you got a local phone book I can look at?" I asked.

"Under the motel counter."

I stepped out into the motel. Worked my way back to the Ls. Ran down the page with the tip of my index finger. Nope. Leonard, then Lopez.

I replaced the phone book and retraced my steps back toward Monty.

"You know a family named Loomis around here?"

"Nope," he said.

I started for the back door. "Thanks."

"Ain't a family; it's a them."

I stopped. "What?"

"Loomis ain't a family; it's a company."

"What kind of company?"

"Somethin' to do with land and real estate."

"And they're local?"

"Hell no," he said impatiently. "Outta Chicago."

"How do you know all this?"

He muted the TV and struggled to his feet. " 'Cause that's who pays Mr. Pinkerton's bill every time." He pushed past me and limped out into the motel, where he pulled a green plastic box out from under the counter. He pawed through a pile of receipts until he found what he was looking for. He handed it to me. A credit card receipt. Michael Pinkerton. Two nights. Room nine. One hundred bucks. Corporate credit card . . . Loomis International. "Who's this Pinkerton guy?" I asked.

"Been coming to town damn near every week for near a year."

"What for?"

"Back when, the damn fool was trying to do business with the Indians." He turned his head long enough to give me a disgusted look. "These days he's got some kinda deal goin' on with the bigwigs in City Hall."

"How do you know he's from Chicago?"

"He tol' me so. Said it was nice to be someplace he wasn't freezin' his ass off. Tol' me Chicago was colder than a well digger's ass this time of year."

"He always stay two nights?"

"Sometimes longer. Don't sleep here much, though."

"He rents a room but doesn't sleep in it?"

"Hardly never." He anticipated my next question. "Got no idea. He drives off in some rental car, and I don't see him again till the next day." He waved a hand. "None of my damn business what he's doin' anyway."

As I stepped out the back door, I had my first lucid moment in weeks. I was kicking through the sodden leaves when I got a hurried little coming attraction of a movie where all of this made sense. I think I may have said, "Shit," as I started for the RV, but I can't be sure.

Carl was where I left him. Robby was gone. "Nothin' new," he said.

"Narva left her cell number. What did we do with it?"

He handed me a torn scrap of paper. I dialed. Voice mail. She probably didn't want it ringing in the Records office. I waited for the tone and left my message.

"Where's Robby?"

"Wiring nine."

I grabbed my jacket from the settee.

"Where you going?" he asked.

"First I'm going to desecrate a grave. Then I'm leaving the country."

"Probably best in that order," Carl said.

They sat on the pile of rocks they'd just moved. Harold wiped his brow with his sleeve and then blew his nose down into the grass. Ralph downed a bottle of Coors in one swig and then reached into the cooler for another. Floyd and I dug carefully, probing the soil with our shovels, as if neither of us wanted to be the one to find anything.

We found the collar first. Moved one way and found vertebrae. Moved the other, found the head. I put on the blue rubber gloves from the house and carefully worked the skull out of the ground. The lower jaw was now a separate piece, but it didn't matter. Didn't need a pathologist, either. I turned the skull toward Floyd.

"Ah," Floyd said. "The rare and elusive three-eyed dog."

32 "THIS IS THE MAN WHO COME AND TOOK CLAUDIA AND the kids back to their people," Juanita said. The guy gestured to the chair at the right of the desk. I took a seat. He wore his hair long. Parted down the middle and braided. Broad pockmarked face stretching a pair of bifocals to the max. Juanita said he was the tribe's legal advisor.

"Leo Waterman," I said.

"Paul Flowers. At least that's the English version," he said.

Juanita grabbed the doorknob. "I gotta go. The kids are coming in for lunch."

He folded his hands on the desk. "What can I do for you, Mr. Waterman?"

"Can I tell you a story?"

"Storytelling is an important tradition among the Hoh people."

I started all the way back on that Thanksgiving afternoon and ran it up to the present. He never moved his hands, and as far as I could tell, he never blinked. He sat there like a rock until I was finished. "And then . . . about an hour ago," I said, "I remembered what Juanita said about the Lummi trying to throw money at the Hoh and I realized that what she probably meant wasn't Lummi but Loomis."

He turned his head and looked out toward the ocean. His braids were held in place by blue rubber bands. "Like any organization, the tribe has politics," he said. "There are as many positions as there are people. But . . . you know . . . for the sake of conversation, let's say that the points of view can be divided into the liberal and conservative elements within the tribe." He looked back my way. "The conservative element—of which I would surely be said to be a member—we look at doing business outside the tribe as a necessary evil. I think it's safe to say that we would prefer to be left alone to live our lives and transmit our values in any way we see fit." He stuck out his lower lip. "Ideally, I suppose, without any outside influences whatsoever."

"Pretty tough here at the millennium," I said.

"To be sure," he said. "Which leads us to the more liberal outlook."

"Which says?"

"Which says that there's a world of opportunity out there. They look at tribal casinos and fireworks stands and cigarette outlets and liquor stores and all they see is the money falling into their pockets."

"Hard to ignore."

He sighed. "Impossible."

"You seem to have stemmed the tide rather well," I said.

He nodded solemnly. "We are still very conservative. The reservation is dry. We don't gamble or sell cigarettes or fireworks." He took off his glasses and rubbed the bridge of his nose. "It's not going to last," he said. "We came within eight votes of leasing nine hundred acres of our land for ninety-nine years."

"To Loomis?"

He nodded. "Next time—and I have no doubt that there will be others—next time, the temptation will be too great."

"What did they want the property for?"

A wry smile bent his lips. "They don't say. Loomis is merely an acquisition firm. They specialize in putting together industrial and commercial properties and then reselling them to principals. They claim not to have a customer, but to be buying purely on spec."

"Claim?"

"Their motives were obvious."

I waited; he didn't disappoint. "Against the advice of their elders, twice in the past five years members of the more liberal elements of the tribe have insisted that we sue both the state and federal governments over petty matters."

"Over?"

He had to mull it over. "Ostensibly, the issues were such gum-on-the-shoe things as the right to fish our tribal waters in any way we saw fit. Or the right to locate the tribal landfill in the area of our choice."

"But really it was over . . ." I pressed.

"Sovereignty."

"Of the tribe?"

"And its land."

"And?"

"On both occasions, we won."

"You don't seemed pleased."

He got to his feet and walked over to the window. "Like most things, sovereignty is a double-edged sword. On one hand, it means that we are no longer burdened by the vast majority of the rules and regulations of the dominant culture." He sat down on the wide windowsill and picked at the twill of his trousers. "Which of course means that the dominant culture is no longer necessarily required to be burdened by ours." He threw up a hand. "A subtlety which escaped a great many of our more impetuous members."

I decided to lay my own burden down. "I'm lost," I said.

He nodded. "What I'm saying, Mr. Waterman, is that someone in Loomis's legal department was quite shrewd. Somebody read about our legal victories and quite cleverly reached the conclusion that any piece of property which abutted only the Hoh reservation was not subject to environmental regulation of any kind."

"So whoever owned it could do whatever they wanted with the land."

"Precisely."

"A copper smelter."

He nodded.

"A nuclear landfill."

And again.

"A maximum-security prison."

"As the law stands now, not only are we hardly in a position to litigate, but the local dominant culture would welcome virtually any enterprise that provided jobs and added to the local tax base."

Flowers was right. The locals would line up for galley slave positions.

"How much did they offer?"

"Ten thousand dollars an acre."

"Nine million dollars."

"Divided by two hundred thirty-five members of the tribe."

"Which comes to . . ."

"Just under thirty-nine thousand dollars per person."

He read my mind. "That figure was for land to which there is no access. No road. No services of any kind. The parcel to which Mr. Springer's property was joined, having such amenities, would be worth, say . . . half again that much."

A shiver ran down my spine as I did the math. I'd walked in knowing who and how; now I knew why. If Flowers was right, that made the thousand acres next door worth at least fifteen million dollars. And the cut wasn't by two hundred or so. No . . . now the cut was down to four or five. And all of a sudden murder became a viable option. All you had to do was get rid of one pesky fisherman whose sin was to show up in the wrong place at the wrong time with a dream he wasn't willing to compromise.

33 FLOYD CAUGHT THE BOW LINE AND TIED IT OFF. "YOU got a call," he said.

I stepped out of the boat onto the floating dock. "Who?"

"The very put together Miss Haynes. Said last she heard you was staying here. Wants to have a word with you. I told her to come on by. That I was a much more charming fellow than the likes of you, but she insisted."

"She leave a number?"

He handed me a scrap of paper. "Thanks," I said and stepped off the dock onto the boat ramp. We walked up the incline together. "Where's everybody else?"

"All that rock moving gave the Booze Brothers a thirst."

"Sunrise gives those guys a thirst."

"They ran out of beer. Started making a pain of themselves. I sent them to town with Boris. They promised to stay in the car. It was either that or kick some ass."

"I'll get them out of here as soon as I can," I promised.

"You get what you wanted from the Indians?"

"Yeah," I said. "Problem is, I don't know if it's going to do us any good."

"Why's that?"

"Because we've only got till Friday to get somebody to break."

I pulled the cell phone from my pocket and dialed.

"Chamber of Commerce, Ramona Haynes."

"I understand you were looking for me."

"Indeed I was," she said. "You're hard to find."

"I'm told that good men are always hard to find."

"Or vice versa," she said quickly.

Suddenly I seemed to be fresh out of snappy rejoinders. Good thing she picked up the slack. "I've thought it over and decided you owe me lunch for keeping you out of jail the other day."

"It is the least I could do, isn't it?"

"We'll call it a down payment," she said.

We settled on the Stevens Falls Bar and Grille at one.

"Glad to see you've regained your sanity," Floyd said.

"I just want to thank her for saving our bacon the other day," I said.

Somehow, Floyd didn't look convinced.

I cleaned up. Brushed my teeth. Put on a clean shirt and a fresh pair of jeans and made it downtown with three minutes to spare.

The place was packed. Maybe a dozen people were milling around the lobby waiting for tables. I excused my way into the dining room and found her sitting at a window table to the right of the door. She wore an emerald-green silk blouse tucked into a pair of blue jeans. Cowboy boots and a silver-trimmed western belt. Earrings matched the blouse.

"Hey," she said. We shook hands as I took a seat. Her hair had more red highlights than I remembered. She made a face. "I really need to use the little girls' room," she said. "I was afraid we'd lose the table." She got to her feet. "Be right back."

She was back before I worked my way to the bottom of the menu.

"Thanks for holding down the fort," she said.

"My pleasure."

"How's fishing?"

I told her about Boris catching the salmon. Left out the gunfire. Poor ambience.

She ordered a chicken Caesar salad and an iced tea. I opted for a Reuben sandwich and a root beer. "You didn't tell me your family owned the mill," I said. She held her glass in two hands and looked at me over the tea. "It's not the kind of story that brightens anybody's day." She put the glass on the table in front of her. "So I imagine you heard about my father shooting himself."

"Yeah," I said. "I'm sorry" sounded stupid, but I said it anyway.

"He felt responsible," she said. "For everyone. For the town." She told me the whole story. How the auctioneers took everything. The mill, the equipment, the family home, his cars, the cabin on San Juan Island, twenty thousand acres of replanted timber. How they even took the clothes in her mother's closet, where they'd hung untouched since her death five years before. How it was just too much for her father to bear. Before I could say something inane, a phone began to ring. We had one of those "is it mine or is it yours?" moments.

"It's you," she said.

I plucked the phone from my belt and put it to my ear. The voice was a shrill tenor. Familiar. Ragged. On the edge of control. "This Waterman?"

I said it was. "This is Emmett Polster," he said. He made a noise like a whimper. I could hear his ragged breathing. "You want to know what happened to Springer, you meet me. I'll tell you." He seemed to gag on the words. "I can't take any chances," he said. "You meet me up at the history marker. On top of Linden Hill." It sounded like he was having trouble breathing. As he gave me directions, he repeatedly stopped to catch his breath. "Two o'clock," he wheezed. "It'll take you an hour." He hung up. I checked my watch. One-fifteen. I hated it.

She read my face. "Trouble?"

"I've got to go," I said. "Sorry." I got to my feet, pulled a twenty from my pocket and dropped it on the table.

"I don't believe it," she said. "I finally get you cornered, and—"

"I'll make it up to you," I said.

She narrowed her blue eyes. "You promise?"

"Scout's honor."

"I'll hold you to it," she said.

"I'll look forward to it," I said. " 'Bye."

On my way to the door, I passed the waitress with our order. She stopped and watched, openmouthed, as I trotted out the door.

I knew Polster was squirrelly, but I hadn't figured he'd break this soon. And while I didn't like the idea of going way out in the boonies by myself, it couldn't be helped. Going back to the homestead for a bodyguard would take the better part of a half hour I didn't have. I'd been picking at the scabs of people's lives, trying to get somebody to bleed, and now that I had my candidate, there was no way I could let it slide. I started the car and pulled out into traffic.

I followed Polster's directions. Out of town toward the east. Couple miles past the Chamber of Commerce A-frame. State Road 1174. Linden Hill Road. Two lanes. Oil over gravel. Potholes big enough to swallow the car. I moved in a zigzag pattern as I avoided the worst of the craters.

For the first ten miles or so, rustic homes, some little more than shacks, dotted the sides of the road. After that, as I began to wind up the side of the mountain, all signs of habitation ceased. I pulled the car to the side of the road, got out and opened the trunk. I took off my jacket and slipped into the shoulder holster. The weight of the .40-caliber automatic felt reassuring against my side. I covered the gun with my jacket and continued bouncing up the road.

Polster was right. It took me a little more than fifty minutes from the time I left the highway until I spotted the stone marker at the top of the mountain. In all that time, I only passed one dwelling, a ramshackle family farm nestled in a break between the hills. A series of gray, leaning buildings that would have been every bit as at home in some Appalachian "holler" as it was among the stumps and scrub oak of the Pacific Northwest. Chickens darted about the front yard and a pair of goats danced on hind legs as they plucked the last withered apples from a tree by the side of the house. Satellite dish.

The bronze plaque on the marker read, "On this spot in 1888, Captain Horace Framer and a detachment of the Ninth Cavalry from Fort Dungeness, although vastly outnumbered, defeated and dispersed a hostile band of Makaw Indians, thus insuring the safety of settlers on the Northern Olympic Peninsula." No Polster.

By two-thirty, I had the plaque memorized, and Polster was yet to show. By three, a thick fog was beginning to settle off the mountaintop and I was fresh out of patience. I backed the car out into the road, managed a three-point turn and started back down, suppressing a chill, hoping that Polster was just late and that maybe I'd see him on my way down.

As I passed the farm, I rolled down the window. Suddenly the front door banged open. An old woman carried an old-fashioned washtub out into the front yard, where she threw the gray water to the ground with a slap. She stood for a moment gazing at me as I drove slowly by, then turned and hurried back inside.

I was still better than ten miles from the highway when I rounded a bumpy left-hand corner and came upon a familiar sight. The Studebaker was trying to back into a small turnout cut into the bank, but didn't have the power. As the truck lurched backward, a light flickered: A small shower of sparks fell to the ground. I heard the motor cough and then shut down, leaving the truck half in, half out of the road. Whitey got out and pulled his cap from his head. He slapped it against his leg and then jammed it back on.

I pulled the Malibu to a stop behind the truck and got out.

He did a double-take. "What the hell are you doin' up here?" he asked.

"It's a long story," I said.

He stood with his hands on his hips, his body language telling me to make it good, but I wasn't in the mood to admit having been on a snipe hunt, so I changed the subject.

"You having that same problem where the battery won't stay charged?"

"Yeah."

"I think I saw it," I said. "When you backed up."

"Saw what?"

"Your short."

I walked over to the back of the truck. "Right here," I said, pointing to a recess in the rear bumper.

"That's the old backup lights. They don't work. Not even wired."

"This one does. It was flickering the whole time you were trying to back the truck into the turnout. I thought I might have even seen a couple of sparks."

Whitey lay down in the road and scooted under the truck. I heard him sputter as mud dropped to the pavement. I listened as he poked around.

"Well, goddamn," I heard him mutter. "Hey, ah . . ."

"Leo," I said.

"Yeah, Leo . . . in the bed in the toolbox . . . would you give me the dykes with the red handles and that roll of electrical tape?"

Two minutes later, he snaked out from under the truck and brushed himself off. "I checked the taillight about twenty times," he said. "No idea that little light was still wired. Must run under the bed somewhere."

"Before we start congratulating ourselves, let's see if it works," I said.

Together, we put our backs on the tailgate and pushed the truck up the little rise, until it sat at the top of an incline. He hopped in. "We'll see soon enough," he said.

The truck began to roll downhill. I heard him pop the clutch and the hiss as the tires slid in the loose rock and then the smooth purr of the exhaust.

I walked back to the Malibu and headed down the hill after him. Twenty minutes later, he was waiting for me at the highway junction. He got out. So did I.

"It's charging like hell," he said. "Thanks."

"No problem," I said, "but do me a favor will you? Next time somebody tells you to run down and set somebody's house on fire, you tell 'em to go to hell. Okay?" His natural inclination was to go with his stupid act. He looked down at his boots, kicked a stone with his toe and then suddenly pulled off his glasses.

He pinned me with his white eyes. "I poured it mostly on the ground," he said.

"I know."

He replaced the shades, pulled himself up to his full height and took a couple of steps back in my direction. "I'm not about burnin' up anybody's babies," he said in a tone of voice that invited me to challenge the statement if I dared. Fortunately, there was no need.

"I know you're not," I said. "Otherwise you wouldn't have gone back after the others were gone and put out the fire."

Above the sunglasses, his head wrinkled like a washboard.

"How . . ." he started. "I never told a single . . ."

"It's the only thing makes sense," I said. "If it wasn't the Springers who grabbed the extinguisher and put out the flames, then, strange as it seems, it must have been one of the shooters. Anything else requires either one hell of a coincidence or direct alien intervention."

He smiled. "My mama'd vote for the aliens." I wondered if she knew Monty.

I gave him the thumbs up and stood and watched as he

pulled out onto the highway and the sound of the truck faded to nothing.

I got in and followed Whitey back toward town, feeling a tad better at having solved the mystery of the reluctant arsonist. That probably explains why I pulled into Linc's Texaco station when I still had half a tank. He came skittering out of the station, wiping his hands. I stepped out of the car. "Fill 'er up," I said. "And let's you and me finish that discussion we started a while back about where it was Mr. Springer got that unleaded gasoline from. Except now we know he didn't buy it himself . . . so . . ."

The last part was wasted. He ran with long strides, his bottom low to the ground. Slammed the station door. I took this to mean the gas was self-service, filled her up, and then went looking for Linc, who seemed to have a disturbing propensity to come up missing at pivotal moments. No Linc. Both the station and the office behind were empty. Gas was eight-eighty. Much as it pained me to leave him a tip, I put a ten on top of the pump and weighed it down with a small rock.

They sent the first team. No rookies, no would-be pensioners. Three cars. Six burly state policemen in body armor. The engine roar pulled my head up. The first cruiser slid to a stop about ten feet in front of me. In a heartbeat, the officers were crouched behind the doors, squinting down sights at me. "On the ground."

I put my hands over my head and dropped to my knees. A hand grabbed the back of my neck, pushing my face into the ground; a pair of knees landed in the middle of my back, driving the air from my lungs, leaving me gasping and shaking my head for breath.

"Leo Waterman, you are being arrested and charged with the murder of Emmett Polster. Anything you say can and will be used against you in a court of law. You have a right to an attorney. In the event that you are unable to afford an attorney, one will . . ."

They didn't mess around. They rolled me over, right then and there, all six of them put me in a waist chain and shackle apparatus. I rode the fifty miles to Port Townsend bent nearly double, the handcuffs on my wrists attached to an eyebolt in the floor of the cruiser. I concentrated on my breathing. Counting in and out and trying to sink inside my skin, until the metal on my flesh stopped burning.

34 I WAS ON SUICIDE WATCH. THEY CAME BY EVERY FIF-teen minutes to make sure that I hadn't decided to cash my chips. Orange paper jumpsuit. White paper slippers. They'd lengthened my wrist chains so I could shrug myself in and out of the jumpsuit, but not enough so I could wipe my ass. They said I'd get over it.

Jed came at nine-fifteen that night. I heard him before I saw him. "This isn't a hospital, Trooper . . . what is it? . . . Franklin. There's no visiting hours for an attorney to see his client." A door clanged. The voice was getting nearer. "You must be accustomed to nursing homes . . . what? How many years have you to go until retirement anyway?" He stopped in front of my cell. The turnkey was fifty or so, working his way toward pear-shaped. First cop I'd seen all night who didn't look like an NFL linebacker. Jed waved a hand at the door. "Well . . . come on . . . open it up."

"No sir," the cop deadpanned. "He's on suicide watch."

"A client of mine? On suicide watch? Are you crazy? It's your local prosecutor you should be keeping an eye on."

"I've got my orders."

Before they could start a full squabble, I said, "Paper and pencil, please."

Jed picked right up on it, reaching in his suit coat pocket and coming out with an eelskin notepad and a black Monte Blanc fountain pen. I wrote: *#1 We need an absolutely secure* *place to talk. #2 Call this number. Find out what's going on. #3 Tell whoever answers that we're going nuclear.* I handed both items back to Jed. His face remained impassive as he tucked them back into his coat.

It took an hour and a half. They had to get Billy Heffernen out of bed. He wasn't amused. What Captain William Heffernen *was* was a hard-ass cop. Fair but completely by the book. If you were looking for sympathy, you better look in the dictionary. Before going out to duel with Jed, he stopped by my cell. He wore his trooper's hat with the strap tight across the very point of his chin, like a Paris Island drill sergeant. He walked to the bars. I stood up and went over to meet him. "Well?" His eyes were trying to bore a hole in the back of my head. I held his gaze. "I didn't kill anybody," I said.

"For Rebecca's sake, I hope not."

"You give me a little help, and maybe I can help you put this to bed."

His eyes never wavered. "If you wish to make a statement, I'll send for a stenographer."

I ignored him. "I need to know what Sheriff Hand did before he became sheriff. And I need the driving record of a guy named Ben Bendixon." I spelled it.

Billy Heffernen snorted once and marched off down the corridor.

At five to eleven, a pair of uniformed Blutos marched me down the hall to Billy's office. Seems Jed had refused the interrogation rooms, and the only other private space was the state police captain's office. They left me standing five feet inside the door, then turned and left. Jed beckoned me over.

"I called that number and delivered your message."

"What's going on?"

"The state cops threw everybody off the property. Ran warrant checks on everybody and of course Ralph and Harold had outstandings. Failure to appear on a failure to appear. Drunk and disorderly. The usual." He waved a hand. "They're already on their way back to King County. I called Evergreen Bonds to bail them out in the morning."

"What about—"

"Everybody else is over at the Twilight Zone, whatever that means. He said to tell you that Narva was running her number as we spoke and it was a sight to behold. Also that they caught a few more things you just had to see. They're holding tight."

"What—" I started.

"No," he said. "It's my turn. Let's talk murder."

"What have they got?"

"It's what *you've* got, and it's problems," he said.

"Such as?"

"Such as about forty eyewitnesses who say you threatened and chased the deceased a couple of days ago."

"Sad but true." I told him the story. "What else?"

"Such as a .38-caliber police special revolver, registered to you, found in a drainage ditch a block down from the decedent's house. Seems the attacker used the gun to bludgeon the decedent and the weapon shows traces of blood. They're running tests on both the blood and the gun as we speak."

"Not good," I said.

"Talk to me," he said.

I did. How last time I actually saw the .38 was the night I offered it to Narva, before we went into Spooner's house to fetch Misty McMahon. How I'd put it back in the gym bag, which I last saw on the night Rebecca and I went over the cliff. I clearly remember reaching down for the shirt to bandage her arm and seeing the bag in the rubble.

His turn to say, "Not good." He leaned in close. "And what's all this about a secure place to talk? We could have been doing this an hour ago."

I checked the walls and ceiling. Over the past couple of days, I'd noticed an interesting phenomenon developing. The more time I spent clandestinely watching people who had no idea their privacy had been compromised, the more paranoid I was becoming. Something karmic, I supposed. I lowered my voice. "I guess I'm getting a little paranoid about . . . you know . . . electronic eavesdropping."

He leaned closer. I put my mouth about an inch from his ear and, without naming names, told him everything. As I spoke, his mouth opened like a drawbridge.

"You've got all this on tape?"

I nodded.

"Audio or video?"

"Both."

"Are these devices still operational and in place?"

"Oh yeah."

His lips curled into something between a sneer and a smile.

"No way it's admissible evidence. Not now. Not ever."

"I know."

"As a last resort, though," he began, "as trading material—"

I interrupted him. "It's not the last resort," I said. "I might have an alibi."

"For two-forty-eight this afternoon?"

He read my surprise. "Stevens Falls police got a call about shots fired. Exactly two-forty-eight." I wasn't surprised. It made sense.

"Yeah. For exactly that time."

"Tell me."

I did. He was incredulous. "Why in hell didn't you tell the cops?"

"Because what they'd do is call out to Stevens Falls, send Nathan Hand out to bring him in for them, which I'm pretty much willing to guarantee wasn't going to get my ass out of here anytime soon."

"So . . . then the sheriff's a question as far as you're concerned."

"No question. The sheriff's a player. Got pictures of that, too."

"But you're not sure whether your alibi will come through for you."

"He's a local. Part of the same group we've tangled with a couple of times. I figure it's a crapshoot. He may and he may not."

"And if not?"

"Then people in high places are going to start getting anonymous videotapes in the mail, and you're going to be defending me on a whole raft of other charges."

Nine o'clock the next morning. French toast and scrambled eggs, my ass. The oiled cow flops and the puddle of yellow bile were right where the turnkey had left them at seven-thirty. A pair of necks I hadn't seen before came waddling down the corridor, opened the cell door and handed me a white plastic bag filled with my civilian clothes. Took me by the elbows and levitated me down the hall and around the corner to the showers, then deposited me back in my cell and disappeared.

Ten-fifteen. The same pair left me unfettered as they escorted me up to the third floor. A lineup. Me and five bruiser cops standing cheek by jowl beneath the bright lights. Jed went postal. Either they had to give up their belts and shoelaces or I had to get mine back. Not only that but he demanded a couple of suspects who, as he put it, "don't look like the state's paying them to take steroids."

Eleven-twenty. I had laces in my sneakers and a belt holding up my pants. Two of the other guys in the lineup now looked human. We did the lineup cha-cha for the fans behind the one-way glass. Step up, step back, stand up, sit down, fight, fight, fight. Back to the cell. But still wearing my civvies, so I felt pretty good about the situation.

Noon. Straight up. I was busting the desk sergeant's balls. Making him double-check every piece of my personal belongings before I would sign the receipt. Just about the time I'd finished stuffing everything back into my pockets, the sergeant's eyes grew wide; he closed the window with a bang and double-timed it out of sight. I looked over my shoulder. Captain William Heffernen. Hat on even tighter than usual. Hands locked behind his back. Parade rest.

"I've got a district judge standing outside waiting for your release, Leo. Why is that?" I reckoned how maybe it was charisma. Billy was not amused.

"I've worked in the same district with the honorable Wayne Bigelow for twenty years, and in all that time, he's never said more than twenty words to me. Now all of a sudden we're on a first-name basis and he calls me every two hours for a progress report about you."

"Judge Bigelow and I are socially acquainted," I said.

He leaned back against the pale green concrete blocks. He had me in a bind. Billy had a bullshit meter second to none, and we both knew it. On the other hand, there was no slack in him. He wasn't going to wink at or ignore anything. Not jaywalking, not littering, not a thing. I had to be careful. I was still pondering my options when he said, "I hear you and Rebecca are having some problems."

If he was trying to push me off balance, he damn near succeeded. I felt the blood rise to my face. "I didn't realize my life was an open book," I said.

"We talk," he said.

I squeezed the words, "That's more than I can say," through my teeth and then broke up a wonderfully strained silence by asking, "She know I'm in here?" He moved his chin about an inch . . . up and down.

Billy gave me a break and changed the subject back to something easier to discuss—like murder. "I'm going to ask you a question, Leo, and I want an answer." He could tell he had my attention. "Have they got a bad cop in Stevens Falls?"

Having Billy Heffernen ask you about a bad cop was like

having your significant other ask you if her butt looks big in a certain pair of slacks. One of those conversations pretty much destined to go nowhere pleasant.

I hedged. "What gives you that idea?"

"The way you sat here all night until you could send your lawyer after your alibi on his own." He didn't wait for me to comment. "And the way this whole thing shakes down. It stinks to high heaven. One minute somebody hands us a case where we've got you dead to rights, and the next minute it comes apart. That's TV, Leo. The movies. That's not how the job goes."

"You're going to hate what I've got to say."

No expression whatsoever. "Well."

"Hand's dirty as hell. Hand and Deputy Russell for sure."

He blew air out through his nose. "How—" he started.

"I can't give you any details, Billy. But I'm telling you . . . he's dirty."

He read me chapter and verse about withholding evidence. I tried not to look bored. "How about, instead of threats, a little quid pro quo?" I said.

"Like?"

"Like you tell me what you found out about Bendixon and Hand."

He stared at me for a moment and then brought several sheets of paper out from behind his back. "Hand had no previous law enforcement experience whatsoever. The closest he ever came to the police was in 1995 when he was charged with negligent homicide in the death of one Alfred Klugeman." He looked up. I kept my face still and my mouth shut. "Seems the old guy refused to move from a building that had been sold out from under him. Hand worked security for the real estate company." Billy turned the page over. "According to witnesses, Klugeman was trying to elude Hand when he and his wheelchair went down twenty concrete stairs and broke his neck in three places." He snapped the pages with his fingers. "You read between the lines on the rest of it and it says they didn't have much of a case against Hand. The company settled out of court with the family. Hand got the gate along with everybody else connected with the acquisition. Top to bottom. No severance, no pension. No nothing."

"Bendixon?"

"Vehicular negligence. Last August. DWI. Blew a two-point-three. Lady in the other car lost a leg. Judge ruled he was too old for a state facility. He's on home detention." I pulled my notepad from my pocket. He read me the address.

"I told you you'd hate it."

He snorted. "I'd rather it was you," he said on his way out.

Behind me the window banged open. The desk sergeant handed me a receipt for my car. "You give that across the street and the officer will return your car." Bang.

Twelve-ten. Rebirth. I squeezed out the door, squinting in the bright light. Jed, Constance Hart, the Honorable Wayne Bigelow. Arm in arm, no less.

The judge clapped me on the shoulder. "For a while there, boy, I thought you were going to make me look bad." Jed offered his thanks to the judge. Constance Hart gave me a hug and whispered that Misty was coming home for the weekend.

Jed and I stood and watched as they meandered across the street toward the courthouse. "Nice job," I said to Jed.

"It was touch and go there for a while."

"Whitey needed convincing?"

He shook his head. "Oh no. Mr. Hunley was quite willing, even anxious to give you an alibi for the time in question. The question was whether or not the authorities were going to consider him to be a credible witness. Without his mother's cooperation, I'm not sure we'd be having this conversation."

"His mother?"

"Picked your car out of the parking lot and you out of a lineup."

I recalled the sound of the dishwater slapping onto the

ground and the moment of eye contact before she turned for the house.

"Said she knew it was after three, because Ricki Lake had already started."

And the satellite dish by the side of the house.

"You're not allowed to leave the state," Jed said.

"Wouldn't dream of it."

We shook hands and then hugged. "What now?" he asked.

"I'm going to see an old man about a dog."

35 "LANDED AT NORMANDY BEACH, YOU KNOW."

"Really."

"Was with Waverly Wray at Sainte-Mère-Église. Stopped the whole damn German Army, we did." He pinned me with his milky eyes, as if daring me to dispute his claim. "Stopped 'em cold. Turned the whole damn tide, right there."

Ben Bendixon was as bald as an egg. The dome shiny and freckled here and there with liver spots. He wore a white plastic transmitter on a left ankle so thin I was pretty sure he could pull his foot out of the thing if he chose. Must be how the cops kept track of his home imprisonment. "Fought the krauts building to building. Tanks'd blow a hole in the garden walls and we'd move from one to another."

I promised the granddaughter I wouldn't mention the accident. Seems he'd gotten shitfaced, run a stop sign and T-boned a woman from Vancouver, BC, who was down in the States visiting her sister. She'd lost a leg. Ben lost everything else. His insurance, his license, his freedom, and, according to his granddaughter, most of his will to live. She said he hadn't done much in the past eight months but sit upstairs in his room and rock and stare out the window. The way she figured it, if he was physically capable of killing himself, he would. But he wasn't, so she let him sit and rock and stare.

"Fought 'em over the rooftops and alleys." He gave a toothless grin. "Stayed in the same cellars at night sometimes.

Too damn cold to be fightin' at night. They stayed on their side. We stayed on ours. In the morning, it was back to the war."

"I wanted to ask you about J.D. Springer," I said.

He shook his head. "He wasn't there. Didn't serve with no Springer."

Before I could respond, the old man continued. "You don't forget the guys you served with. No sir. Ain't nothing in the rest of your life as real as those guys."

His ancient eyes again dared me to disagree. "The guys you fought with . . . hell, you cain't never trust nobody like that again."

"Yes sir," I tried.

"Ain't no sir. No spit and polish. Just a rifle grunt."

"I meant the young guy you sold the homestead to."

He slapped his knees with his leathery palms. "The Springer boy," he said. "Hell of a fisherman, that boy. Knew his damn rivers."

We'd gotten this far a couple of times before. Right up to the point where he remembered who J.D. was . . . and then he'd go fishing in his own river, back fifty years to the beaches and hedgerows of France, and I'd have to start over.

"He's dead," I said this time.

He slapped his knees again. "Hell, they're mostly all dead now. Those that ain't just waiting for their time to come."

"The fisherman's dead," I tried.

For the first time since I'd entered the room, he stopped rocking. Behind the cataracts, I imagined his eyes rolling like a slot machine. Unless I was mistaken, we were about to make another extended foray into the past.

"Shot him down just the way they shot your dog," I said quickly.

He rocked harder now. Chewing his gums and picking at his pants with his long yellow fingernails. "My fault," he said. "Shoulda just let the sons a bitches kill me."

"Who?"

"That Hand fella."

"Why would he do a thing like that?"

"Wouldn't sell out. Said if'n I give it to my grandkids, they'd come and get them, too." A tear ran down his stubbled cheek. Then another. "Kilt my dog just to make his point," he said. He wiped at the tear but missed.

"So you sold out to J.D."

"Be damned if those sons a bitches was gonna get my place."

"They won't," I assured him.

He took a shuddering breath and seemed to calm himself.

"Seemed damn strange. Tryin' to kill each other all day and then trying to keep each other warm all night, so's we could go at it again in the morning."

36 | I RECEIVED A SITTING OVATION. CARL, ROBBY, FLOYD, Boris, Kurtis and Narva all packed into the RV. All monitors off but one. Watching Oprah. The incessant rain pounding on the metal roof. Carl read my mind. "Nobody home at City Hall," he said. "We're running on sound activation." I turned my attention to Narva.

"I thought you had a class," I said.

She showed both palms. "Could I miss this?" she said. "Besides, they took a vote and said I could be a criminal, too."

"Democracy een action," Boris said.

Floyd shook his head. Made a buzzer sound. "*Ennnnggg* . . . Language barrier," he said. "We voted that she *was* criminal, not that she could *be* a criminal."

"What I do is illegal," she protested.

"If it ain't," Carl growled, "it oughta be." He put a hand on top of his head. "You oughta see what she did to Tressman."

"Got some great stuff since you been gone," Robby said.

"We ready for thermonuclear destruction?" I said hopefully.

"Fuck no," said Robby. He looked over at Narva. "Excuse my French."

She waved him off. "It's a verb I'm familiar with," she assured him.

"What's the holdup?"

"Your girlfriend won't get lost. She's been camped out in the Chamber of Commerce office since ten this morning."

"Who, by the way," Narva said, "I saw at the courthouse yesterday afternoon." She whistled, shook her right hand like a chimp. "A looker . . . for a woman of her advanced age, that is."

"What advanced age is that?" I demanded.

She smiled and said, "Never mind."

"Miss Haynes is making her promo tape for next week," I said.

"I need daylight," Robby said. "It's not flashlight work and Kurtis says the place has nothing to cover the windows."

"No curtains, no shades, no nothing," Kurtis said.

"You gotta get her the hell out of there," Carl said.

"And keep her out of there for a couple of hours," said Robby.

"Either that or we wait till tomorrow, and I've spent about as much time in this shithole as I'm gonna," Carl said.

"You're right," I said. "We've worn out our welcome."

"Shouldn't be hard," Floyd said. "That girl's got a big-time hard-on for our boy Leo here." He looked over at Narva. "I mean, like, you know . . . figuratively, rather than, like . . . you know . . . anything . . ."

"You were right the first time," she said. "Haven't you ever looked at the . . . ," she began, then stopped. "Is he blushing?" she asked. "He's blushing, isn't he?"

"Either that or he's been boiled," offered Kurtis.

Much to his displeasure, we all agreed that Floyd was indeed a tad more rubicund than normal. "Hot in here," he mumbled as he stepped out into the thundering rain.

I wagged a finger at Narva. A girlish laugh escaped her throat.

"I'm always amazed about how men can be so totally fixated over something about which they generally know so little." She giggled again. Kurtis joined in. Boris opted for the typhoon, closing the door behind himself.

I did the only sane thing and changed the subject. "What did you find in the records?"

She pulled her planner from her purse, walked her long fingernails to the back of the book. "Like you figured, Gretchen Peabody of the hundred and sixty-five acres is none other than the late mother-in-law of our late friend Polster."

"The mayor's not involved in the scam," Carl said.

"Really?"

Carl nodded. "Tressman, Weston and Polster call each other every five minutes, but nobody calls Her Honor."

Robby dialed the phone. "Is this Alice? . . . Oh . . . oh . . . I'm sorry." Hung up.

"She's still at the office," he said to me.

"Do your stuff," Carl said.

"I have a nice collection of latex condoms," Narva offered.

Robby growled. "Sic 'em tiger," he said.

"Some in lovely pastel colors."

"How much time do you need?" Robby asked.

"Something with studs?" she persisted.

"Two hours minimum."

Narva held up a hand. "Careful, now. Don't put that kind of pressure on him."

37 THE EXPRESSION ON RAMONA HAYNES'S FACE RE- minded me of how the other cartoon characters look at the moment when they realize Casper is a ghost. She stopped in her tracks and then reached out and put one hand on the doorframe. "What in hell . . . ?"

"I'm like the bad penny," I said.

"But . . . ," she sputtered "they said you'd been . . ."

"I was, but it didn't stick." I read her the *Reader's Digest* version.

"Two murders in as many months. I mean, this just doesn't happen around here . . . maybe in . . ." She moved the hand to her throat. "Kind of makes that mush I was pedaling about small-town life sound ridiculous, doesn't it?"

A bit too much color had returned to her cheeks. Her chin was pink.

"Not really," I said. "That scene at the supermarket the other day would never happen in Seattle. Most people wouldn't want to get involved. They'd be afraid of getting sued or shot or something."

She walked out into the outer office and leaned her elbows on the counter. "What is going on around here?" she said.

I winked. "Don't worry. Unless I'm sadly mistaken, we're about to find out."

Her forehead wrinkled. She straightened up. "What makes you say that?"

"Oh . . . just a premonition," I said in my best conspiratorial tone.

"Come on," she snapped. "Don't be so damn mysterious."

"Us detectives are like that."

She waved a hand at me. "You're just blowing smoke."

I grinned for all I was worth. "Whatever you say."

She hated it. I had her going I could tell. So I jumped in. "If you let me take you up on that invitation for dinner," I said, "maybe you could worm it out of me."

She looked me over. "So . . . you'll sing for your supper, will you?"

"The cuisine at the Peninsula County Jail left a great deal to be desired."

She laughed. "I'll bet," she said.

"I decided that 'previously eaten' was the best description of the fare."

She pulled the corners of her mouth down. "That's awful."

"How's about it?" I said.

She stuck her hands in the back pockets of her jeans. "Worm it out of you, huh?"

"An unfortunate turn of phrase," I said.

"Let me finish up here. You can follow me."

She swirled the remaining wine in her glass. "It's what happens when people get desperate," she said. "They can't see any further than tomorrow."

"But," I countered, "it shouldn't have been a surprise. For as long as I can remember, the world has been telling the timber industry that the party was about to be over." I'd had a bit too much merlot and was babbling. "I mean . . . the rise of the environmental movement alone should have told them . . ."

"It's not just an industry. That's what outsiders don't get. It's an entire way of life. In my high school class, there were a hundred forty kids. Know how many of them went off to college?"

"How many?"

"Eight." She let it sink in. "Because they're backward? Stupid?"

"Don't forget inbred," I suggested.

She sneered at me. "Because the rest of them knew where their lives were going. They knew who they were going to marry and who they were going to work for. And what area of town they wanted to build a house in when the time came."

"Sounds absolutely terrifying," I said.

She got to her feet and began to clear dishes from the table. I joined in, and in two trips we managed to get everything into the dishwasher. I was leaning back against the kitchen counter. Ramona was wiping her hands with a black-and-white-striped dish towel.

She rested her hip on mine as she draped the towel over the faucet. Outside, the wind had something squeaking. Slanting rain hammered directly on the windows.

She stepped in between my feet and looked up at me. I could see the faint hair on her cheeks and smell scented soap. "So . . . what's this big secret you're harboring?"

I tried to look offended. "Is that all you think of me? You think a great steak dinner and a couple of bottles of good wine will loosen my tongue?"

She reached around me and pulled the chain on the overhead light.

"I had something else in mind for your tongue," she said, sliding her arms around my neck, pulling me down toward her face and the smell of flowers.

38 KURTIS SIPPED COFFEE FROM A WHITE MUG. "THIS thing with the cameras is creepy," he said. "There's something about watching people who don't know they're being watched . . ." He waved a hand. "I don't know. It's weird."

Boris added what I thought to be a particularly Russian idea. "Vat eef de people doing de surveilling are also under surveillance?"

"Stop it," Narva said.

"Lotta tape," said Robby.

"You have no idea," said Carl with an evil grin. "Every tanning parlor, every locker room, dressing room, bathroom. Every bridal suite in every hotel . . . hell, they're all wired. Have been for years."

Narva looked at Robby. "He's kidding, right? Tell me he's kidding."

"If that's what you want to hear, I'll tell you," he said.

"Noooooooooo," said Kurtis. "You can't be—"

"Countdown," Robby said above the conversation. "Ten, nine, eight . . ."

Carl reached up and switched on a monitor.

". . . three, two, one."

Chanel Fourteen. Stevens Falls TV. Time: seven A.M. The date. A community calendar began to scroll by. What had begun the morning as thick mist now pounded the metal roof of the RV.

"We didn't start right off with the good stuff," Carl said.

"A little of them, a little of us," Robby added.

"The shit hits the fan in four minutes," Carl said.

"Everybody ready to roll?" I asked. They said they were. I'd already paid everybody but Carl. "What about you?" Floyd asked.

"I'm gonna take a quick swing by the homestead and then head out."

"I'm staying with you. Boris can take the car," said Floyd.

I started to argue, but he wasn't having any of it. "Everybody in this crew did what they signed on to do. Am I right? I signed on to get your ass back to Seattle in one piece, so I hope you don't mind if I earn my money." When he put it that way . . .

On the screen, Redwood Farm and Garden, for all your landscaping needs. Family owned and operated for fifty-three years. The whole Brady clan smiling into the camera.

"You find the switch?" I asked Robby.

"Big as life. We're broadcasting all over the peninsula."

"Here it comes," said Carl. "You seen this one before."

MONDAY 8:46 A.M.   CAMERA 1—TRESSMAN

The lower half of Nathan Hand paced in and out of camera range. "I don't like it," he said. Mark Tressman sat at his desk and began rolling a paper clip around in his fingers. "It's just a burglary."

"You haven't been up on the roof."

"Don't start any conspiracy theory with me," Tressman said.

"No conspiracy. It's that Waterman and those hardcases he's got out there with him. I think they're trying to queer the deal."

"He admits as much. So what? He's got nothing. And there's nothing in this building that would advance his cause in any way. If I was going to worry about anybody, I'd be more inclined to worry about Loomis."

Hand leaned down and put both hands on the desk. "I don't get it. Loomis wants the deal to go through as bad as we do."

"Maybe they're getting nervous. Maybe they're checking up on us. We blew it once before. Maybe they don't trust us to get it done."

Eight-fifty-four A.M. Another voice. June the receptionist. "Is Sheriff Hand back there?"

"Be right out," Hand called.

"Ten days," Tressman intoned. "Just ten days."

Dewitt Davis of the Davis Funeral Home, looking somber, as a mortician should. Recommending the Purple Cross program so your loved ones won't be burdened with the bother of giving you a decent burial.

The next insertion was a split screen. Tressman on the left, Weston on the right.

"How cool," Narva said.

TUESDAY 9:03 A.M.

On the screen, Nancy Weston looked older than I recalled.

"He's out of control, Mark. You know he had an accident. Hit some man out in front of the Country Corner."

"I heard."

"Something has to be done."

"What's that supposed to mean?"

She put a hand to her throat: her voice rose. "What it means is that I've spent some of my prime years here. Doing my end. Putting this together."

"As have we all," Tressman said.

"Which is why something has to be done. I'm not getting

stuck here, Mark. Loomis is my ticket out of here and I'm taking it."

On one side of the screen, Nancy Weston banged the phone down hard. On the other, Mark Tressman winced, depressed the button and dialed. Robby zoomed the camera in. Last four numbers were 9595.

Polster is pacing back and forth. Weston is trying to calm him down. "It's not esoteric like bridges or sewer systems. They're going to know right away."

"You really think he's got state inspectors coming in on Friday?"

"Damn right I do."

"I think he's bluffing."

Polster paced the room, biting on his thumb. "It's pretty goddamned easy for you to think that. It's not your ass in the wringer."

"Will you relax?"

Polster raised his voice. "No, goddammit, I won't. You damn well better get behind me on this one, you hear me. I'm not going to be anybody's whipping boy here, Nancy. You and Mark and the rest of them better get that straight right now."

"Rest of them?" Carl said.

I shrugged.

Back to our regular programming. Doug's Auto Repair and the Steelhead Tavern.

"You haven't seen this next one," Robby said. "This is the one where the clerk melts down."

Split screen. Tressman left. Weston right. "Is that what you told Emmett Polster?" she asked. Tressman massaged his forehead.

"Will you just—"

"If you think I'm going to wait around until Nathan Hand puts a bullet in my brain, you better think again."

"Nancy, come on, now . . ."

"I've got all the checks." She pulled open the drawer in front of her and pulled out a handful of checks. She fanned them out on the desk. "Springer, Manson, Enos, Howard, McNulty. Every one of them. Every one of the people we claimed didn't pay their taxes. I've got them all. If the authorities want proof, I'm the one who's got it. And don't you think I won't, either."

"Nancy . . . ," Tressman started again. "We're almost there. All we have to do is stay calm."

"Calm?" she screamed into the mouthpiece. "Calm like Emmett?"

"We—"

She hung up on him. Stuffed the checks into the pocket of her dress and disappeared from view. Tressman laced his fingers together over the top of his head and sat all the way back in his chair.

A loud knock on the RV door. Everybody flinched. Boris stepped behind the door. Floyd opened it a crack. Monty. "Ya said I should tell ya if the sheriff drove by."

"Yeah," I said.

"Just went roarin' off for all the car was worth. Fire truck hot on his heels."

We were twenty minutes into the tape. I was guessing that by now phones were ringing all over the county. The later it got, the more they were going to ring.

"I'd love to see their faces," said Kurtis, "when they see

that steamroller parked in front of the door." He hoisted his mug at me. "A stroke of genius, Leo."

"What if they have extra keys?" Narva asked.

"They do," I said. "They're on a board inside the station."

"They'll have to go in through a wall," Floyd said.

"Steel-reinforced concrete," Kurtis said. "Crew of four . . . six hours."

"Ta-da," sang Robby. "The main attraction."

The screen is black for a moment and then slowly lightens into the interior of room number nine at the Black Bear Motel. Narva and Mark Tressman. In living color. Narva's face is electronically blocked out. Mark Tressman's is not.

They're standing at the foot of the bed. He's all over her like a cheap suit. Slobbering into her neck while he gropes behind her, trying to figure out how her dress is fastened. "You're wonderful," he gargles. She squeals and begins to unbutton his shirt, which she then yanks from his trousers and pulls from his torso, until it hangs from his wrists. He's haired all over like a gibbon. While Tressman is busy trying to unbutton his cuffs without putting the shirt back on, she undoes his belt and drops his trousers to the floor. Briefs, not boxers. Black. She squeezes him. He closes his eyes and groans piteously. She takes him by the shoulders, twirls him around and sits him down on the bed. One foot at a time, she maneuvers the pants over the wingtips, so, in less than a minute, he's sitting there wearing brogans, briefs and black socks. More or less every man's nightmare. She pulls him to his feet. She takes him in her hand. Nods toward the bathroom. Her voice is breathy. "You go put a helmet on that soldier. I'll be waiting for you." With those words she loosens the top of her dress and folds it down. Tressman makes a dive for her cleavage but is rejected. He kicks his pants off, finds his wallet and scoots for the toilet.

Quickly, Narva gathers both of their clothes. Pulls open the dresser drawer, produces a folded piece of paper, which she leaves on the bed. Hustles over to the door to the adjoining room, opens it and steps out of sight. Two minutes of an empty room nine.

"We left it in," said Robby. "Figured it would give people time to call their friends."

Tressman comes out of the bathroom wearing a glazed expression and a black condom. At first he thinks it's maybe some little hide-and-seek game, so he takes a lap of the bed. Halfway around he realizes his clothes are gone, tries the closet. Empty. The adjoining door. Locked. Sees the paper on the bed. Picks it up. He's at half mast. I can read it over his shoulder. Big letters. Red lipstick *SMILE, YOU'RE ON CANDID CAMERA*. The condom heads for the floor like a dowsing rod over a water main. Fade to black. Wild applause.

"He drove home wearing the bedspread," said Floyd.

"It wasn't his color," Narva added.

Carl turned off the monitor. "It's been swell," he announced. "Unplug me on your way by, will you, Robby?"

Robby said he would and stepped out.

"Let's roll," I said. "The shit has officially hit the fan."

I walked Kurtis, Boris and Narva around the front of the motel to their cars. I shook hands with the fellas and watched as they bounced out of the lot. As Kurtis faded from view, first the cherry picker, then the RV came rolling out from behind the building; rocking in divots, they eased out onto the highway. Carl tooted. Robby waved.

Narva stood by the side of the Miata. "You were back early, last night."

"You know us old guys."

She gave me the eyeball. "Yeah . . . sure," she said.

"What . . . are you fishing for a story again?" I said. She laughed. Handed me a card with a phone number. "If you'd like to talk sometime," she said. I took the card and gave her a hug. The little Miata U-turned in its tracks. She tooted the horn and purred off down the highway.

Monty appeared at the motel door. "Ya gotta see what's on the boob tube," he said.

39 THE RIVERS RAN CHOCOLATE BROWN. THE VOLUME OF water ironed out the riffles and eddies, turning the flow fast and featureless. Between the river and the rain, I practically had to shout to be heard. "I'm going to close up and get my gear," I said.

Floyd patted the rifle hanging from his shoulder. "Except for this, my stuff is already in the car," he said. His curly hair seemed to keep the rain at bay, like wool on a sheep, while mine seemed to serve no purpose other than to funnel the water more efficiently down my neck.

"I'll grab mine and be right with you." I started for the cabin.

"We leaving the birds?" he asked.

"Huh?"

"The motion sensors."

After two weeks of throwing Claudia Springer's money around, I had a sudden spasm of frugality. "Why don't you get them while I close up?"

I jogged inside, dripping all over the floor, stuffed all my gear into the black Nike bag. Sat at the kitchen table and tried to call home. Forwarded, forwarded and then finally offered voice mail. The joys of technology.

I turned off all the lights, locked the front door. Changed my mind. Unlocked. Turned on the porch light and then locked up again. I ducked my head into the roar of the rain and ran for the car. Got halfway there before I looked up and saw Nathan Hand's black and white sitting in the driveway. I kept walking and tried to look as honest and nonchalant as a guy wearing a shoulder holster could look. Bobby Russell stepped out of the car and aimed the riot gun at me over the top of the car. Hand got out of the car like he was going to the beach. I watched as the rain began to cover and darken his hat.

"You got a warrant?" I asked.

Hand emitted a bitter chuckle. "We're not playing that charade anymore, Waterman. This isn't about the law anymore. Isn't about you or any of your smartass dirty tricks or any of that shit. This is about survival."

"Where's that son of a bitch spit on me?" Russell demanded.

"Gone," I said, as loud as I dared. Hoping like hell that, somehow, above the rush of water, Floyd heard what was going on. I had an overpowering desire to look up at the tree line but bit my lip and squelched it. I kept my eyes on the deputy as he walked over to me. He stopped in front of me. Gave me a smile he didn't mean and then dug the butt of the shotgun hard into my ribs. I gasped for breath.

"Bobby," Hand growled.

The deputy reversed the weapon and gave me a matched set. I bent forward at the waist, hugging myself, massaging my ribs.

"Yes sir."

"Gimme the shotgun. Get Waterman's gun."

Bobby did as he was told, laying the automatic on the hood of the cruiser next to Nathan Hand. "Check the house and the cabins," Hand said.

He kept the shotgun trained on my middle as Russell went through the house and then worked his way through the cabins. "There's no point in this, Hand," I said.

"Shut up," he said. He put the riot gun on the hood and picked up my automatic. Checked the safety and the load.

Satisfied about the Glock, he put it on the hood of the car by his elbow. His hat was three shades darker now. A steady stream of water ran from the front of the brim.

"What's the point?" I asked. "It's over."

I kept my hands in sight and moved a couple of steps forward. Floyd was my only chance. I had to make sure that whatever happened next wasn't shielded by the house. Huge drops of silver rain drummed on the hood of the car. "You just don't know when to quit, now, do you, Waterman? Just couldn't let things be, could you?"

"I don't know what you're talking about," I said.

"You probably think that stuff you put on the TV is funny, now, don't you?" he said.

"What stuff on the TV?"

I saw pure hatred in his eyes. "I learn from my mistakes," he said. As he picked up the shotgun, his eyes darted about like spotlights at a prison break. Out of the blue, he said, "They've got nothing. They've got nobody to put me at any crime. Nobody who can say they ever heard me admit a damn thing."

Bobby Russell stepped down off the porch of Cabin Number Eight. "No people. No gear," he announced and started our way.

Hand looked over at the deputy. "Nobody but Bobby Russell there. And he's hardly in a position to tell anybody anything. Is he, Bobby?"

Russell swabbed his face with a handkerchief. "What's that, Sheriff?"

"I was saying how you were hardly in a position to be saying anything about some of the unfortunate instances we've had around here lately. Especially considering you're the one who screwed up and shot your friend Springer in the face. Huh? Lethal injection don't sound any better to Bobby here than it does to me, does it, Bobby?"

"Dumb shit shouldn't of grabbed my gun."

Hand shook his head sadly. Water ran off the back. "Another goddamn month and Springer would have gone on his own. And none of this would have been necessary."

Russell turned my way, as if he felt some inner need to explain. "We was just bustin' his chops. The sheriff was tellin' him how much better his life would be if he'd just sell out. How much safer it would be for his wife and kids . . . and the dumb shit reached out and grabbed the barrel." He shrugged. "Next thing I knew, he was all over the place."

A bitter laugh escaped Nathan Hand. "Turns out it was an accident after all."

"Kind of like Bendixon's dog," I suggested.

"Nah," the kid said. "Sheriff shot that old cur on purpose."

"Bobby," Hand said. "Get me the flashlight."

"The flashlight?"

"You heard me."

I admit it. Hand had me fooled. It wasn't until Bobby Russell leaned into the passenger side and bent down for the flashlight. Then Hand picked my automatic from the hood of the car. Then I got it. So did Deputy Russell.

When Russell straightened up holding a black rubber flashlight in his right hand, the sheriff shot him in the chest. He pointed the gun my way. "You just stay nice and easy, now," he said. "Nice and easy."

He kept the automatic trained on me as he backed slowly around the front of the car, talking to himself as he moved. "Just going to clean up after myself a little here," he muttered. "Give those state boys something they can get their teeth in." He bumped his butt off the hood and began to step around the open door. I moved forward. "Easy. Easy," he chanted. I moved again. Three steps this time. If I figured the scene correctly, there was no way he was going to shoot me with my own gun. He fired again. Down at the ground and then momentarily squatted out of view. I hurried up to the corner of the house, stepped around. Bobby Russell lay on his side. The second shot had entered his head just beneath the hairline. Nathan Hand held Deputy Russell's revolver in one hand and my automatic in the other. He set the Glock on the roof of the car, moved the revolver to his right hand and thumbed back the hammer. I began to cringe in toward myself like a dying star. His hand was steady as he brought the gun to bear. I couldn't tear my eyes form the single bead of water that dripped from the yawning end of the barrel.

The exit wound exploded his upper lip before I heard the crack of the rifle. His nervous system instinctively moved his left hand to the back of his head, as if he'd been stung by a bee, dislodging his hat, which landed upside down at his feet. The hand came away red, but even as he held it in front of his face, I don't think he saw it. He was dead before he hit the ground, first with his knees, where the revolver slid from his fingers, and finally, awkwardly, over onto his back, where his body came to rest half on, half off Deputy Bobby Russell. I began to breathe again.

Floyd ran down from the tree line. Pine needles and oak leaves were plastered all over his soaking jacket. "What the hell was that about?"

"Our friend the sheriff here was going to stage a fatal shoot-out between me and the deputy. Russell was the only one who could put him on death row. I guess he figured with the two of us gone, he might be able to take his chances in court."

Floyd paced in a circle. "Son of a bitch," he snarled. "This is deep shit, man."

"Let's fix it," I said.

"We got two dead cops here, man. Tape isn't going to patch this shit."

I told him what I had in mind. By the time I was finished, he was standing still.

"Still leaves us a big problem," he said.

"What's that?"

"Each other."

"Oh . . . you mean the fact that one of us would be a lot safer if the other guy was in the trunk with Hand and Russell."

He smiled. "Crossed your mind, too, huh?"

I said it had. "Until you found yourself fresh out of weapons," he said quietly. The tone suggested that whatever I said next better be good.

"No . . . until I thought it through."

"Yeah?"

"There's no way they'd let anybody plea-bargain for two dead cops."

"No matter how dirty," Floyd said. "Sure as hell we both get the needle, and they clean up after their own."

"That's the way I read it," I said.

"Kind of makes us blood brothers," he said with a touch of irony.

"Let's do it," I said.

It took an hour. Longest, wettest hour of my life. Working like hell and waiting for a squadron of state cops to come and put an end to life as I knew it. If they showed up before we finished, we were both doing twenty to life. End of story. If we got it done right, we might walk. As far as motivation goes, it was real simple.

We dug a couple pairs of rubber gloves out of the cruiser's medical kit and drained everything we could find. Oil, coolant, transmission fluid. Didn't need any oil slicks floating around the river. Took every loose object out of the cruiser, put it in a plastic bag and threw it in the trunk with Russell and Hand. Dug up three square yards of blood-covered driveway. Shoveled the soil into the trunk with the rest of it. Replaced the dirt with some of Chappy's. Spread gravel over the top. Closed the lid. Locked it shut and then wired it for good measure. Rolled down the windows.

"You sure?" Floyd yelled above the rain. "The other day when the water was clear, I could sorta see the bottom. That car goes down there and ends up being visible, our ass is grass."

"When you're standing in a boat, you can feel the hole under your feet."

"What if it's not deep enough?"

"J.D. said it was at least twenty feet deep."

"What if he's wrong?"

"You got a better idea?"

I slid into the driver's seat, pulled the gearshift out of park. Floyd put his back to it. The car began to roll on its own. I eased the Crown Victoria down the boat ramp until it was about six feet from the water. I didn't want the car to hit the water with any speed. I wanted to ease it in and let the current do its thing. I set the emergency brake and got out. Looked back up the incline at Floyd. He gave me the thumbs up. I reached into the car, popped the brake, slammed the door as it rolled by . . . watched.

The big car drove slowly into the river, lurching slightly as the front tires slipped on the slick stones of the river bottom. And then for a moment it seemed to stop moving altogether. Then to float. My heart stopped beating for a second as the car began to turn to the right, following the current toward the ocean.

Suddenly, as if gripped by some massive hand, the cruiser straightened and stood on its nose, the whip antenna now parallel to the water, as the car began to bounce forward on its front bumper . . . grinding over the rocky bottom . . . turning a hundred eighty degrees until the roof and the red and blue lights were pointed my way. Then, with the grace of a dancer, it began to sink nose down into the rushing water, turning on some invisible axis, shuddering occasionally as if it were being sucked down some vast cosmic drain. And then . . . it was gone. Quiet again, except for the silver hiss of the rain.

I waited. The Stephen King in me expected the car to bob

to the surface, lights ablaze, siren wailing, corpses pointing fingers, but it didn't happen. Just more silence.

I turned and trotted to the top of the ramp. Threw him the keys to the Malibu.

"Get out of here," I said. "Take the rental."

"You?"

I'd thought about leaving, but there was no way it would float. In the next couple of hours, state cops were about to start pulling electronic surveillance equipment out of city offices. Half of city government was on the lam. Two city cops were going to turn up missing. "I leave now, they'll be waiting in my driveway for me when I get home."

He nodded. "They're really gonna hate misplacing two cops."

"Yeah," I said. "I'll probably be a while."

Floyd wiped his dripping face with a soaked-through sleeve. Grimaced.

"Don't forget the bag," I said, pointing to the pale green pillowcase resting on the lawn. All the guns were in the bag. Floyd's rifle and the police riot gun we'd broken down into pieces and thrown into the sack on top of the three handguns.

We shook hands. A trickle of water fell from the flattened tip of his nose.

"I'll see they get half a ferry ride," he said.

40 THE TRUCK WAS RUNNING AND SO WAS SHE. RAMONA Haynes staggered out the back door of her house carrying a suitcase nearly as big as she was. She used both hands to swing the bag up onto the edge of the bed and then pushed it over the side. She looked up, breathing hard, and finally saw me standing there.

"You sorry son of a bitch," she shouted. "What are you doing here?"

"Just wanted to see you off," I said.

She started to lie, to tell me it just looked like she was leaving town, but changed her mind. She went back into the house. I'd changed into dry clothes. Found a yellow rain jacket in the cabin. Probabaly Claudia's. It was too small to fasten, so I held it closed at the neck, listening to the rain smacking the hood. She came back out with a matching garment bag and rolling suitcase. Threw them into the truck.

"I'm going to—"

I cut her off. "You're going to get your ass out of town while you still can," I said. She started to open her mouth, but I kept talking. "It had to be you. None of the rest of those dolts could plan their way out of a paper bag. You're the only one with the drive and the initiative to put something like this together." She set her jaw and kept silent. "Your chin is red," I said. "Must be the exertion that does it."

She put her hands on her hips and sneered. "Well . . .

that's the only way you're going to see it, isn't it, then . . . you pathetic, impotent bastard?"

"Whoa, now," I said. "I said I wouldn't, not that I couldn't. What say we don't confuse the two?"

The rain rolled off the plastic jacket, wetting my jeans from the knees down.

She turned and started for the door. Stopped and turned back my way. "Do you have any idea what it is you ruined? I mean, do you have even the slightest glimmer about how many lives you've screwed up?"

"Like the Springers'?"

She began to shout. "They didn't amount to anything," she screamed. "They were afterthoughts. Nothings. Their families didn't give their whole lives to settling this valley. They haven't spent a hundred thirty years trying to wring some sort of a life out of the land." She waved her arms about. "They just show up one day and expect everything to come to a halt because they want to start their little fishing business." She dropped a hand disgustedly to her side. "If you'd just stayed the hell out of it, we could have saved this town. We could have revitalized this whole end of the valley. And you—"

"And become millionaires in the process."

Something in her snapped. She began to shout. "Why not? It's my birthright. That stupid son of a bitch lost everything. Gambled it away in some stupid Indian casino, until I was left with nothing . . . nothing but"—she waved at the house—"this hovel and a few hundred useless acres of land that still technically belonged to my mother . . . or they would have taken that, too." She kicked the door closed. "Everything. The idiot lost everything."

"You saw a way to put it all back together, didn't you?" I prodded. "But you weren't sure it could be done altogether legally. So you kept the property in your mother's name and brought in Nathan Hand to handle any complaints."

"It should have been easy," she said. "Just one old man."

"An old man who wouldn't sell."

"All we had to do was wait. He was ancient."

"Except Nathan Hand got impatient and tried to hustle things along. So he shot the old man's dog."

Her surprise was visible. "How . . ." she started.

"Pissed the old man off, so, just to spite you, he sold it to the only guy he knew who wouldn't sell it back to you at any price. A guy he figured you couldn't run off, either."

"We had him, too. He was no more that sixty days from going under."

I already knew the answer, but I decided to say it anyway.

"And, just in case his life wasn't fucked up enough already, you started running your number on him, didn't you? And nobody escapes from that tender little trap of yours, do they?"

She brushed her hair back from her face. "He was easy," she said. "Just like the rest of you little boys. Stuck out there with those snot-nosed kids and that cow of a wife. His life coming apart. J.D. needed a shoulder to cry on." She smiled. "Unlike you, his equipment worked."

"Same way you kept the Pinkerton guy from Loomis hanging around, while you kept trying to put the deal back together. Coming back over and over. The deal must have been good, or else the company wouldn't have kept footing the bill, but I'm betting you were a whole lot better."

"*You'll* never know, now will you?" she sneered.

"I'm figuring maybe Nathan Hand, too." Despite her best efforts, I could see that I'd hit a nerve. "The way he deferred to you in public," I said, shaking my head. "Money or no money, most men I know only put up with that level of crap from women they're sleeping with." Her lip curled as she opened her mouth to speak.

I'll never know for sure if my guess about the sheriff was true. As Floyd and I knew only too well, Hand wasn't going to be filling us in, and before she could utter another word, her eyes went wide; that pulled my head around. State cops. Two cars. Four cops. No guns this time. For questioning. Both of us.

41 BILLY HEFFERNEN DUMPED THE PLASTIC EVIDENCE BAG out onto the table. Five cameras, five mikes. All wearing little white tags that told where they'd been found and by whom. Jed reached over and touched the back of my hand. *Don't touch*, was the message.

Billy's ears were bright red. "And you're going to sit there and try to tell me that you don't know anything about this."

"Perhaps you should take notes," Jed suggested. "We've answered this query at least four times. My client has no knowledge of either that equipment or how it came to be found in whatever nefarious locations your minions supposedly uncovered it."

Billy kept his eyes locked on mine. "We're going to sort this out. Count on it."

Jed yawned mightily into the back of his hand. "Sorry," he said. He shot a glance my way. "It's been a long week."

Billy started in on a litany of the technological innovations by which the state crime lab was going to link the surveillance gear directly to me and thus seal my doom. I tried not to look smug. They were going to find nothing. No sales receipts, no fingerprints, no hairs, no nada. Whatever the crew's moral failings, they were professionals. Way I saw it, if crime lab threats and hoping I'd touch the evidence were the best Billy Heffernen could muster, then Jed must have been right to begin with.

*　　*　　*

Jed had arrived at the Peninsula County Jail at about seven-thirty Thursday night. Maybe six hours after they'd hauled me in for questioning. He'd looked tired. His tie was pulled down, the seat of his pants sagging a bit. He ran his hand over his head.

"Sorry it took so long," he said.

"Thanks for coming again."

"I've been out there for an hour," he said.

"Doing what?"

"Being threatened."

"With?"

"Oh . . . a waltz before the judicial ethics committee . . . possible prison time for conspiracy . . . accessory both before and after the fact . . . which, of course, means . . ." he let it hang in the air like smoke.

"Yeah?"

"I mean, they brought out the first team, Leo. Hell, the Peninsula County DA himself is out there casting aspersions about both our mamas."

"Which means?" I prompted.

"They don't have shit," he said with a smile. "I've never heard such a raft in all my life." He patted me on the shoulder. "Stonewall," he said. "You know the drill. You'd prefer not to speak other than in the presence of your attorney, and your attorney is going home for the weekend." He started for the cell door.

I hated the idea of spending the weekend in jail. "Am I under arrest?"

"You're being held as a material witness. As things stand right now, you're not charged with anything."

I did the math. Material witnesses can be held without bail or charge for seventy-two hours. I counted on my fingers. Thursday afternoon till Sunday afternoon, which, in the jurisprudence business, was the same thing as Monday morning.

"Yeah . . . go home," I'd said.

338 | G.M. FORD

* * *

Billy now scraped the electronic gear back into the evidence bag. Jed yawned again and got to his feet. "I take it we're finished, then?"

Billy looked over at the assistant DA, who stood against the far wall. The ADA said, "Yes . . . for the moment, you can go." Heavy on the "for the moment."

I stood up and followed Jed toward the door. Billy stopped me with a hand on my chest. "May I have a private word with your client?" he asked Jed.

Jed looked back at me and raised his eyebrows. I nodded. Jed and the ADA closed the door behind them. "I'm going to give you one last chance, Leo," he said.

"For old times' sake."

"Call it anything you want." The muscles along his jaw looked like knotted rope. He stood there staring holes in me. He was a good cop doing what the state of Washington paid him to do, so I tried to help him out.

"All I'll say is this, Billy. There's an old man here in this town who's sitting in a rocking chair waiting to die, because everything that mattered to him is gone. And there's a family over on the mainland whose husband and father doesn't come home anymore because somebody shot him in the face and then burned his body to a cinder." I took a deep breath. "As far as I'm concerned, other than them, everybody else connected with this case is getting exactly what they deserve."

Billy's voice rose in this throat. "I've got two dead bodies. I've got a couple public officials upstairs pointing fingers at each other. A couple more who seem to have packed up and taken unscheduled vacations. And most interestingly, I've got two missing cops, who you claim are dirty, and who don't seem to have packed a damn thing before they went missing in a city patrol car. You want to help me out here?"

"Justice has been served as well as it's going to be," I said.

"That's not your call, goddammit," he snapped.

"Sometimes . . ." I began. Thought better of it. Stopped. "I said everything I've got to say, Billy. Can I go now?"

He walked over and put his face in mine. "Listen to me, you arrogant bastard. I put my best crew on this. There's no way—" Same old, same old. I interrupted.

"Me, too," I said and headed for the office door.

For the first time in four days, the rain had stopped. The air smelled like it had been washed and hung out to dry.

My get-out-of-jail party had dwindled to one black Lexus. I got in.

"Where to?" Jed asked.

"Home," I said.

42 | WE STOOD ON EITHER SIDE OF THE KITCHEN SINK, where we could keep an eye on Alicia and Adam running around the backyard. Claudia Springer held her cup of tea with both hands. "I got a card from Rebecca," she said tentatively.

"New address and phone number?"

She nodded and blew the steam from the top of her cup.

"We're going to try something different for a while."

Anyway, that's what we were telling people. I still wasn't sure what the problem was, so I was definitely a bit fuzzy as to why we needed separate residences in order to process the situation . . . whatever the hell that meant. She'd been gone when I got back. She rented an apartment somewhere in ever-so-trendy Belltown. Hired movers to come and get the stuff she wanted. Said it was only temporary, but my insides told me different. Except for the past year, I'd spent the majority of my adult life living by myself. And yet I felt totally unprepared for the empty feeling inside my body. It was as if there was no place in the house that was mine, just a succession of spaces that invited me to move on to the next. We'd agreed to let a couple of weeks pass before we talked about it. I figured I could live with it for that long. At least, that's what I was telling myself.

"I saw on the news"—she took a sip of tea—"about the scandal in Stevens Falls. The TV station and how everybody was bugged and everything. And the steamroller thing block-ing the door and that naked guy with the note."

So had everyone else in the Pacific Northwest. The tape had played for the better part of nine hours before a city maintenance crew had managed to jackhammer their way through the wall. By that time, half the people on the pen-insula had recorded the juicy parts. The media were having a field day. The cops found Tressman holed up in a roach motel in Aberdeen, trying to work up the courage to blow his brains out. Yesterday, when I spoke with Judge Bigelow on the phone, he said that he'd heard they were rolling over on one another like trained seals. Blaming each other for the scheme and the dirty work on Nathan Hand.

Claudia set the cup on the counter. "Was that . . . uh . . . us?" she asked.

The question seemed vague enough, so I nodded.

"You can't talk about it, can you?" she said.

"If you want, I can tell you why it all happened," I said.

"Go ahead."

So I laid it out for her, filling in the gaps with my best guesses. Part fact, part fiction. About people who wanted to get out of a dying town so badly that they were willing to bend the rules a bit. How I figured that the Pinkerton guy from Loomis probably stopped at the Chamber of Commerce on his way into town. Probably even told her why he was there. I was guessing that Ramona had bestowed her fair charms on Pinkerton early in the game. That scenario fit with Monty saying Pinkerton never slept in his room and ex-plained why he blabbed to her about the lack of environ-mental regulation. Haynes was a smart woman. She saw the possibilities right away. Loomis or no Loomis, her mother's property was worth fifty times what anyone else imagined. As long as they had the whole thousand acres.

It didn't take much imagination to see how Ramona Haynes convinced Tressman, Weston and Polster that this was their big chance to get out of town with their pockets full. All they had to do was buy up the rest of the property. Anybody who didn't sell, they'd foreclose on. Of course, the sheriff had to go. They needed a sheriff of their own. I was betting that when it came out in the wash, Haynes had known Nathan Hand from her time in Chicago. Maybe even worked with him before he was fired. Told her how Hand hired Bobby Russell so he'd have an endless supply of unemployed thugs at his disposal for things like shooting up houses and tearing out fences.

Things fell into place. The Hoh dragged their feet for eighteen months and then turned Loomis down. That gave Haynes and Tressman and the rest of them time to acquire the remaining property. "Except for Ben," Claudia said.

"Except for Ben," I repeated.

"Who—" she started.

I held up a hand. "I can't do *who* for you," I said. I'd rehearsed this part, so I was ready. "All I can say to you, Claudia, is that I believe the disposition of those people directly responsible for J.D.'s death would satisfy you."

"You know who did it?"

"I didn't say that."

"But you know what happened to them?"

"I didn't say that, either; I said I believed you would be satisfied."

She picked up the cup. Took a sip and set it back down on the counter.

"Okay," she said. "Maybe somewhere down the road, when this is all ancient history . . ." I kept shaking my head until she stopped.

She took a deep breath. "Was J.D. having an—"

I cut her off. I'd put in a lot of time on what I was going to say when we got to this point. Maybe it was like Floyd had said. Maybe trust was just an illusion we used to keep the darkness at bay and we'd all be better off barricaded in doorless buildings. Or maybe old Ben Bendixon was right when he said that trust was real, but only the horrific specter

of war and death was sufficient to bond men in a truly in-
separable manner.

While I wasn't sure of the answer, I knew I wasn't about
to send this young woman out into the day with any less
faith in mankind than she'd walked in with.

"No," I said. "If you noticed any change in his behavior,
it was just because he had more than he could handle."

Claudia cocked her head. She was about to do that
search-my-eyes thing when the kids burst through the back
door and saved my ass. I picked Adam up and set him on
the counter beside me. Alicia ran to the refrigerator and
threw open the door.

Claudia was still searching for eye contact. I gave it to
her.

"You sure?" she persisted.

"Trust me," I said.